Edgewise
Publications

Appalachian Carnival

by

S.M.Fernand

Appalachian Carnival

Published by
Edgewise Publications
P.O. Box 472
Benzonia MI 49616
U.S.A.

First Edition
ISBN: 978-09858070-7-8

Acknowledgments

I heartily wish to thank the estate of Jean-Claude Flornoy for their generous permission to reproduce images from his restoration of the Jean Dodal Tarot. Below, I quote an excerpt from Jean-Claude's *The Journey of the Soul* — stating his view of what the Tarot is, which I envision it to be as well:

The 22 Major Arcana of the Tarot are a coded description of the journey through life, from incarnation to liberation, of an individual soul. It is a geographical map which describes the inner itinerary of a being.

Each Arcanum represents a stage along the way, a level of achievement. By examining them in order, one after the other, each of us can feel the particular energy which emanates from these images. One may "play at remembering", and find oneself saying, "I, too, have experienced this...." In the end, perhaps he will realize that the Tarot is telling the story of his own life

This is the teaching which the Ancients, master builders of the Medieval cathedrals, chose to entrust to a game of cards. Because of its modest form, because the game was a way to make money, because it spoke through images and not in words, and for doubtless other reasons as well, the message has come down to us.

(© 2000 Letarot.com Editions)

I also want to thank several friends in Benzie County, Michigan, who read the early drafts of *Appalachian Carnival*, and who gave me much-appreciated critical advice.

And most of all, I thank my lovely lady, Susan Koenig, for allowing me to spend so much time in her presence with my attention focused on the writing.

S.M.Fernand

0

LE·FOL·

With muddled array and a bundle of fancies over a shoulder, The Fool leaves the past behind — spurred on by hopes and fears, and pushed forward, or perhaps held back, by naked animal urges. The Fool's eyes are fixed on choices to be made, fateful and forthcoming, unexpected and important, bringing both reward and misfortune from taking risks both sorely needed and dangerously foolish. Lacking a number, or in some decks assigned the number zero, the Fool's position in the procession of Trumps is at the beginning, at the end, or wandering throughout.

I aimed to stay home that Friday night, May Day, 1970, and not traipse down the hill to the carnival. I'd even scribbled in my diary that carnivals were for kids, and for yokums without sense enough to poke acorns down a peckerwood hole. Flipping through stale magazines, I sat sullen in my sour bedroom—the lights and sounds of the show bouncing into my window, and Maw sprawled on the couch in the sitting room, snoring again in front of the snowy TV.

Me, Annabelle Cory, nineteen-years young and looking mighty fine, and where in hell was I? Clandel, West-by-God-Virginia.

To get shut of my mulligrubs, if only for a few hours, out the door I flew in a burnt hurry down the treads, down the steep street, down the hillside our slattery apartment clung to. Fetching up at the sidewalk along US-52, the main blacktop snaking through Clandel, I leaned over the rusty pipe rail and took in the carnival below.

On the bottoms by the train yard, colored lights danced in the night's chill. The heap of folks on the midway kicked up a flickery dust cloud, with whiffs of fried food, hot sugar, and diesel exhaust floating in the familiar taint of coal—all swoggled full-tilt by the iron arms of monstrous rides, roaring and whirling through laughs and screams, through bells, bangs, buzzers, and barkers—all amid one golly-whopper ruckus of full-blast 8-track rock-and-roll.

With no money for the front gate, I ducked under the railing and into the bushes—my feet finding and remembering the stony rut carved by years of us young'uns scrambling down this nigh cut to the weedy lot between the railroad tracks and the wide bend in Black Creek. There we used to play our games, and there the carnival would set up each spring. Then we'd play their games. Skidding down between the bushes, grabbing at the budding leaves, I recalled other times with no money—my sister and me, sneaking into the show together, giggling till our sides smarted.

I clambered out of the brush, and up and over the bed of slack and cinders, the oily wooden ties, the gleaming steel rails. Ahead, between the lonesome tracks and blaring midway, the carny camp lay huddled in trembly shadows. Several cars and pickups and a pair of beat-up two-ton trucks crouched nearby a jumble of house trailers, a few curtained windows glowing like foxfire.

I put on like I wasn't sneaking in, smiling and strolling into the camp as if I knew where I was going. But in a blink, fear stole my breath, my heart leapt, my lips tightened. I spied a bright gap in the backside of the line-up of booths surrounding the midway, and tiptoed toward it.

Just before I got there, a bench-kneed Chihuahua charged out from underneath a nearby house trailer, snarling and snapping at my ankles. I kicked at it and fled to the gap, but it jumped at my leg and chomped down on the cuff of my favorite bell-bottom jeans. Hopping on one foot, I swung my leg and the dog around and around, trying to spin it off, its pointy ears and bulgy eyes darting back and forth—the puny bastard in a fright about where I had it right then.

I soon spun myself dizzy, and when I tottered and slowed and grabbed the corner of a tent, the dog let loose, rolled off—no doubt dizzy too—and it wobbled back under the shabby green trailer. As I stood there, getting back my breath and my bearings—one eye on the dog, and the other eye on the crowd shifting by in the bright hullabaloo a few steps beyond the gap in the tents—the battered door of the trailer squawked open, and an old gypsy woman leaned out from the flutter of candlelight within. For a spooky stretched-out moment, she eyed me up and down—gold hoops dangling from her earlobes, red kerchief tied atop her long gray hair, a black shawl over a colory and billowy dress.

Then her squinty gaze softened, as if she'd easily figured me out. I turned tail and stumbled out onto the midway.

1

· LE BATELEVR ―

Behind his table of tricks stands Le Bateleur ― the mountebank ― which in some decks is named The Juggler or The Magician. He conjures up confidence in himself by wielding his skills to mold the world to his will. Perhaps he shall transform his audience as they hope for any miracle at hand. Or maybe he'll bamboozle them into giving back to his own ego what he has brought forth with his creative power. At number one in the Tarot, he begins the parade of Trumps along the path of life ― the first of the steps to become who we are, both divine and diabolic.

"Hey! It's you!" he hollered, grinning wide, eagerly waving come here, leaning out from behind the counter of a bushel-basket game set up in half an over-lit metal trailer. Behind him on the booth walls, all sorts and colors and sizes of stuffed animals hung higgledy-piggledy.

I stopped short and eyed him. "Say what?"

With one hand cupping an even wider grin my way, and the other juggling two softballs, he said, "It's a secret. Come here, and I'll tell you."

I scowled, stepped right up, and huffed, "What?"

He leaned into my ear. "You're the one I see in my dreams. My dream come true."

A dither prickled all through me. "You're full of way too much coal, mister."

"Walt. Walt Ryder. Mighty pleased to make your acquaintance. And I swear on a two-dollar bill, if I took my Instamatic camera into my dreams and snapped a shot of my dream girl, it'd come out to be of you. Mmm, hmm. You, with that curly red hair bobbin' 'round those wide sparkly-green eyes. Yes indeedy, you, sweet and petite, that teeny snoot, the pouty lips. Mmm, hmm. You be the one."

"So you say."

"If I'm lyin' my mama's cryin'."

All aflutter and a mite offput, I leaned back on one leg, my hands on my hips, and told him, "You know what else, mister. A galloopus lays square eggs."

Lifting that ear-to-ear grin higher,

he stood up ramrod straight, raised his right hand as if taking an oath, and swore, "I've seen a million pretty faces pass by out here. I've known a few gals like wives. Yet every night I dream of you. You, who I'm huntin' for among all the others. Measurin' them up to you. Leavin' them 'cause I knew I'd one day find you. And now here you be."

Yeah, sure—I thought, as I looked him over. Though several years older and kind of lanky, I admired his big smiley jaw, his long sun-tanned nose, and his wide shoulders in a pearl-button cowboy shirt and brown leather jacket. Yet I wasn't so partial to his greased-back sandy hair, Elvis forelock and all.

I crossed my arms and stared hard at him. Awaiting my answer, his feathery eyebrows wrinkled up his wide forehead like an actor's—his crafty eyes startling me with how sincere they appeared, how blue they were.

Curious, I asked, "So now what happens?"

"I buy you dinner and drinks at the Mountaineer tonight after the show closes."

Even though I ought to have reckoned this feller to be some sort of spitting snake or worse, he just point-blank felt good to me—then and there, wham, a mountain shaker. He likely was dangerous. But all I cared about was when it wouldn't be too soon to say yes. What did I have to lose? Either I see what goes with him, or I go back to the apartment. Slowly, my phony scowl lifted into a feisty smile.

He shouted, "Yes! Oh my. My dream come true. Hey, ha. You, ya!" He yelled it so loud that some in the crowd stopped to gawk at us, and a few carnies leaned out of their tents in the line-up to see what the commotion was all about.

We sniggered and smiled for a short piece until an awkward hush fell between us for a few dozen heartbeats. Then we eyed each other up and down for a long look... and saw that we each admired what we were seeing.

A half-dozen junior-high kids, boys bragging to the girls, tromped up to the counter, and Walt whispered in my ear, "Baby, the boss has a rule about dream girls hangin' 'round the counter, what ain't winnin' him his money. So me oh my, I gotta get back to the ball-in-the-basket business. Have you seen the show, my sweet dream?"

"No money, honey."

"Well, hell.... What is your heavenly name?"

"Annabelle."

"Annabelle, heaven's dream, looky here...."

Reaching behind his money apron, he dug into the front pocket of his black jeans and pulled out a thick fold of cash money. Thumbing off a ten-dollar bill, he handed it to me and whispered into my hair, his lip brushing my ear, "You be right sure to see the show tonight, Annabelle, my dream.

Leery of the money, I didn't take it, and looking him straight in the eye, quizzed myself on why this feller was giving me ten dollars. When men gave you something they were likely to want something back. Ten dollars was more than I'd earn at the diner on one bad night after another. Did he think he was buying a ticket to ride here? Or was he just a genuine mister-nice-guy? Boys had bought me beers before, but none had ever handed me money. I studied his face for a clue, yet all I could cypher from his grin was that he sure was glad to see me. When he pulled the apron aside to stuff the bankroll back in his pocket, I snuck a peek at the bulge of his prides.

He took ahold of my hand with both of his, pressed the ten in my palm, gently squeezing my fingers around it, and said, "Have some fun. But don't drop more than a buck or two at any of these games. Okay, baby? Come back for more when that's gone. Come back for me, Annabelle. See? For me. Okay? Okay, baby?"

I shrugged, and said, "Sure... why not? Thanks. Reckon I'll be seeing you later then, Walt Ryder."

I waved goodbye with the crumpled bill, winked, and sashayed off into the midway crowd—waggling my backside likely a bit too much. Glancing back a few times, I caught him watching me from the corner of his eye—his arms gesturing, pitching his ball game to the schoolboys, their prettied-up girlfriends leaning in close behind.

The crowd swept me down the midway. To our left roared the Spider, the Tilt-A-Whirl, the Zipper, the Rock-O-Plane, the Scrambler—all lifting and spinning loads of laughing and screaming riders amid the ruckus, the flashing colored bulbs, the full-tilt rock and roll. Lined-up along our right stood the razzle-dazzle of games and sideshows blaring out their ballyhoo side-by-side—a glitzy wall surrounding the trampled midway, awnings propped high, banners strung between poles, barkers calling in all afoot.

I puzzled on what was up with this Walt feller? At other springtime carnivals, I'd seen plenty rascals like him swap off all the money they could from boys trying to win teddy bears. They sure enough were of a kind who spoke right up. A thousand times, I'd ignored their ceaseless, pushy, sing-song come-ons. Most of them plumb downright nasty, out for all they can get—and then, "Who's next?"

But this feller was another guess. The air about him somehow felt cleaner or fresher, like being near cedar in a swamp. He likely used that dream-girl line every week in every town. Yet he appeared to handily mean it.

Whatever he had a mind to, I reckoned I was cagey enough to find out. If only a rollick in my straddle—well, if he was nice enough about it, I had sense enough to be on the pill, and might could be nice about it too.

A year now out of high school, my childhood world was petering out. Three years before, Pap had left out to Charleston with one of his doney-gals, and Maw now drank herself to sleep in front of the TV most every night. My big sister, Rosalie, had married-up last summer to a brush-ape named Lenny, and I scarcely laid eyes on her anymore. My best friend, Karen, had gone off to college, and other friends had married-up, or taken-on jobs and bank loans. Most of the smarter boys were long gone—to school or to cities, or carted off to Vietnam. The not-so-smart worked in the mines or downtown, and now saw me as a possible wife. To think I might marry into these hills made me cringe like a mule eating briars.

When not earning eight or nine dollars a night as a waitress at Jake's Diner two or three times a week—most of which I gave to Maw to help with the bills—I'd read novels or magazines, or stare at TV talk shows, or yarn on and on in my diary. Most folks thought me bookish, over-fattened on reading, which for a fact I was—too keen on pronouncing things properly, and often using words seldom spoken aloud within a two-day's ride.

At the library, I chose my novels by closing my eyes and running my fingers over the books on the shelves until one felt of the one to read. Then, back in my bedroom I'd wolf it down, love it or not. When I came across a word I didn't know, I'd look it up in my tattered dictionary and whisper it in a made-up sentence.

Vaulted inside the novels lurked notions that thereabouts scarcely saw the light of day—stories pretending to be tall tales, but which appeared to ring much truer than what's what in Clandel. Both saved from and damned to my forlorn desolation by pages and pages of spellbound ink, I'd read for hours on end to conjure up what else might be possible in the wider world.

Though I would paw through any magazine within reach, celebrity slicks were my favorites. Their photos and stories proved that far beyond these hills—up in New York City and out in California—folks talked about things other than the price of coal or Mary Sue's new lover, or custom headers on a Chevy, or the Pittsburgh Pirates, or drinking beer and shooting pool. Or the mines.

Clandel, a clapboard and brick town cleaving to the hillsides, was the county site for Black County—a small-time parcel in southwestern West Virginia—so named after one Hiram Black, who a hundred years before made his fortune mining both coal and people. Much has blackened-up around Clandel ever since. Black Creek ran inky from an eroded strip-mine up the cove. Soot laid low in the grooves between the bricks of the dingy buildings downtown. Faces came up from the mines smudged like minstrel players.

And on that first night of May, beneath a ceiling of diamonds and coal, a fat crescent moon, floating low above the jagged ridge, shone through the thicket of trees—rocky-top high, yet ever so near. Each spring, for as long as I could remember, McCain's Magic Midway had come to Clandel, and if not rainy or too cold, it'd fetch a jam-up crowd. The soft air, breathing promises of the new season, brought out carloads of creek-and-hollow folks from forty miles around, wheeling down the twisty roads to the show— hundreds of kith and kin afoot, circling the midway. I'd been there many times before, with friends or a beau, with Maw or Rosalie, and with Pap long ever ago.

But that night I was there alone. And that's how I'd been lately—lonely, even among my oldest friends. Scuffing through the crowd, I saw faces I'd known forever. So why did I feel like an outsider, an oddling? Who were these people to me now? Shoot, I didn't even know who I was. I just knew I couldn't be one of them.

At the back end of the oval midway stood several sideshows lined up in a broad turn—tents, trailers, stages, and banners. In front of a smaller tent, blown-up clippings of newspaper stories were laminated onto a sign board—one headline screaming in thick letters, FROG BABY! BORN ALIVE!

Behind a ticket counter with an orange-and-blue-striped umbrella overhead, a chuffy feller sat smiling—forty or fifty extra pounds on him, thirtyish, with a round pink face and short curly-blonde hair. Next to him up on the counter squatted the ugliest dog I'd ever seen.

I pointed at the dog, "Is this The Frog Baby's brother?"

"Nah. That there's Sharpy. Frog Baby's inside for a half-buck," he told me with an out-of-state drawl, the smirk on his fat cheeks squeezing up the corners of his gleeful eyes.

I dug into my back pocket for Walt's ten-dollar bill.

"Sharpy's a Chinese dog," he told me. "They breed 'em for eatin'. Hairless."

Bald gray folds of skin encased the dog's squabby thirty-or-forty pounds, and the only fur it had were silvery tufts on its feet and at the tip of its thick curly tail, and a ridiculous cowlick flopping forward like eyebrows atop its hippo-shaped head. Bloodshot brown eyes rheumy and sad, it panted happy dog-breath at me.

I handed over the ten, got my change and a half-torn ticket, and went into the tent. On a table inside stood a two-gallon glass jar. Beneath its lid floated The Frog Baby, pickled in brine. It had a head like a frog, but the body and limbs of a human baby. I studied it, and puzzled how in God's world could this be? My innards sunk at the notion that someday maybe I'd give birth to such a monster. And then what? Put my baby in a jar in a sideshow? No way. I'd raise it as best I could. The sign out front said it was born alive. Well then what did they do? Kill it and put it in a jar? I shuddered and turkey-tailed out of the tent.

Stopping in front of the ticket seller, I asked him softly, "How did that ever happen?"

His cheeks squeezed a smile so high his eyes became slits, and he said, "You've heard tell of the Frog Prince? Who got kissed by a princess and turned into a human? Well, this here Frog Baby is their direct descendant."

Taking this as plain-old sideshow point-blank tale-telling, I shunned his jolly face, and looked hard into the pitiful eyes of the dog—likely no Chinese eating-dog, as well. Huffing a little snort, I showed them my back and strode off.

A few sideshows down, on the awning over the back end of a trailer painted up with dozens of mysterious symbols, a neon sign stopped me flat. In yellow tubes of light surrounded by flashing red-and-blue bulbs, it read: INSIDE! THE 3-ARMED MAN! ALIVE!

Fixy wrought-iron treads led up to a curtain of colory beads veiling the entrance. I dug out the half-dollar admission and handed it to a gum-chewing girl in the ticket booth. Pushing the clattery beads aside, I went into a dim hallway for a few steps and then turned left through another curtain of beads. Spreading them cautiously, I faced a wall filled with photos, newspaper articles, and posters—all about this so-called three-armed man. Paying them little heed, reckoning it all to be just more carny ballyhoo, I stepped on through and turned to see what else was in the room.

I squeaked when I saw him there, swiveling in a black leather high-back armchair, like a boss man in his office. Large colory cards were laid out in front him on a carved crescent-moon-shaped table. For a fact the little old feller had three arms!

Two normal hands along with a smaller weirder one busied themselves shuffling and flipping the big cards of a thick deck onto the table. With a black beret, scraggly white hair, a suntanned wrinkly face, and a scruffy goatee, his noggin held a favorance to a moldy acorn. A lackadaisical look in his droopy eyes browsed over the cards he shuffled and flipped, shuffled and flipped. The somehow-cute little freak sported a turtleneck sweater onto which was knitted an extra sleeve to fit the extra arm—a smaller arm that sprouted from the armpit of his other, near-normal-size, left arm, which set higher on a humpy shoulder. His right side appeared almost ordinary, though a mite lopsided.

He lifted soft brown eyes to me, and offered kindly, "May I read your fortune in the cards?" His calm metallic voice had a strange echo within it, like a kicked tin can.

"I... I don't know," I stammered. Then, realizing I was gawking at his third arm, I turned away and fluttered my eyes around the room for something else to land on. In a corner nook stood a small statue with four arms, dancing on one foot and kicking up the other.

"Don't be uncomfortable. You paid to look at me, so look. I'm quite used to it."

I studied his extra arm. It was for real. He swept up the cards and shuffled and cut them mickety-tuck, again and again—his third hand not near as limber as the other two, but shuffling cards better than any hand of mine might ever could do.

I asked, "What's the price to read my cards?"

"It costs your purse three dollars for three cards, and ten for ten. But what it'll cost your soul to know what shall be, that's a whole other deal."

"What does your soul spend on knowing what?"

He didn't answer—his eyes puzzling at a flipped-up card on the table, which had just popped out of the deck, a miscue from a shuffle. When he realized I was standing there waiting for an answer to my question, he said, "Pardon me?"—cocking his extra arm and cupping its tiny hand behind a long earlobe.

"You said that it'll cost my soul something to know what shall be. What does a soul spend on knowing that?"

He set the deck on the table and leaned back into the squeaky leather. With a sly little smirk he thought on this for a piece, scratching the scruff of his neck with both left hands, and murmuring, "Hmm, good question." I stood rigid by the table, like a possum in headlights.

Then he answered matter-of-factly, "Your innocence. When you gain knowledge, your innocence is spent in the bargain. Then you must thereafter make your own choices. Ignorance is bliss. Blessed be the pure of heart. And when Adam and Eve ate of the fruit of the Tree of the Knowledge of Good and Evil, the innocence of the Garden of Eden was traded in for our ability to decide for ourselves what is right and what is wrong."

Appearing pleased with his answer, he leaned forward, shoveled the deck into his third hand, and shuffling cards in and out of his other two, he asked, "Three cards or ten?"

"Three," I breathed.

"Three dollars, please," he said, quickening the pace of his fifteen fingers.

I dug the money out of my jeans and set it on the table. At the high point of one joe-darter of a three-handed card-shuffling exhibition, he slapped the deck onto the center of the table and swept the three dollars into a small drawer that smoothly slid open and shut. I winced some, remembering what Walt had told me about spending no more than a dollar at a time.

"Cut them into three piles," he said, leaning back to watch, his arms woven together atop his potbelly.

The deck was huge, bigger than any deck of cards I'd ever seen—over an inch thick, and near the size of postcards. I reached out shyly for them, but I felt that since I was going to do this, then I might as well do it justice. So I held my hand palm-down above the cards, and pinched my eyes shut to gather myself in that magically expectant way I would before tossing a penny into the wishing well at Stone Hollow Park. Then, carefully with my fingertips, I split the deck into three nearly equal piles.

He glanced an approving smile up at me, and as he lowered his drowsy eyes, he lingered them on the make of my hips. Leaning forward over the three piles, he flipped over the top cards—one with each hand.

"The Fool, The Lovers, and The Wheel of Fortune," he announced. And with his shaggy eyebrows lifting a look of surprise, he added, "Hey, good ones."

I stared at the cards. On the left, painted in bright colors, The Fool—a jester with a bundle on a stick over his shoulder—steps off a cliff while a small dog bites at his leg.

Pointing at the dog on the card, I told him, "A yappy chihuahua bit onto my pant leg not an hour ago."

"You don't say."

I leaned over and studied the card in the middle, The Lovers. A young man turns to an old woman on his right, but reaches toward a young woman on his left. Above, in a cloud under the sun, a plump little angel aims a bow-and-arrow downwards.

"I just met a new feller tonight, too."

"No kiddin'," he whispered.

On the third card, The Wheel of Fortune, three creepy animals with human faces ride around a spoked wheel—much like on the rides out on the midway.

Drop-jawed, I gazed down at the cards. Right there was close to what was happening to me that very night. How could cards do this? How could this freak know what was happening to me?

I eyed him warily. He shook his head and said, "I've been turning these cards for more than thirty years and they still never cease to astound me."

"What do they mean?" I asked. But I felt what they meant, and I knew it was important. An omen.

Draping the upper of his two left arms over the wing of the chair—the extra arm dangling, its childish fingers twiddling with one another—he gestured to a card with his right hand, and said, "Well, the first card is The Fool, and it signifies you. The Fool is the wanderer. His number, zero, is at the beginning and at the end. His force comes from spontaneity. The Fool chooses without thinking, sometimes foolishly, sometimes fortuitously. Into new experience, he strides unaware off a cliff.

"The dog, a symbol of intellect—being an animal that transcends its natural state to live in a higher world—pounces at The Fool, maybe holding him back, maybe driving him onward.

"This card is upright, not reversed, not upside-down, as are all three of your cards, and this means that the inner force driving The Fool is positive, not negative.

"The second card, The Lovers, is another card about choice—and again, a choice not by reason. Its number, six, is a number of ambivalence and tension. You see here on the card that the lover doesn't know whether to choose the mother's world or that of the beloved's. Will it be the old or the new? Yet there will be no indecision if Eros releases his arrow of destiny. This card indicates the forces to be soon about you.

"The third card indicates your future. The Wheel of Fortune is the symbol of the ever-turning ups-and-downs of life. Your task is to be at its center, turning the crank, not riding up and down on the rim. Its number, ten, the first double-digit number, begins a new cycle of progression."

He paused, flipped each card facedown, gathered up the piles, and added, "So from what these cards are telling us, it looks quite auspicious as to this feller you've just met."

Bumfuzzled, I could only ask, "Auspicious?"

"Yeah. That means it looks good for you kid. Good luck."

Feeling that I'd been dismissed, I thanked him, turned away, and went back out onto the midway. The flow of the crowd pulled me along between the antic game-booths and the whirling jam-packed rides. Dazed, I scuffed through the jumble, ignoring the insistent pitches hollered at me from each booth. I had to believe the three arms and the three cards, but whatever else I believed, suddenly appeared to be not so certain.

I shuffled into a crowd around a red-and-orange-striped tent out in the center of the midway—twelve-foot square, awnings propped high on four open sides—counters lined with folks putting quarters down onto numbered circles. On the upper rails of the glossy-red wooden tent frame hung dozens of fuzzy stuffed mice in several colors, big as possums, with ropey tails, pointy ears and nose, and goofy eyes and grin. On a platform in the middle of the tent, slowly spun a laid-flat four-foot wheel upon which a live white rat turned near the spindle, sniffing the air. The man running the game— short and wide-shouldered under a dusty-black cowboy hat—raised a beat-up trumpet to his thin lips, tooted a ta-da, and the rat scooted over into one of the many numbered holes around the rim of the wheel.

Trading the trumpet for a tinny bullhorn, the cowboy announced, "Number eighteen!" Then he and a teenage girl with long black hair, quick as chicken hawks, swept handfuls of quarters off the counters and into their apron pockets.

"Hey! We got a winner this time on number eighteen right over here," he drawled into the bullhorn and pointed to the winner at the far corner of the tent. "Pick out what flavor teddy-mouse you want, young lady." His sun-browned middle-aged face was near the color of his pricy leather vest—it all carved with curlicues and stitched-up like the sides of western boots.

"Hey! Who knows the number of the mouse house this time? A quarter on your lucky number wins the big teddy-mouse prize," he drawled again and again into the bullhorn, the squint in his eyes searching the folks around him, while he and the girl made change for paper money waved at them by the crowd. "Hey! Who knows the number of the mouse house this time? A quarter on your lucky number wins the big teddy-mouse prize."

The woman who had number eighteen—a fixy piece with a drunk-eyed bruiser at her side—pointed out a purple mouse. The longhaired girl knocked it off the rafters with the slim end of a baseball bat and handed it over. By then, twenty or thirty quarters laid down around the board marked a new round of bets.

The Juggler

"Hey! Who knows the number of the mouse house this time? All the quarters down? We're gonna do it again. Watch the mouse. Last chance to get your quarters down. When the horn blows, folks, no more money on the board. So get 'em down now. Watch the mouse. Here he comes!"

He grabbed hold of the slowing wheel and slid a drawer, shaped like a slice of pie, out from beneath the hole the rat had last run into. The little critter lay curled up in the drawer, until the cowboy gently dumped it out onto the center of the wheel and gave it a spin. The red-eyed rat squirmed onto its tiny pink feet, its bald tail searching for balance, its whiskers sniffing. Some around the counters yelled out their numbers, cheering it on as it turned slowly at the center of the wheel. The last few players hurried down their bets, and after a few more spins of the wobbly wheel, the cowboy blew the horn and the white rat scampered to the rim and into a hole.

Just like in the cards, The Wheel of Fortune was smack-dab in front of me. And there, that rat was me.

I sidled up to the counter, took a dollar bill out of my pocket and held it up. The girl came over and quickly made change. I put a quarter on number ten. Twenty-one numbers in colored circles were painted onto each of the four counters.

"Hey! Who knows the number of the mouse house this time? Get your quarters down on your lucky number and take home the big teddy-mouse prize. Hey! We're gonna do it again right now, so get 'em down. Here comes the mouse. Watch him go!"

This time the number was eleven—so close to ten that after they swept the counters I straightaway put another quarter on ten. Standing next to me, taking up room enough for two, a broad-bottomed and middle-aged black woman, with rhinestone eyeglasses and badly dyed copper hair, had won with number eleven, and took her sweet time picking out a red mouse from the rafters, clapping her hands in front of her hesitant smile.

The winner of the next go-round was number twenty. Nobody had it. I played ten again. By this time, the magical bedazzlement that I'd wandered under the awning with had been lost to the cheap thrill of betting on a rat on a wheel.

While waiting for the next spin, I watched the girl working the counter—tall and shapely, near my age, her straight black hair swaying halfway down the back of her red blouse, the curve of her bum held tight by black stretch-pants, a thin brown cigarette dangling from her heart-shaped lips and face. She hustled back and forth around the counters, making change and adding to the cowboy's megaphone banter with her own lackadaisical sing-song—"Who needs change. Get 'em down afore it goes around. You can't win iffen you don't play. Change for a buck can change your luck. The more you bet, the more you get."

I had half a notion that it might be fun to run a game like this.

The rat again turning in the middle of the wheel, the cowboy tooted a 'ta-da', and it scurried into hole number ten.

"I won!" I shrieked. I saw faces around the tent swivel to me—some looking sore about their bad luck, others happy for my good luck. The girl scooped up the quarters, then hurried over to me, and asked, "What color, hon'?"

"Oh, gee...I guess that pink one."

She hefted the baseball bat and poked at the one I'd pointed to. It fell off the hook, she caught it, and handed it over, hollering, "There goes another big prize for only a quarter. Let's get 'em down for another round."

I stepped back from the counter and admired my trophy—the first thing I'd ever won in my entire life. Its happy eyes and lopsided grin no doubt mirroring mine, I nuzzled its fuzzy nose, and sauntered away.

Before I got thirty steps up the midway, a big gruff rascal, his left eyelid at half-staff over a bulgy eyeball, leaned out to me from the corner of a tent in the line-up, croaking, "Say, Red! Did you get one of these when you came in?"

He held out a card, and waved it at me with come-see gestures. Behind him on stepped shelves sat some radios and tape players, a small TV, his-and-her watches, and several huge teddy bears. Two other rascals stood to his right—all three on a platform behind the high counter—a pair of shaggy, yard-high, red-and-white stuffed dogs sat between them upon the counter, dividing it into thirds.

He reached out as I neared, and handed me the card. It read:

~ GOOD FOR ONE FREE GAME ~

~ AT THIS STAND ~ TODAY ONLY ~

"No," I said, searching his good eye, "I didn't get one."

His hound-dog jowls beardy, he heaved up his swaying bulk and growled toward the far end of the counter, "Hey, Boss. She didn't get a ducat at the gate."

The slick slouching there whined, "Give it to her now."

"Okay. You're the boss." He took back the card and handed me a leather cup, rattling under my nose the half-dozen red marbles in it. "Just spill 'em out into the box, and we see what you get. Free game. No money."

I took the cup and dumped the marbles into a wooden tray, about a foot square with short sides, and numbered holes in rows on its bottom. Each marble rolled to rest in a hole.

After quickly adding up the numbers by each hole—"Eleven, nineteen, thirty-one, forty-four. Check forty-four."—he scooped the marbles back into the cup and pointed to a red number 44 on a plastic-laminated chart next to the tray, a checkerboard of out-of-order numbers, some black, some red, some of which had amounts of yards printed along with the numbered squares. Big letters across the top spelled out: PLAY FOOTBALL and 100 YARDS OR OVER WINS.

"Why this be your lucky day, you pretty little thing you," he grumbled low, like a tired steam shovel digging into a seam of coal. "A forty-four wins you fifty yards. A hundred yard's a touchdown, which takes home the big radio back there. Another spill, to go for fifty more yards, just fifty cents."

He slammed the leather cup down in front of me. Behind him on the shelf, the radio was a good-sized one, but had a cheap look to it. Still, it appeared worth the chance, so I dug out a five-dollar bill, collected my change, which he was slow to hand over, and I dumped the marbles again.

"Four, seven, nine, thirteen. Thirteen! That there's your lucky number tonight, little lady. Check thirteen." He pointed to a red 13 in a square on the chart and scooped up the marbles. Under the number it read: 30 YARDS.

"Thirty more makes eighty yards total. Only twenty to go for a touchdown, and the radio's yours. You're almost there now, Red. Just another fifty cents."

He'd grunted "just another fifty cents" stone-cold cocksure that I'd go again. I cast a suspicious eye from him to the chart and to the radio, but shortly handed him two quarters, and spilled the marbles again.

"Eight, fourteen, twenty-three, twenty-nine." He counted them in a blur, and then said, "I don't believe it. You count 'em with me, to check." So we slowly added together the numbers under the marbles—twenty-nine. On the chart, 29 was set in big black print in a box alone atop the other numbers. Under the number 29, was printed: BONUS INSURED. And at the bottom of the chart, in small dark print, it said: No. 29 DOES NOT WIN and ALWAYS DOUBLE ON No. 29 and BLACK NUMBERS DO NOT WIN.

"Well, darlin', I'd say you're the luckiest player yet tonight. A bonus means that a touchdown now gets you the radio and the big blue teddy bear, or fifty dollars in cash. A dollar shoots for the bonus," he said, again with that cocksure tone, his hand held out for the dollar.

I hesitated... and explained, "But the feller who gave me this money— he works in a game over on the other side—he told me not to spend more than a dollar on any game."

"What?" he bellowed, his grimace shifting from fake helpfulness to a look of genuine rage, his slack eye nearly popping open. "Just say you're with it, Red. Don't waste my breath. I got goddamn money to win!" His thick throat gurgled with anger. "Get out of my face. Go find a ticket booth to park your tight little ass in."

"Suck a polecat dick, mister," I hissed at him and backed away.

"Haw! I'd druther tongue your waggly keister," he said, now smirking like a pervert.

He swiveled to the rascal next to him—who was leaning out over the counter, slick as a peeled onion with his Clark Gable mustache—and he guffawed like a jackass, "Haw, haw. Hear her, Ray? 'Suck a polecat dick,' she tells me. Haw, haw. Her whang, a fuckin'carny, dukes her a bean to blow at a joint, and she comes to me. Then she tells me, 'Suck a polecat dick.' Haw. A juicy lickin' around her sassy brown-hole's what I oughta give her. Yeah. Haw, haw, haw.... Hey, Pops! Did you get one of these when you came in? Come here. I'll show ya."

I stormed up the midway, twisting through the crowd, muttering cusses through clenched teeth. I just about kept on going right out the front gate, when I bumped into Johnny Bob Clark.

"By grabs, Annabelle. Where you headin' off to, mad as fire?"

I stopped short, turned on my heels, looked daggers up into his big-eared face, and told him, "Some damn one-eyed bastard just cut a rusty over me playing with his fucking marbles."

"Girl, them carny japes 'll swap you off bad. Best keep a far piece from 'em. Say, tell me, what're you a-doin' here all alonely? Ain't nobody brung you out to the fair?"

Johnny Bob owned a longtime hankering to get into my panties. A few times, due to my boredom, or his pestering, I'd let him.

"Johnny Bob, are you saying I can't get here by myself?"

"Well, shoot girl. I hear they won't let you git on that crazy Zipper ride lest you take someone to hang onto. C'mon, let's you and me go git all turned round, then go drink some beers in my car."

"No thank you. I already have a date for later," I said, smugly nuzzling the ears of the stuffed mouse.

"Well, let's cooter 'round some till then."

"Maybe next year."

"They ain't a-gonna be no next year for me 'round here."

"What? Why?"

"I done hitched up with the Air Force. I'll be long gone, like a turkey through the corn, in five weeks. So how 'bout me and you a-havin' a few more one-more-times afore I go?"

"Lord's sake, Johnny Bob. Who in hell do you think I am?"

"Annabelle, I reckon I know who you..."

"No. You just think you know who I used to be."

"Ahh, girl don't kick the cat on me. What kindly poot is that?"

"The kind I'm telling you. Are you listening? Bye-bye, Johnny Bob. I hope you fly high as the moon and make a golly-whopper hero of yourself."

I twisted him a mock smile, flittered my eyelashes, and marched off—mostly to escape showing him my mulligrubs. Here was another one leaving out. It wasn't likely I'd miss Johnny Bob much. He was more a botherment than anything else. His hog-and-panthering had paid off a few times, and I'd let him have some of what he wanted. But I hadn't gotten much from it—just a taste of what I knew I didn't want. Beer and sex in the front seat of his rust-bitten car was a big night out for Johnny Bob, but it did little for me.

Sometimes his buddy, Luke, had pot, and I'd ride around with them getting stoned. Sitting between them, passing a joint, the world would appear different for a while—more antic, yet somehow having more importance. We'd fun on and on about things, until a silence would come over us. Then I'd ask to get out of the car—before Luke would want out, leaving me alone with Johnny Bob—and I'd bogue up and down the streets, until I found myself home once more.

As I drifted into another turn around the midway, the sight and scent of sizzling meat and fixings brought me over to a cook tent—a smutchy canvas top fitted to a wooden frame, maybe twenty-foot by twelve, with folks under the awnings along both sides hunched atop wooden stools at low counters. Up front behind steamy glass and beneath a chest-high counter, a table-sized griddle fried a dog's bait of jibbled-up white onions and green peppers, greasy gray burgers and charred hot dogs and coiled links of Italian sausage—all tended by a bulky old cook, a chef's mushroom-hat square on his roundish head, one cheek humped with chaw. Out in back, folks sat on fold-up wooden chairs around beat-up card-tables beneath a canvas stretched from the cook tent to what once was a milkman's truck—a kitchen window now set into its side.

I straddled a vacant stool and found myself next to Suzy Gaithers and her little girl. I used to go to school with Suzy until she got bigged-up at fifteen and quit.

"Hey, Annabelle."

"Hey, Suzy."

"Well I swan, ain't you the lucky one. How'd you win that pretty pink mousey?"

Suzy was a pleasingly plump sort of girl, whose lilt of voice often got a mite worked-up over one trifle or another—but with a glint behind her mascara that often left me doubting that she was for real.

"Oh, over yonder. Betting on the wheel where a rat runs in a hole with a number on it."

Suzy's slightly cross-eyed, pig-tailed daughter, Maggie, wriggled off her stool and came over to pet the mouse's fur. "He's so soft. Can I hold him?"

"Sure, Maggie." I handed her the prize and turned to a wiry feller wiping the counter in front of me, who asked in a nasal singsong, "How many? What kind?"

"A hot dog with onions and peppers, please."

"One pup in the garden," he sang toward the cook at the griddle and then scurried down the counter, wiping and chanting, "How many? What kind?"

The griddle man, swaying his bulk side-to-side, jabbed sputtering sausages with a two-foot fork in one hand, while the other tended burgers and heaps of fixings with a long-handled pancake flipper. Working hard at his wad of tobacco, he spurted amber into the muddy sawdust at his feet. Then with a hulky grace he set down the flipper, grabbed a bun from a pile stacked like cordwood beside the griddle, stabbed a singed hot dog, stuffed it into the bun, forked on some onions and peppers, and set it atop the counter on a square of wax paper. This he did while taking an order from some folks out front for burgers with and without this and that, while also taking another order for two pups bare from the wiry feller at the back counter, who shortly hurried my dog over to me, and gave me a quarter change from my dollar.

"What ya been up to?" asked Suzy, chewing on her Italian sausage, twice as thick as a hot dog, spicier, and in a bigger bun.

I saw she'd put on more weight, in her face and elsewhere—not chuffy-girl weight, but a woman's measure—and I said, "Not much. Working at the diner. Cootering around."

I bit into my hot dog—the warm and greasy fixings nothing short of salvation on the doughy bun and overdone meat.

Suzy brayed, "Girl, I wish I had time to do much o' nothin'. All day and all night, if it ain't one thing then anothern. It's either the young'un, or my man, or the house, or the vittles, or my kilfliggin sister with her connipity kids. Laws a mercy, I ain't got a lick of time enough for me."

She bit off an inch of her sausage, and chewed out through it, "Mama tells me, 'Suzy, you gotta take the time to do what you want.' But soon as I try, my time gets took away. What to do? I hardly know anymore, Annabelle. Just keep on doin' what needments be, I reckon."

I said, "I've got plenty time, but hardly know what to do with it."

"So when you gettin' married, girl?"

"Yeah, sure. And then what? Have no time for nothing?"

"So what other you gonna do?"

"I don't know... take the mountain, most likely. See the world. Travel."

"Oh sure, there's one bodacious fortune to be made a-travelin'. Travelin' takes powerful cash money. Why last year me and Lenny and Maggie went down to Virginia Beach for just one week, and it cost us nigh on three-hundred dollars just to sleep and eat and have a few drinks. Just to lie on the beach we had to run back to the car to feed the dad-burned parkin' meter every hour."

"I don't mean that kind of traveling. I mean go to some city and get a job. Something like that."

"Somethin' like that takes money, too."

"Staying here will cost me a lot more than money."

"Oh yeah... well, let me tell it to you, missy. This a-here's my home, for better or worse till death do us part. I got no hankerin' to carry myself off and get all citified where nobody knows me. No family, no friends. And work my hind end off to end up the one-in-the-same I am today—but lonesomer." She crammed the end of the sausage and bun into her mouth and wiped her hands on the back pockets of her jeans.

I asked, "How do you know you'd end up being the same person there as here?"

After chewing for a spell on her mouthful and my question, she told me, acting like I was some sort of squackhead, "Cause I am who I am. I ain't 'xactly tickled silly 'bout my life, but I know it's mine. I know there ain't no fairytale out there in the big city what's gonna turn me into Cinderella.... Hey, maybe it might could happen with you. But Lord's eye on it, that's nary gonna happen with me. So me and Lenny and Maggie here, we're a-takin' it as it comes. And lately it ain't been half bad. Lenny's workin' steady. Maggie's gettin' to be so upheaded. Ain't you, Maggie?"

One eye appearing to look elsewhere, Maggie gazed into my face, suck-ing at the straw in her Co-Cola, and clutching the goofy mouse to her skinny ribs, rocking it like it was her baby.

"Well, we gotta git," Suzy declared, and hauled herself up off the stool. "Be seein' you, Annabelle. Nice talkin' at you. Come on, Maggie. Give the mousey back to Annabelle. One more ride, and it's a-home to bed."

Maggie stroked its snout and gave it a goodbye kiss.

"You keep the mouse, Maggie," I said.

Her eyes went so wide aglee they nearly straightened out as she hopped up and down at her mother's feet. "Can I, Maw? Can I?"

"Girl-child, you got more 'n enough toys already. And I'm always the one a-pickin' 'em up. Come on, let's git."

Maggie sadly gave me back the mouse, and they walked off. Slowly eat-ing the last of my hot dog, I lingered awhile, watching the griddle man work, until the counter man, wiping in front of me with a bleachy rag, asked again, "How many? What kind?"

I shook my head and went back out onto the midway. Not yet ten o'clock, I had over an hour till my date with Walt. Across from the cook tent, the Merry-Go-Round turned its load of kids, its mechanical organ toot-ing a waltz. Next down the midway, the Ferris Wheel rolled tall and grand, nigh on fifty-foot high. Red-yellow-and-blue fluorescent tubes spanned the spokes and rims, some flickering from loose connections. Around between the two rims wheeled two dozen seats, each wide enough to squeeze three teens into, and all full of folks full of smiles.

In front of the loading ramp, a dozen others awaited their turns. I bought a ticket and stood in line. The Ferris Wheel's operator unloaded and loaded one seat at a time, and shortly I got waved into the next by hairy tattooed arms, very tanned and very dirty, muscling out of a loud and yellowed T-shirt smudged with grease. He swung a steel bar across the front of my seat, hitched it with a pin, and accidentally, or so he tried to make it appear, a few of his grimy fingers brushed against the left bubby pocket of my denim jacket.

When I jerked a scowl up at him, he flapped a sly wink at me—his beardy face leathery, his black eyebrows and curly hair salted with grains of sawdust and sand—and he growled, "Hi, doll. My name's Buck. What's yours?"

I shot him the evilest eye I could muster. He sucked in his gorilla gut, yanked his baggy jeans up a hitch, and bent an arm against the lever beside him. The motor groaned, puffing gassy blue smoke, and backward and upward I went, clinging to the shiny bar, swinging up into the night amid the tubes of light, the bolts and pig-iron, the turnbuckles and rods. The wheel stopped with me on top, the opposite seat unloading and loading at the bottom. As my seat gently rocked, I gazed over the show and around at Clandel upon the hillsides.

Below, folks floated around the oval assemblage of writhing machines roaring in the middle of the hullabaloo—the folks encircled in turn by a razzle-dazzle line-up of games and sideshows. Up high, it all appeared so far away, yet somehow easier to pick out each voice, each sound. Surrounding the carnival, Clandel sat hushed in a dim cloud of streetlights, quivering slightly from the show's pulse. And above it all, a slice of moon hung in the star-spangled night. Hunting the hillside for sight of our apartment, I made it out among the other tired houses—even spying the pale window of the room where Maw likely still dozed on the couch.

The motor groaned and the wheel lurched forward, and down I went— faces in the crowd milling at my feet, and my innards turning, too. Then I swept back over the loading ramp to a stop, as Buck let off and took on riders on the seat in front of me. Several starts and stops later, the reloaded wheel rolled nonstop a few dozen times around, and then took in again unloading and loading.

While the pink mouse and I rode the Ferris Wheel, I puzzled over The Three-Armed Man's cards, and how strange it was that those cards appeared to echo what was happening to me. But what was happening? Was I now riding on The Wheel of Fortune? Something felt of something new—like my life had more of a chance to maybe happen. But nothing had actually changed. Or had it? This Walt was likely just another carnival clown, like that Bozo with the marbles. Or was he? And what about that other card— The Lovers? Maybe I really was his dream girl. Yeah, right. But was he the man of my dreams? And what would that man be like anyway? Well, maybe someone who'd take me away from Clandel—someone who'd be nice to me, and who looked good, and felt good.... Maybe something wonderful was happening, and I didn't yet know it. But then there was The Fool card—and that dog biting my pant leg.

My seat stopped at the bottom, and Buck steadied it and swung the bar open. I ignored his pruney eyes and steered clear of him as I stepped down the ramp and headed back down the midway, hunting for Walt's booth. Halfway down the row of games, there he was, leaning over the counter, one hand on a big feller's shoulder, the other handing him a softball. Keeping my distance, I moved over by a pipe fence around the Zipper ride—

tumbling its load of shrieking hillbillies around and around, rattling and roaring, colored lights flashing, rock and roll blasting from six-foot speakers.

I watched Walt talk the man into buying another chance. I couldn't hear what was said, but I could see Walt was good at what he did, what all these rascals did, which was talk people into doing what they didn't want to. The man, a head taller than Walt, and a hundred pounds heavier, paid for another shot, gingerly weighed the ball in his hand, and took aim at a tipped peach basket. He tossed, missed, threw up his arms, and twisted away, kicking the dust.

Walt called him back and leaned out over the counter, saying something into his palm cupped by the player's ear. With a look of misdoubt, he studied Walt, but then fingered his poke for another bill and gave it over. Walt handed him three balls this time. The man—with a chest like a rain barrel, a fresh crew-cut, and black-rimmed eyeglasses perched on a hooked nose—set two balls on the counter, and working up his focus, tossed the other ball up and down in one hand.

My pink mouse tucked under an arm, I slowly neared the booth to watch the game better. I gathered that the object of it was to toss a softball so it did not bounce back out of a peach basket, which was nailed to a wide board at the back of the booth with three other baskets—each tipped forward so the player at the counter looked straight into the bottom—tipped just enough to cradle a ball on the low side of the basket.

The man flipped his first toss into the basket and the ball bounced back out almost quicker than it had gone in. Walt caught the ball, waved it in front of the player, and laid on him, thick as sorghum, a pantomime of how to toss the ball in an arc, soft and high, with some backspin, so it fell hitting the basket on its side and not bounce out off the bottom slats.

"Soft and high. Soft and high. Flip it with reverse English and drop it in the pocket," Walt told him, and then demonstrated with a toss of his own, which plopped into the basket's low side and rolled to rest there.

Walt removed that ball, and the big feller weighed his second toss. Then, trying to do what Walt had shown him, with an awkward twist of his wrist he flipped the ball, soft and high, and the ball thudded onto the trailer floor a foot short of the basket.

"Dadgumit," he muttered, and grabbing the last ball from the counter he reared back to heave it at the basket.

Walt stepped in front of him, and both palms up, hollered, "Hold it!" The man lowered his arm.

"Listen," Walt said calmly, "I know you can do it. You got one more shot at it. Let me show you one more time. Lift it soft and high and come down just over the front lip. That's where the end of the rainbow is. Just like this." And Walt again showed how to do it, plunking the ball in.

Suspiciously looking around, like Papa Bear after his porridge had been eaten, the man caught me watching him from one end of the counter. He held the last ball out to me, and said, "Here. You toss it for me, hon'. Looks like you've been lucky tonight."

I stepped right up, took the ball, leaned over the counter, and promptly chunked it into the basket. It stayed in!

The man clapped a fist into a hand, and with a sight of satisfaction he pointed to a fuzzy blue-and-white elephant hanging on the trailer wall. Walt jumped up on the floor, grabbed the trophy, and lifting it high, hollered out to all walking past, "Hey, there goes another one to another lucky winner."

Walt awarded it to the man, who inspected it, thanked me with a short nod, and said, "Good shot, girl." Then he brought it to a plump little girl leaning her face against her mother's hip, off from the booth some. The girl nuzzled its floppy ears as the family strolled away.

Walt searched my wary eyes for clues. "Annabelle. My oh my.... Did you win you a prize tonight?"

"Yeah." I held the mouse's silly snout up to Walt's toothy grin. "I won it where a rat runs into holes in a wheel."

"Well then, you surely are the lucky lady tonight."

"Did that big feller just get lucky, too? Or did you do something that made my ball stay in?"

"Well... he was lucky you were here to take the shot for him. A five-dollar shot, at that. Strange way to sell stuffed animals. No?"

"So how come I made it so easy and he couldn't?"

"Because you look much better to me than he does. And I left the cop ball in."

"The cop ball?"

A teenage couple neared the booth, as he whispered, "Gotta educate you later, because yonder comes another financial opportunity."

Waving a ball at them, he struck up his spiel. "Hey, what d' ya say? Here's the one to play. Come on in. Here's the one to win. Give it a try. You know why. Boy, win that gal a teddy bear toy. Here you go, shoot one for free. Take a practice shot on me. Free. On me."

The boy—low and little with it, and glassy-eyed from the chaw in his zit-speckled cheek—sized up the game from under a John Deere feed cap. His squirmy girlfriend—with a make like a potato bulging out of purple hot-pants and an ill-fitting halter-top in some god-awful shade of pink—shoved him forward and drawled, "Win me a b'ar, Merle. Go on, win me one."

In brand-new Dickie-gray work shirt and trousers a size too big for him, Merle stepped up to the counter, and asked respectfully, "What d' ya gotta do here, mister?"

Walt put a ball into Merle's hand and told him, "Just chuck a ball into the basket so it stays in. Give it a try. Free practice shot, on me. Toss it just like this. Now listen and watch, and then you do it. Arc it soft and high, and land it on the bottom side of the basket." And with a swoop of his arm, Walt flipped the ball right into the pocket of the tipped basket.

Merle, with a hard grip on the ball, measured the toss, then flung it straight into the basket, and out it flew.

"No, no. That's not the shot," Walt told him. "Here, let me show you."

He took a ball, and leaning backward over the counter, demonstrated again. "Underhand. Bring the hand up with the ball high as you can reach before you let it fly. Watch. Arc the ball high, so it plunks down on the side of the basket. Then it doesn't bounce back at you off the bottom."

With a flourish and a backspin-giving flip of his hand, Walt tossed the ball high and it plopped onto the low side of the basket and rolled into the pocket.

"Here, try it again. Free practice," he said, handing another ball to Merle—who chunked it the same way he did the first time. But this time the ball stayed in.

"There you go. Now just do that twice for fifty cents and you win the little lady her choice of a fuzzy prize. Two in, you win!" Walt leaned to the girlfriend and asked her, "Which one you want, girl?"

She circled her pasty arms around Merle's middle and stood on tiptoes, her Avon-gaumed face twisting right and left to survey her choices. As Merle reached to his back pocket for the poke chained to his belt, she heaved him off balance and they near about fell over together. She giggled like she had the hiccups, but he turned dead serious as he traded Walt a dollar bill for two quarters and two balls.

Merle tongued his chaw around to the other cheek, elbowed away from his girl's arms, spurted some amber off to his left, and weighed the toss with his death grip—then he flung it the same way again, straight in and right out.

The girlfriend gave Merle a heavy shove, and complained, "You didn't do it like he tol' you."

Merle's chaw-glazed eyes just stared at the basket. Walt again demonstrated the proper way to toss the ball. Merle flipped his second shot a jag higher and a grain softer, and this time the ball didn't bounce out.

"There. Now you got it. Just another fifty cents, get two in, and pick out the prize."

"Naw. I can't get no two in there. There's a squirrel up this a-here tree somewhere." And he walked off, girl in tow, her finger in his belt loop.

"Hold on!" Walt hollered. They stopped and turned. Walt said, "Tell you what I'm gonna do. I'll split the difference with you. You pass me one dollar, and you get two shots to get one in. You'd chance a dollar for her to do what you just did. One out of two. Won't you?"

The girlfriend dragged Merle by the belt back to the counter. He chewed his tobacco twice on the offer, spurted some amber, looked Walt dead in the eye, and said. "Okay, mister. One out of two for a dollar." He dug it out of his poke, handed it over, grabbed up two balls, and quickly chunked both shots in and out.

"Dog my hide," he cussed, spat, and stomped off, leaving the girlfriend at the counter.

Wanting to get in on the game, and figuring on Walt again doing whatever he does to make the ball stay in, I said to the girlfriend, in my best drawl, "Tell ya what *I'm* a-gonna do. Shoot twicet, for two dollars. And iffen you *don't* get one of 'em in—I say, *don't* get one in—you win this-a-here pink mouse."

The girl puckered up her face, and measured my offer against the goofy mouse on the counter. She eyed Walt sideways, asking, "That be so?" Walt shrugged and nodded yes. She ordered Merle back to the counter and demanded two dollars. Merle protested with half a word or two, but dug it out while she waited, one hand held out to him, palm up.

She paid Walt, took two balls, one in each hand, and without even trying to pretend that she was trying to get them in, she flung them both at the same time, missing the baskets way high, one boffing a teddy bear on the noggin, and the other thunking up against the metal wall.

Then with a hardy-har-har smirk, she snatched the mouse off the counter, turned her broad back to me, and wobbled off on worn-down high heels, leading Merle away, who glanced back a few times till they were out of sight.

Walt chuckled, and said, "That's what they'll do to you if you let 'em."

I faked a sour face, and whined, "Why, she didn't even try to get them in the basket."

"Would you?"

"Well... I likely would've at least tried to look like I was trying."

"That I believe. So... easy come, easy go. Does you miss your fuzzy pink prize?"

"Nah. I don't know what I'd do with it anyhow."

"And we got a deuce more from that gomer. Thanks. I bet you could've asked for five."

"Well... you gave me the money I won it with in the first place, so..."

"So, what goes around comes around. Good deal, eh? Win, win."

"Sure. What comes around next?"

"Next, I'm back to work. Like I said, the boss beefs when I'm not grindin' the tip."

I smiled up at him, waggled a few fingers bye-bye, and said, "Okay. See you after a while."

"Another hour or so and we are out of here and on our way, baby."

I strolled down the midway to the back end, where on a long narrow stage under a row of canvas banners strung up in front of a large tent a barker held high a blazing torch. Decked-up in a dusty black tuxedo, sparkling with sequins and hanging loose on his gaunt frame, he yelled out over the heads of the people, a squinty smirk across his raw-boned horse-face, "Sev-en shows for the price of one! Sev-en shows for the price of one!" I sidled over near the belly-high stage, and joining the gaggle of other folks, gawked up at him.

"Sev-en shows for the price of one," he chanted again and again while waving the torch, striding back and forth, cock of the walk, with a hint of a limp. After a few dozen folks had gathered in front of the stage, he announced, "Ladies and gentlemen!"—his voice pitched high and urgent, but cracking wearily—"Under the big top behind me,"— he swept the torch backward, casting a dancing light onto the tent's patchwork of repairs— "you shall see, absolutely alive and in person, you shall witness, agog and in absolute awe, seven of the most extraordinary exhibitions you shall ever come face to face to. I say, ever! And every and all, all seven shows, for the price of only one ticket. All seven shows for just ninety cents. Just a dime less than a dollar, and you shall witness seven expositions of eclectic eccentricities utterly unseen today in the whole wide world. Here! Now! Not just one. Not two, or five. But, seven. Yes, seven!"

Like a preacher selling salvation, he hollered, "You shall see swords of cold steel swallowed to the hilt." And he waved the leaping torch-light in front of one of the canvas banners, big as bed sheets, hung on ropes and poles behind and above the stage. Painted in cracked and weather-drinted colors, and drawn like something belonging in a comic book, a bare-chested sheik at a desert oasis plunged a huge sword down his upturned gullet.

Next to me in the crowd, a schoolgirl drawled, "Yuh-uck," and her huddle of girlfriends all giggled.

He crowed, "You shall behold The Human Pincushion," striding over to another canvas and waving the torch at it—this one painted even cruder, but in fresher paint, and no doubt by a different artist—of a cockeyed swami in a diaper, sitting cross-legged on a bed of nails, his body run through with dozens of hatpins.

The schoolgirls twisted their faces and rolled their eyes at each other, and followed the prettiest one away from the stage.

He swung the torch to a chipped canvas of a curvy lady getting zapped in an electric chair—eyes bugging out of her head—and shouted, "The Battery Woman shall electrify you with her amazing powers."

Leaning forward, he swept his hand over the crowd and stabbed the torch toward the colory cartoon of an aired-up feller tied above the tent tops like a blimp. "Be carried away by The Human Balloon."

"And... you shall not believe your eyes when you witness The Human Blockhead." On this banner, a goofball with a claw hammer was pounding a spike up his big nose.

"Yes! All for the price of one ticket. Oh, and how can I forget? In the tent behind me, obesely corpulent with stupendously pendulous blubber, sets Lula, The Fat Lady. The chuffiest cherub this side of Charleston." And he waved the torch under a sitting portrait of a long-haired red-head, wider than she was tall.

"And now...." He held the torch in front of his face, and paused for drama. "I shall give you a taste of what can be experienced inside for only one mere dime less than a dollar."

He grabbed an unlit torch from behind The Fire Eater's banner—center-stage on a newer canvas, by a better painter—of a man blasting dragon fire out of his mouth into the carnival night, and who looked a lot like the feller up on the stage. He lit this smaller torch from the other, and held it high over his upturned head, the larger torch held an arm's length away beside him. Lowering the small torch slowly, till fire nearly kissed his sneering lips, he licked at it like an ice cream cone—the little blue flames dancing on his tongue. Snapping his mouth shut, snuffing the flames, he then licked the torch again for more fire to eat.

After a few minutes of this, he raised the torch high, threw his head back, lowered the flame into his wide-open mouth, and closed his lips over it. Sliding the snuffed torch out, he tilted his head down to the crowd, pursed his lips, and puffed out a smoke ring the size of a wheelbarrow tire. Then with a flourish he lifted high overhead the torch ablaze in his other hand and blew a mighty breath into it. A blowtorch blasted from his mouth up into the night, just like the picture on the banner. The crowd shrunk back from the tongue of fire—some raising their hands to fend off the heat and light, some shrieking, and many breathing, "Ooooh!"

The Fire Eater bowed, and announced, "Much, much, more inside. The show begins in a few minutes. Step right up and get your tickets. Seven shows for the price of one. Plenty of room for all inside the big top. Step right up!"

He hopped off the back of the stage, doused the torch in a bucket, and ducked into the tent. A shaggy-haired boy—in a black leather motorcycle jacket studded with chrome, and with 'Born to Lose' lettered across its back—pushed forward from the edge of the crowd, waving a dollar bill. At the tent's entrance, he bought the first ticket from a pimply girl behind the bars of a ticket booth window. A dozen or so sifted out of the crowd to also buy tickets, and get a dime back from their dollar—myself among them.

Inside, on a knee-high stage just past the entrance, The Fat Lady squatted atop a low stool. Beside her stood a large scale. She sure enough was fat—but not all that fat. The small stool made her appear bigger, and the silly pink tights she wore under a flouncy red tutu ridiculously exaggerated her huge big bummy and thick thighs—but Natty Jones from up by Three Hills was a heap sight fatter than this woman.

We all gawked at her anyhow. Her bloated face held a neglected prettiness behind her pasty mask of makeup, and her hair wasn't red like on the banner outside—it fell to her shoulders in golden ringlets. Nearby me, a scarce-hipped woman bent to her little girl, and hissed, "See how fat she is?"

The Fat Lady, putting on as if she couldn't care less, munched from a bag of potato chips and searched our faces, one by one.

Shrugging at each other and looking around the tent, we took in wondering what else was going to happen in this show. A few dozen naked 200-watt light bulbs hung spaced out on a electrical wire strung between the two poles that heaved up the saggy twin-peaks of muddy-brown canvas. A second stage stood along the backside of the tent. On it were set a sheathed sword on a stand, a bed of nails, a pillow-size pincushion with long needles stuck in it, and a bicycle pump. At the far end was a smaller third stage with an electric chair upon it.

On a cue of growing impatience, and with nobody else straggling in from outside, The Fat Lady, sighing and grunting a mite too much, heaved herself to her feet and waddled over to the scale. It was the kind of scale with an arrow on a big dial at eyelevel, but the dial was on its backside facing us. She loaded herself onto it and the arrow spun around the dial a few times—then whirled off, clattering to the boards. Sniggers and laughs rang out from some of the spectators. One heavier couple just cut up a-giggling. The Fat Lady swayed off and around the scale, and bent over to pick up the arrow—her huge bummy wagging wide in our faces, and near about to split a seam of the pink tights. A few mountaineers whistled and guffawed.

While she fumbled putting the arrow back on the dial, The Fire Eater came out onto the second stage, now with his tuxedo jacket off—yet still all a-sparkle in a glittery blue vest over a silky black shirt with puffy sleeves. In a master-of-ceremonies' voice, he called to us, "I'm afraid we're going to have to get a bigger scale for her, folks. Right now, come to center stage and prepare to witness the astounding."

We all shuffled over.

"In my many journeys to the Far East, I've acquired from the ancient masters the methodology of the power of mind over matter. Mind, it is said, is the ultimate substance of the universe. Matter is but the effect of mind's cause. Cause is the real truth, but most of mankind is infected and affected by the errors of effects."

A hillbilly or two swiveled their faces around to see if anybody else knew what in tarnation he was talking about.

"This ancient wisdom is evident only when an adept, as I am, performs exercises demonstrative of the power of the ethereal mind over solid matter. Those who have eyes to see, shall behold."

He yanked a shiny sword out of its sheath, swung it around some, and then stabbed it into the stage boards to prove it was solid matter. Taking a black silk handkerchief from the sheath stand, he wiped the blade clean, up and down, again and again. Then with a grand gesture, he hoisted the sword high, its point above his upturned mouth, and let it drop slowly down his goozle—to the hilt.

We all squirmed. Someone behind me whispered that the blade goes up into the handle. The Sword Swallower bowed to us—his backbone ramrod straight, his mouth open wide—and he slowly pulled out the sword. Standing right up front, I could plainly see that the blade had not gone up the handle. As he wiped the sword down and slid it back in its sheath, there arose a small patter of applause, along with some mutterings of disgust.

"My next demonstration shall be to riddle my flesh with hatpins while sitting upon a bed of nails. Great concentration is required to conquer the excruciating pain. Absolute silence is requested, please. Behold, The Human Pincushion and The Human Blockhead."

He tore off his vest and shirt, went over to the bed of nails—a three-foot square of plywood bristling with rows of nails—and he ever so carefully lowered himself onto it in a cross-legged pose. A tiny gray-haired woman beside me said to her potbellied old miner—a mite too loudly, as he was likely half deaf—"He's a-wearin' nail-proof trousers." The man sucked his lips in over a toothless jaw, nodded once, and grunted agreement.

One by one from a pillow, the Human Pincushion plucked long sharp pins, wiped them off with another black handkerchief, and slowly pushed them all the way through pinches of flesh, up and down his pasty arms, his hairy chest, and his flabby belly.

Some of the onlookers turned away their faces, gritting their teeth. Others gasped or gulped. I usually went a jag dauncy around doctor's needles poking me, yet I found myself standing there drop-jawed, wondering if this feller had ever been in Ripley's *Believe It or Not*, or on TV.

After he had more than a dozen hatpins through him, The Fat Lady waddled up onto the stage, and taking on the role of The Human Blockhead's assistant, handed him a claw hammer and a six-inch spike. The Human Blockhead slid the spike into a nostril, and tapping it with the hammer, he drove it up his nose a full five inches.

Several witnesses to this marvel twisted their lips with groans of disgust.

The spike and needles, as slowly as they went in, were pulled out, wiped off, and stuck back in the pillow. He bled only a tiny bubble here and there, and then rising from the bed of nails as his spectators turned restless, he hollered out, "And now I shall demonstrate the technique of intra-duodenal inflation. Behold, The Human Balloon."

The Human Balloon's assistant, again The Fat Lady, waddled over with a bicycle pump. The Human Balloon lay down on the stage and put the end of the pump's hose into his mouth. Then his assistant bent over the plunger and took in pumping. His belly bulged. She and the pump huffed and wheezed—her mounds a-jiggling, his belly strutting larger and larger. Then with his middle big as a basketball, he took the hose from his mouth, rolled onto his side and pushed himself to his feet, and in an eerie bullfrog voice, he belched, "And now you have seen how mind conquers matter. Betake yourselves back to your world and ponder these wonders." He took a bow, and let loose a stout burp that wouldn't quit.

We laughed and applauded almost loudly, plainly relieved that our lessons in such wonders were over with. But now, where was the rest of the seven shows? Was this all there is to it?

"At the next stage," announced our master of ceremonies, reading his audience well, "The Battery Woman shall demonstrate her marvel to you forthwith."

Throwing on his vest, he led us to the next stage, where The Fat Lady, now evidently The Battery Woman, squeezed herself into the wooden electric chair. He buckled her down with leather straps, and taped wires onto her forehead, her saggy ankles, and the backs of her porky hands.

"And now I shall turn her on."

Milking more drama, he gripped and re-gripped the lever of an over-sized knife-switch mounted on the side of the chair. Then he jammed it home. The house lights dimmed and sparks crackled across rods atop the chair. The Battery Woman quivered and quaggled. He threw the switch to off. The sparks stopped, the lights came up, but she still quivered and quaggled, all charged up. He got out an electric shaver from behind the chair and plugged its cord into her nostrils. The shaver hummed. He trimmed his chin while we all hooted and hawed. Then he plucked the wires and straps from her and heaved her out of the chair. They took a deep bow to our patter of applause and hurried off the stage out through the back of the tent.

The born-to-lose feller in the studded motorcycle jacket—who before the show had stepped up and bought the first ticket—he yanked the drape open at the exit, and said like a tough guy, "Okay. Show's over. Next show in fifteen minutes. This way out."

As we shuffled out, an old mountaineer next to me yelped to him, "But whar's The Fire Eater?"

"Ain't you seen him out on the bally?"

"Yeah..."

"For free?"

"Yeah..."

"Well, what more d' ya want, old timer? Burn the top down? Huh? Is that what ya wanna see? Let's go. Everybody out. Next show comin' up. Let's go. This way out."

On my fingers I counted the seven shows—Fire Eater, Fat Lady, Sword Swallower, Human Pincushion, Human Blockhead, Human Balloon, Battery Woman. I'd say we'd gotten our dime-less-than-a-dollar's worth.

An hour or so later, after shuffling around and around the midway through the dwindling crowd and plunking a few quarters down on a game here and there, I got joggled out of my daze when the colored lights and the ride motors quickly shut down and the carnies jumped out of their booths and dropped their awnings.

I found myself not far from Walt's trailer, past which in the last hour I'd ambled by again and again. Spying on him between the rides and through the crowd at every chance and angle, I'd watched him work his game. Unable to keep my eyes off him, I studied him and hunted for faults. He plainly appeared to be just a happy-go-lucky feller, handily having a good time—and giving one out, also—foisting his game onto folks. And I admired what I saw—the fluid way he moved, the cagey look in his playful eyes, the easy grin across his square jaw. When I'd catch sight of him, a fluttery bearm would set astir my innards. When he'd now and then catch my eye, I'd go all of a twitter and turn away, my heart throttling the breath in my throat.

I scurried over to him as he pushed up with a pole the hinged aluminum awning, which was the trailer's sidewall when shut—as was the other half of the trailer already. While Walt propped the awning off its braces, a short-legged but broad-shouldered feller—with clean-cut wiry-gray hair, two-tone-green polyester duds, and a yellow-billed meshed cap—stepped atop the counter, and at each end pulled hitch pins out through holes in the steel bars angling up the awning. Then he hopped out of the trailer, and Walt, with the pole, lowered the awning into his hands. Appearing even shorter down on the ground, he swung the side of the trailer shut, slid the bolts to, and set the padlocks.

Walt took my elbow, and I pressed against him as he ushered me through a gap in the line-up, to out back behind the tents and trailers, and along a dark maze trampled in the grass between parked cars and trucks. When we came to a red-and-white Mercury—the model with the back window slanted inward at the bottom—he swung open its door, and we slid across the wide front seat.

At once, we latched onto each other and went at it as if eating the other alive. With hungry lips and frantic tongues, we feasted on our necks and faces. He didn't grabble at me like all the others boys would do. He stroked me as if he treasured my make—caressing and fondling my curves with an admiration I'd never before been given.

Soon, the almighty power of this magic moment scattered like birds at sunrise. And as a remedy for the goofy awkwardness that set in, I took to giggling.

"My oh my, Annabelle... Woo-wee, baby... Wow. I mean, I never... You know? I never."

"Me neither, Mister Dream Man."

"Oh yeah. Yes. You know it," he said, and, reaching in his soft leather coat for his pack of Raleighs, added, "Tell you what, baby. I ain't ate much of nothin' since yesterday, save some bacon and eggs and a corn dog. And Barnett at the Mountaineer shuts down his kitchen at midnight, which is near to soon. So how 'bout you and me scoot over there right now for some eats and drinks."

I nodded my agreement. He lit a cigarette and offered the pack to me. I shook my head—it being one vice I'd managed to shun. We slid out of the car and marched off toward Clandel's two-and-three-story downtown, huddled between the hillsides a few-minutes' walk away. Clinging to each other, we crunched through a gravel parking lot and strode onto Main Street's sidewalk, a lone pickup truck rattling past. The canyon of bricks echoing our heels, our reflections on plate-glass storefronts followed alongside—from one window to the next our likenesses shape-shifting, near to far.

I'd walked past this picture show many times, in sunlight and streetlight, peeking at myself growing from girl to teen. Often, who I'd sullenly view in the glass was not who I'd want to see—I wanted to be older, be prettier, be more knowing, be with somebody else, be somebody else. But there with Walt, his arm across my shoulders, our reflection thrilled me to no end. I was no longer that sulky girl with yet another big-eared boy. Walt, for a fact, was one hunk of a man. And there beside him, somehow I'd become more of a woman.

I stopped him in the middle of crossing the street, reached up behind his stout neck, and lifted my lips up to his. He muscled me off my feet, twirling me in circles like a carnival ride, laughing in my ear while I nibbled his, carrying me clear of a hopped-up Ford rumbling past with two acorn-crackers eyeing us, their radio booming out a Merle Haggard tune.

Across the street, by Johnson's Shoe Store, he set me down, and I followed him through a swinging door and into a stairwell, where we stomped up a flight of creaky wooden treads to a dented green steel door. Walt fingered the buzzer button next to a small sign that read: Mountaineer Club ~ Members and Guests ONLY. Bars serving hard liquor in West Virginia, legally, could only be in private clubs, by state law. Shortly, a small panel in the door slid open, and a woman's eyes, lined with hard living and dark mascara, peered through with an ashy squint.

She asked, "Y'all got a card?"

Walt said, "We're with the show."

Her eyes narrowed even meaner. "Ya gotta have a card."

Walt pushed his face up to the open panel, and told her, "Get Barnett."

Backing away, she said, "He's behind the bar."

"And so... get him here. Please."

She slammed the panel shut, her hand flashing cheap rings and bright red fingernails. Walt shuffled around some, grumbling. "Goddamn West Virginia. If it weren't for a good-old boy like Barnett, show folk couldn't get a decent drink. One more month and we're on to New York, where you can sit down at a table and buy whiskey like a civilized human being."

"New York City?"

"Nah. Upstate."

The panel slid open hard, and puffy eyes peeped through. The panel slammed shut, and the big door squawked open. Paunchy, with grizzly shocks of hair over ruddy ears, Barnett stepped out onto the landing. The Friday-night hullabaloo and country-music jukebox spilled out the door, held ajar by Barnett's heel. He asked, "Got a card?"

Walt shrugged and apologized, "Sorry, Barnett, I left it in my other pants or someplace."

Barnett pulled from his shirt pocket a pen and a thin stack of membership cards. Scribbling on one, he asked, "Walt, ain't it? Walt what?"

"Ryder. R-y-d-e-r."

"Here ya be, Walt Ryder. The sheriff's been on me like a big dog, bitin' my ass 'bout everybody's gotta have a card. So, duty be done, this here's your lawful scrap of scrip. Your beauteous guest here... she twenty-one?"

"More than that to me."

Barnett swung the door open and waved us in with an honest, "Good to have ya again tonight. Y'all want somethin' to eat?"

Walt took my elbow and led me through the door, saying, "Yessir, sure do. What's good?"

"Got some T-bones I could do. Or a burger? Some tasty shrimp cocktail. No taters left. There's some turnip greens I could warm. Everythin' else is put up, run out, or too much to fuss with."

"T-bone, rare, and some greens. What you want, baby?"

"I don't know... I never had shrimp before."

"Shrimp cocktail for the lady. Bourbon on the rocks for me. And you?"

"Um... Stroh's?"

"And a Stroh's for the little lady," Barnett said, with a short nod and a welcoming sweep of a hand. "Help me out, will ya? And take a table down near the kitchen. Busy night."

The jukebox thumped out a Johnny Cash tune through the narrow and smoky room. A brown Formica bar along half its length, the rip-roaring Friday-night crowd elbowed up to it, as others bunched around a clattermint of chairs and tables—their laughs large, their slurred words rowdy, their poses cocky, their downcy faces all aglee.

The end of the room by the kitchen held two rows of booths upholstered with mallyhacked red plastic. Walt steered me toward one, and as we went through the room, several faces turned to watch us. Some boys I knew from school were at the bar, and I saw one nudge another, to look see who'd just walked in with what. The volume of the ruckus left off a piece, as we slid into the booth, our backs to the gather-all. We wrassled our jackets off, and Walt stroked my thigh, the room returning to its hullabaloo.

I cocked an elbow on the table, leaned an ear into my hand, and said, "It must be nice to walk into someplace and know nobody. Nobody making it their business who you're with or what you're doing. Tomorrow, half this town will've heard from three-quarters of these egg suckers in here that Annabelle Cory was up at the Mountaineer with a carnival man last night. Not that I set one ounce of owl turd over whether I'm in here with you or not.... But what aggravates me to no end is them benastying me in their hillbilly minds."

Firing up a cigarette, Walt said, "Baby, people got nasty minds everywhere. They put you down to prop themselves up... no matter where you go and what you do. It's one-million-percent unbelievable what kind of shit stinks up people's heads in this world. I see it every day, everywhere, in every way. And it's my job to figure out what's goin' on in their noodle, so's I can play their game while they play mine. That's how I win my money. And don't we have fun.

"But I'll tell you what, baby. When people have no clue who you are, you can be anythin' you want. You pull into a town, and till they find out you're a carny you might be anyone at all. I've told people that I was things, from a priest fired for hanky-panky, to the son of John Wayne—just for shits. For somethin' other to say when they ask me where I'm from and what I do. If I tell 'em I'm a carny, they jump to the usual kinds of conclusions about who the hell I am.... So why not play games with it?"

I whispered, "In Clandel, everything is everybody's business. I mean, there's scarce anything outlandish to do around here. But when you *do*, do something, folks make a big foofaraw of it. And most times what was done amounts to nothing much at all.

"Now I ain't that wild a girl. But I read a mess of magazines and watch my share of TV, so I know what-all goes on out there in places like New York City and California. Now there's some folks worth talking about. Me, I do something a jag different 'cause there's nary else but the same old same-old, and folks get all briggity-britches blabbering about it."

I sighed, glanced over my shoulder at the liquored-up rowdydow, and asked, "So, where are you from? And what do you do that makes folks talk about you?"

"I'm from lots of places, and I'm in show business."

"Ever been to New York City?"

"Once. Just passin' through on a bus."

"What's it like there?"

"Oh... it's like another planet."

"Where do you like the best?"

Turning to give me that big grin and look me straight in the eye, he said, "Here, now. With you."

"Hmmm... I mean if you hankered for someplace else to live, where would you move to?"

"Baby, I move to live, and live to move. The only place better than the place I'm leavin', or the place I'm goin', is everywhere in between."

"But where's home?"

"Here's home. Where's your home?"

"Up yonder in an apartment on the side of the hill."

"You're not at home right now?"

"No."

"Well, I'm right at home, right now. This is my table, and fat old Barnett, my servant tonight, will shortly bring me my dinner. My bed's in my hotel room. And baby, I buy this home of mine with the same green money that you buy your home on the hillside with."

I thought on this for a short piece, before saying, "That sure is another way to look at it."

"That's how I see it."

"So where haven't you been?"

"I ain't been in love lately."

"Oh? And when's the last time you were?"

He stubbed out his smoke, his eyes searching the blistered blue wall paint for the answer. Then he said, "Baby, I don't know if I can say that I've ever really been in love. You know, like you hear it's supposed to be. Wonderous and all....

"I'll tell you, I've pitched woo to loads of women, and I still love 'em all. But I can't remember a one who I could flat-out say I fell into somethin' magical with."

He turned his sly blue eyes to mine, and added, "But with you I feel somethin' different comin' on.... Do you feel somethin' different?"

I shrunk back a bit, and stammered, "Um... I've never met a body like you before. And I... I haven't ever been in love like they tell in tales, neither. But I don't even know yet who you are, mister."

"Well, what say we get to know each other a lot better tonight?"

"And then what?"

"And then we see what then."

Barnett set our drinks down on the table, and scooted into the kitchen. Walt poured the can of beer into the glass in front of me, swoggled the ice cubes in his whiskey around with a finger, and then raised his glass to me, toasting, "To the beginnin'."

I clinked his, and whispered, "To the beginning." And we drank to it.

Things went quiet between us for a spell, until I asked, "Is that three-armed man for real?"

"Yessirree-Bob. Trips is for real. Born that way, and'll die that way. And I'll tell you what. For small-town West Virginia, McCain's Magic Midway is one first-rate show. Not just a respectable roundup of rides and games, it's got one of the better back-ends in the business nowadays. That's because old Eli McCain treats his freaks right proper. Good friends with many of them. Sees to their special needs.

"All day Trips shuffles those fortune-tellin' cards in his joint trailer. Then every night he deals poker in the G-top. Isis, our tattooed and genuinely bearded snake woman, is his squeeze. Imagine that, baby. And both of 'em way out into some sort of hocus-pocus.

"Old Eli's got a glommin' geek, too. And always one, sometimes two, kootch shows. Now that's what brings out the people. Sonny McCain, the old man's only son, he's out eatin' fire and swords on the bally every night, workin' the tip with his wife, Lula, The Fat Lady."

I said, "Yeah, I saw their show, and Trips read my cards."

Walt fired up another cigarette, and asked, "So what's in your future, baby?" After I didn't answer that straightaway, he added, "Doesn't take a crystal ball to see you ain't too copasetic with life here in Clandel. What do you figure on doin' about that?"

"Oh... I don't know. I'd sure like to leave out of here, though, and find out. There's nothing around here but coal. If coal wasn't here, this town wouldn't be here. Folks either work in the mines, or work in a business that makes its money from miners. Of course, there's no women down in the mines. But there's plenty sitting home with nothing for it. Their men all tore up with the black lung. There's got to be someplace better than this."

"Then why don't you go there?"

Scarce of an answer, I just shrugged—but it felt more like a cringe.

"Well, I'll tell you what, baby—if you don't know, then what can I say?"

"Yeah... really."

Walt sipped his whiskey and smoked his cigarette, tapping it on the ashtray more than need be. After an awkward silence, I asked him, "How did you ever get hooked up with the carnival."

"Well, at the Mardi Gras in New Orleans about five years ago—just off a lobster boat out of Marathon in the Florida Keys, which didn't catch much—I was down to my last twenty-dollar bill, so I answered a newspaper ad for parade vendors. Pushing around a grocery cart loaded with peanuts, popcorn, cotton candy, and candy apples, hawking it to the parade crowds for the two weeks, for a quarter of my gross, I came out fairly flush. The two brothers who ran the operation saw I could hustle, and asked me to come on with 'em and work their joints. Half my twenties later, here I be. Settin' here with you."

"Where were you born?"

"Rhode Island. Grew up there. Got thrown out of high school. And after a stretch in the army, I hit the road."

"Why did they throw you out of school?"

"Ahhh... some smart-ass teacher tried to teach me a lesson, but I taught him one instead. Hell, I'll tell you what—any human can learn more about what's really important in one week out here on the road, than in any amount of years of schoolin'."

"But in school you learn different things."

"Sure you do. Same out here. Out here you learn what people are really like, and what a dollar is worth. What you are worth. And how to stay alive. And what feels good and bad. And who you are. And what to do and what not to do. All those things. In school they never told me nothin' I needed to know so far, except maybe my three R's. And all that I learned in a few years of grade school. Baby, there's too many kids wastin' too much time, costin' too much money, goin' to school year after year after year."

"That's for sure," I said. "I can't think of a thing they taught me that's doing me any good today—save reading and writing."

Walt waved an arm around, saying, "What do people do in life? Talk about history? Write book reports? Do geometry? Shit... school don't teach you how to make money. And it don't teach you how to make love."

"Nobody needs to school me in love-making," I bragged, fibbing. "But I sure wish I could find out how to make some money."

"You don't say..." He lowered his voice, leaned closer, and grinned. "I'm just the contrary. I always had a natural talent for hustlin' a buck. But I sure do need loads of help from a pretty gal like you when it comes to makin' some good lovin'. What say we teach each other what we know. Hmm?"

"Maybe."

He stroked my thigh, kissed my ear, and murmured, "Baby, you know it's more than maybe."

I shied off some, and asked, "So, where you going next week?"

He leaned away into a sip of whiskey, and said, "Stuart."

"Stuart..." I sighed. "You know, Stuart can't be but a few hours from here, but I've never been even near there. The only far piece I've ever been was Capital City once. We used to go over to Welch, now and then. We got kin over there. Once I took a ride with some boys into Kentucky and back. That was fun.... But otherwise, I've hardly been out of this cove at all."

"Stuart and Clandel are the same towns," he said. "They're just in different places—which are pretty-much the same, too. With different people, who are really the same people, doing the same things. I hear Stuart's wrangier than most. More jigs, too."

I said, "But at least there's different folks to meet, who don't know you. So like you say, you can be what you want to be, instead of what people think you are."

"Yeah, baby. Like I said. When you're a stranger you can be anything or anybody, or nothing or nobody. You are what you do, what you say, what you act like, whether that's really you or not. You meet someone new, there's no expectations, only surprises. That's what I do every day to make my money—I surprise people. Granted, most of 'em know what to expect from a midway joint, but they don't know what to expect from me. Most of 'em want to find out who I am, as much as they want to beat the joint."

"And who are you to them?"

"Either Satan or Santy Claus. Dependin' on whether they win or lose. Most lose. Then they tell me to go to hell."

I whispered, "Aren't those games fixed?"

"Some are, some ain't. Most of them don't need a gaff because the joint alone is hard to beat. Some joints throw out stock on a percentage. You won that pink mouse at a percentage joint. Twenty-one-to-one shot on the lay-down. Twenty-one quarters is five-twenty-five. Crazy-ball stock runs eighteen bucks a dozen, a buck-fifty apiece. Pay the nut, the juice, the patch, the gas, the stock bill—and what's left goes in your poke.

"Carnies ain't out here to lose. We're out here to make a livin'. And the only way to do that is to win more than we lose. A lot more. Some agents don't want to lose at all. That's their business. My business is the amusement business. Give the Clems a good time, and a few teddy bears, and end up with as much of their money in my apron as I can. Ah. Here comes the food."

Barnett swayed out of the kitchen, his hands full of plates and silverware, and hurried it onto the table. Walt ordered us two more drinks, and sat up bolt-straight, rubbing his hands over the slab of meat and wad of greens steaming on his plate.

After slicing off a corner of the steak and chewing on it some, he declared, "That Barnett sure does you up right. He likes show folk—or at least he likes the way we spend money in his club. I've been here four nights now this week. When the show rolls into town, he goes around the midway droppin' a few dollars here and there, and fillin' out membership cards for the carnies. He does God's work keepin' his kitchen open late. Mmm-hmm. How's the shrimp?"

"I don't know. I never had them before."

"Well then, let me try one out for you." He pinched a pink curl of shrimp out of the crushed ice around the rim of the plate, dipped it into tomato sauce set in a small bowl in the middle, and bit into it carefully— baring his teeth in a sidewise grin. Chewing as if studying the taste, he set the tailfins on the side of the plate, and said, "Top shelf."

I picked one up, scooped some sauce onto it, sniffed its fishy scent, and took a teeny bite. Its exotic flavor spread over my tongue. I sniggered, and took a bigger bite.

"Good, huh?"

"Mmmm.... Do you eat this good all the time?"

"Only when I can get it, baby. Can't get it this good everywhere."

While we ate, he did most of the talking, slicing, forking, and chewing his food eagerly, saying a thing or two and then scarfing down the next bite. I nibbled at the shrimp, until its taste became too rich—the last of it going down slow as sorghum.

He told me, "What you get, is what they got, where you're at. One night it's a bowl of beans at the cook house. Another, it's a meatloaf special at a diner. Tonight was a good night in the joint. I won near a hundred-and-a-quarter for my end. So it's the best in town tonight for you and me."

"You made a hundred-and-twenty-five dollars in one night?"

"Tonight I did. Last night I made thirty-seven. My end's a percent of what I grab. Wednesday night was only eighteen dollars in a cold rain. Tomorrow should be real good. Clandel's a decent spot.

"One week I won eighteen-hundred dollars in a bust-three at the state fair in Nashville. Then, a few weeks later down the road, it might be rainin' in no-wheres-ville, U.S.A., and I pocket forty-four beans for the whole week, with motel and meals addin' up to a yard note or more. That's the way it is in this business, baby. You gotta squirrel your nuts.

"Last season I drove a Cadillac. An eight-year-old one, mind you—but Cadillac it was. I go tap city in January and sell it, and next thing I know I'm grinding a hanky-pank at the Florida fairs, barely makin' eatin' money, and sleepin' on the counter of the joint.

"So then I meet Nickel Nick over whiskey and snooker at the Showman's Association in Gibsonton. Two days later, after an all-night poker game, I'm tapped out again, and Nick offers me a hole in his basket joint, going north the next week.

"Nick books his pitch-till-u-win, bushel baskets, and nickel pitch with the McCain show in Albany, Georgia, late February. Then we hopscotch north, town to town, week to week, through the Carolinas—where I bought the Merc' after getting flush again. By early April, the show doubles up in size. Each week, more and more joints and rides booking on. And after Mt. Airy, the caravan climbs into West Virginia for seven still-dates till Memorial Day.

"Nick plays McCain's spring route on his way to his summer line-up of county fairs in Ohio and Indiana, where I hear tell he flat out shovels in the nickels. McCain jumps up into Pennsylvania and New York. Then in the fall, he drops back to Florida through the Carolina fairs.

"After West Virginia, I'll prob'ly find some other hole on McCain's midway, and head north with 'em. All that flatland corn in the Midwest just don't set right with me.

"But I'll tell you what—over the years, the people in these towns have gone home with armloads of Nick's cups and saucers. He moves tons of glass—truckloads of the stuff. And yes indeedy, he wins tons and tons of nickels, thank you kindly.

"These hillbillies are good shots with their nickels. They take dead-serious aim, pitchin' nickel after nickel till one plunks into the piece they're wantin'. I watch 'em at the center joint tossin' nickels all day long. Nick likes to locate it smack-dab in front of his joint trailer, so's he can keep an eye on everything at once. I spot the Clems who like to toss things, call 'em over after they're done with the nickels, and hand 'em a ball. The glass pitch out front's been workin' for me all spring. I'm just startin' to thick up the fold of yard notes in my pocket again."

"Yard notes?" .

"Hundred-dollar bills, baby."

"You carry hundred-dollar bills around with you?"

"What else do I do with 'em? Give 'em over into some two-percent bank that's miles from here?"

"Let me see them," I said, not believing it.

"What, you think I flash my bankroll to...." he stopped short and eyed me. Then he peeked over his shoulder, and groping down into the left front pocket of his jeans, he pulled out a fold of powerful cash money nigh on an inch thick. He peeled back a horse dose of twenties, and tucked in the middle were some fifties and several hundred-dollar bills.

"Why there's more than a thousand dollars there," I whispered.

"Baby, this ain't nothin'. A few years ago I fell into a good hole and worked four state fairs, won a barrel of scratch, and then got lucky on a dice table, and carried nine G's into winter quarters, down in New Orleans that year. Spent every dollar on a good time. The best time."

"That sounds great."

"You know it, baby. There ain't nothin' like spendin' easy cash on a good time. Except maybe easy lovin'."

"Would you do me a favor?" I asked gently.

"Why, sure. What?"

"Would you not call me baby, and call me Annabelle, or just Belle?"

"I surely shall, Annabelle"

"Thank you, Walt."

"Your wish is my command," he said, grinning huge.

"I wish there was somewhere else we could go,"

"There is, my dear Annabelle," Slipping some dollars beneath his plate, greasy with remains of the T-bone, and cramming the bankroll back down into his jeans, he suggested, "My hotel?"

I hesitated. Things were moving here a mite too fast. He saw me shy off, and he stood up saying, "I'm off for the plumbin' in this joint. Be right back."

I twisted a pretend smile up at him, and then stared at my beer and fretted while he walked away. For a fact, I admired this Walt feller. He looked good and felt good and sounded good and smelled good. I hankered mightily for more of a taste of him. But a one-night stand with a carnival barker? I'd best chew on that twice.

Well, I'd had some one-hour stands before, with boys I hadn't admired half as much. But I'd known those boys, and I'd only known this feller just a few hours. Yet why was I tortured with such a powerful yen for him?

Then, reckoning how I hadn't much fancied any of those other boys, I asked myself—so what's right and what's wrong? Corresponding with somebody you don't much admire, or with somebody you don't much know?

The only thing I could figure for sure was that if I didn't go with Walt now, I'd forever lose what might have been—even if only for one night—a chance for some real magic.

With a feel of somebody else saying it, I muttered, "I'm getting some tonight, come hell or high water." My swivet ceased, and in floated a flood of cagey glee.

When he came back, I slid out of the booth, my heart hammering up one golly-whopper of a smile, and I said, "Let's go."

Half the room eyed us as we made our way toward the door—the ruckus quieting from a roar to a hum. Clenching my breath, my steps feeling clumsy, I glanced from one familiar face to the next. Walt appeared to sense my unease. A hand at my elbow, he stopped us in the middle of the room. I looked up at him for a clue and watched him stare down several of those eyeing us. Then he spread his sly grin wide and jabbed a thumbs up out to Barnett—who, behind the bar, said loud and clear, "Thanks, Walt. See ya'll next year."

He steered us through the door, and down the treads we clattered, the rowdydow behind us stirring back up as the door swung shut. Out on the sidewalk, I clutched his arm as we strolled to the hotel. He pulled me into the plate-glass entryway of a storefront, shadowed from the streetlights beneath a metal awning, and he kissed me like a sailor come to shore.

I'm not one to kiss and tell, but when Walt pulled me up into his arms there, it was like nothing I'd ever yet known. Not just a kid anymore, fooling around, stealing some sugars, each lusty kiss somehow fetched up the woman inside me all along—now set free by my surrender to him.

Clinging to each other, we staggered the few blocks over to the Grand Hotel, one of downtown's older and larger buildings—half a block of bricks piled square and plain, three stories high over Harper's Mercantile. At the hotel entry, up a steep side street to the second floor, he held the door open for me as I shied off—unsure once more, dropping my eyes—and then, with half a shrug, half a shudder, and chill bumps thicker than warts on a pickle, I scooted inside.

We clomped up some treads to a landing, where behind a desk sat the night clerk, who leaned back in his chair, and said, "Another person in the room'll cost you extry."

Walt steered me past the desk, telling him, "We'll settle up in the mornin'."

Up another flight of creaky treads and down a stuffy corridor lined with numbered doors, we came to room 22 and he unlocked it. Then, dropping an arm behind my knees, he swept me up, carried me into the room, and lowered me tenderly onto the squeaky bed.

2

II

· LA·PANCES ·

La Pances — a French word for belly or womb — is in many decks known as The High Priestess or La Papesse. Keeper of mysteries, she cradles a book that contains understanding of what is hidden by the veil behind her. Serene, regal, an image of feminine grace and strength, she is receptive and intuitive — possessing a woman's way with the world. She passes on what wisdom she gathers from high and low, which can bring forth both enlightenment and darkness. Her number, two, indicates this duality — as well as a myriad of other ironies, coupled like male and female.

I hardly slept a lick that night. For hours I lay open-eyed next to Walt, listening to him breathe, hoping he would wake up and make love to me again. When he stirred in his sleep, I sidled up against him, expecting his caresses to renew, and when he slept on and did not reach for me, I tortured all the more, tossing back and forth between fidgety wakefulness and jumbled dreams, tangled with puzzlements echoing the doings of the night before.

One dream I remembered because it woke me up hard. I'm wading upstream in a rocky creek, and I come upon a man with a blurry face, who may or may not be Walt, standing bare-naked atop a slab of shale. He's waving one hand at me, beckoning me to come closer, and with the other hand he's pointing back downstream. I slosh up to him, and he reaches his arms out to me. But I bow down, scoop up some branch water, and take in washing his feet. Suddenly, the run dries up, and dozens of snakes gather around me—nuzzling their cheeks against my ankles like cats might. I panic with terror, unable to do anything, and I woke with a gasp.

Near sunrise, I gave up hope on sleep, stared up in the mornglom at the cracked plaster of the smoke-yellowed ceiling, and thought about the likelihood of carrying myself off with this man next to me. One voice in me said that I didn't know him at all, and was bereft to think I'd light out with him and his carnival after just a one-night stand. Another voice said that Walt was the man I'd been waiting for, and if I let him go without me, I'd maybe miss the boat—the boat carrying my tomorrows. And another voice jowered that even if Walt turned out to be a three-hundred-and-sixty-degree son-of-a-bitch, then at least I'd be long gone from Clandel, and that would be one giant step forward.

But long gone to where? To some sideshow in a carnival? No, I might could travel with the show a while, maybe make some powerful money like Walt does, save it up, and buy a ticket for California or New York City.... But they were both a far piece, and what would I do if I got to one or the other? Well, maybe get a job in a fixy restaurant and make big tips, for one. And on and on I puzzled over what to do now.

I tossed and turned, with half an aim to wake Walt, and after a while when this didn't rouse him, I reached down to his straddle and fingered his okra. It strutted solid, fast as skim milk through a tow sack. He hummed a randy moan and popped an eyelid open. We mooned across the pillows for a spell, until he hauled himself above me, and we took in at it again—slowly, quietly, and gently at first. Then we set the bedsprings to squawking, raising the dust to glitter in the sunbeam that poured through the window. As our frenzy blazed, I melted like hot sugar—cotton candy spinning in the depths of me, a deliciousness oozing between us—exalting our endmost moment to a sweetness that tore the stars out of heaven, and carried me near a glory I never thought possible.

After we calmed our squirming, and before dozing off like pigs in sunshine, a feel of redemption settled on me. Though not any wedding night, somehow in less than half a day I'd hitched up with a man, who for a fact vowed nary an 'I do' at all, but who did do it to me nevertheless—handily ringing the bells atop my steeple, blessedly pealing knells of salvation through my jingle-jangle puzzlement. If Walt weren't the man for me, he sure enough felt of it so far.

My eyes, though heavy with scarce sleep and tuckered-out pleasures, wouldn't stay shut because they couldn't get enough of the sight of his face, inches from mine—so close I could study the way the beardy stubble peppered his lean cheek, his big-boned jaw, and his firm-set upper lip, proud with a slightly curled-up corner. In novels and movies, heroines would fall in love with their heroes—alakazam—and follow them through the middle pits of hell, and then on to seventh heaven. The enchantment I felt of as I gazed at him lying there, was this love? If it was, it was brand-fire-new to me, and the chance that love had finally come to me filled each breath with hope I drew deep down within.

An hour or so later, with me snuggling up to his sturdy and fuzzy chest, he mumbled, "I gotta go open the joint pretty soon.... So, what're you gonna do, my lovely Belle?"

"I don't know. Go home and change my clothes. Then go see you."

We lay there for a spell in awkward silence, struck dumb with questions that begged to be asked. I itched to ask him to take me with him. But how could I abide that? I didn't rightly know if I ought to leave out with him and his carnival, and I didn't want him to tell me that I couldn't go if I did ask.

Then, maybe reading my mind, he asked, "How're you gonna get out of this town, Annabelle? I mean, I hear you sayin' how you hate it so, but I'm not hearin' any evacuation plan."

"That's because I don't have one."

"So when you gonna get one?"

"I don't know. Got any suggestions?"

"Well... tonight we jump to the next spot, Stuart... and I'd... I might be able to help you out."

I sat up against the headboard, crossed my arms over my mother-naked bubbies, and looked keen at him. "How?"

"Well... I prob'ly can get you a hole in one of Nick's joints. And I suppose I could show you the ropes, about bein' out on the road and all."

"And me be a carny?"

"Maybe... give it a try. If you don't like it—that's why the road goes both ways."

"And what about you?"

"Same deal. Give me a try. And if you, or I, don't like what's goin' on, then off we go down the road in different directions. What've we got to lose?"

I thought on that a piece, and then said, "You've got nothing to lose. But as for me, I could lose... What?.... My respect?"

"Baby—Annabelle—respect is two things. One's what people think of you, and the other's what you think of you. Personally, I don't give a rat's ass about what anybody in this hick town thinks of me. Exceptin' you, that is. I care what you think about me. I'd like your respect. And the only way I know how to get your respect, and keep mine, is to be real. Real to myself and real to you. No bullshit, no alibis, no jive. If I bullshit myself, I'm not being real, and I don't respect myself. So, no bull—I'd respect you if you ran off with me and McCain's Magic Midway. But I wouldn't respect you if you weren't real to yourself, and stayed here where you really don't want to be. Does that make any sense? You get what I'm sayin'?"

"Sort of.... But if I do go with you, then half the town will soon know, and they'll be squandering opinions about it from here to Christmas, which will make me feel like one sorry squackhead if I ever come back."

"Then you won't want to come back, Annabelle. And won't that be about the best thing that's happened to you since you were born?"

"I don't know. I've got my maw and sister here. Though most of the time they're a misery. But they're family. And there's my friends... and, you know, my reputation."

"Belle, your family, friends, and reputation are all yours. I used to carry my load of that, too. But I left it all behind for my freedom. I'm no longer who others want me to be. I am what I am and that's all that I am. And I ain't Popeye the sailor man."

I sniggered nervously, then asked seriously, "Who are you really?"

Walt breathed a sigh, reached for a cigarette from his jacket on the bedpost, and smoked while he told me with his answer.

"I'm really just a regular kind of Joe. No devil. No angel. Just your typical lucky boy who's lookin' for somethin' better in life than just the typical. That's why I glommed onto you. You're miles from typical. You're the most beautiful gal I've ever laid eyes on. No lie. I had to reach out for you.

"And also, I'm in show business. It's way more alive than the sucker life, much more free. I'm my own man. I say whatever I want. And as long as there's dollars in my pocket I go where I want, when I want. Sure, sometimes I'm not where I wanna be—I get someplace, then find out I don't really wanna be there. But I know that soon I'll be goin' down the road again.

"So I guess who I am is a traveler. A travelin' man always on the way to someplace new, maybe someplace better, maybe someplace worse. I won't know till I get there. Then off I go again.

"This here carnival business, I can take it or leave it. Scads of times I've quit and gone off someplace else, to do somethin' else. But carnies say that once you get sawdust in your shoes, you don't get it out.... Hell, who knows what and where I'll be in ten years? Or next year? Or even next month?

"Today I'm a carny, and I'll work my joint out on that midway. Tonight I'll slough, load up, and haul it all to the next spot. I told Nick I'd do that, and tonight that's what I'm gonna do. But hey, I've flipped burgers in hash houses, and pounded nails, and sold insurance, and made change, and done lots of other things, too."

I asked, "Who am I to you?"

"You're my dream girl." He laughed, and blew a swirl of smoke into the sunbeam. Then, with a serious tone, he added, "Annabelle, to me this mornin' you're a mystery. I hardly know who you are, or what will be. I do know that I've been feelin' mighty fine about you these last dozen hours. And I do know I'd take the chance and take you with me, and see what comes of it. I suspect you want that too, Annabelle. But... it's hard for you to just pack up and leave."

I searched his eyes for clues. "And what would you want from me if I did leave out with you?"

"I'd want you to be you," he said. "What you want to be to me is what I want you to be. If you wanna be my sex slave, go for it. If you wanna just be buddies, go for it. If you wanna be a sword swallower, go for it. If you wanna be President of the United States, go for it. But whether I'd wanna be with who you wanna be, I won't know till we get there.... What can I say?"

"Can you say you love me?"

"Hoo-hoo.... Look, I said won't bullshit you, Annabelle. I like you, loads, so far. How the hell do I know you enough to tell you I love you? I'll say this, though—there's somethin' about you that's switched on somethin' inside me. When I saw you out on the midway last night, I absolutely had to call you in, and not for no softballs in no peach basket. After the first time you walked past the joint, I cussed myself out for bein' so hang-jaw stupified—just watchin' you walk by, maybe never to see you again. When I spotted you comin' around the second time, there was no way I was gonna let you go by. I would've jumped out of the joint right then and there, gotten disqualified, and followed you around all night. And Belle, after we talked a few minutes, I knew we'd be here this mornin'. Now I got this feelin' we'll be together tomorrow, too.

"And what's more—you know last night when you asked when was the last time I was in love? Well, I've been thinkin' that, yeah, I'd been with lovers before, for a few days, few weeks, or months..."

"How many?"

"Oh, I don't know. A couple dozen or so. But what I was thinkin' was that none of 'em ever gave me much of an urge to stick with them. You think maybe that's what love is?—the glue that sticks people together?"

"There's lots of people stuck together who ain't in love."

"You got that right, Belle."

I said, "I know what love is."

"What?"

"Love is the good of one's soul giving itself to another soul's goodness, for the good of both."

"You think so?"

"That's my guess."

"You think we've got good souls to give?"

"You don't?"

"I'd say we've got bodies to give, thoughts and feelin's to give, lives to give, time and money and things to give. And all that to get, too."

"That's not love," I said, "that's some sort of barter. Love has to do with the soul."

"And where's our souls?"

"In our hearts."

"Hmm.... And who told you this?"

"I don't know. I likely read it in a novel."

"Oh yeah?... And have you given the goodness of your soul for love yet, Annabelle?"

"No. I reckon not."

"Why not?"

Unsure of what I felt and how he'd take it, I shied off, and said, "Because love hasn't happened to me yet."

"So you don't love me. Eh?" he said with comic scowl. "Well, what'll happen next is I'm gonna take my broken heart down the hall to the plumbin'. Then get dressed, go find some eggs and coffee, check out of this dump, and go open up my basket joint for the matinee."

Walt hauled himself out of the bed—leaning back to kiss me once more, his eyes gleaming with an adoration I took to be unduly lavish—and he gathered up a towel, razor, and toothbrush, pulled on his jeans, and went out the door, shirtless and shoeless.

I rose from between the warm sheets and yawned and stretched—mother-naked, up on my toes, arms over my head, hands bent back. I went to the flyspecked window, pushed aside the torn plastic curtain, and looked out over the sunny morning. The hotel sat higher on the hillside than the rest of downtown. The view over the roofs made Clandel appear to be not quite itself. And to be up in the old Grand Hotel, with its sinful reputation, tasted right salty.

Dancing like a ballerina across the gritty linoleum, twirling amid sparkly dust in the sunbeam, I waved my arms up at the narrow sky over the town, hummed some notes of no particular song, shook my bubbies, and took a bow.

A half-hour later, I led us to a booth at Jake's, the railroad-car diner where I'd waitressed part-time since I was sixteen—Jake and Loretta, the mom-and-pop owners, Jake on the grill and Loretta at the counter. Jake was a good old boy, mid-sized and middle-aged, with a few side teeth missing in a good-natured face beneath a waxed-up flattop haircut. A machine at his griddle, he took orders by memory and shuckled them out handily, with nary a one done wrong. From behind her counter, Loretta handled the money and oversaw everything else, lording over the customers on the dozen chrome-and-black naugahyde stools—always a hairnet over her blonde bouffant, and a flowery bib apron over a baggy jersey in any shade of red, and blue jeans way too tight for her big bum. Once, she was chaperoning at a teen dance I went to at the Church of God, all decked out in her frippery, and I didn't even know it was her until she spoke to me. She looked like some fine-haired lady on Easter morning, and appeared shrunken, out from behind her counter. But after I'd gotten my focus back, I recognized her greedy eyes beneath her blue eye shadow.

Barbara—who waited on the booths along the window, which was my job, too, on my shift—she clacked over in her always-shiny-black low-slung patent-leather heels to take our order, and asked me, "How you doin' this mornin', honey?".

"Mighty fine. Barbara, this here's Walt. He works with the carnival that's in town."

"You don't say..." she said. Mannerable as a crow, and withering away already at fifty—her disagreeable face made even more peevish by the heavy eyeliner and fire-red lipstick she always wore—Barbara tapped her pencil on her pad and scowled down her long nose at Walt.

Walt lifted his huge grin up from the menu, and said, "Two hen fruit, over easy, with gravy, grits, and coffee, barefoot. And what you want, Belle?"

"Two scrambled with toast, and coffee with socks on."

Barbara sternly scribbled that down. I knew her moods all too well, and she clattered off, misput something terrible. Walt leaned to me and whispered, "When you tell the good townsfolk that you're with the carnival, it's like tellin' them you're a goat raper."

I whispered back, "Barbara never has a good thing to say about nobody no how."

"Most people don't," Walt said, lighting a cigarette. "But I sure got somethin' good to say about you, though."

"Yeah? What?"

He took a long pull on his Raleigh, and blowing a cloud out the side of his mouth, head back, squinting at me with one eye, and half that cocky grin, he said a mite too loudly, "You know."

"Stop looking at me like that," I told him.

"Stop lookin' away from me like that."

I whispered, "What am I supposed to think. You asking me to leave out with you like it was nothing."

He leaned to me, lowered his voice, and said, "Sooner or later you're gonna go, Annabelle. Why not now? With me? I'll at least get you out of here. Even if you don't stay with me, you'll at least be on your way to some place besides workin' in this dump."

Barbara came with the coffee, plunked the mugs down, eyeing me hard to let me know she'd heard some of what he'd said, and then she clacked away to see to her other tables.

"It's not so bad here," I muttered.

"Yeah, right. It looks big-top copasetic—your career here. Huge future in this show. Look where it's gotten Barb the Bitch"

I hissed, "Shush. She's not a bitch."

"Oh. Pardon me. To what would you attribute her warm-hearted ways?"

"I don't know."

He whispered, "Yes you do, but I'll tell you anyway.... Once she had other dreams, just like you do, Annabelle. But she chose this instead. She don't want to be here, either. But here she is, and here she'll stay, because she ain't got what it takes to do what she wants."

We sipped coffee and stared across the table at each other. Though ashy from his straightforwardness, I had to ask, "And what does it take?"

"Guts and gumption. Most people are afraid to take a chance with their lives."

I said, "That's for sure," and we sat there silent for a spell—him pulling on his smoke, and me staring out the window.

Barbara thumped down in front of us the heavy plates steaming with our breakfasts. Walt scoffed up his food up like a hungry hound, nearly done before I'd even jellied my toast.

Wiping his mouth and fingers with a paper napkin, he said, "Annabelle, I gotta check out of the hotel and get over to the lot and raise the awning. You think on what we've been talkin' about and come see me later today. Things slow down around late afternoon, so maybe we can get together some then."

He gulped down the rest of his coffee, reached over for my hand, looked across the table into my eyes, and said, "Even if I never see you again, last night was the best. At the least, let's have tonight, too. Then, maybe who knows.... Will I see you later?"

"Yes."

"Good."

He laid some dollars on the table and hurried off.

Beat out with all of what had happened to me since last night, I just poked at my breakfast. Barbara, swooping up to grab Walt's plate, cup, and money, said, "Honey, you best steer clear of those carnival rullions. They ain't nothin' but trash."

I looked up at her, and almost said, "And what the hell are you?" But I held my tongue and turned back to my eggs.

When I got up to go, Loretta waved me over to the cash register, and told me, "Annabelle, we'll be needin' you to work tonight. That carnival's bringin' a heap of folks down from the hills, and last night we was swamped."

"But I have something planned for tonight."

"Well, we'll be needin' you here. Six o'clock. Okay?"

"I guess."

I scuffed out onto the sidewalk. For another half-hour or so, I wandered through the Saturday-morning hubbub—folks going about their business, many down from a long and chilly April up in the hollows, big-eyed at the spring day, buying their hardware, getting their hair cut, paying their insurance man, towing along young'uns raring to go to the carnival. Up and down the streets, cars and pickups rumbled while a coal train rattled down between the ridges, setting the whole town to trembling.

I sauntered along my usual downtown circuit, a walk well known by my feet. I'd go down the low end of Main Street, its two-lane one-way traffic crawling uphill between the brick buildings. I'd march by the courthouse, its concrete square lined with humdrum offices of lawyers and realtors. Then I'd climb up Church Street to High Street—a one-lane one-way winding downhill through town—where on the uphill side of the street, smaller storefronts shouldered against each other, facing the fire escapes on the backsides of Main Street's buildings.

More and more of the shops on High Street were gone out nowadays. Some still held businesses that had been there forever, their windows never changing—a shoe repair, a barber, a second-hand store. A new shop that sold baby clothes—lacy curtains in the window and a fresh-painted sign over the door—looked lonely and doomed to be worthless.

Toward the end of the row, there sat one shop that had been empty for a spell, which I thought to be right cute. Now and then, after smoking pot with Luke and Johnny Bob, they'd drop me off downtown, and I'd bogue by and peep in its window, and speculate on what kind of business I might chance in such a place—a store with magazines, comic books, and paperback novels, or maybe a fashion shop with cool clothes or shoes. But before I'd get too far along in these pipe dreams, I'd figure there was no way someone like me could even get started on something like that—never mind make a go of it, or ever make a living at it, here in fruitless Clandel. You load sixteen tons and what do you get....

So what the heck was I going to do with my life? For that matter, what had I done so far? After nineteen years of folks telling me what to do, now it was all up to me. I had no skills to speak of. Twelve years of schooling taught me reading, writing, and arithmetic, some history, civics, and science. But besides the basic three R's, what good was all that in a place like this? I could likely find a job as a sales clerk or a receptionist, or keep waiting on tables, but where would that get me? The only thing I really had going for myself was my looks. If I played that card right, maybe some feller who had something going for him, other than digging coal, would give me a decent life. Maybe all I was good for was fucking and making babies. Yet I wasn't much experienced in that, neither.

After weaving up and down a few of the side streets that connected Main and High, I found myself trudging once more up the dead-end street our apartment perched on—the sign at the bottom telling all: NO OUTLET. I stopped flatfooted, peering up at the whitewashed wooden treads leading to our second-story door, rough-cut into the downhill face of that big-old lap-sided and lop-sided house. Then I scurried back down the street and turned left, climbing out of town along Highway 52.

About a quarter mile up, the sidewalk ended at a bridge over Black Creek and the railroad, a tight fit for two cars over rusty girders. Usually I'd walk no further than there, and often I'd sit on a rock and watch the run splashing by, or maybe a train clickety-clacking past. But this time, I waited for a gap in the rumble of cars and trucks over the bridge, and scurried across.

On the other side of the creek, a narrow blacktop carved its way up the cove. I trudged along the right berm, the traffic coming up from behind, crowding me against the crumbling outcrops of shale. So I crossed over to the left side, the cars coming at me head-on down the hill, keeping me close to the guard rail—a pair of cables strung between chipped concrete posts—the creek tumbling below. Carloads of faces rushed past carrying all sorts of looks at me, one after the other—surprise, caution, amusement, anger, curiosity. I eyed the drivers to be sure they saw me. Here I am, my face said back at theirs, don't you dare run me down, and don't ask me what in hell I'm doing traipsing up the side of the road. Their guess was as good as mine. A mile or so up the corridor, my stiff-necked pace slowed. Then I just turned around, crossed the road, and hoofed it back to town, kicking at pebbles and litter along the way.

I stomped up the treads to the apartment and into the kitchen, where at the chipped white-enamel table, Maw, in her plaid flannel bathrobe, sat hunched over a *National Enquirer*, between a half-eaten baloney sandwich and a can of Co-Cola. After Pap left out, she'd let herself go, far too much. Down with a horse dose of mulligrubs, lately she'd taken to stump liquor.

Folks would always tell me what a pretty girl I was, and they'd often say I'd gotten my good looks from Maw. Long ever ago, she'd deck out in a gingham dress, pile her red curls atop her head, and we'd take walks through town on Sundays, sometimes to services, or a church picnic, sashaying with Rosalie and me in hand, sometimes Pap in tow. I'd watch folks admire her, and I'd press the back of her hand against my cheek—the many rings she wore cooler than her fingers, her nails polished pink and filed to perfect ovals. I'd gaze up and study the bluish tinge of her freckled skin under her proud chin leading us about, her pleased smile raising the blush into her high cheekbones.

Now her saggy face glared up at me through grayed and uncombed hair, and she snarled, "Don't you tell me where you been all night, 'cause I already know!"

"What do you know, and how?"

"I know you been out a-strollopin' with one of them no-account carnival losels. And I know 'cause it's all over town. Two long-tongues done rang me up about it so far. How many more you reckon are noratin' it around right now?"

"I ain't been strollopin' with no losel. And I don't give a hate what any blatherskites squander opinions on."

"Well, missy, they say you have, and I say I do. And from what I heared, you been japin' him all night long at the Grand Hotel. Kate Wither's husband's the night clerk there. He told her, and now her biggity pie hole is yammerin' it all over the whole goddamn county."

"Maw... it's true I was there with a feller last night, but he's real nice, and I like him, and... well, you know, it just happened, and it was wonderful. Not at all nasty like you're making it out to be."

"Well I'll be dipped in shit and rolled in breadcrumbs. I didn't want to believe it. My girl-child's a-diddlin' rullions down at that chippyhouse hotel. What in tarnation did I do to come to this? Iffen your pappy was here, he'd whup you somethin' terrible. You know that, missy? And this losel works at that goddamn carnival?"

"Yes. And he's handsome and smart, and he makes a lot of money traveling around."

"And he's likely braggin' on his buddies right now about the tight satchel he got into last night, and you'll never be seein' his tallywags again."

"He wants to see me again tonight, and..." I almost told her that Walt had asked me to go with him.

"You stay clear of that japer. You hear me?"

"I'll see him if I want to."

"Don't you peart off to me. You hesh up and git to your room, girl. I can't abide your sorry face. Git!"

I charged into my room, slammed the door behind me, fell onto my bed, and stove my face into a pillow. Burning from downright disrespect, I jumped to my feet to stamp it out, back and forth between the walls, like a panther in a cage. Then tears sobbed onto my itchy hot cheeks, and I crawled head first under the blankets, curled up into a ball, and in the warm stuffy dark, moist with my breath and tears, I shut the world away and soon fell into a fitful sleep.

A few hours later, I woke with a startle, threw off the covers, jumped up and showered, brushed my teeth, combed out my tangled hair, prettied up my face, and pulled on fresh clothes. Then without a word to Maw—laying silent on the couch, a bowling show on TV—I snuck out the door and tiptoed down the treads. Stealing into the back of the carnival again, over the rails and through the camp, within a few minutes I stood in front of Walt's booth.

He had two players tossing balls at two baskets at the same time, and as he moved side to side, working one then the other, he twisted sly grins my way— rolling his eyes and winking, a curl of his greased-back hair dangling over his forehead. He waved me over, and leaning out over the end of the counter, told me, "I'm way too busy right now. Dreamy, this be one jam-up matinee. I'm near a yard note already for my end. Listen, I can't talk now. I told you how Nick gets all hot and bothered about dream girls hangin' around his joints. I get relieved in about two hours. So I'll be seein' you then. Okay?"

"Yeah. Okay."

"Belle, what's the matter?"

"Oh... I had a golly-whopper of an onset with Maw. And my boss wants me to work tonight at the diner."

"You listen to me. I'll be seein' you in a few hours, and I'll make it all better then. Okay?"

"Sure."

"No. Much more than sure. Hang in there. I've been thinking about you all day. Just a few more hours now." He held two long fingers up between us, then brushed them along my cheek, which eased me some, so I lifted a little smile to him. He grinned wide as the sky on a hilltop, winked once more, and turned back to his players.

I strolled off down the midway toward the sideshows, and came to a tent in front of which hung a banner picturing a bearded and tattooed busty brunette in skimpy clothes, with a huge snake wrapped around her. I dug seventy-five cents out of my jeans, and from a wiry teen with a bushy Afro and round brown face, I bought a ticket for "Isis, Queen of the Amazons."

Pushing aside the red velvet curtain over the entrance, I warily went in. The tent, about twenty-foot square, felt way too warm inside—heated by a rattly pair of electric space heaters and insulated with heavy drapes, purple, blue, and red that hung in pleats along the sidewalls. At the far corner on a low triangular stage, a tiny old woman sat cross-legged like a swami upon a pile of rugs and pillows. Her peaceful face smiled, half hidden behind a silvery white beard, which, like the wavy hair on her head, fell to her collarbone. A silky red robe with gold trim hung loosely over her shoulders, revealing a black leather bikini and a patchwork of tattoos. On her lap lounged a seven-foot snake, as thick as a fire hose.

Her gentle eyes peered up at me from her book. "Come in, dear," she said, singing the words in a kindly manner.

I shuffled over in front of the stage and gawked at her. The fine curls flowing from her dainty jaw and thin lips were, for a fact, rooted in the wrinkles of her face. Swarms of tattoos, faded with age, covered her wrinkly skin, partly bared by the robe and bikini. The snake raised its head and turned its gaze to me. I took a step or two backward.

"Oh, he won't bite you," she warbled and smiled. "My name is Isis. Would you like to look at my tattoos? I can tell you all about them."

"Okay."

"Here, sit down on the edge of the stage," she said—and I did, on the side away from the snake's head. Then in a melodic voice, chiming in rhythm to the words of her story, likely told a thousand times, Isis rendered her tale.

"My first husband was a great tattoo artist. I met him on the boardwalk in Atlantic City in 1928, and we got married a week later. He died in a car crash in '49. Bob Dodd was a wonderful man, he loved tattoos, and for twenty years he decorated my skin with his art. All of my tattoos are by him, done with the utmost care and thought. My skin is etched with his allegory of the life of the world. My husband was not only an artist, he was also a mystic. My tattoos contain the symbols of his contemplations.

"My feet carry the whirlwinds of the suns that gather the cosmic dust into fire, earth, water, and air." She uncrossed her legs out from under, leaned back on her hands, and lifted toward me one tiny foot, then the other, for my look-see—their tops dizzy with red and black spirals, their un-tattooed soles blue-veined, flakey-white, and starkly contrary.

"At my ankles are the crystals of formation." There—the flesh puffy and the tattoos drinted and stretched—was drawn a zigzag geometry of cubes and diamonds, shaded to appear 3-D.

"My calves and shins depict the birth of the world." Though she didn't shave her face, Isis did shave her legs. On the left splashed a blue wash of waves of water, and on her right leg, craggy brown volcanoes burned red with lava.

She slipped the robe off her shoulders, and stood up in her bikini—her slender make still in pretty good shape, but for its elderly swag. With both hands, she raised the snake high over her head, and chanted, "On my knees, the spark of life. On my thighs, its birth." Jagged black and yellow lightning bolts wreathed her knees. Low on her scarce thighs swarmed a mess of puny one-celled things, with and without tadpole tails, like in a biology book. Halfway up they came together into living blobs—green on her right, and blue on her left. Nearing the edge of her bikini bottom, the shapes turned into fish, crabs, starfish, and eels, swimming onto her bony left hip. On her right side, gnarly roots grew out of the green shapes below, stems weaving upward and branching out into a jungle of red and purple flowers.

She slowly turned all the way around, the snake still held high. Girdling the small of her back, a spider's web tangled up all sorts of beasts and birds doing all sorts of things—a tiger killing a lamb, a grasshopper biting a leaf, a bird swooping down on the grasshopper, a grazing cow suckling a calf, horses humping, rabbits hopping, hummingbirds tending a splash of flowers that grew from a dead dog.

"On my belly lies the Garden of Eden." Out from under the top of her bikini bottom, a thick tree reached up into the sag of her belly and branched out over her ribs. Aside the tree, posed in the raw except for fig leaves, stood Adam and Eve, each with one hand pointing at Isis's belly button and the other gesturing upward. Around the tree trunk, a horned dragon coiled. Apples and pears hung in the lower branches, but as the limbs reached outward over her ribcage, there also hung books, tools, weapons, pots, wheels, fiddles, and trumpets. Above, reaching down for these fruits, stretched the arms of a canopy of entwined men and women—Isis's swaggy bubbies weighing the leather bra down onto them.

She lowered the snake to her waist and turned halfway around, saying, "My back bears the labors of mankind." There, tiny stick-figure people built up larger and larger buildings, which in turn were drawn smaller and smaller—grass huts with totem poles to log houses and stone idols, then palaces and temples and pyramids, and across her shoulder blades were cities, bridges, and skyscrapers. And above all that flew airplanes and rockets to the tops of her shoulders, which were spangled with stars, and moons, and planets with rings.

She turned to face me, and sat back down cross-legged onto her pillows. Draping the snake on her lap and gesturing to the black bra, she said "My left breast has the New Moon and the Evening Star. My right breast, the Sun rising with Mercury. Signs of the Zodiac lay under this yoke.

"My heart carries the signature of the man of my life, the artist of this masterpiece upon me—my love, Bob Dodd."

Tucked into the fold of her cleavage, across a heart tattooed in red and blue, was Bob Dodd's bold signature.

"Above my heart are the three interpenetrating astral planes of heavens and hells—those of the ill, the healing, and the kingdom of health." A swarm of devils, ghosts, and angels wove a bizarre shawl over her chest and up and down her arms. Her wrists and hands had no tattoos.

"And on my neck lies the ultimate meaning of life—veiled by my beard."

I could make out only a few lines and colors through her well-kept curls. I waited for more of her tale, but when she just sat there smiling at me with her calm eyes, I realized that the show was over.

I hollered, "Holy cow!" I bounced up on my toes, clapping my hands like a cheerleader whose team had just won State. "Wow. Butter my butt and call me a biscuit. That's the out-doingest dang thing I ever did see. You've got more tattooed on you than what anybody around here ever learned in school, or in any god-almighty church. I ain't never seen the likes of such, ma'am. I do declare, I am impressed. Thank you for showing me. I'm plumb fexatiously whipped out."

"Well, thanks for your appreciation." Her soft voice rose an octave to ask, "Would you like to buy some photographs of me?"

"Yes, indeedy. How much are they?"

"Well for someone who truly appreciates these tattoos for what they are, as I see you do, just four dollars."

I searched through my pockets for the remnants of Walt's ten dollars, and came up with only two. I told her that was all I had. She said that would do, and traded for an envelope of photos, telling me, "You know, mostly I sell them to men who care nothing about what the tattoos mean. They only want to see me naked, to see if I'm really a woman."

I said, "Shoot, men are mostly polecats."

"Oh no," she disagreed in a kindly way, "they're mostly just primitives. Us women, too."

I stood corrected, a heat rising into my cheeks. It was time to go—the show was over—but I didn't want to. I wanted to talk more to this strange old woman, so I blurted out the first thing I could think of to ask. "What kind of snake is that?"

"A very nice snake." She smiled through her beard and reached down to stroke the snake's head. "His name is Solomon, because he's very wise. He's a python from Borneo. We're very good friends. And he protects me.

He doesn't attack people or bite or anything like that. But most people are so afraid of him that they wouldn't dare do me any harm."

"Can I touch him?"

"Sure. He loves warm hands. He's why I keep it so warm in here. Well, it gets a little chilly wearing this bikini, too." She warbled a giggle as she pulled the red silk robe back on.

I warily reached out, and when I touched his cool scales, the yellow-and-brown striped snake rose under my hand. He wasn't slimy, as I thought he'd be. He felt strong and firm, from a place far away and long ago.

Solomon turned his head to fix the slits of his orange eyes on me, his tongue licking the air. I stroked the snake with more confidence, but when he started to slide his head toward me, I shrunk back and moved away from the stage.

"Oh, he won't swallow you."

"What do you feed him?"

"He eats little animals whole. Mice, chipmunks, squirrels. I set out live traps at each spot. He really doesn't eat much at all. Once or twice a week is plenty. Sometimes I'll find a pet store and buy him a white rat or a hamster for a treat. He loves hamsters. He just had a hamster yesterday. Didn't you Solomon. See the bulge in his belly right there? That's why we feel so good today."

The snake coiled into a more comfortable position in his mistress's lap. I said lamely, "I had a turtle once, but it didn't live long."

"Poor dear.... What's your name?"

"Annabelle."

"That's such a nice name. And you're so pretty. Well you know, Annabelle, reptiles take a lot of very special care and attention to keep them healthy."

"Yeah, I guess.... Can I ask you how you got a beard?"

"Why sure. When I was a teenager, it just started to grow. Just like what happens to the boys. Except I was a girl. Oh, the doctors have a name for it, and they think they have a reason for it nowadays. But what that name and reason is, I couldn't care less.

"Other than Bob Dodd, the best thing that ever happened to me was this silly hair on my face. It's allowed me to travel all over the country for nearly fifty years. I even did a tour of Europe one winter. While the world looked at me, I saw the world."

"What's it like traveling with a carnival?"

"It's been the best for me, Annabelle dear, but it's not for everybody."

"There's a feller who wants to take me with him when the show leaves out tonight."

"And what do you think about that?"

"I don't know.... I'm not sure. For a fact, I disgust being stuck in this town, though. And I haven't been offered any other ticket out of here lately."

"Who is this feller."

"His name's Walt. He runs a softball game with peach baskets."

"Oh, I know Walt. Why, Walt's a nice young man. There's a lot of trash that hangs around these midways, but Walt's not like that. He's so handsome, too.

"Annabelle, when I met Bob Dodd, I was a kid from Jersey who had to shave twice a day and wear heavy make-up just to go out in public. Bob had a small tattoo parlor in Atlantic City, but soon we went out on the road and booked in with circuses and carnivals. Oh, we had a wonderful life, traveling, exhibiting, making loads of money—just because I can grow a beard. And he'd work his tattoo joint. Did thousands of tattoos for thousands of people.... My, do I miss him so."

I said softly, "I can feel the love you still have for him."

"Yes, yes... I've had two husbands since, but nobody will ever be anything like Bob."

The fact that this bearded lady had three husbands startled me—creeped me out somewhat—and I stood there mute and awkward, head down, watching my foot push around a tuft of trampled grass.

She suggested, "How about I take a break? Kiddie matinees are always slow for me. If you'd like, we can go to my trailer for a cup of tea, and talk about your predicament?"

"Okay. Thanks. Please."

She picked up a small brass bell and shook a jangle from it. The ticket boy quickly poked his frizzy head through the drapes at the entrance. "Tyrone, this young lady and I are going to the trailer for some tea. Shut it down for a half hour, and you go get yourself something to eat."

"Yes, Miss Isis," he said, throwing a leery look toward me, before pulling his head back behind the drapes.

Unwrapping herself of the snake, she lowered it into a box beside the stage with a lid and holes in it. Then she pulled on a thick velvety emerald-green robe, flipped its hood over her hairy head, and slipped her feet into felt clogs. Pushing aside the drapes at a gap in the canvas sidewall, she said, "Come, dear," and led me out the back, where just a few steps behind the tent she swung open the door to a house trailer.

Up in the trailer, she gestured for me to sit at a blue-tiled table hinged to the wood-paneled wall, and I slid in one side of the nook onto a bench seat upholstered in black leather, my back to a pantry. I looked around at the kitchen, admiring its shipshape space—ample enough for Isis to scuff back and forth from sink to counter to cupboard to stove, and make tea. Dark brown drapes hung over a three-sided picture window at the hitch end of the trailer—a black leather couch set wall-to-wall there, with pillows on it matching the drapes. Above the windows, wooden cabinets, built into the corner between ceiling and wall, were crammed with books behind leaded glass doors.

Isis sat on the other side of the nook, and gently asked, "Now, what is it that makes you want you to leave this lovely valley?"

I thought on this for a piece, and then told her, "I don't appear to belong here."

"Well," she said, "I guess that's as good a reason to go as any."

"Yeah. I reckon.... But I've got no money to speak of. And, well, it's scary to really leave out, and not know where you're going."

"Where would you like to go?"

"Oh... somewhere bigger and better. I don't know for sure. New York City? California?"

"Annabelle dear, some people search for that better place, and maybe find it or maybe not. Some people stay where they are, for better or for worse. That's what people have been doing forever, and forever more will do. Some take what's given, some seek what they don't have, and some seek what they want—each ending up happy with it or not. We all eventually enable ourselves to be in a world we choose, whether we know it or not. Everyone's personal world is their own portion of all that is."

"All that is?"

"All the worlds. We're all simply part and parcel of worlds within worlds—bits of all that is—portions of God, or All That Is, or The Great Spirit, or whatever else you might call It."

"What does God have to do with me staying or leaving?"

"You're your own little piece of God. You need to be true to this, to yourself, and to Itself."

"You think so?"

"Oh, I know so. How else could it be? Why are you not like your other townsfolk? Doesn't life need both those who remain and those who go forth? Those who tend these towns and those who widen life throughout the world? That's The Great Spirit's plan. It must be. Isn't that what's been happening since before history began?"

"Well... yeah. I guess."

"Okay, so all you need to know is what kind of person you are. Are you one who remains and sustains, or one who seeks out more than what's been given? And then, once you've recognized which you are, you either stay or go."

"You know, Walt told me something similar.... But go where?"

"It doesn't matter where. What matters is being true to what is in you. You go to *who* you are. Then your life will unroll out of the needs of each day. You may be happy there. You may be not. Until you get there, who knows? At least you'll know that you've tried to become who you are. Take it from me, Annabelle, being who one is not is no way to live."

The teakettle whistling higher and louder, she leaned forward, elbows on the table, and gazed curiously at me for a spell. Then she slowly pushed herself up, and shuffled over to the stove to pour the tea. The china and spoons clinking, I sat there trying to weigh what I'd just been told—that there wasn't any particular place I needed to go to. The going itself would bring me where I needed to be. No, I wasn't the sort to be content with what already is. What could be is what's better to me. And what could be is always changing.

Isis set the teacups on the table, sat, and added, as if reading my mind, "Yes, dear, it's what you do and how you do it—not where or when—that are important. That's why you must."

My eyes sobbed up a smidgen. I sipped at the tea, and said sincerely, "Thank you."

"Annabelle dear, you just ask the little old bearded lady anything you want to, anytime. Okay?"

"Sure." I snuffled, and snorted a clumsy snigger.

Isis said, "Now let me ask you something. What's going on with that handsome Walt feller?"

"Well... we're getting along fine enough so far."

"Fine enough to run off with him?"

"I don't know.... Do you?"

"Do I what?"

"Know how fine it needs to get before you run off with somebody."

"Depends on where you're at, dearie," she said, and laughed like birdsong. "I'd say if you're a damsel in distress imprisoned atop a horrible tower by some dastardly villain, then any old hero would do quite well right then, thank you. But if things are not so bad, then Prince Charming may have to work a little harder to carry you away on his charging steed.

"After Bob died, there were all kinds of heroes vying for my hairy kisses. Young lady, let me tell you, it's odd how men want me so bad. Some women, too.... With this or that Prince Charming, we'd set off together into a sunset. Then along comes the sunrise, and all of a sudden it's a different day."

She sang a laugh again, and went on, "Oh, for a while there, I wandered around on shaky ground. Even took up shaving a few times. Then I'd be rescued again by some knight from one round table or another. I married two of them. But were they another Bob Dodd? I guess I wouldn't have known unless I'd found out. And most times, that takes time, Annabelle."

"Do you have a knight in shining armor now?"

"Well, I'm getting a little old for that nowadays, but I do now have a very good friend, with mutual interests, who I love dearly, and who is very sweet. He's not the type I usually go for. He's a freak like me. He's got three arms."

"The one with the fortune-telling cards?"

"Is there any other three-armed guy around here?"

"He read my cards last night, and it was really strange."

"Oh.... How do you mean, 'strange'?"

"It was just so true."

"What were these cards?"

While we finished our tea, I told her my story of the dog and the fool and the lovers and the wheel.

"Well, what do you know," she said, then stood, gathering the cups and spoons, telling me, "What's happening to you now is not something to ignore."

"What do the cards mean?"

She set the china into the sink, swiveled her head to me, and looking me straight in the eye, said, "They mean that you had better pay attention to whatever they mean to you. And also they mean that you are someone, somewhere, extra-special right now—to experience such clear and powerful synchronicity."

"What's synchronicity?"

"Synchronicity is coincidence with a message. Omens. Symbols coming together for a moment of deeper meanings. Or at least that's my two-cent interpretation of the concept." She chuckled at that and put the box of tea back into the cupboard.

"How do you know so much?" I asked.

"Dearie, I've been reading for half a century. I don't get out much, you see." And she chuckled again. Then, changing her tone, added, "Nevertheless and notwithstanding, my public awaits. Back to the grind for this freak. The show must go on."

I slid out of the booth, and with my hands on my hips, I craned on tiptoes to look at the bookshelves. Some of the titles crammed spine to spine behind the leaded and beveled glass were, *The Great Secret, Magic and Myth, The Great Mother, The Tibetan Book of the Dead*. I'd never seen books like these before. Appearing somehow forbidden, I wanted to reach up, unlatch a cabinet, and touch them, feel of which to read. One title stopped my eyes, *Isis Unveiled*.

"What's *Isis Unveiled* about?"

"It's about lots of things, Annabelle.... Well, you know it was real sweet talking with you. I do hope you decide what's best for you."

She swung open the trailer's steel door. As I moved toward it, I asked her, "If I go, will you be my friend?"

"Oh dearie, I already am your friend."

"You know, I just might leave out with you all."

"Of course you will. You're one gone girl. You just figure out what the next step is, take it, and go from there. There's a saying about a journey of a thousand miles beginning with a single step. There's that first step, and then there's the last one. But it's all those steps in between that makes the walking worthwhile. So you get along now, and good luck to you, Annabelle."

"Thank you, Isis."

"Anytime, dear. Bye-bye."

I stepped down into the late afternoon shadows, and Isis shut the door behind me. I went behind the line-up a short piece, back up toward Walt's booth, until I stopped flatfooted and asked myself what to do now? My mind appeared closer to being made up. Or was it? And if it was, now what?

Through a gap in the line-up, I spied at my townsfolk wandering past on the midway. Though I'd likely seen most of them most of my life and a few I knew by name, their faces carried a look I'd never before seen on them— on the lookout for fun, but with a pinch of caution. On the other side of this border of tents and trailers they strolled warily through another world—a world within a world, like Isis had said. Leaning onto a truck fender, I watched them reel past the gap in the tents, which seemed a gateway between these worlds. If I went through and joined them walking in circles, would I ever get anywhere?

Then the notion came to me that I should climb up to my special ledge on the side of the ridge above the apartment—the overpeer where I'd gone when other big questions had put me in a pickle, where I'd answered some questions and questioned some answers.

So I hurried off the lot, over the tracks, and up the hillside. At the dead end of my street, I climbed into the woods and zigzagged up the steep rocky path. My breath burning deep and Clandel looming below through the greening trees, I clambered onto the shale outcrop jutting out above a lightning-split dogwood tree. The crag wasn't easy to get to. I had to lower myself onto it, like going down a ladder—my feet breaking off shards of ancient shale, hands grabbling at branches and roots.

Below among the treetops, in the deep fold of the earth where I'd forever been, the roofs of Clandel huddled puny and unbefitting amid a misty ocean of warped and gnarly ridges under the huge blue sky. Down on the cove floor the carnival whirled—rides, tents, trucks, and trailers like toys— the people, just dots, moved like weary bugs in a flea circus. Black Creek ran glistening, snaking around the bend where downtown sat. Then away it slithered—pushed into its stony bed by one hill after another, taking with it as it went a touch of each hillside. To the west, the stormy sea of hazy ridges stretched out under the lowering sun.

I sat at the edge, my legs dangling, knocking shale loose with my heel. Raising my face to the springtime sun, I closed my eyes and basked in its power and warmth. Fading in and out of the tree-rustling breezes, smidgens of Merry-Go-Round music floated up through the faint bustle below. When after a spell I opened my eyes, I saw the shadows had grown beneath the ridge across the cove—the sun with three hours yet in the sky, but already a cool darkness spreading below.

One summer evening, when I was twelve or thirteen, the clouds in the narrow sky above Clandel had turned a bodacious gold, and I'd clambered up here just as red turned to purple and the sun-ball sank beyond the far ridges. There was such a magic in that moment—I felt as if these colors when daylight died was why I lived. Then, watching the last glow fade, I lingered too long, and climbing off the ledge and fumbling down through the dark woods scared me spitless.

Today I had plenty of time, though—hopefully, time enough to figure what to tote fair. I knew I had to leave out. But I just needed to have it all make sense to me. Or maybe I just needed to come up with a good excuse not to go. Though surely someday I'd carry myself off somewhere, what really needed reckoning here was whether or not I'd leave out with Walt tonight.

No suitcases were packed yet—nobody told about it, save Walt and Isis. I could simply forget about joining up with this carnival, forget about running off with this man, and it all becomes just something wonderful to remember.

Well, forgetting about joining up with a carnival appeared simple enough, but to not go with Walt wasn't as easy. Yet what did I really know about him after less than a day? I knew I admired him a heap sight, so far— the way he spoke and moved and looked and smelled, and especially the way he made me feel like a woman—the way he touched me, the way my twitchet tingled just being near him, the way he knew how to bring me to a tizzy that no other boy had come near to, to pleasures that only my own fingers had ever conjured up. In his eyes I saw he admired me even more than I did him. He'd likely be kindly to me. So it might could just work out all hunky-dory—for a while. Maybe forever. It was just so damn quick for something this big to happen in only one day.

I reached nearby for a pie-sized chunk of shale, and with the edge of a smaller stone, scratched onto it:

2 BIG 4

1 DAY

I put it aside, dug out a bigger slab, and etched on that:

ANNABELLE

LEFT OUT

WITH A CARNY

I stared at the scrawled words. What would folks think? Up and down the creek, every long-tongued blatherskite would take in norating tales and squandering opinions about me.

"So what?" I muttered. Then I yelled down at the town below, "So what?"

A muffled echo carried back the answer—so what....

What was it to me what folks said? Tomorrow I could either wake up in Clandel with my regrets, or I could be out on the road with Walt. Maybe someday sooner or later, I might wake up with both Walt and regrets. But all that was just jags of maybe and maybe not. Tomorrow, still here in Clandel without Walt, I'd most likely be more than sorry about missing that train, long gone around the bend.

Well then, I'd best leave out with him. But how could I so soon? Because that's all the time I had. Too big for one day? Yes, but one day was all there was. I'd already swallowed a horse dose of regrets in my short life. I knew that missing a chance was easy to do. Taking a chance, that was all the harder.

I stood up, and one by one, like Moses in that movie, *The Ten Commandments*, I held the slates with both hands over my head and heaved them down at Clandel. They crashed through the treetops, clattered down the hillside, and stopped silent with their messages somewhere below. Lying back on the hard ledge, I gazed up at the wispy clouds. Yes, I'd go. I had to. I sat up and yelled to the sky, "Damn it. I'm gone!"

I clambered off the ledge, scrambled back down the ridge to the carnival lot, strode up to Walt's booth, and waited a few fidgety minutes at the end of the counter while he finished up with a player. Spreading that big handsome grin while juggling three balls two-fistedly, he moved over to me, and I told him, "I want to go with you."

"Yee, haw!" he brayed like a Kentucky mule, and flung the balls backward into the wall of teddy bears. He jumped over the counter, hefted me belly-high to his face, and danced us around in a spry jig. Then he slid me down till our laughing lips met and kissed.

Marching up in a huff, the short feller who had helped Walt drop the awning last night squawked, "What's goin' on here?"—his oversized forehead wrinkling with aggravation under the visor of his yellow golf cap, his double-knit slacks and jersey sporting two tones of blue polyester, crisp as brand new.

"Nick," said Walt, "This here's Annabelle. Out of my dreams and come to life. Annabelle, meet Nickel Nick, independent concessionaire and owner of my basket joint."

"How do, Nick." I offered him a handshake after wriggling away from Walt.

"Fair to middlin', young lady." He took my hand in a clammy grip while his eyes searched back and forth between Walt and me, and then he said, "Walt, give me your apron and go get something to eat."

Walt untied his money apron and gave it over. "Thanks, boss. An hour?"

"Half an hour," Nick told him.

"Three-quarters?" Walt asked.

Nick grumbled, "Yeah, okay."

We hurried off hand-in-hand down the midway toward the back end. Then Walt pulled me through a gap in the booths, and out behind a tent he pressed me up against the canvas and kissed me long and strong—sparkles dancing across my closed eyelids, my lips hungry for his.

He whispered, "Want a ride in The Tunnel of Love?"

I nodded yes, and he led me behind the booths to the backside of a semi-trailer—sections of it folded out into staging and panels. We squeezed through a gap around to the front, where painted across the panels were jagged mountains under a stormy night sky—THE DARK JOURNEY, splashed in huge purple letters along the whole length, and here and there the words, PERILS, HAZARDS, DANGERS, CHANCES, dripping with phony blood.

We stepped up the iron-grate treads to a balding fat man on a stool. Walt slipped him a ten-dollar bill and got back no change, just a sly wink from the man's bulgy red eyes. Then Walt ushered me into a cute little two-seater boat on wheels.

"Ten dollars for a carnival ride?" I whispered to him as the boat jerked to a start along tracks to a door painted up to be a cave.

He said, "You wait and see where we're off to."

The little boat pushed through the cave door and rattled us into the dark. Then it took a hard left, which threw me against Walt, and we turned into a low and narrow tunnel, where lights flashed like lightning, thunder boomed, wind howled, and the boat rocked gently over the warped tracks through a stormy sea painted on the walls and ceiling—waves churning under clouds stabbed with jagged bolts. At the end of the corridor, before it took another left turn, the boat stopped, and a door popped open in the wall.

Walt took my hand and pulled me out of the boat and through the door to a dim-lit room, nearly wall-to-wall with a waterbed, made up with red sheets and piled with purple pillows.

The boat rattled away without us, and the door swung shut by itself. I asked, "What in tarnation is this place?"

"Blackie's nookie nest. It's clean. His wife takes care of the sheets."

"And how many dream girls have you had in here?"

"Aw come on now, Belle. You're my only dream now." He laughed and tumbled onto the sloshy bed, pulling me down with him. We wrassled, tickled, and giggled. Then in a heartbeat, we took in ravishing each other again.

Several boats rattled through the thunder on the other side of the thin wall. Our heat spent, the waterbed cool, I clung to his warmth, and whispered, "Who knows about this room?"

"Pretty much most of the show folk. Dark rides usually don't have anythin' like this. This joint's Blackie's own little sideline. He runs the G-top for the front office, too. A dark ride grinds steady money as is. But Blackie makes an extra sawbuck here and there off a carny or two when the tip is slow. I hear tell that now and then, if the patch is in, he'll spring open the door for a pair of smootchy marks. You'll see 'em goin' in, but not comin' out for a while. He pushes a button, the cart stops, the door pops open, and they go in, or not. Then, fifteen or twenty minutes later, Blackie gives 'em an 'all aboard' through the intercom. Out they scramble, all smiles, and Blackie dings 'em for housekeepin' at the end of the ride. Some joint, eh?"

We pulled our clothes on, and Walt pushed a buzzer by the door. A few minutes later, up rattled a boat, and we stepped out into it after the door swung open. The rest of the ride I gave little notice to—cutout devils swinging out to laugh at us diabolically, ghostly sheets wailing and brushing by. I nuzzled the collar of Walt's leather jacket, and felt heavenly in this fake hell.

Walt thanked Blackie as we climbed out of the boat. We clanged down the metal treads, and he towed me up the midway, weaving through the people, and he brought me to the cook tent, where we sat out back on fold-up chairs at a small round table.

"I gotta get somethin' quick to eat, Belle. You want somethin' too?"

"Like what?"

"Well, let's see." He turned and hollered over toward the crowd around the counter, "Hey, Squirrel." The little man who had served me a hot dog the night before scurried over to us and asked, "How many? What kind?"

"What's the soup?"

"Butter beans and fatback."

"Two bowls, on the Q.T. And two coffees, one barefoot and one with socks." As Squirrel hurried off, Walt turned to me and asked, "That okay?"

I shrugged, and he added, "What the cookhouse cooks is what we eat today. I just got a few minutes till I gotta get back to the joint.... So tell me, what's the plan, Belle?"

I shrugged again. I had no plan.

He offered, "Best way to do something is just do it."

"Yeah, so you say," I said, still in a swivet about it all. "But what am I getting into here?"

"Belle, what are you gettin' out of here?"

"Good question."

Walt lit a smoke, looked around, and nodded a greeting over to a feller at a nearby table.

I said, "I reckon I'll just go home and pack up some things. What's your plan?"

"Midnight we slough. Then I pull Nick's trailer joint with his truck through the night over to Stuart, while his wife drives my Merc'. We catch a sunup nap at the new lot. We get our location. We set up the joints. We get a room. We eat. We drink. We be merry."

"We slough?"

"Yeah, we slough the show. We break it down and load it up."

"What's in this for me?"

"Me, Annabelle. I'm in this for you."

"And what do I do while you're being a carny?"

"Whatever you want to."

"How about some options?"

"Stay, leave, work, don't work, sleep, wake up, eat, fuck, party. Same as every day. Whatever you want to."

"And... are you going to take care of me?"

"Belle, we're both on the same road here. And it ain't no one-way street. Like I told you, the road goes both ways—toward somethin' and away from somethin'. You're with me tonight. Tomorrow, I'll watch your back till you know what's what. Till we know what's what."

"My, how romantic."

"Now that's another story. What I'm dreamin', I'm genuinely dreamin'. How the dream's gonna end—how the hell do we know now?"

Squirrel hurried over with red plastic bowls—a slice of corn bread perched on each rim. Then he brought plastic spoons and paper napkins, along with two styrofoam cups sloshing with coffee, and gathered up trash from tables around us while Walt dug out a couple dollars for him. Walt crushed his smoke in a tuna-can ashtray, warily spooned, smelled, and tasted the steamy beans, and took in gobbling them up.

Between mouthfuls, he told me, "Annabelle, if you want to work, Nick's always needin' help in his pitches. The glass pitch, you just make change, pick up nickels, and throw a piece of stock to a mooch now and then. His pitch-till-u-win is in the same trailer as my basket joint, right next to your dream man. Toss hoops at blocks with prizes, little prizes and big prizes, fun for the kids, a winner every time. I don't know what Nick'll pay you in the glass pitch, but in the pitch-till-u-win you'll get twenty-five percent of what you grab, cash each night. You spend your money where you want, Belle. I'll cover the room and eats for next week or so. Till we see what's what."

I nibbled at the greasy beans on my plastic spoon and watched him wolf his down. His proposal wasn't much of what a white knight might declare to a damsel in distress, but it was as good as I was going to get right then. I knew he couldn't yet say he loved me—but neither could I say that I loved him. I almost wanted to, but I couldn't. Our eyes hunted in each other's for clues. He lit another cigarette, sipped his coffee, lifted an ankle onto a knee, and asked, "So what's it gonna be, Annabelle?"

"Well, Walt, I guess we'll just have to see."

"Yes we will. Yes we will. Just like in dreamland."

He smoked while I ate, and we said no more until he got up to go and told me, "I gotta get back to the joint. You do what you need to, and I'll see you later. Okay?"

"Yeah. Sure."

But I wasn't so sure about any of this. I was supposed to go to work at the diner at six, which it nearly was already. Maw was likely still mad as all get-out and now wondering where I was. My stuff was at home. I had to go there first.

I dumped the rest of my coffee into the dirt, and the cup and bowl with half the beans into a trash barrel, and trudged out the front gate and up the hill to the apartment. At the top of the rickety treads—the chalky whitewash scuffed off the middle of the warped boards—I turned around, took a few steps back down, and sat.

I'd watched the night fall over the roofs of Clandel many times from there—the streetlights flickering on, the last shouts of kids at play, the traffic rumbling homeward, the scent of vittles cooking. I'd sit on those treads, misput as a cat in a carton, and hone for the day I'd be gone. Now that day was here.

Yet these surroundings that used to vex me so, now appeared so peaceful and beautiful. This here was my home—maybe seeing it for the last time. With the sun sinking over the ridge, I felt shadow-shy about the unknown road ahead. But there'd be no forgiving myself if I backed out of going. I had to fetch my stuff, and say goodbye to Maw.

Slowly opening the door, I peeked around it, and tiptoed inside. The TV wasn't on, and she wasn't on the couch, nor in the kitchen. The door to her room was closed, which meant that she could be in there, or she could be out. I went into the kitchen and swung the fridge door open. There was little to eat in there, and I wasn't hungry anyhow—it was just what I always did when I came into the house. It struck me how many thousands of times I'd hunted for something to eat in this fridge, into which I put little to nothing, and in which there was not much for me now.

I went to my room, lay face up on my bed, and stared at the familiar cracks in the splotchy ceiling. Once, with a borrowed stepladder, I tried redding up that ceiling, but found it was beyond washable.

The big question right then was whether I would tell Maw I was leaving out, or would I just steal away without fessing up. If I told her face-to-face, there would likely be a cuss fight. Well, maybe we ought to raise a ruckus about this—then some things that needed saying might get said. What if I just left out and didn't tell her? No, I'd have to, or she'd likely call out the sheriff, figuring me kidnapped or worse.

I shied off wanting to go nose to nose with her, after how she'd cut such a rusty earlier. So I reckoned a note would do the deed. Though I would daily fill page after page in my diary with my yarning, I'd never written Maw more than a few lines on paper scraps—messages about where I was, when I'd be home. I dug a pad and a pen out of a drawer, and wrote:

Dear Maw,
First, I want to thank you for all you've done for me. I know it hasn't been easy. You're the only mother I have in the world.

I reckon it's just time for me to go off on my own. I know
you don't cotton to what I'm doing. But believe me, I feel that
he is the man for me right now, and whatever happens with
him and me, I point-blank know I have to go now.

This carnival thing for me is just a ticket out of here.
What I'll be doing next week, next month—I'll write or phone
and let you know. I love you and I hope this doesn't hurt you
like when Pap left out. That was mighty sad for all of us, but I
knew it was powerful sad for you.

I'm going to take the mountain, make a mess of money,
and hunt up a new home. Be happy for me.

Love, Annabelle

I read it over and over, and nearly dropped a tear onto it. Then I tore it
out of the pad, folded it up, and wrote on the next sheet:

Dear Loretta and Jake,
Thanks for the job. You two, and Barbara, are the best.
I'm taking the mountain, so I quit. I figure you owe me some
back pay. Please get it to my mother.

Bye, Annabelle

I put both notes on my dresser, and then gathered up things to take,
throwing them onto the bed. Pap had left his army duffel bag in the hall
closet. Stuffing it with some favorite clothes, both dirty and clean, the bag
shortly grew full and heavy, but not yet near to all I wanted. I reckoned I
ought to take only what I could tote, so I settled down and arranged things in
piles on the bed, from most-needed to least—my best green sweater, two
pairs of newer jeans, a dressy pair of black slacks and black shoes, my
strappy sandals, some shorts, skirts, tops, and bras, and enough clean panties
and socks for a few weeks—and I shoved them into the duffel bag. Bathroom needments went in an old purse of mine. And that, along with some
other odds and ends, I crammed into my schoolbook rucksack—though its
Clandel High red-and-gold colors clashed horribly with the olive-drab duffel.

Hefting the rucksack up on one shoulder and the duffel bag over the
other, I paced around the room, weighing the load. Feeling it to be not too
heavy, I shoved in some extra tops and my dog-bitten bell-bottom jeans. In a
small red leather purse with a thin shoulder strap, I put my driver's license,
some small change, a comb and compact, and Pap's old wristwatch, missing
half its gold-chain watchband. In the rucksack I stowed my latest, near empty, diary—a lined notebook with thin black cardboard covers, which I'd
been partial to using lately, sold at McCrory's.

On my closet floor sat a box stuffed with old diaries filled with words about what had been my life, and I wondered what to do with them all. I couldn't just throw them out, but I was shy about leaving them. All my secrets were there—no telling who might open the box and just start reading. Yet there was nothing else I could do right then, save leave them to chance, and maybe one day come back and fetch them.

Then I counted the money I'd vaulted above the closet door frame— eighty-seven dollars. Tucking it back into its cotton drawstring poke, I buried it deep in the rucksack. I'd saved this money a few dollars at a time, putting it away for the day I'd leave Clandel. Even when I was scarce of two nickels to rub together, I would not reach up and peel off nary a dollar. Once stashed above the door, I'd vowed to spend it on nothing else but leaving out. And now, here it was, ready to go.

But was eighty-seven dollars enough to get to who-knows-where? Maybe I ought to go collect the back pay that Loretta and Jake owed me. Or maybe I ought to work the night just one more time. If I didn't show, Loretta might not want to pay what she owes me. Any extra dollars might soon be handy.

I studied on this while I traded the top I wore for another on the bed, and my beat-up red sneakers for my sturdy pair of brown cowgirl boots— yanking them up over my pant leg and stomping them on. Then I looked myself up and down in the mirror. In the mite-too-tight, low-cut, green blouse, it wasn't likely I'd be waiting tables in the diner tonight. I poked at my unruly curls, searched the freckles on my face for any blemishes, dabbed some lipstick on, and twisted my hips to view how my jeans rode on my hind end. I declare, there I was—one gone girl.

I pulled on my denim jacket, put Maw's note on the kitchen table, and with the bags over my shoulder, my boots clattered down the treads for maybe the last time. Striding along the sidewalk downtown, I felt that the eyes of everybody who drove by were on me.

I hiked over to the diner, only aiming to drop off the note, but Loretta, standing at her lookout at the end of the counter by the window, did a double take when she spotted me with my bags, and before I reached the door, she was out on the stoop.

"Well dog my hide," she said. "I ain't never afore seen abody show up late for work a-totin' an old army bag."

"Loretta... I aim to quit the diner. I'm right thankful for the job and all. But I hear a train a-coming, and I'll be jumping aboard. I figure you owe me some back pay, and I'd appreciate us settling up."

"Why you briggoty little red-combed strumpet. You're a-lightin' out with that carnival rascal you were with this mornin'."

"Who, or what, I'm lighting out with is my business, Loretta. I quit the diner and I need my money."

"I'll fetch you your money," she snarled, her lip curling mean and nasty, uncovering her gold tooth. "And you'll get your comeuppance, I'll allow. I heard your name norated around the counter more 'n once today. Folks don't take kindly to sorry girls."

"Loretta, I don't aim to stand here jawing about it. I just want my money."

She showed me her back, and tore inside waving her arms and squawking about it to Jake at the grill and the half-dozen customers inside, who swiveled their faces from their plates to me out on the sidewalk. She jabbed at the cash register and snatched up some bills, but then thought better of it and took a minute to peer at a calendar she kept by the coffee urn, on which she'd note the hours the help worked. She poked some numbers into her adding machine, swapped money in the till for what she'd cyphered, and slammed the cash drawer shut, hard enough for me to hear it ring outside.

She swaggered out on the stoop, handed over a used envelope stuffed with my pay, and told me, "Annabelle Cory, you're drivin' your ducks to a poor puddle."

I said, "Can't be much poorer than this puddle," and I hefted my bags and marched off. When I got around the corner, I stopped and counted my pay, $23.50, mostly in dollar bills, near what I figured she owed, and then I stomped away.

At the front gate of the carnival—'McCain's Magic Midway' spelled out across a twenty-foot banner hoisted up on poles and guy wires—a sad-eyed feller in a ticket booth there tried to get me to pay the seventy-five-cent admission. I said I was joining up with the show. He asked who with, and I told him Nickel Nick and Walt Ryder. He squinted at me and my bags with some misdoubt, but shortly waved me past.

I went down the midway to Walt's booth, and announced, "Here I am."

He moved over by me while a player weighed his next shot, and asked, "Remember where my car's parked?" I nodded. "Here's the keys. Go put your gear in the trunk."

I stepped out behind the booths and found the car, a red-and-white four-door with a coat of dust, and threw the rucksack on the back seat and the duffel bag into the trunk. Mercury Monterey was spelled out in chrome on a trunk lid big enough for a family of ten to sit around for Christmas dinner. Heavy with chrome on bumpers, grill, and fins, the car had taillights like something from a rocket ship, and a back window that slanted inward at the bottom and that whirred up and down at the touch of a button. An uncle of mine over in Welch drove a '63 like this one, only it was all rust bitten and stoved in at a rear door. Walt's appeared in fine shape—the upholstery clean, the trim all there, sleek and tidy save for the dust.

Before I could figure what to do next, Walt was beside me, one hand rubbing my bum, the other taking his keys back. "Now you're with it, Annabelle. And with me, too."

"So now what do I do?"

"Well, I work the baskets till we slough. You can help out then. But for now, just hang out, I guess. You can't work a joint in your hometown, Annabelle. If you want, you can snooze in my car. Tonight'll be a late jump.... Here's some eatin' money."

He gave me five dollars, kissed me quickly, and then backed off saying, "I gotta get back in the joint. Oh my, Annabelle, we're on our way to dreamland now. You hang in till midnight."

Off he went, leaving me there behind the booths with four or five hours to kill. Maybe I ought to have gone to work at the diner, and made a few extra bucks. I was in no mood for a nap in his car. So I wandered out onto the midway and strolled around the show several times.

"I did it." I said to myself, over and over, hardly able to believe that I was really leaving out.

With each step around the midway, I felt all the farther from Clandel. Here and there, I saw a face I knew—from high school, downtown, or the hillside—and I had half a mind to brag on my adventure. But I figured they'd just twist up their faces with unsure smiles, or frowns, with no clue of what to say next, reckoning me to be even more funny-turned than they'd thought. Soon enough, they'll hear about my doings, but not from me tonight. Then they'll squander their opinions. They'll say that I'm off my box, or I'm so contrary I'd float upstream, or that I'd taken up with Old Scratch—Annabelle Cory, over-fattened on book reading, upheaded and briggoty, half the time talking like an outlander.

As the daylight drained from the sky and the carnival lights burned brighter and brighter, I scuffed again and again past Walt's joint—as he called it. Often with two or three games going at once, winning his players' confidence and money, he'd shift his eyes back and forth from them to me, and wink or grin. When I'd smile back at him, a throb would hop into my heart for several beats, and at that moment he was the handsomest feller I'd ever seen—the pointblank fetch of manhood, the hero rescuing me from my dungeon, my knight in shining armor.

I puzzled on how, in only a day, I could feel of such trust, and such lust. The day before, he was nothing to me, and now he was everything—like some magic switch had been flipped on. I couldn't call it love at first sight, because I was chary of him right off. But now, it was as if he'd fit a key into what was locked up in me, and that treasure chest was now wide open, to share my jewels with his.

Then he'd turn back to his player, reach for another ball, and become just another carny surrounded by teddy bears. As I strolled along, I watched the other carnival folk, sitting in the ticket booths and running the rides and games, and I wondered what sort of people would they be to me. What kind of person would I be to them?

Up by the front gate near the kiddie rides, at a small square trailer, white and bright with too many light bulbs, I stopped to buy a bag of popcorn. Kernels erupting from a popper—its glass sides smoky and oily—their fresh scent sliced through the sticky smell of hot sugar in a cotton-candy machine. A gray-haired woman sprinkled salt over the popcorn, her flabby arm jiggling and jangling with an overloaded charm bracelet. In tidy rows on a stainless-steel tray, a dozen shiny red candy apples gleamed inside a glass case, their wooden sticks poking straight up. Plastic bags stuffed with pink and blue cotton candy hung from wires strung across the ceiling.

As we swapped my twenty-five cents for a warm bag of popcorn, the butter bleeding through the paper, she asked, "A pretty girl like you all alone tonight, hon?"

"Just for a while," I said, tossing a pinch of popcorn into my mouth.

"A date later?" Her smile appeared gentle and honest—her light blue eyes wrinkling happily at their corners, in which I could spot a kindly snoopiness. Her peppery hair was cut short and straight atop her roundish face—like it was trimmed beneath a soup bowl.

"Well, actually," I told her, after shortly wondering whether or not to do so, "I've got my bags packed, and I'm joining up with the show."

"You don't say.... What kind of hole do you have?"

"Hole?"

"Where are you working?"

"Um, I don't quite know yet. I'm leaving out with Walt Ryder. He runs the softball-in-a-peach-basket game over yonder."

"He works an alibi joint?" she asked, her face twisting with suspicion.

"It's the one where you toss the softballs into the basket."

"Yeah, the bushel baskets.... Honey, you watch out for those alibi agents. They'll tell you anything to get you to play their game, and then they'll tell you something else when you do."

I stood there frozen, my mouth full of half-chewed popcorn, and stared up into her scowl.

"You be careful, young lady," she said, pointing a candy-apple-red finger down at me.

"Yes, ma'am."

I turned and walked away and didn't know what to think of this. Here was one of them warning me about him. What was I getting myself into? As I wandered by Walt again, busy with a counter full of players, he didn't notice me walking past, and a flutter of fear grew in my middle. The popcorn went dry and hard to swallow. I turned around a few times, stepping backward, and tried to catch his eyes with mine. But he just kept on working the balls, in and out of the baskets.

As I took the turn around the back end again, I met a crowd of men gawking up at a belly dancer atop a stage attached to the side of a two-ton box truck. She looked to be maybe in her late twenties, long straight blonde hair, and she wore a skimpy two-piece outfit with bangles and tassels sway-ing over her poochy belly and meager thighs. Next to her, a barker with a Fu Manchu moustache and scraggly nut-brown hair talked up the show through a bullhorn, which exaggerated even more his nasally voice, crowing about what all could be seen inside for only two dollars. On panels that swung out from the side of the truck, and spelled out in red foot-high letters burning in golden flames, was painted: THE HAREM.

Feeding myself popcorn, kernel by kernel, I watched the dancer shimmy in her black fishnet stockings, a cagey smirk on her hawkish face. Her mas-cara-gaumed eyes went from face to face of the men below, teasing them with winks, her glossy red lips making kissy little pouts. Waggling her swaggy bummy, and shaking the bangles of a bra that barely covered her puny bubbies, she swayed her arms as if treading water in a lusty swimming hole.

I fancied that if I were up there on that stage doing that, I'd be packing them in. I loved to dance. At the several high-school dances I'd gone to, most of the boys reckoned themselves to be too cool to ask a girl to dance. So I would just walk up to one or another and tell him to dance with me. He'd get flustered some, and then straighten his spine, wink at his buddies, and follow me onto the floor. Now there's just about nothing as goofy look-ing as a lanky hillbilly jerking around to rock and roll. But I wouldn't care a hate about what he was doing—I'd lose myself in the music, and move to how it felt. While I danced to my own drummer, and the other couples would be doing their second-hand version of one juba or another, I'd watch them watch me as I whirled, my arms weaving the air—the boys going slack-jawed, and the girls with that there-she-goes-again look.

As the barker egged on the men to step right up, the belly dancer shim-mied her way through a curtain at the stage door cut into the side of the truck. I wondered what went on inside The Harem in front of the men after they'd paid their two dollars. No doubt the bra came off. But did the pant-ies? And then what?

Several men shouldered their way past the ticket booth and through an entrance cut into a panel hinged to the left of the stage. I wandered back up the midway, dumped the un-popped kernels into the trampled hay, balled up the bag, and tossed it into a cluster of litter.

Up ahead, I spotted Maw, mad as all get-out, and hunting for me. I froze, and seeing that she hadn't seen me yet, I scurried off the midway through a gap in the line-up and ducked behind a trailer with a machine-gun shooting gallery in it. The rat-a-tat of the BBs whacking against the metal of the trailer made me skittish, so I made my way around behind the tents, aim-ing to get over to Walt's car on the other side of the show and lie low in it for a while. I had no hankering to jower with Maw. That would only get ug-ly. Nothing she could say or do would make any difference now. And what I had to tell her, she wasn't going to listen to.

Sneaking along behind the line-up, I found myself outside the back of The Harem—a tent pitched up against the truck. Inside, whistles, laughs, yells and hoots accompanied a scratchy boogie-woogie record. I spied around to see if anybody could see me, and then where two sections of the tent sides were laced together, I separated the canvas with two fingers, enough to peek through with one eye.

Between the heads and shoulders of the men, I saw the dancer on a waist-high stage. Unhitching the catch in the back of her bra, she jiggled her little bubbies further and further out of the cups. The feller with the Fu Manchu now stood off to the side of the stage with a baseball bat over his shoulder, his eyes on the men.

Behind me, a hoarse and crusty voice croaked, "Hey. What you doin'?"

I spun about, and lurching toward me through a patch of floodlight limped a gangly old giant with gray nappy hair, rheumy blue eyes, a liver-spotted yellow-brown face, and a beaky nose above African lips. Agley arms swung at odds with his huge and filthy hands. His sweatshirt was riddled with holes and his pinstriped overalls smutchy with stains.

"Nothing," I said meekly. Then, lighting out like a scalded dog, one eye making sure he wasn't chasing me, I racked through the paths behind the tents, and wound my way around to the other side of the show.

I found Walt's car, crawled into the back seat, and with my rucksack as a lumpy pillow, I curled up and stared at the stitches in the red vinyl upholstery. That half-breed feller had scared the bejeebers out of me. And damn it, Maw was likely still out on the midway prowling around in a hissy-fit.

Someone traipsed by the car. I didn't dare look up. Beams from a light tower slanted through a side window and onto my face. I flipped around to the dark end of the seat, and nestled my forehead into the vinyl and shadow.

As big a pain as Maw was, I worried on her getting all worked up over me. She was my mother, and I loved her as best I could. I had no need to hurt her—yet I didn't want to hurt myself, neither. I just plumb could not talk to her. She was a natural quiet type to start with—though her and my sister would blather together well enough—but when Maw would switch her attention to me, we'd soon get to bickering over one contrariness or another. Then shortly we'd simply hush up, rather than go at each other again.

Muffled loops of sounds from the midway soothed me—barkers chanting their pitches over and over, the rattly racket of the whirling rides, the Merry-Go-Round tooting its waltz, the pounding rock and roll, the voices of the crowd floating in and out. It had been a long day, with scarce sleep the night before. I curled up and closed my eyes. Trying to quile the prattle in my head, I stared into the blackness behind my eyelids, and searched for the floating faces that arise before I fall asleep.

When I woke with a startle, the feel of things around me had changed. Metal clanged on metal, and the roar and rock and roll of the rides had ceased. I dug a hairbrush out of my rucksack and tidied my frazzle in the rearview mirror. The clock on the dashboard neared midnight. I squeezed the rucksack under the back of the front seat and slid out of the car to go hunt for Walt.

The awnings of the bushel-basket trailer were closed down and locked. Out in front of it on the midway, Walt and Nick were removing and folding up the orange-and-blue striped skirt around the side rails of a car-port-sized tent—its awnings on all four sides propped open. When he saw me approach, he shuffled over to me, pecked a kiss onto my sleepy frown, and asked, "You want to help slough the center joint?"

"Do what? Sure… I guess."

"Just wrap the glass in newspaper and pack it in the boxes. If you find any nickels, they go in that bucket over there."

"Will I get paid?"

"Prob'ly not tonight, Belle. But show Nick how you can work, and it'll be easier puttin' you on tomorrow."

He squeezed my elbow and turned away as Nick called him to the other side of the tent. I set myself to wrapping and packing cups and saucers, plates and glasses, carefully and quickly as I could—now and then peeking over at Walt talking to Nick, no doubt about me. Nick, now wearing tan coveralls, didn't appear all that happy about it.

Packing up tableware along with me were three others—a blonde woman, tall and wide-bottomed, maybe thirty, her straight hair in a long ponytail, and sort of pretty but for eyes set a mite too narrow—her hefty six-or-seven-year-old spitting-image daughter—and a dumpy dumb-looking feller with a flat-top crew cut and even narrower eyes, darkly deep-set. He stood swiping dust off a plate with a rag, and staring at me like a dimwit. The blonde woman sat on a low stool, wrapping dishes, her thick thighs bulging in pink sweatpants, and wearing a dark-blue nylon jacket over a yellow sweatshirt. The little girl, also with a blonde ponytail, and so cute in her nearly-outgrown Bambi jump suit, hunted for nickels on the carpet between the stacks of tableware. She dropped a handful into the nickel bucket, and then came over to me.

"What's your name?" she asked sweetly.

"Annabelle. What's yours?"

"Jenny.... You workin' for my daddy?"

"I hope so."

"Me too," she said, and then went back to hunting nickels.

I glanced over at her mother. She showed me a tight smile. Then she hefted herself off her stool, came over, peeked into the box I was loading, and told me, "Looks good. Pack 'em tight so they don't rattle around."

"Okay. Hi, I'm Annabelle. Walt said I might could get a job with you all."

"You'll have to talk to Nick about that. But I'll tell you what—I've been at Nick for weeks about putting someone on. My name's Brenda, and that's

73

my brother Fred over there," she said, jerking a thumb toward the feller with the crew cut, who still stared straight at me, a creepy glint lurking within his addled gaze. "You been on the road long?"

"I grew up here in Clandel... and I want to put it behind me."

A corner of her thin smile twitched as she said, "Oh. Well... we'll see." And she went back to her stool. I gathered she was Nick's wife—maybe twenty years younger than him, as well as a foot taller and forty pounds heavier, which struck me as slightly uncommon.

A half-hour later we had all the tableware packed up, and took in toting it a carton at a time to a two-ton truck parked behind the bushel-basket trailer, where Nick, up in the truck box, stacked them tight. That done, Brenda and Jenny strolled off with the bucket of nickels, and Walt and Nick rolled up the carpet on the crushed grass beneath the tent, and shouldered it over to the truck. Leaning against a tent leg, Fred eyed me with his daft grin half-cocked to one side of his doughy face. Without a word, he just kept leering at me, like I had nothing to say about it. I showed him a peevish scowl and shortly turned away, avoiding his eyes and uneasily shuffling my feet.

The blaring music and flashing lights now gone until next year, a pair of thirty-foot light towers slanted hard shadows past the dusty pig-iron arms of the Octopus as two ride boys muscled them into its traveling pose. The show was coming down piece by piece—the seats off the Ferris Wheel, the pipe fence around the Scrambler, the ticket booth of the Zipper—loaded onto trailers, metal clanging and lumber slamming, whole rides folding up to go.

Walt returned with a battered sledgehammer, and at each corner of the tent he swung it upside the inch-thick steel stakes that anchored the canvas to the ground with heavy ropes. The stakes loosened after a few clangs, and Walt yanked them up, the steel ringing a note out of the dirt.

Nick and Fred pulled hitch pins from hinges attaching the diagonal braces of the tent's frame—half a hinge was bolted on each end of the blue-painted two-by-four lumber, with the other halves bolted to the legs and rails. Then, one end of the tent at a time, Walt, Nick, and Fred swung the legs under and lowered the top to the ground. Next, they untied the canvas from the frame, folded and rolled it up, wrassled the bundle into a big canvas bag, and hauled it into the truck. Within another fifteen minutes, all the hinge pins had been pulled from the skeleton of two-by-fours, the pieces unhooked, and the lumber loaded.

Walt fired up the truck and backed it to the hitch end of the joint trailer—the tents that were in the line-up there, now gone—Nick waving and hollering, "Cut to the left. Hard to the right. Straighten it out. Easy.... Half a foot. Stop!" Then Fred cranked the trailer hitch down onto the ball, hooked up the safety chain, and Walt wheeled the trailer off to the edge of the lot.

He hurried back and told me, "Get what you'll need in the mornin' out of the Merc', and wait for me in the truck."

I fetched my rucksack and climbed up into the truck cab—its upholstery split open here and there to the stuffing and springs—and a lengthy quarter-hour later he jumped in the driver's side, grinning to his ears, and he slid over to me across the wide seat. Somewhat huffy from waiting for I knew not what, my arms folded and my legs crossed, I pronged an elbow in his ribs, which he ignored, and pushed a kiss onto my face.

I squirmed away, and asked, "So what's next, Mister Ryder?"

"Give me a smooch and I'll tell you," he said, puckering up goofy and cross-eyed.

I wrinkled my nose and stuck my tongue out at him. He licked the tip of it with a flick of his, and then slid behind the wheel and turned the key. The truck turned over, grumbled to a roar, and he hollered to me, "We be gone, Annabelle. Adios, Clandel." And he sung a shard of, "Vaya con mio, my darlin'," adding, "Not con dios. Con *mio*, my darlin'."

I shouted back, over the motor, "So what's the plan?"

"The plan, my beautiful Belle, is to get this rig a-rollin' and make the jump to Stuart tonight. Brenda tends to piss and moan about pullin' a trailer, so she's drivin' my car, with Jenny and Fred, and followin' Nick in his Oldsmobile towin' the house trailer. Nick's got this early-bird-gets-the-worm thing about bein' on the lot before locations get passed out. Plus he's always hell-bent to get his joints up on Sunday. Glass pitches are a ton of set-up. Me, I'd rather get there when we get there. But he pays me to drive his rig, so off we go."

Walt kicked in the clutch, shoved into gear the big-knobbed stick shift wobbling up from the floor between us, gave it the gas, let out the clutch, and the truck groaned and jerked forward, bucking against the trailer. He muscled the big steering wheel back and forth, eyeing the trailer in both rearview mirrors as we snaked around what remained of the show. Rolling out onto US-52, he pushed the truck through the gears as we wound up the hill past my street.

Tempted to lean into the windshield and look up at my home, maybe for the last time, I instead held tight to the armrest on the door, the hard ride of the truck jolting me on the springy seat. I didn't want to look back. All of a sudden leaving out wasn't just something I might do—I'd done it.

But where was I off to? The apartment up on that hillside had been the center of my world for most of my life. Fairly cozy in the winter, and in the summer with a few windows open it had a nice breeze through it. Though the privy was cobbled into what once was a hallway, it was decent enough. And there was usually something to eat in the kitchen.

Jouncing atop the truck seat, I now had to pee. Also, I was a jag hungry. When and where would I pee or eat next? Living with Maw wasn't all peaches and cream, but what kind of barrel of apples was I jumping into here? They say that one rotten apple spoils the barrel—well what sorts of apples were in a carnival barrel?

We trundled along up Black Creek for a few miles and then climbed switchbacks on the ridge—Walt working the wheel and gearshift, the motor so loud it flooded over my fearful silence. At the crest of the ridge, Walt swung into a turnout and stopped, and took a wadded-up plastic baggie out of his jacket pocket.

"I need a little help from my friends, Annabelle." In the low-hung moonlight and the backwash of headlights on the trees, he rolled a skinny joint from the fixings, and asked me, "You smoke reefer?"

"Yeah, sometimes."

"Well now's a good a time as any. We got a long and twisty jump ahead and there ain't nothin' much to look at but asphalt, guardrails, and tree trunks. So, my Belle, I'm gonna alter my outlook with this here maryjane, and perk up my eyelids with a few little white pills. You want some uppers, too?"

"Um... no, I don't think so." Though partial to a pot buzz, I'd tried speed only once, a black beauty that kept me awake for two days. After these last couple of days, I had no yen to maybe stay up for two more.

Walt tossed a pair of pills into the back of his throat and swallowed them dry. Then he lit the joint and sucked on it hard, the ember crackling red, glinting off the moist pearl of his wide-open eyes. The sweet stink of the smoke fetched from my innards the familiar hankering for some of it, and I reached for the joint. He passed it over, holding his breath, his cheeks ballooning out and smoke flaring from his nostrils.

I took a few short tokes and passed it back. The dope strutted heavy in my lungs, spilled through my blood, and rushed to my eyes. The truck cab loomed larger, but somehow nearer. The headlight's glow through the trees thickened their shades, like colors in the Sunday funnies. The motor grumbled from deep down, tingling the soles of my feet. We passed the joint back and forth, sipping at the smoke as it dwindled, thirsty to get all of it we could.

When it burned too tiny to handle, Walt flicked it out the window, swung his big grin to me, and said, "My Belle... I could kiss your Anna-bellybutton right now. But—and your butt, too. I could kiss your beautiful buttocks now and forever. But, Annabelle, my Belle, we'll be comin' around the mountain, so let's get on down the road."

He whooped out a Kentucky yeehaw, levered the truck into gear, and over the mountain we went. A heart-thumping bearm of hog-wild exaltation rushed through my doped-up blood.

The rig picked up speed, winding down the side of the ridge, the gearbox wailing a complaint against the grade, the trailer shoving the truck's rear end back and forth from curve to curve. Shortly it appeared we were going a mite too fast. I stiffened up and clung to the chewed-up armrest on the door.

Just as I wondered if Walt knew what he was doing, he said, "Uh-oh."

"Uh-oh, what?"

"Uh-oh, we're losin' our brakes."

"What?"

"Hold on, baby. I think there's a seatbelt over there. Cinch it up."

I fumbled around for the belt, and found the buckle wedged in the crack between the seat's back and bottom. I yanked it out, jammed my hand into the cranny for the other side of the belt, and found only a grimy pencil. Grabbling around behind the seat, I dug out the other end of the belt, gritty and greasy, and taking a bit of doing to pull it from the tangle of tools on the floor. After clicking it onto the buckle, I felt a measure safer. But then, wide-eyed at the steep blacktop calahooting under us, I wasn't so sure.

Walt leerily pumped the foot brake—slowing us some, yet not nearly enough. His face went taut in the greenish glow of the dashboard lights as he wrassled the big steering wheel left and right. The zigzag two-lane had no guardrails—a drop-off to who-knows-what on one side, a wall of rocks and trees on the other. Bealed with chug-holes, the blacktop jolted us with growing spite. Bucking at the hitch, the trailer shoved the back of the truck one way then the other. In the rearview mirror on my side, I watched the trailer take a curve nearly tilting off its wheels—and I reckoned we were done for.

We barreled down to where the grade eased off and the road climbed for a short stretch. Walt pumped at the brake pedal, grabbed the handbrake lever on the floor next to the stick shift, and hauled back on it. Then, as the road again turned downhill, he stomped on the clutch, revved the motor to a scream, grabbed the shifter, and fought to coax the truck down a gear. Metal skived metal in a god-awful gnashing of teeth. Walt gunned the motor even more, booted the clutch pedal twice, and jammed home the shifter into the lower gear. Gas to the floor, he slowly let the clutch out, the motor about to burst, the gearbox wailing like a siren. But as we took in downhill again I felt the motor braking us some, slowing us from way too fast and getting faster, to just too fast.

Walt eased up on the gas, the motor working against the hill, and he wrassled the steering wheel through the next stretch downhill—not as scary as the last, but we weren't out of the woods yet. As we neared a switchback, the road flattened out for a piece, and Walt revved and double clutched it once, twice, grinding gears all to hell, and found the lower one on the third try. We whipped around a hairpin turn, the motor grabbing hold of the squealing tires, the shriek of the gearbox falling in pitch, the truck tilting way over to my side, Walt off the seat and on his feet, leaning hard into the wheel, the trailer shuddering behind us.

We snaked downhill another half mile—on my side of the road, just a drop-off to bushes, treetops, and darkness. The lower gear slowed us more, the howling motor dropping to a tired growl as we leveled off some. When the road mercifully lifted uphill for a stretch, Walt brought the truck all the way down to first gear, and we lumbered along, half throttle, at five miles an hour.

"We gotta find a place to pull off the road," he said, turning a worried smile my way. "Nick'll be along soon, so we'll wait to see what he wants to do.... You okay?"

I looked over at him and had no words. One hand still in a death grip on the armrest, a charley horse knotting my leg from mashing it on the floorboard, a lump the size of an walnut throbbing in my goozle, and in sore need of a privy—I hadn't a clue if I was okay. It was near as I'd ever come to being killed. The reefer up at the mountain top had played second fiddle during our downhill rush toward the grave, but now it struck up a tune to beat the band. A powerful dread threw a fright into me that set my fingers to tremble. I'd known pot paranoia before, but this was another guess. My terror felt of a nightmare exploding into reality, blown out of my mind by dope smoke.

We crawled along the road, slow as a turtle. A car, honking and flashing its lights, came up behind. Walt slowed even more, rolled down the window, and waved it around us. At the next switchback, we came to a turnout big enough for the truck and trailer, so Walt wheeled the rig into it. He pumped up the brakes and mashed the pedal to the floor—but we were not stopping. Pulling the wheel hard to the right, heading us for some thick brush on the edge of the turnout, he heaved on the handbrake with both hands. We crunched into the brush, bent some saplings over, and jolted to a stop against a thicker tree.

"Woo-wee!" he howled. "Baby, that was one hell of a ride."

I wanted out. Now. Clenching what breath I had, and fumbling to unlatch the seat belt, I yanked at the door handle, kicked it open, slid out of the truck and into the brush, and took in panting to keep from barfing. The motor smelled burning hot. I waded out of the brush, ran over to the other end of the turnout, and paced back and forth until I chose a place to drop my jeans and pee in the dirt.

Walt backed the rig out of the bushes, leaned out the window, and hollered to me, "Get a big rock, or chunk of wood, and wedge it under a tire."

I found a rock that I could hardly lift, struggled it over to a wheel, and chocked it on the downhill side. Walt stopped riding the clutch—the big tire crunched the rock into the gravel—and he set the handbrake and killed the motor. Jumping out, he grabbed a few more rocks and jammed them under a couple more tires, and then scouted around the rig and the turnout, before he came over to me, fetched me into his arms, and took in laughing out loud like he was off his box.

I snapped, "What's so funny?"

"We made it, Annabelle. In one piece. That don't make you happy?" And he laughed all the more, hoisting me off my feet and swinging me around.

"Well, I wouldn't call it happy.... What the hell happened?"

He let loose of me, scratched behind his ear, and said, "I told Nick those brakes were a little spongy, and he just said, 'Nah.' Well, I guess he'll have to do somethin' about 'em now. He'll be along in a few.... You okay?"

"I wouldn't call it okay. But I'm a lot better than a few minutes ago."

"That's worth at least half a smile... if not just a little chuckle."

He turned away, got a flashlight out of the cab, and crawled under the front of the truck, stabbing the light here and there, and cussing now and then. I sat down on the trailer hitch, crossed my arms and legs, and thanked my lucky stars. I felt I'd gotten into a wreck but couldn't yet find the damage. I rubbed my elbows and my knees, and got up, paced around, and sat back down.

A carnival rig hauling the Rock-O-Plane came around the bend, slowed, stopped, and blasted its horn. Walt scrambled out from under the truck, went over to the driver, and told him we were all right for now, and were waiting on the boss.

Near a half-hour later, Nick wheeled around the switchback, his big green Oldsmobile hauling his long blue-and-white house trailer—Brenda, with Fred and Jenny, following in Walt's Mercury. He spotted us sitting on the trailer hitch and rolled up beside us, his window whirring down.

"What's this jackpot?" His beady eyes blinking with surprise and searching for a clue.

"Brake line shit the bed," Walt told him.

"You don't say," Nick said, his head twisting out the window, eyeing the length of the rig. "You two alright?"

"We about got ourselves killed comin' down the mountain. Annabelle here is gonna take a bus back home."

"I didn't say that," I said, punching his shoulder.

Nick shut off the Oldsmobile and got out—kicking at the gravel and spitting cusses as he went back to the Mercury to tell his wife what was up.

I heard her squawk, "I told you to get those brakes checked out," which riled Nick up even more so.

I could see that Nick held his aggravation close, just behind his customary grimace. He swung a punch into the air, stamped back to Walt, grabbed the flashlight, and crawled under the truck. Walt told him the leak was by the right front wheel. Nick flashed the light around underneath and cussed it all to hell. Then he went silent—thoughtfully clicking the flashlight off and on. Brenda switched off the Mercury, and suddenly the whole huge night went quiet.

Nick scrambled out from under, brushed off the dirt clinging to the sleeves of his clean-cut windbreaker and the seat of his perma-press pants, and said, "Goddamn it, ain't this a kick in the keister? We gotta get this rig over to the lot tonight and get our locations in the mornin', or we'll be settin' by the donniker all next week. Looks like just a small hole in the brake line. Me and Fred'll nigger rig it and bleed 'em. You drop both trailers and hook the joint trailer to the Olds'. I'll pull the house trailer with the truck. It's got trailer brakes, so if the truck brakes go again, that might keep my sorry ass from tumblin' over the fuckin' mountain."

Walt asked, "The Olds' is all right haulin' the joint trailer?"

Nick said, "Yeah, sure," then hurried off to bark orders at Fred, tell Brenda what was going on, and fetch his overalls out of the house trailer. Brenda hauled herself out of the Mercury, and arched her spine back, her hands at the small of her back. The dome light inside the car dimly shed light upon Jenny's sleepy curiosity. Fred climbed out of the back seat, trudged over to the truck, and while rubbing his eyes with his fists, stole peeks at me.

Walt told me, "Belle, you can ride in the Merc' with Brenda, Fred, and Jenny if you want. Or you can ride with me.... Haulin' the joint with the Olds' and no trailer brakes might be a little touchy."

"Touchy?" I asked, sliding over upon the cold hard frame of the V-shaped trailer hitch, to make room for Walt as he sat down next to me.

"Well, when you're pullin' a heavy trailer with no trailer brakes and you got dual rear wheels and a two-ton truck, it's hardly a problem when the trailer shoves you around the road. Behind the Olds' we got a different story goin'. I just gotta be careful, Annabelle. But if you wanna ride in the Merc', I hear you. Go on over and set a spell with the wife and kid, and check 'em out. They won't spit in your eye. You're with it now—with us."

I whispered, "Brenda seems a mite young and large for Nick."

"They can't all match up to the likes of me and you. I hear tell she's Nick's third or fourth wife."

We stood, and he patted my bum. I had a yen to reach up around his neck and hold him tight, but that somehow felt awkward there and then. He lit a cigarette, grabbed the crank of the hitch jack, and spun it around a hundred miles an hour—the jack's post screwing slowly down to a few inches off the ground. Then he fetched the keys out of the cab and unlocked the side door of a plywood box—nearly the size of a coffin, and strapped beneath the frame of the truck—that Walt called the possum belly. Out of it, he got a short piece of thick plank, slid it under the jack, and cranked the trailer up off the hitch ball. After hollering at Fred to move the stones out from under the tires, Nick rolled the truck away from the trailer, rocking the clutch in reverse for a brake, and yelled again at Fred to re-chock the stones under the tires.

Walt went to crank the house trailer off the Oldsmobile, and I shuffled over to Brenda—her wide hind end sprawled atop the front fender of the Mercury, her big feet swinging dusty white sneakers, heels bouncing off the tire. As I sidled up next to her, she leaned to look past me and into the car to check on Jenny.

"Hi," I said.

"Hey.... You alright?"

"Well, after being nigh to dead and done for, and now I'm not, things are looking up."

"I told Nick that truck needed work. He just drives 'em into the ground. If it ain't broke, he don't fix it. The cheap little squirt."

From inside the car, Jenny cried, "Mama, don't talk bad about Daddy."

"I'm not, dear," Brenda sang over her shoulder, then turned to me and whispered, "Haulin' us all over these hills through the middle of the night so's he can beat out some cotton-candy wagon for a better location at the next nowhere spot. All he's got to do is throw the McCains an extra forty or fifty beans every week or so, instead of all the time pissin' a fuss about every location they give him. Nickel Nick, the shortest small-time nickel-and-dimer on the road today. Welcome to the big top, honey."

I tried to change the subject. "Walt saved us from crashing off that mountain. He brought that rig to a stop with only the gears and the hand-brake."

She pulled a pack of Winstons from a pocket of her blue nylon jacket, lit one up, and whispered through the smoke, "Now that Walt, I've been watchin' him. What he's doin' here grindin' out still-dates in these devil-forsaken hills, I ain't got clue number one. He ain't nobody's fool. But there he is bustin' Nick out of this jackpot like he had a piece of the action. You two ought to be ridin' along together in Walt's car here, or in a cozy motel bed—anywhere but here, almost goin' off a cliff. Instead he does Nick's biddin' like he was his boy. Twenty bucks to drive that ramshackle rig through the middle of the night. No thanks, if I was him."

"Walt told me he was driving the truck because you don't like to pull a trailer."

"I don't like to pull 'em, park 'em, clean 'em, nor raise my baby in the contraptions. Give me a house without wheels, anytime. I was born on a carny lot. I married a carny. But I don't have to like it. Do I?"

"Well, I suppose not."

"You bet not.... And here you are, nearly killed first night on the road. Why in hell did you sign onto this?"

"Would you want to stay in that fruit-jar-sucking coal-town we just left?"

"Honey," she said, losing the whisper and leaning into my ear, "there's other options in this world other than either Clan-fuck, West Virginia, or joinin' up with this sideshow."

"Well... it doesn't appear there are for me right now." I looked away to Walt, scuttling blocks under the tires of the house trailer, then turned back to Brenda, and said, "I'm right partial to Walt, fact be told. And I don't want to miss what might could happen with him—with us."

"Lordy, good luck on that. I'm a-rootin' for you. I like Walt, too. He's got somethin' all these other grifters out here lack. What it is, I can't quite figure. Somethin' else besides his good-lookin' charm. Maybe somethin' decent inside."

"Could be that's why he's helping Nick out," I offered.

"Is it good when good lard's used to fry bad eggs?"

I had no answer to give her for that—and she added, "Honey, you're too nice a girl to be out here. I can see that with my eyes closed. You won't last a week before somethin' chases you off. Not likely someone. But somethin'. And I'd guess you won't be goin' back to that town we just left, because if you're jumpin' on this bandwagon then you must really want to get the hell out of there."

"That's for a fact, Brenda.... So maybe I last a week, so maybe I don't. But what's for sure is that I'm long gone from where I was."

"For certain, girl. You be with it now.... Turn that spunk into what you want to happen, and nobody'll be pitchin' nickels at you."

"Mama," Jenny whimpered from inside the car, "I'm cold and I want to get in bed."

"We're not there yet, Jenny. I'll get you a blanket and pillow out of the trailer."

"Bring Jocko, too."

"Okay." She sang "okay" with two notes sounding sweeter than I'd expect from her. Sliding off the fender of the car, she granted me a warm smile. Plucking her pink sweatpants out of her butt crack, she explained, "Jocko's her plush monkey," before waddling off to the house trailer.

I shuffled over to the edge of the turnout where several big boulders bordered the overpeer. Far across the dark cove, above the ridges from here to yonder, the half-moon hung low, buttering the western rocky tops. I reckoned Brenda to be just one big fat-ass pain. Still, a pain-in-the-ass is often right about things. Especially things we don't want to hear.

I found a boulder to sit on and leaned back onto cold hard stone, the grit digging into the back of my head. I closed my eyes, still buzzing from Walt's reefer—or from the close call with the grave. The grunts and curses coming from under the truck, the clanking of the tools, all sounded nearer, clearer, and more startling than they ought to be. I heard Nick bossing Fred around, like I was right beside them under the truck, but they were fifty or sixty feet away.

After a while, I opened my eyes and watched the moon drop slowly beyond the edge of the world. The boulder grew colder and harder. I jumped off, and found Walt hitching the Oldsmobile to the joint trailer.

"You ridin' with Brenda in the Merc'?"

"No thanks," I whispered. "I've heard enough of her complaints already. And that Fred creeps me out."

"Brenda's alright," he whispered back. "She likes to bitch about things, but she's a real sweety when you see through all that."

"You think?... I'd rather ride with you."

"Okay. Nick's meltin' solder around the hole in the brake line. Then he'll wrap it tight in duct tape, and bleed the lines. We should be rollin' again soon.... Go lie down in the Olds' if you want."

After fetching my rucksack from the truck cab, I crawled onto the back seat of the Oldsmobile, and tried to find some comfort in sleep. An hour or so later, Walt slid onto the front seat, fired up the car, and led the way out of the turnout—Nick and the truck and house trailer behind us, and behind him, Brenda, Fred, and Jenny in the Mercury.

The going was slow, especially downhill. Often we pulled off the road where we could, to let a rig from the show or a rare car pass. Walt would then jump out of the car and run back to check on Nick and the brakes.

On the back seat I'd nod off, and shortly wake with a start, sitting up and watching the back of Walt's head swivel back and forth from the road ahead to the fender-mounted rearview mirrors—the headlights of the jerry-rigged caravan sweeping in and out of them—until I'd topple over again.

Near daybreak, we lurched off the road and onto a field, the brush scraping the car, and we swayed to a stop. Half awake, and unsure if this was a dream or not, I pretended to be fast asleep. Walt's leather coat creaked on the seat as he turned around to look at me. He brushed his fingertips lightly over my hair, and I faked a dreamy little squirm. Stretching out on the front seat, he tossed and turned some, wobbling the car. Then all went still.

3

IMPERATRIS

Cradling the eagle's shield, The Empress holds an orbed scepter upon her womb. Queen of All, she rules from her throne of angelic wings. She begets and fosters the world's children — who must eventually leave her domain, or be devoured by her love. The Empress gazes at her sphere of influence, surmounted by the cross of Christ, and her eyes show a concern born from ancient inner wisdom. She knows what shall become of her realm, were she not to demand her due — which when mocked, turns pride into vanity. In her crown of triangles, the number three symbolizes her strength.

Through the dewy car window, the morning sun poured onto my sweaty face. I rolled over, stretched head to toe, door to door, and slowly sat up to look around. Cars, trucks, trailers, and semi rigs with folded-up rides sat scattered about. Walt wasn't in the front seat.

I flipped open the door handle, slid out, rubbed my eyes and arms, and staggered away. We were in a scraggly field aside a narrow blacktop road, surrounded by unfamiliar ridges with greening trees, speckled white with dogwood bloom.

I had to pee bad, so I set off for some nearby bushes. Combing my hair with my fingertips, I waded through the wildflowers and grass, my shins plowing the tangle apart, its keen scent bursting up at me. Behind some wax myrtle, I ducked out of sight and did my business, but had nothing to wipe myself with. Spotting a small creek gurgling nearby, and with an eye out for anyone watching, I crouched low and hobbled over to it—my panties at my knees, one hand gripping my jeans at half-mast, the other one pushing aside the brush.

I came upon a little pool where the run tumbled over a ledge of shale. Nobody in sight, I pulled off my boots, socks, jeans and panties, and squatted over the pool—one bare foot on the sand, the other out on a stepping stone—and dabbled branch water onto my satchel. The pool silted up, and a frog croaked, leaping underwater. I dried my bottom with a cuff of my jeans, and then made myself decent.

Hunting upstream for a fresh pool to wash my face in, I spied a pour-off spilling down against the ridge on the other side of the creek and made my way toward it—tiptoeing across from stone to stone, and weaving through the mouse bush and saplings to where the trace splashed down out of the laurel onto mossy stones. I leaned over and, palms up, reached in and scrubbed my face with the cold water. I had half a notion to strip naked and take a shower right then and there, but it was far too chilly for that. Tilting my head up and catching a trickle on the tip of my tongue, I lapped at it like a critter—the mountain's taste in it sweet.

Slow to quit this place, I meandered back down toward the run, and gathered up some mayflowers into a little posy. After hopping back across the stepping-stones, I found a huge flattop boulder to sit on in the sun. With some green twigs, I set to fashioning the flowers into a circlet to wear for Walt.

Then something stirred in a patch of devil's apple near the boulder. A water moccasin? Still as a statue—but for my eyes hunting for what it was beneath the wide leaves—I couldn't see what it was, yet heard it slither again. I flung the half-made circlet at it, scooted off the other side of the boulder, and high-stepped through the brush and grass, back to the jumble of rigs by the road.

At one end of the fairly level field, three sun-tanned carnies—shirtless in smudged gray overalls, bare arms muscly and tattooed—hoisted and hung a section of the Ferris Wheel rim. One of them was Buck, the grease monkey who'd swiped a feel of my bubby.

Small wooden stakes with pieces of paper stapled to them stubbled the lot, apparently marking what was to go where. Squealing and rattling as it swayed through the grass, the Zipper rig lumbered over to its location. The Octopus, with two long-haired ride boys unfolding it from its trailer, sent loud clangs above the other sounds of the camp—the dim mix of voices, someone hammering, a tinny portable radio with a country song, a dog yapping, a motor purring, a door creaking and slamming.

I wandered around hunting for Walt, but couldn't find him. Spotting Nick's blue-and-gray house trailer amid the camp set off to the side along the edge of the woods, I drew nigh. Hearing Nick out back, barking orders at Fred, I peered around the corner by the hitch. Fred, down on his knees, jammed a shovel into the bottom of a hole, while Nick, squirming on his back beneath the rear of the trailer, stacked short-sawn planks under a screw jack.

I got down on my haunches, and asked Nick, "Have you seen Walt?"

Screwing the jack up tight against the trailer frame, he said, "Not this mornin'. When you find him, tell him we get our locations at noon."

"Okay."

He grabbed the jack, shook it to check how tight it was, and asked, "You gonna work a joint for me?"

"Well... I surely would appreciate a job."

"What've you done before?"

"Waitressing at a diner."

"Can you make change for a dollar?"

"Yes, sir."

"Okay.... I pay twenty-five percent of what you grab, cash each night. If I catch you boostin' even a nickel, we're done."

"Boostin'?"

"Stealin'. You're not a thief, are you?

"Oh, no sir."

Looking me up and down after scuttling out from under the trailer, he said, "Let's see if we don't turn you into one," and added, brushing off the backside of his coveralls, "And no goo-goo eyes with Walt when you're in the joint."

"I can do that," I told him, and reckoned myself hired. Fumbling for something else to say, I asked, "What's that hole for?"

He looked at me like I was behind the door when brains were passed out. "It's for piss and shit. A donniker hole."

I watched for a few minutes while Fred struggled to shovel up dirt from the bottom of the hole, about two-foot wide and three deep. Then Nick told him, "Good enough," and uncoiled a benastied four-inch hose out from a storage hatch on the side of the house trailer. He hooked it up to a spigot there, dropped the other end into the hole, and covered up the opening of the hole with scraps of plywood and clumps of sod, while Fred leaned on his shovel, and stared straight into me—some breed of squackheaded fancy lurking behind his deep-set eyes.

Escaping his creepy gaze, I shuffled away as they finished up. Nick hollered to me over his shoulder, "Be there noon at the joint trailer."

Threading my way around the lot, I hunted again for Walt. A quarter-hour later, I realized that the Mercury was gone, too. I leaned up against the fender of the Oldsmobile, still hitched to the joint trailer, and waited for him to find me. Yet another long quarter-hour later and still no Walt. Had he run off without me already? And there I was with nary a notion of what to do next. Chill bumps crawled all over me as I sat down on the trailer hitch, elbows on knees, chin in my hands.

Then I scurried off, jumpy as a pregnant fox in a forest fire, hunting around the lot for him one more time. He wasn't there. Many of the carnies watched me, with questions in their eyes, as I nosed around the lot again and again.

A fat woman sprawled across a beat-up over-stuffed loveseat set in the grass on the sunny side of a two-ton truck asked, "You lookin' for someone, darlin'?" She wore dark glasses and a Hawaiian mumu, her blonde head lolling back in the sun—a gentleness showing in her bloated, but still pretty, face.

"Do you know Walt?"

"No, I don't. Who's Walt?"

"He works a bushel-basket joint for Nickel Nick," I said hesitantly in this strange new lingo.

"No, I don't know him." She heaved her bulk toward me, and then I recognized that she was The Fat Lady in the sideshow Friday night. She asked, "What's the deal with Walt?"

"Well... he brought me here, from Clandel, and now I can't find him."

"Oh darlin'. Do you think he's left you?"

"I don't know. I can't figure why he'd light a shuck just like that."

"Then I'd wager he's not gone," she said kindly. "Here, set with me a spell, and tell me about yourself."

She scootched over against one end of the sofa, and though it was a two-seater, there was hardly room for me. Not wanting to be unmannerable, but shying off from squishing my tail up against hers, I sat half a cheek on the edge and leaned back against the armrest. Still, her soft thigh pressed against mine, and her moist arm quaggled a mite too near. She smelled of perfume, sweat, and beer.

She asked my name, and told me hers was Lula. Her voice warbled very high in pitch, somehow appearing to do so on purpose. But when she'd chuckle, which she did after most everything she said, her cheery laugh rang out much lower.

"My name ain't really Lula. That's just my stage name. I'm the fat lady in the seven-in-one."

"I know. I saw your show the other night."

"Ain't much to it. Is there? The tall drink of water swallowing swords, that's my husband, Sonny. Only son of Old Eli McCain—the show's owner. He's got a daughter that lives in Tulsa, but she wants nothing to do with carnivals. Quite a pair—huh?—Sonny and me? Fat and skinny had a race, up and down the pillowcase. Jack Sprat could eat no fat, his wife could eat no lean."

I added, "But betwixt them both they licked the platter clean."

She chuckled hard at that, until she choked with a coughing fit. Tilting her bulk sideways, she reached over the arm of the sofa and down into the shade, and raised a can of Stroh's beer to her flubby lips, drowning the cough with a long pull.

"I'd offer you a beer, darlin'. But they're way over in the trailer."

"That's mighty kind of you, but no thanks right now."

"So tell me. What you got goin' with this Walt feller?"

"Well, he came on to me strong, Friday night, and now here I am."

"There's gotta be more of a tale to it than that. A fine-lookin' gal like you just don't up and run off with a show the day after she meets a carny. What's this Walt look like, anyhow?"

"He's in his mid-twenties, near six-foot tall, wide shoulders, wears a brown leather jacket and black jeans. His hair's sandy brown and slicked back like Elvis. He's got a long nose and a big jaw, with a huge grin half the time."

"A big goofy grin cocked over to one side?" she asked.

"Kindly. Sometimes."

"Yeah, yeah. Now I know who you're talkin' about. I see him in the G-top all the time. He seems better than the regular run-of-the-mill 'round here. But whatever made you want to up and go off with him? I'd guess that all the studs were pawin' at the ground for you back in that coal town."

"Well, I reckon it's not so much because of him and me, as it's more about Clandel and me. I grew up a mite bookish, a loner in school, and my make didn't bloom until late. So by the time boys took notice of me, I became more partial to reading stories in novels than listening to their sorry tales. My pap lit out a few years back, and left my maw and sister and me to fend for ourselves. My sister married up, Maw took to drink, and I hankered just to get away from it all."

"But darlin', what are you gettin' away from?"

"I'm getting away from there. Where there's nothing for me."

"And there's somethin' for you out here?"

"Well, I don't rightly know yet. Do I?"

"What I'm tryin' to get at, is what is it about your hometown that's set you to leave it so?"

I thought on this for a piece, then answered, "When I look around at folks there, I don't feel like, nor want to be like, one of them. Yet they want me to be like one of them.... I say thanks, but no thanks. So then they're not so partial to me—nor me neither to them. I just have no feel of belonging."

"And you're gonna fit in here?"

"Ma'am, I reckon I don't rightly know that yet," I told her again, a tad testily this time.

"Now don't get yourself in a pucker. It's just fat old Lula tryin' to help you figure out what's what."

"I appreciate that."

"Anytime, darlin'. Do you have a hole yet?"

"A hole?"

"A job in the show."

"Yeah, I guess—with Nick, Walt's boss."

She looked me up and down, studied my eyes, and then said, "Well, if you need a plan-B, I'll bet we could make the seven-in-one into a genuine ten-in-one with a looker such as you. Sonny could work up some of his old tricks—saw you in half, or make you disappear. It's been a long time since I fit into any of his magic boxes. If it don't work out with Walt or Nick, you come see what we have to say then. Okay?"

"Sure enough."

"I'll tell you one thing, darlin'. Out here, we all gotta stick together. To the rest of the world carny folk may be a tribe of tricksters and thieves. But among our own, you don't find better folk—once you get to know 'em. We're no different than anyone else, makin' a livin' doin' what we do, helpin' out our own—each of us our own peculiar selves, in our own particular manner—some good, some not so good.

"My hunch is that your Walt ain't the worst devil out here, and wouldn't be leavin' an angel like you for no good reason. So he'll be findin' you shortly. And we'll be seein' you around the show.... Good luck to you, Annabelle."

I thanked her, got up, and offered a handshake. In how she held mine— her thick soft paw warm and moist—I felt of her goodness. She leaned back into the sun and I scuffed away.

After hunting for Walt a couple of turns around the lot again, and feeling less and less likely to find him, I sat with my back up against a white birch tree at the edge of the field. Plucking sullenly at a patch of Venus' looking glass, I figured Walt must have left out—left me. Notions of what to do next fluttered through my head like bats from one end of an unknown darkness to the other. The hundred-and-ten dollars I had wouldn't likely get me far. With Walt gone, Nick might not look so kindly on giving me a job. And I wasn't too partial to being sawn in half in a sideshow.

But what had happened with Walt? Did he just do me a wham-bam-thank-you-ma'am, and now he didn't have the cods to deal with it? Was he just a bucketful of ackempucky that I'd swallowed whole? I shook my head with disgust at what a fool I was.

At a nearby box truck, while unlocking its back door and lifting it open with a rattle, a muscly and wiry feller—in tight-ass checkered bell-bottom pants and a big-collared half-unbuttoned paisley shirt—caught me shying my eyes away from his. His Fu Manchu moustache appeared familiar. After yanking some steel tent stakes out of the truck and clanging them onto the ground, he spun on the heels of his clunky platform shoes and clomped over to me.

"You're a dancer, and I know it," he said, his thumbs hooked in his white belt, his stringy brown hair framing a wise-guy smirk, his moustache cocked to one side.

"I like to dance," I said warily.

"Do you like to be watched when you dance?"

"Who wants to know?"

"Me. I'm Danny. I got the kootch show."

"The what?"

"For six nights this week there'll be tentfuls of men right over there," he jerked a thumb toward the truck behind him, "payin' their dollars to watch women dance."

Now I remembered where I'd seen him—the barker on the Harem stage.

"Bare-naked?" I asked.

"If they want."

"If who wants?"

"If the law wants, if the front office wants, if the dancer wants, if I want. Dancin' bare-ass in public is a complicated business in the good old U.S.A. Even so, every red-blooded man throughout all time and space, sure as hell-fire, owns an itch to watch naked women dance.... Do you like gettin' naked in front of men?"

"I never much tried it."

"I'll tell you the truest fact I know. If a beauty such as you danced in my show—even just half naked—men would be your toys."

"What good is that?"

"Good money. Good show."

I twisted my face up at him, eyed him like he was a pervert, and I had nothing more to say—though his offer sparked a heat in my blood that chilled me to the bone with shame.

After an awkward silence, he read his answer in my eyes, and told me, "Scrumptious, anytime you want your panties stuffed with cash—dancin' naked or not—you come talk to Danny. I'll be settin' right over there all week." And he strutted, banty-legged, back to his truck.

I turned around and there was Walt hurrying toward me, a sight for sore eyes. Heaving a sigh of relief, I jumped to my feet. Then, slapping the dirt off the back of my jeans, I dropped my grateful smile. With no clue of what he'd been up to, I was riled enough to kick a cat.

"I got us a room in town," he said, beaming wide and eager.

"Say what?" Confused for a moment, I gathered that in. Then I snarled at him, "You left me here alone and I didn't know where the hell you went."

His toothy grin fell from his face. "Annabelle, I whispered to you where I was goin' when I got out of the car, but I guess you were dead to the world.... What? You thought I'd gone down the road without you? I figured I'd let you get some sleep."

"I didn't know what to think. Couldn't you write a few words on a note telling me where you went?"

"Damn, I guess I could've, and prob'ly should've.... I thought you heard me, baby." Turning a touch misput himself, he added testily, "I didn't know we got married so quick."

"We ain't married, mister. You scared the lizards out of me. And don't call me 'baby'!"

"Okay, okay," he said, and put his hands on my shoulders, pulling me close. "I'm sorry.... I'm sorry I scared my Belle."

"I'm tired. I'm hungry. I'm in yesterday's sweaty clothes. And you go off to I don't know where. Don't ever do that to me again. You hear?"

He held me tighter, and nodding his chin on my ear, murmured, "Yes.... Yes I hear you."

Before I had time enough to quile my hissy fit, he asked, "What was Danny talkin' to you about?"

I squirmed out of his arms and said snippily, "It appears he's offered me a job dancing in his harem."

Walt slowly lit a cigarette, and then told me point-blank, "There ain't no hootchy-kootchy tent with you and me in it, Annabelle."

I saw the edge of the pit that I could shove this down. So I backed off with stone-cold silence, folded my arms across my middle, and poked at the grass with a toe.

He studied me for a spell, his eyes probing mine while he blew smoke. Then he just said, "Let's go into town."

I followed him to his car, and grit my teeth the three miles into Stuart—the narrow road snaking between greening hills that crisscrossed ten-o'clock high. As we neared town, slattery box houses sat scattered alongside a creek, their low-pitched roofs slung over galleries yopped up with clattermints. Concrete-slab bridges over the creek appeared hardly passable enough for a half-ton pick-up hauling half a load. Up behind the box houses, mobile homes of every breed and age perched in the hollows—many no more fixy than a semi-trailer with a door and a few windows cut into it, and a scrap-wood stoop cobbled on. Around every third or fourth curve of the road sat twice-abandoned businesses—one a caved-in gas station with a hair-salon sign in drinted paint on its cracked plate-glass window, another a boarded-up restaurant with rusty scrap metal strewn about its parking lot. Here and there, a scattering of cars and pickups gathered around several churches set in most anything save a real church with a steeple—in trailers and second-hand buildings, with made-up names on hand-painted signs.

We climbed into Stuart, some forty miles northeast of Clandel as the crow flies—yet with all the winding switchback roads, twice-again further by car. Clustered upon a stretch of top land, the town had more sky than Clandel. Its buildings were spread out lower, not as huddled shoulder-to-shoulder, up and down a double-barreled main street a half-mile long.

Walt wheeled into a motel parking lot—The Corridor Inn. He parked, and without a word or a smile, he grabbed his bag and mine out of the trunk, and led me up the treads to the far end of the balcony, to room 16 at the top-right corner of the two-story redbrick motel.

He keyed open the door, saying, "We got this for the week," and I followed him into the room.

On the bed was a box of chocolates, and on the nightstand a dozen red roses in a sparkly cut-glass vase. A note leaned up against the vase. I folded it open and read, 'Welcome to my dream. xxx—Walt.'

He said, "Do you know what I had to go through to get roses and chocolates on a Sunday mornin' in this town?"

So that was what he'd been up to. I melted in shame onto the bed. He crawled above me. I reached up and pulled him close. And off we went at it again.

This time I took the lead, and did things I'd never done with a man, things I'd only heard tell of. With a mind to make it up to him for my being such a pissy bitch, I fetched something out of myself that I never knew was there—a lusty gratefulness that strutted my heart to welcome what he had to give, like a flower in sunshine.

An hour later while I showered, Walt shouted through the steam into the bathroom—as if to prove he'd told me this time—that he was going down the street to the Kentucky Fried Chicken for some takeout. When he came back with the food, smelling so good, we sat cross-legged on the bed, the Colonel's bucket between us, and gnawed bare-fisted on the crispy and greasy chicken—me, just in panties, arms jostling my bubbies—Walt, grinning huge, his eyes adoring the sight of me. For dessert, from my box of chocolates we picked out our favorite ones.

He showered while I fixed my hair in the mirror over the chest of drawers, and we were back to the lot by noon, where we found Nick in a stew, pacing back and forth by the Oldsmobile, which was still hooked up to the joint trailer. I followed Walt's lead and sat beside him, mute on the trailer hitch. Walt smoked and Nick fretted, while I watched the horses on the Merry-Go-Round get pulled out of a truck and attached to poles on the whirligig by two carnies—one, a short and shirtless teenager with a rolled-up red-and-black bandana tied around his crewcut, and the other was the gangly old giant who had scared me off from peeking through the backside of the girly show.

Three-quarters of an hour later, nothing had happened yet—just a wisecrack now and then from Walt, told to try to lighten up Nick, who twisted a lopsided little smile at a few of them, but mostly just grumbled and paced. I sniggered skittishly at Walt's jokes, and didn't have much else to offer. I gathered we were waiting to get our locations—where to set up Nick's joints.

The bestower of locations was a small but buxom older woman driving a golf cart around the lot. She wore her puffy and silvery hair piled atop her head and proudly carried a graceful angular face, though sagging and sun-dried. When she'd stop to read from her clipboard, she'd lift tiny gold-rimmed glasses up from a chain around her neck and perch them on the tip of her up-turned nose. Her ample cleavage, bursting up from a lacy blue low-cut top, and her meaty hind end, sleek in black slacks, jounced on the seat of the cart as it whirred back and forth. I asked Walt who she was.

"Julia's Eli McCain's second wife, I hear. The old man's got a couple of kids from his first wife. One of 'em, his boy Sonny, swallows swords and eats fire at the show's back end. And eats shit from Julia in the front office. She pretty much runs the show for Old Eli now. He just sits out in front of the office trailer, diddling with his cane most of the time. But Belle, I gotta hand it to her, the lady Julia sure runs one tight ship. Yessiree, Bob."

Another quarter-hour later, Julia curled a finger at us, and Nick strode off, following her cart. Shortly, he returned and fired up the Oldsmobile, and pulled the joint trailer around to the other side of the oval of rides taking shape in the middle of the field. Walt and I followed on foot behind the trailer, which swayed across the field, leaving a trail of crushed mayflowers.

Nick jockeyed the trailer back and forth and back and forth, longways into a space between two stakes—jumping in and out of the car to eyeball how it lined up. When he got it where he wanted, he cranked the hitch up off the ball and unlocked the awnings. Then he wheeled the Oldsmobile over near his house trailer, and returned with the two-ton truck, parking it along the backside of the joint trailer.

Meanwhile, Walt cranked the trailer down close to level, chocked its tires with short chunks of two-by-fours, and steadied it under each corner with some screw jacks that were stowed inside the trailer. Fred wandered over, and digging in an ear with his pinky, stood staring at me until Nick told him to open up the back of the truck.

Before long the three of them had the trailer awnings propped open, and they took in unloading the frame of the center joint out of the back of the truck. I helped carry some lumber around to the front, where we set it down in its location, staked out in the grass midway between the joint trailer and the half-assembled Tilt-A-Whirl.

Brenda and Jenny, hand in hand, strolled up to Nick. Brenda appeared to caucus with him about me—voices low, glances sneaking my way. Jenny clung to her mother's arm and squirmed, shyly looking me over, twisting her head away, then turning to scowl another peek at me from beneath her downy eyebrows.

She let loose of her mother and clambered atop a huge and dusty canvas bag stuffed with the tent, as Brenda came over and told me, "We're gonna try you in the pitch-till-u-win. Jump into the joint."

The pitch-till-u-win sat next to Walt's bushel-basket game in the other half of the joint trailer. I backed my hind end up to the counter, hopped onto it, swung my legs over, and stood on the trailer floor between the counter and several rails of wooden blocks—large and small, with a prize attached to each. Under the blocks hung a red cloth, swagging end to end with dozens of four-inch-wide wooden hoops. Brenda leaned over the counter and pointed to three panels cut into the floor and fixed with sliding bolts. She told me to slip the bolts open, lift the trapdoors out of the floor, and stow them on the grass beneath the trailer. I struggled with the first one some, but soon had all three stashed under the trailer.

Brenda pointed at a yellow-and-white-striped tarp rolled-up on the floor of the basket side of the trailer, and said, "Set that bally cloth on the counter and jump out with me."

I did so with all the haste of eager to please. She unrolled the bally cloth—three-foot wide and the length of the twenty-four-foot trailer, with snaps along its topside—and she told me to hold it up out of the dirt while she snapped it on beneath the counter from one end to the other, as a skirt to hide the wheels. With the awnings up and the bally cloth on, the aluminum trailer became a pair of carnival games, easy as that.

Brenda hoisted herself into the peach-basket side, and on her hands and knees hunted under the counter and brought out a rag and a bottle of spray cleaner. She told me to clean off the bally cloth, dust all the blocks, and straighten out the prizes. Then, leaving me to my tasks, she joined Jenny beside the tent bag, where they watched Walt, Nick, and Fred assemble the frame of the glass pitch.

I went at the bally cloth with all the elbow grease I could muster—spraying and scrubbing to beat the band. Most of the grime was long set into the canvas, and nigh on impossible to get out. But I busied myself with trying, and at the least, wiped off slathers of coal dust from Clandel.

Then I hopped back into the pitch-till-u-win and took in dusting the blocks and the prizes—transistor radios, plastic whistles, hunting knives, Chinese finger-traps, wrist watches, tin sheriff's badges, costume jewelry, rubber spiders, and more, all latched with rubber bands to the blocks—big prizes on the big blocks, little prizes on the little blocks. Under the counter sat several boxes filled with hundreds of the little prizes. I straightened them out some, and then gathered up all the wooden hoops in the cloth slung beneath the blocks, and neatly arranged them in two long rows. Working hard to look busy, I wiped everything down again. When there was nothing else to red-up, save do it all again a third time, I swung my legs out over the counter and sat there dangling my heels against the bally cloth.

More and more of the carnival was coming together. Encircling the rides, other tents and trailers took shape in the line-up. The Ferris Wheel seats swung into the sky one after another. Sledgehammers rang down on inch-thick-steel tent stakes. Motors groaned and rumbled to life. The arms of rides unfolded into their poses—getting readied for their dizzying rounds by grimy men clambering over the pig iron and muscling huge wrenches. Walt, Nick, and Fred unrolled the center joint's heavy canvas over the hitched-up frame, and shortly hoisted each end into the air—swinging the legs out from under the corners, and levering up the top.

Walt came over, patted me on the knee, and said, "I'll slough the glass to get on down the road. But I don't flash no glass. The center joint's in the air, so I'll be done soon. Then we can go back to the room."

I hopped off the counter and told him I was going to take a stroll. After a few dozen steps down the midway, Julia McCain whirred by me on her golf cart. She eyed me as she passed—then stopped, backed up, and asked me, "Who are you with?"

Trying to sound with it, I said, "I've got a hole with Nickel Nick."

"What's your name?" she asked, and I told her.

"Get in," she told me, and I did. She looked me up and down, stepped on the gas pedal, and the cart jerked forward.

"Where you from, Annabelle?"

It crossed my mind to make up a story—tell her I was from Arkansas or someplace—but I thought it best to just say, "Clandel... the town we just left out of."

"And what are you doing on my midway?" she asked gently as we lurched along, her blue eyes probing the carnival's half-done jigsaw puzzle.

"I'm going to run a game."

"And why?"

"To make some money, and get out of state. To get someplace else."

"You decided to just up and do this by yourself?"

"Well, Walt—he runs the bushel-basket game for Nick—he's kindly helping me out."

"How old are you, Annabelle?"

"I'm nineteen."

"I suppose that's old enough in this state to run off with a man. What's your people think about that?"

"I reckon Maw is kicking the cat this morning. But soon as she gets into her stump liquor, she'll settle down. My pap is long gone. My sister's got a husband and her own problems.... That's about all there is to it."

"You in any trouble with Johnny Law?"

"Oh no, ma'am. Never been. And never aim to be."

"So, you want to be a good girl, eh?"

"That's for certain, ma'am."

"Well then, young lady, let me tell you what. This is my show, and the fewer jackpots I have to deal with, the nicer I am. I can see that you're one fine buttery biscuit—which means that more than a few of my boys are likely to get their rut riled up, lookin' to spread their marmalade on you. However, I hate a soap opera. I've seen too much good help go down the road after one another feisty episode. Good help is hard to find. And harder to keep. You keep your nose clean, and you keep these hound dogs around here from sniffin' your tail, and gettin' wrangy over you with each other. Then you've got yourself a carnival. You catch my drift?"

"Yes, ma'am. I surely do. And I ain't no hussy."

"Miss Cory, you don't have to be a hussy. All it takes is bein' young and good lookin'. You just watch out for yourself."

"Yes, ma'am."

She stopped the cart, and said, "All right. Go on. I'll be keepin' an eye on you. And if ever you be needin' help with somethin', you come and see me, Annabelle. You hear?"

"Yes, ma'am. Thank you."

Hopping out, I stumbled a step or two, puzzled why she would offer me help after reading me my rights and putting the fear of damnation in me.

She mashed down the gas pedal, and as the cart whirred away she spun her head back to me, and said, "And no drugs neither."

"No, ma'am."

I scuffed around the lot a few times—the midway taking shape in the warm and bright Sunday afternoon, the frenzy of moving the carnival fading. Resting now in yet another spot sat the same oval of rides, surrounded by its ring of tents and trailers, surrounded by a jumble of vehicles, surrounded by yet another cluster of West Virginia hills.

Sprawling on their monstrous machines and lounging in the sun, ride boys smoked and joked—several trying to catch my eye as I strolled past. At the cookhouse, carnies chatted over their bowls of chili-mac and cups of coffee. In lawn chairs in front of a trailer marked 'OFFICE', a fat old man under a straw hat like the ones worn by a barbershop quartet—Eli McCain, no doubt—leaned forward on the silver knob of his cane and talked business with a deputy sheriff sitting beside him. Several local teens bogued about, checking out the show, their hands shoved into the front pockets of their tight jeans.

I came upon Isis's tent in the line-up—her boy, Tyrone, putting the finishing touches on his ticket booth—and I went around back to her house trailer, where I found her kneeling in the grass and shoving a wire trap under her trailer.

She looked up and said, "Oh, my! Look who's made it to Oz." Tottering to her feet, she brushed off her robe, and smirking beneath her beard, added "I was thinking about you. Wondering if you'd have the get up and go."

"Yes, ma'am. I reckon I did. Now here I be. With a job in a game and a man in a motel room."

"My oh my. Aren't you the one coming along.... Would you like some tea?"

I said sure and we went inside. While she got the tea going, I scanned again the titles of the mysterious books on the shelves behind the glass doors above. On my tiptoes, with my head cocked sideways and my eyes upon *Isis Unveiled*, I asked if this book was about her.

She laughed in her warbling hee-hee way, and said, "Oh no. Oh no.... Well come to think of it—sure it's about me. And about you, and about everybody."

"Can I read it?"

"Annabelle dear, that book's one of my favorites. And what with the way life is out here in the sawdust, sometimes people and things go down the road never to be seen again. So I don't lend out my books. But I do have a little booklet that I've put together, and made some copies of, which I hand out to curious souls, now and then."

"You mean you wrote it?"

"I didn't re-invent the wheel or anything like that. It's just a little guide-book to what I've found important in all these books—and in life."

I told her I'd love to read it, and she fetched me a copy from a drawer. The title, *All Was, All Is, All Ever Shall Be*, was handwritten in red ink across the cover—a manila file folder—to which was stapled a quarter-inch-thick sheaf of shiny paper with purple mimeograph print.

I slid into one side of the table nook, opened it to the first page, and read aloud, "If you think that you know, then you do not. Whoever knows knowledge to be unknowable—who knows that truth is simply too much for our minds to grasp, and is thus always misunderstood—knows the truth that sets one free."

I thought on this for a short piece, and then asked Isis, "Haven't scientists got things pretty much figured out?"

Her back to me at the stove, she shrugged and said, "Once upon a time the world was flat. Then it was round. Then Einstein said space was curved. And next it was all just vibrations. Now I hear that everything may be made of strings. It seems that every time the scientists figure it out, something else comes along to change their minds."

She brought over the teacups, and told me, "There's an old Hindu story that goes something like this.... Three blind men encounter an elephant. One reaches out and feels its trunk, another reaches out and feels its leg, and another reaches out and feels its ear. So, one says that the elephant is like a snake, the other says it's like the trunk of an oak, and the third says it's like the broad leaf of a palm. They each assume that what each can sense is the elephant. But what they each perceive is only one part of the elephant."

I hunted for something to say while she poured the tea, and came up with, "But if the three blind men got together and compared notes, wouldn't they get a better picture of the elephant?"

Setting the teacups down, she said, "You'd hope so," and sat across the table from me. "But what are they comparing notes with?... With words. And what are words?... Just symbols. Words are merely symbols for bits of what we see and feel. What we see and feel is not the whole elephant. And often it's not even the same elephant that someone else sees.

"Words are symbols for thoughts. And thoughts are as unique as each person is—in each land, in each time. When you think that you, or anyone else, speak the words of truth, then you delude yourself. If you teach, or preach, what you think you know to others, then you delude others. Which is even worse. So don't believe a word I say, dear."

She sung a little laugh, and added, "For what it's worth, take it or leave it from my own illusory perspective. All we have are symbols that may, or may not, get us any nearer to what we want to know."

"Then what's the sense of figuring anything out?"

"Oh, it's just what we do—being human beings. Who knows why we're the only monkeys who have to know why, when, what, who, where, or how.

Or maybe we're not. Maybe even the cockroaches have answers for their questions. Who knows? Who will ever know?

"My best guess is that figuring things out is just plain useful to us. We learn that the tusks of that elephant are useful to slice into piano keys or carve into ivory crucifixes. We make footstools from its feet. We train it to do circus tricks. But we don't really know or understand the elephant. A scientist observes its behavior, measures its length and weight, cuts it up and labels each piece. Yet when we look an elephant in the eye, we meet a mystery.

"Honey, when we look at the person next to us in the eye—even if it's your husband of forty years, or your own mother, or one's own face in the mirror for God's sakes—what do we know? We only know what we think we know, and most of the time it's mostly wrong, and often enough dead wrong."

"So what's the use of even knowing what you're telling me?"

"So you'll be cautious. So you'll not delude yourself and others. So you'll know that words are not answers. Like all symbols, they represent the mysteries that we live with. And like all idols, these symbols can replace those mysteries with creeds like the one that once built the Tower of Babel. Symbols aren't the answers—they're tools to shape our questions."

Puzzled about what to think of all this, and shying away from any more mumbo jumbo, I respectfully put her book down next to me on the bench seat, lifted a mannerable smile to her, and said, "I'll give it a read."

"Please return it to me."

With her tattooed elbows on the table, and both hands tipping her cup to her beardy lips, she sipped at the tea and studied my eyes, until she asked, "So, my beautiful young friend, how was your first day on the road?"

I blurted out the story of the truck and the brakes, and made it sound like Walt and I were on the edge of death, which likely we were.

Her whiskers bristling like the cat that ate the canary, she smiled wide and said, "Sounds like you got yourself one able-bodied hero there. How is he in the sack?"

"A heap sight better than those tater-grabblers back in Clandel."

She rang a laugh off the plywood-paneled ceiling, and added, "You think men are grabby with two hands? Try three!"

We sipped tea, and I told her how Walt had disappeared that morning, and I'd thought he'd gone and left me already, but then found out he was in town getting us a room and hunting up flowers and chocolates for me.

Then we heard the clank of the trap under the trailer. Isis snapped her fingers and rushed out the door. A minute later she came back in with a terrified field mouse scrabbling around inside the wire mesh, making pitiful little jingle-jangle sounds. In the corner of my eye, I sensed something moving. I turned and saw Solomon slithering his way out from under the black leather couch at the window end of the trailer.

Isis said, "It seems that Solomon likes the looks of his furry little lunch. Do you want to watch me feed him?"

I said, "No, thanks," and then gulped down the rest of my tea, slid out of the nook, and arsled sideways to the door.

"Don't forget my little book"

I snatched it up, thanked her for it and the tea, and let myself out.

I found Walt waiting beside his car. "Where you been?" he asked, a mite testily.

"Talking to Isis, the bearded lady. She gave me this little book that she wrote."

He glanced at it in my hand, walled up his eyes, and said, "Come on. Let's go back to the motel."

Back in the room, I stashed Isis's booklet in the nightstand drawer, which also had in it a Bible and a pad and pen. Walt turned on the TV and plopped onto the bed in front of a basketball game.

Nibbling on a chocolate, I re-arranged the roses in the vase. To see where I admired my bouquet the best, I moved it around the room—beside the TV on the low-slung chest of drawers, or atop the TV, or on the back of the commode, or on the nightstand by the bed, or by the window on the wobbly round table with two squarish chairs. I spread open the drapes—the daylight pouring in through half a wall of glass—and I tried the roses atop the air conditioner beneath the window. There felt of the place, my flowers to be seen from both outside and inside.

When I fetched a wad of moist toilet paper and took in wiping the dust off the window sill, Walt, lazily shifting his stare from the TV to me, said, "There's a maid what does that."

"Looks like she didn't."

Then I went at scrubbing the tabletop and the top of the dresser, with an air of well-I'll-show-you, until I had to toss the tattered wad into the waste bucket. Fetching more, I wiped down the bathroom mirror and the sink, scouring with no success at a rusty stain around the drain. Taking my measure of the bathtub—the plastic curtain still spattered from our showers, the wall tiles moldy here and there, and the paint damply peeling from the ceiling—I saw there was little help for it from me. But after my redding-up just that touch, the room felt more mine.

Next, I unpacked my bag, laying my clothes out in a dresser drawer. While arranging my toothbrush and make-up atop the commode and sink and in the cabinet behind the mirror, it struck me that this was the first place ever, other than my room at Maw's, that was mine. Mine and Walt's. Here, even if only for a week, I was the woman of this home.

Walt had plopped his beat-up suitcase half-open onto a foldup stand in the corner behind the door, and when I took in loading the other dresser drawer with some of his socks from it, he told me, "Belle, leave my stuff be. If I gotta move quick, I like to have it all in one place."

I tossed the socks back in his suitcase, and hoping we wouldn't be moving anywhere neither quick nor soon, I scootched up next to my man on the bed. His droopy eyes turned from the TV to me, and he spread his mile-wide grin. For a spell, we watched the basketball bounce from player to player and through the hoop... and soon fell asleep to the announcer's voice, the referee's whistle, and the cheers of the crowd.

We woke with a startle to a rap on the window, now filled with night. A chuffy face peered in through hands cupped on the glass. Walt jumped up to the window, and then swung the door open.

Traffic sounds rumbled past as a spoony jingle on TV advertised a furniture store. Scratching the back of his head, Walt said, "What it is, Cheeks?"

"Who you got in there, Walt? Make with the intros, man."

Walt stepped out to the balcony rail, and peering down into the parking lot, asked him, "You couldn't see us sleepin'?"

"Ahh... don't disqualify me for that. It looked like you two were watchin' TV. Who's the gash? She with it?"

Walt stretched his spine and rubbed his neck, then came back in, swaggered into the bathroom, and slammed its door shut. The commode seat clanked upright, and his branch babbled into the bowl.

"Hey. I'm Cheeks. And you are?"

I told him my name and recognized him as the feller with the ugly bald dog at the Frog Baby sideshow. He stood there wide as the doorway, a cheeky grin sliced across his pumpkin face.

"I got the room next door," he said. "Girl, we all gonna par-T!"

"Not now we're not," Walt hollered from behind the bathroom door, and after blowing a honk from his nose, he added, "We need some eats."

Cheeks offered, "There's this A-1 joint two blocks downhill. Big jigs deep-fryin' chicken. Bona fide."

I said, "Thanks, but we had fried chicken today for lunch. Or was that breakfast, Mr. Ryder?"

Walt swung out of the bathroom and said, "That was what we could get, where and when we could—which is what we'll go find now. I'm near hungry enough to eat scraps off a buzzard's beak."

Then he pulled on his brown leather jacket, went to the window, yanked the shades shut, and bellied up to Cheeks at the door, backing him out onto the balcony. Walt turned to me, winked, and said, "You pretty yourself up, and I'll see if I can't hunt up a decent restaurant." And he shut the door behind him.

I washed, and changed into black satin slacks, a sparkly red blouse that slung low on my left shoulder, and my strappy red sandals. I hurried on some make-up, brushed out my hair, and when I came out of the bathroom, Walt was slouching in a chair, browsing through a brochure.

"The desk clerk gave me the dope on the eats in town," he said, unfolding the brochure, his eyes flashing from one panel to another. When he glanced my way, he tossed it on the table, and grew one of his ear-to-ear grins. "Mmmm, mmm. You look better than good enough to eat, Anna-belle." And he tongued a wolf whistle off his front teeth.

I flashed him a feisty eye, and asked, "That chuffy guy at the window—Cheeks—he's got the tent with The Frog Baby, doesn't he?"

"Yeah. The pickled-punk joint."

"Is that thing for real? A baby with a frog's head?"

"Nah. It's a bouncer. Made with genuine latex. And settin' in a jug of Tetley tea. Sometimes you'll see a baby show that's the real deal—a fucked-up fetus in formaldehyde. But sooner or later a local lawman disqualifies it, maybe confiscates it, 'cause the fool carny has a dead body in his joint. La-tex lasts lots longer."

"And nobody cares that it's fake?"

"What ain't fake? This is the amusement business, Belle. Not a science museum. Let's go."

Out of the room, into the car, down the street, and a few turns later, we parked in front of Mama Maria's restaurant. As we went in, I thought of Maw—how she'd likely be so out of heart. I saw a pay phone by the door, and had half a mind to call and tell her things were fine. But I knew she'd spit nails at me. Wanting none of that right then, I figured I'd call her after she quiled some—maybe toward the end of the week.

Mama Maria's was done up Italian style—red-and-white checked table-cloths atop small square tables, a scratchy record of a mandolin plinking in the background, dozens of fat-bottomed and straw-wrapped jugs of wine, along with bundles of dried garlic, hanging across the stucco walls between arched doorways and windows. A handful of folks sat in twos and threes, scattered about, eating, drinking, and talking—their voices hushed among the clinking of knives and forks on their plates, the swinging door of the kitchen muffling the clang and sizzle of pots and pans.

A waitress, not much older than me, in a pleated black skirt and a low-cut white blouse with puffy sleeves, led us to a table and set down two red-and-gold menus. When Walt pulled my chair out for me and slid it under as I sat, I felt like a princess in a fairy story. I'd never eaten in a fancy restau-rant before—with cloth napkins that matched the tablecloth—and no beau had ever pulled a chair out for me.

The waitress asked us if we'd like to see the wine list. Walt, his face to the menu, shook his head. I ordered a bottle of Stroh's. Her curly black hair hanging to her shoulders, she eyed me with obvious doubt behind her mas-cara, and asked, "Can I see your I.D., please?"

"I don't have it with me."

"Then I'm sorry, I can't serve you," she said, one side of her mouth ap-pearing apologetic, the other with a hint of a smirk.

Walt looked up at her and said, "I'll have a Stroh's, and a bourbon on the rocks."

She told him, "I'm sorry sir, but hard liquor's served only in private clubs in West Virginia."

Walt dropped his jaw, as if shocked by the news—though he already knew it was so. "Just bring one of those jugs of wine like you got hangin' all over the walls."

"I still need to see her I.D. if she's drinking any."

"I'm gonna drink it all," he told her.

Her eyes narrowed as she thought on that. Then she flashed us a phony smile and hurried off.

Walt winked at me and went back to studying the menu. She came right back with a bottle and a single fancy wine glass. After working hard at screwing the cork out, she poured the glass half-full of the red wine, and, play-acting being happy as a songbird, she asked, "May I take your order now?"

I had no idea what to get, so I simply smiled up at her, shook my head, and she promptly went away. Walt pushed the wine glass over to me, then stuck a thumb through the straw cord around the jug's neck, tipped it over his shoulder, and took a pull on it, moonshiner style. I sniggered and stole a sip of the tart wine. I'd had wine before, Boone's Farm, with the boys three or four times. I didn't much like it. I'd wake up in the middle of the night with a throb behind my eyes and a thirsty tongue that felt of licking the sole of a coal-miner's boot. Yet now, here I was, out on the road, getting what I could get, where and when I could get it.

The menu listed fixings that ended in the letters 'i' and 'a'—spaghetti, lasagna, ravioli, linguini. I'd eaten my share of spaghetti, mostly out of a can, so I had a mind to taste something different. The prices were steep, some plates near seven dollars. Money didn't appear to trouble Walt, so I picked out the fanciest and longest name on the menu, Fettuccini Alfredo—and then I took in fretting about how I'd pronounce it to the waitress without me sounding like a hillbilly.

I leaned to Walt and whispered, "Do you reckon Mama Maria's out back in the kitchen cooking this all up?"

"I'll lay you forty-to-one that no Mama Maria's ever been near this joint."

"How can they name it that then?"

"Annabelle, this here's America. And not only that, it's West-by-God-Virginia. So you can name a restaurant anythin' you damn well please."

"But isn't that false advertising?"

He slapped his knee and hooted a laugh. "Hoo ha! False advertising? That's a good one."

The waitress returned and asked if we were ready to order. I pointed on the menu to what I wanted. Walt asked if they could do him just a steak without all the Italian fixings. Her eyes flashed back and forth from her pad to Walt, and forcing a smile, she shook her head. He ordered spaghetti with sausage.

I asked the waitress, "Is Mama Maria cooking tonight."

"I ain't seen nary a Mama Maria since I been here. And that's nigh on two years now. Leland Gates started up this place, maybe five years back, and I know for a fact his mama's named Alice."

"Then why's this place called Mama Maria's, if it's not."

"Honey, you'll have to ask Mr. Gates about that one. And he ain't here tonight."

She shrugged, did that apologetic half-frown-half-smirk thing again, and grabbing up the menus, marched off to the kitchen with our orders. Walt held his hand over his mouth, squeezing mock laughs into his ears. I sipped some wine with nary a bother about anybody's mama putting a stop to it.

Walt hooked the jug with a finger, bumped it against my glass, and said, "And they beef about a carny's gaffed-up joint. Four-ninety-five for spaghetti noodles? Five bucks buys me a tank of gas for the Merc'. Phony Italian name, phony Italian wall-to-wall flash, jugs of wine wrapped in straw, waitresses dressed like peasants and workin' for tips. What a racket."

He poured me more wine, and swigged a lengthy pull off the jug. Right then, a pair of fixy pieces clattered through the front door in pointy high heels, both prettied up a sight too much for this town. They looked around the room, saw us, and fetched up, all full of smiles.

"Why what the hey, Walt," said the smaller one, way too loudly. "Who's this you got here?" Everybody in the restaurant turned from their plates and stared at us.

Walt said, "Trudy, Janet, this here's Annabelle. She's come to me straight out of my dreams."

"Why, I didn't know you could dream, Walt," joked Trudy—a hawk-billed, straight-haired, slinky blonde with too much make-up gaumed on her wide-set eyes, pinched cheeks, and pouty lips. "Hey there, Annabelle. You best wake Walt up now." And she laughed out a loud cackle, as if inviting me to laugh, too.

I mannerably lifted a smile. I'd seen her somewhere before.

Janet said, "Annabelle, don't you pay Trudy's cracks never no mind."

Her wavy-brown short hair streaked with blonde, Janet was a smidgen on the heavy side—her boobs like muskmelons, the cleavage squeezing out of the top of her low-cut tight-ass jump suit. Her face carried a cheery air, yet appeared somewhat squared-off and mannish, as if all her smiling had muscled it up. Both of them were decked out like they'd just stepped off the bus from Hollywood, their perfume loud enough to drown out Mama Maria's oregano.

Janet asked, "Mighten you care a hate if we set with y'all?"

I shrugged and said, "Why not."

Walt shot me a glance that looked like a warning.

They dragged over two chairs, sat on down, and pulled off their jackets—Trudy's, shiny white plastic with black trim on its wide lapels, and Janet's, red leather with silver conchos along the bottom edge. Under the jacket, Janet wore the jump suit, also black, with no blouse beneath it, and Trudy had on a sleeveless jade-green knit dress, which clung to her spare make from neck to knee, and had a slit up one side to mid-thigh.

"Trudy and Janet dance in the kootch show," Walt said.

That explained it all. I'd seen Trudy up on the stage of the Harem the night before. I told them, "That feller with the Fu Manchu—Danny?—he tried to sign me up for The Harem this morning."

Way too loud for Mama Maria's ears, Trudy shrieked, "That fuck-face! He's always tryin' to work one angle or another on someone. He needs more dancers like he needs another asshole full of shit."

Janet said, "Maybe he's wantin' to eighty-six your nasty mouth, Trudy."

"Could be it's your fat ass he's lookin' to D.Q.," Trudy shot back.

"Now ladies," Walt said, lighting a cigarette, "Annabelle's no dancer."

"I like to dance," I corrected him, and then asked Janet, "How much money do you make dancing in a girly show?"

"Depends on the spot. What do you say, Trudy? What do we average? Maybe four-or five-hundred a week?"

"It oughta be lots more, but for that bullshitter, Danny."

"Each?"

"More or less," Janet said.

"And do you take all your clothes off?"

"Depends on what the sheriff has to say about that."

Trudy added, with a snort, "Yeah, and if him and his beat-meat deputies get their free show."

I had to ask, "Do you do anything else, too?"

"Like what?" Janet cocked her head sideways at me.

Trudy hissed, "She's asking if we fuck 'em."

Walt explained, "These two ladies are lovers, Annabelle. Of each other."

"Oh... I'm sorry."

"Sorry about what?" Trudy snapped.

"I'm just saying I'm sorry I asked a personal question without knowing the first thing about you."

Janet said, "Askin' questions is how you find out things, darlin'."

Thankfully, the waitress came over with our food right then. Janet ordered a bottle of wine and asked for menus. My plate had a dog's bait of noodles on it, but I was let down to see that Fettuccini Alfredo was just flatter and wider spaghetti in a slather of pale cheese sauce. Walt's plate had a heap on it, too—the tomato sauce and sausage set steaming on top.

Trudy cracked, "Looks like some asshole squeezed out a bloody shit on your spaghetti, Walt."

Walt tucked his checked-cloth napkin into his shirt collar, and said, "Trudy, you really know how to perk up a man's appetite."

She said, "That's not all I can perk up on a man," and then laughed like a banshee.

As I twirled noodles onto my fork, Janet turned to me and asked, "Where're you comin' in from, Annabelle? I ain't seen you on the lot none."

Walt said, "She's green—genuine First-of-May."

The two strippers eyed me differently, and then looked at each other as if to say, now I get it. Then they ignored me while I dug into my noodles, which weren't much to write home about. They caucused with Walt about how Clandel had been down some, but still decent, and about how Stuart was a wrangier spot, and a jig spot—which I took to mean that the locals were more fractious, and lots of them were black.

We had some blacks in Clandel—not many. They lived mostly up a hollow down the creek a short piece. I went to school with several, and had a black girlfriend, named Sharla. We'd often play at recess, and in classes where the teacher would sit us alphabetically she'd be in the desk in front of me, her last name being Cobb. When we got to high school, something between us changed, and I sorely missed Sharla's big-eyed smile. I never knew whether it was because of her, or it was something I said, or it was the pig-headed grits and their ill-bred racism that withered our friendship. Yet I can handily say I never held the bad blood that most of the whites in Clandel had with blacks.

There was no mystery what Trudy had to say about them. And along with too loudly squandering her opinions about "all the mother-fuckin' jigs," she also blessed out "these bum-fuck towns," and the "shit-ass service in this fuckin' joint."

While she went on and on and on, Walt and I kept our mouths full of noodles and our eyes wandering around the room. Janet just shook her head and chuckled as if there was nothing to be done about Trudy's ways.

Before long, a balding man—dressed in his Sunday best, with his stringy hair combed over the top of his round and shiny head—came over to our table and said, "What say you keep down the cussin'? The wife and I aim to enjoy a pleasant meal here, and your benastied language ain't allowin' it."

Trudy scowled up at him and snarled, "What say you aim your puny jemison up your wife's ass, and fuck shit."

He just stood there, jaw and fists clenched, with no answer for that. Chairs squawked on the floor, and from a nearby table a pair of squat and muscly miners got up and swaggered over.

Janet stood up and moved between them and Trudy. Walt just walled his eyes back, shook his head, and twirled spaghetti around his fork.

Eyeing the two miners, Janet said, "Now Trudy, that wasn't a neighborly thing to say, was it?"

"I ain't no neighbor of this dick-head."

One of the miners, the meaner-looking one, said, "Y'all are trash from that carnival outside of town. Ain't ya?"

Trudy said, "What of it?—you egg-suckin' squirrel-turner."

He moved to get around Janet, but she sidestepped in front of him.

Walt yanked his napkin from his collar, flung it down on the table, and said, "For Christ's sake, Trudy. Why're you always stirrin' up a jackpot? Chill it. Or it'll be me kickin' your kiester."

"Fuck you too, Walt."

Just then, out from the kitchen, up charged a burly black woman in a bib apron over baggy-ass jeans. A cast-iron frying pan in one hand, and the other waggling a finger at us, she spit out, "There'll be no bitin' and gougin' round here. Y'all just set yourselfs back down and hold your taters."

The whole room stared at her. I could see she meant business with that fry pan. When nobody moved quick enough, she shrieked, "Git! Git back to what you come in here for, so's I can git back to my kitchen."

Trudy said, "Damn. You must be Mama Maria. You tell 'em, Mama."

"I ain't your mama! But iffen I was, I'd be a-scrubbin' your mouth with soap, right here and now. I can hear your cussin' clear back in my kitchen. You either hush it up, or git on out of here."

Trudy looked around the room, all eyes on her.

Walt said, "Drop the awning, Trudy. Will ya? So I can finish my spaghetti?"

She stood up in a huff, grabbed her jacket from the back of the chair, and clacked her high heels through the silence, to plunk down at a table at the empty end of the room. The old feller with the comb-over and the two miners shook their heads with disgust and disbelief, and shuffled back to their seats. Janet went and sat with Trudy. And the cook toted her fry pan back into the kitchen.

Walt muttered, "That damn Trudy is flat-out crazy-bitch trouble."

"They're lesbians?" I whispered.

"I'd say Janet is. But Trudy would fuck just about anythin' that squirms. She rides with Janet because no man'll have her. Let's eat up and get the hell out of here."

We gobbled down the remains on our plates, and Walt swigged the rest of the bottle. When we got up to go, I glanced over at Trudy. She sat scowling over her wine glass, one foot up on another chair, the slit in her dress baring her leg, a knee cocked to show the whole room her shaved satchel. Janet sat across the table from her, smoking a little cigar, and threw us a smile, waggling a few fingers goodbye.

Back at the motel parking lot, we got out of the car and heard laughs and voices coming out of the open door of the room next to ours. Walking by on the balcony, we peeked in on nearly a dozen carnies—wall-to-wall with beer and cigarettes, twice as many men than women, most in their thirties or forties, a portable eight-track playing some Rolling Stones, the TV on with no sound, and a loud scent of marijuana cutting through the tobacco smoke.

Cheeks sat cross-legged on a pile of pillows up against the bed's head-board, and doled out cards to four carnies sprawled atop the coverlet. Aside him lay his ugly dog, half tucked under the sheet. Another half-dozen car-nies sat around the room—atop the dresser and on chairs at the table by the window. Some greeted Walt with, "Hey, Walt," and "What it is, Walt?"

Walt waved a hand at them, and said, "It's a Sunday night in West Vir-ginia. What it is with you all?"

"Copasetic, man. Copasetic," said one, sprawled sideways on the bed with his cards at his elbow, and wearing a cap like Peter Pan's, topped with a turkey feather stuck in it. He twisted his head around to study me, his face narrow, weathered, and buck-toothed as a rabbit. He asked in a voice high and tight, "Who's this gorgeous gash with you, Walt?"

"Everybody, this here's Annabelle."

Not everybody said how-do—but enough for me to feel welcome.

Walt asked Cheeks, "What's the action on the blackjack?"

"My house. A fin limit."

"Deal me in." Walt dug some bills from his pocket, and sat down on the edge of the bed. Turning to me, still at the door, he said, "Get yourself somethin' to drink, Belle."

Cheeks added, "Yeah, gorgeous. Bar's in the donniker. Beer on ice in the bathtub. Only three-two, though. The jug on the back of the commode's some angel-teat moonshine I scored last week from a barrel-dogger. Mix a jigger in a can of beer, and then you got somethin'. There's a pop machine down by the office, too, with other mixers."

I thanked him for the hospitality, fished a can out of the bathtub, and tipped a splash of splo, both into the beer and down my gullet. Angel-teat, it wasn't—being more like kill-devil stump liquor. As it quickly seeped into my bellyful of cheesy noodles, its warm shiver becharmed the air of the roomful of carnies.

Beer in hand, I found an empty corner and listened to the hearsay. Like at any gather-all back in Clandel, it was mostly moonlight talk—the braggy ones squandering opinions, the jokey ones cutting up. Only the particulars had changed. They caucused about shows, towns, joints, and weather, both good and bad. They norated about what had happened with who, where, when, and why. I just leaned against the wall, with nothing yet to share with them, eyes and ears open, my lips eager to return a smile.

Walt kept an eye on me, and showed me a grin now and then, but the card game got much more of his attention than I did, and he appeared to be losing. On the bed, along with Peter Pan, sat a porky couple, cozying up against each other as they played their cards and made their bets. Also in the game, a big beardy frizzy-haired hippie sat on the floor, his legs stretched out under the bed and his back against the wall.

The others in the room were in two groups, three at the table and chairs by the window, and three sitting atop the dresser. The three at the table, were doing most of the talking—two clean-cut slicks in crisp clothes, one swarthy, with a pencil-thin moustache, and the other tow-headed, his ashy eyebrows heavy with menace—and also a girl, near my age, with straight black hair hanging down to her bum. I recognized her to be the girl that ran the game with the rat and the wheel.

The other three sat squished together aside the TV on the long and low chest of drawers—an older woman, laughing loud and often, and still looking pretty good—a younger woman in her early twenties, likely her daughter—and between them, a baby-faced feller, near the same age as the daughter, and nattering into the older woman's ear a sight too cozily. He had a mollycoddled conceit to him—tousled corn-silk hair, sleepy eyes, a pinched turned-up nose, a slight pout on his puffy lips—and he paid much more attention to the older woman than to the younger, who sat there hunched forward with her elbows on her thighs, appearing forlorn.

Everybody had beers in their hands or within reach, and half of them a cigarette going. I stood there not knowing what to say, and nobody saying anything to me. Before long, the cigarette smoke got too thick, so I went out on the balcony for some air.

My elbows on the railing, I looked out over the parking lot, my eyes following the cars rolling up and down the street, past the hodge-podge of storefronts. Had anything really changed for me? And if it had, was it for the worse? Here I was, still an outsider—even more of an outsider—without a clue what would happen next. At least back in Clandel I held the hope that when I'd left out, things would change for the better. Now I was gone, but gone into a world of strangers—and strange strangers at that.

Give things a chance, I told myself. It's only been one day.

"What's out there, Annabelle?" said a voice behind me. I turned to the girl from the rat wheel. A widow's peak above her wide forehead and pointy jaw, her heart-shaped face, fixy with makeup, carried something shrewd within her dimply smirk—something older than she appeared.

"Not much," I said, showing her a warm smile.

"I'm Madeline. You just come in?"

I nodded, and didn't say from where.

"For spring still-dates, the McCain show is better than most," she told me matter-of-factly, but not a bit briggoty.

"So I hear," I said. Then, groping for something to say next, I asked, "What do you know about Walt?"

"I know he looks mighty fine to me. I see him around the lot. We say 'Hi' now and then. But that's about it. I never seen him with any gal before, but we've only been with the McCain show three weeks now."

"What can you tell me about the others in there?" I jabbed a thumb toward the room.

Loud enough only for my ear, she said, "Well, let's see. Cheeks, the big guy dealin' blackjack, he's got the pickled-punk joint. He's a sweetie pie—generous, funny. That dog of his, though, is ugly enough to scare buzzards off a gut wagon. I thought maybe Cheeks might be queer when I first met him, but I don't think so now. He's just a fat and happy feller travelin' around with his weird dog and his baby show. A bit of a doper, too. So if you're needin' anythin', he's likely to have some, or find it for you."

"That's good to know," I said, my eyes coaxing her for more.

"The guy with the feather in his cap they call Robin Marx. He's the roughie for Tall Paul, who's got eight or nine hanky-panks and alibis booked in with McCain. Robin's always bustin' a crack about somethin'. He's got a cute little squeeze who works one of Paul's joints. She's usually around, but I ain't seen her tonight. Robin knows everythin' about whatever happens around the lot. If you want to find out about somethin', or if you want somebody to find out about somethin', talk to him. Why he wears that stupid hat is a mystery to me. Maybe so everyone will think he's Robin Hood."

"He could be Peter Pan, too," I said with a lame smile.

She chuckled charitably, and continued, "The two agents by the window are flatties. The one with the moustache, Ray, he works one of the front office's count stores. The other one, Jimmy, works a pin store. They're just bona-fide thieves, and proud of it. Ray's one hell of an asshole most of the time—always braggin' on how much he beat one mark or another for. Jimmy's nicer. Or at least he is to me, 'cause he's always hittin' on me. But if I took up with a flattie, Pa would whup the shit out of him and me, both. I wouldn't have nothin' to do with one anyway. They're always flush with cash, but there's somethin' not right with someone who'll beat someone out of their last dollar, and then laugh about it."

Though not catching the gist of much of what she said, I shrugged and shook my head, as if I did.

"The hippie by the bed, Hairy Larry, just came in last week. He works a swinger for Paul. I don't know anythin' about him. I'd guess he's just another alibi agent bustin' from hole to hole."

She dropped to a whisper. "The three on the chest-of-drawers—Linda, Lorraine, and Tom—they work some of Paul's joints, too. Now there's a bizarre trio for you. Tom's married to Linda, the young gal, but he's fuckin' Lorraine, Linda's mother! How that's goin' down is a wonder to all. Jesus, Mary, and Joseph, it makes me sick just to tell it. They ought to buy a tent and book their freak show at the state fair. Hurry, hurry. Step right up and see the motherfucker. I've no idea why Linda don't get herself a pistol and shoot 'em both."

Bereft of what to say about that, I sucked my teeth, and muttered the old saw, "Everyone to their liking, as the old woman said when she kissed her cow."

Madeline squinted a questioning look my way, then said, "The other pair on the bed, George and Diane, they're good folk. They've got a grab joint—elephant ears. The gomers they just line up for that fried dough. George and Diane are the quiet type. My guess is they hang out with Cheeks 'cause he's always got reefer.

"And me, I've been on the road since before I can remember. My pa's got a mouse game. We're out of Texas—Waco, where my ma lives. They split up when I was six or so. She went back to Waco, and I'd stay with her for the school year—then I'd work summer fairs with Pa. Well, I quit school, and quit Waco, and now here I be. We're doin' all right together. Pa likes east-coast shows better than those long jumps out west. We winter in Florida, after workin' our way to Maine and back.

"Usually I stay on the lot in the house trailer, but now and then, like to-night, I need to get a motel room for myself. I try to stay wide of jackpots, but I like to find some fun, too…. So that's my story. What's yours?"

I had half a notion to make something up, but nothing came quick to mind. Plus, I liked Madeline. I didn't want us to get off on the wrong foot with a phony story. So I just told her, "Yesterday I left out from Clandel, my hometown, with Walt who I met the night before last. And tomorrow will be my first day running a hoop-toss game."

She let that sink in, and then asked, "You mean you're totally green?"

"If green means that I've never run off with a man and worked in a car-nival before, then I'm as green as a Christmas tree at Thanksgiving."

With eyes that appeared knowing, she gave me a sideways glance, and after some thought she said, "Annabelle, tell you what I'm gonna do. Me and you are partnerin' up. I'll show you the ropes and watch your back. How's that sound to you?"

"Madeline, that sounds mighty fine. Mighty fine indeed."

"Okay. First thing we do is boost some beers from Cheeks' bathtub. Then we go to my room and talk."

She fetched the beers, while I whispered to Walt where I'd be. He looked up from his cards, searched my face, and said, "Go in our room, Belle. Okay?"

He gave me the key, and I told Madeline, "Let's go in my room, it's right next door."

In the chairs at the table by the window, the waxing moon in view, we popped the beers, and she asked, "Did Walt get you the roses?"

"Yeah. Chocolates, too. You want some?"

"Not with beer. That was mighty nice of him."

"For a fact," I said, proud of my beau.

"So, Annabelle, how did you get from there to here?"

I told her the tale how Walt had come on strong to me, and how I'd gone along with it because he'd lit a spark in me, quick as greased light-ning—though, truth be told, it was likely more because I was fed up with living in Clandel, with Maw, with scarce prospects, save marry up with some hillbilly.

"It was like I was the only one in town that thinks the way I do. I'd tell someone something important to me, and they'd look back like I was speaking a foreign language. Then when someone would go on and on, about one thing or another, I'd have no clue why they'd give a hate about it. It felt of... if I stayed, I'd have to give up being myself, and turn into a fake one of them."

"So now you're gonna become a carny?"

"Girl, I don't know what I'm going to become. I'm just out to make some money, somewhere other from where I was, and see what comes of that."

"What hole have you got?"

"Walt got me a job in Nickel Nick's pitch-till-u-win."

She shrugged, took a pull of her beer, and said, "You won't make any big scores in that hanky-pank, but if you work the grind you can do okay."

"The grind?"

"Just work the joint hard. Grab every quarter you can. Call 'em in, call 'em in, call 'em in. Try it again, try it again, try it again."

I said, "That feller with the Fu Manchu, Danny, he asked me if I wanted to dance in the girly show, and make big money. But in the restaurant tonight, Trudy and Janet, who dance there now, sat down with us, and Trudy got nasty as all get-out with some folks who just wanted to eat in peace."

"Annabelle, you don't want to go that route. Danny's nothin' but a pimp, and Trudy is about the wrangiest bitch I ever done seen. If you got any kind of respect for yourself, stay far from that jackpot."

"Yeah, I figured that. But the money's tempting."

"That's what money does. It tempts you into jackpots. Just stick with the hole you've got. Grind the joint and squirrel your nuts. And before you know it, you'll be foldin' yard notes together. Workin' a square joint is where the steady money is out here. You don't have to be a thief. Just run the game by the rules, and the rules are made for you to win."

"What about other jobs around the show?" I asked.

"Carnivals have a peckin' order just like anyplace else in the world. And bein' a hanky-pank agent ain't at the top of the heap, but it's as near as you'll soon get, honey."

"What's the pecking order in a carnival?"

"At the top, sets the front office. They own the power plant, and most of the rides, and some of the joints. They book the routes and grease the bull geese. The McCain show is a family operation. Old Eli's been puttin' shows on the road since the forties. His wife, Julia, she runs most of the day-to-day now. Charlie's their advance man. Carl's the patch. Dave, head roughie. Garland's the electrician.

"Next comes the independent concessionaires, like Nick, and my pa, Tex. They own their joints—games, sideshows, and grab joints—and book 'em in with the front office. They pay the front office so much a foot for midway frontage. Plus they pay for juice. And if their joints work strong, they pay the patch."

"Can you translate that?"

"Each joint pays for electric hook-up. And if the game is gaffed to never lose, then the patch ices any heat with the law, with cash."

"Oh," I said, but still didn't quite get it.

"Next down the totem pole are the agents workin' the games. Each one pockets a percentage of what they take in. Sometimes they'll win more money than a joint owner, because they don't have to pay the nut, the stock bill, all the dings, the gas down the road, the truck, and whatever else.

"There's three types of joints—flat stores, alibi joints, and hanky-panks. No mooch will ever beat a flat store. Either it's gaffed strong, or the mark get out-counted. Alibi joints can be beat, but the agent might disqualify the shot because of a foul line, rim shot, or some other rule. Hanky-panks are percentage joints. They blow a certain amount of stock for a certain amount of dollars, day in, day out. Pa's mouse game is a hanky-pank. Nick's pitch-till-u-win is a hanky-pank."

I was about to tell her that I'd won a stuffed mouse at her game the other night, but before I could, she went on.

"Somewhere in the peckin' order, above or below the games and grab joints, dependin' on who you talk to, are the sideshows—the freak show, the kootch show, the illusion show, the pit show, the workin' show, the what-not show. They're usually independently booked. Though who knows what sort of deal Sonny, Old Eli's boy, has with his string show."

I told her I saw Sonny eat fire and swallow swords, but she just shrugged it off, and said, "Annabelle, this show's got a geek in the back end who fills the tent twenty times a night with Clems watchin' him eat a frog. He books his own joint, and his wife nurses their baby while she sells admission. Then there's our bearded lady with her witchy tattoos and humongous snake. Plus we got the kootch show. And a genuine three-armed man. Who's to say who's higher in the food chain, the sideshows, or the games?"

Answering that with a shrug, I only knew she liked to talk, so I just let her go on.

"Whatever and whichever it is... next, there's the bottom rung of the ladder—the ride jockeys. They draw a salary, sleep in the trucks—or under them—eat beans at the cookhouse, and end up each week wearin' old sweat and fresh grease, tap-city once more. Half of 'em on payday pissin' away their week's draw on G-top booze, and the other half lackin' sense enough to add up the numbers on a pair of dice. If a ride boy keeps a girlfriend, she plops her usually fat ass inside a ticket booth, where she chomps on gum, short-changes the punks, and sulks.

"Now I ain't sayin' all ride jocks are gazoonies, nor that there ain't none such in the front office and in the joints up and down the midway. What I'm tellin' you is that for the money, a ride boy ain't never gonna make the kind of scratch an agent can, and an agent usually won't win the dollars a joint owner will, and nobody makes what the front office does. And don't it always come down to who does what, for how much? Back in your coal town, ain't it the same thing? Just different people doing different things, some better off than others? Because of more or less money?

"And even the ride monkeys got someone to look down on—Hank, the donniker man. You seen him? That big old lanky half-breed? Walks like Frankenstein, and tends the show's donniker? I call him Hankenstein. He also sets up and sloughs the jenny. Sleeps in it too."

Before I could tell her he'd scared the bejeebers out of me the night before, she went on.

"Jockeys, jointies, and management pretty much mix only with their own kind, save in the G-top and the cookhouse—just like everyone next door in Cheeks' room tonight. The ride boys are no doubt back at the lot passin' their pop-skull whiskey around. And the management is settin' back on their easy chairs in their new house trailers, or over at the sheriff's house fattenin' up the pig."

I asked, "You're telling me that the law is in on it when the games are crooked?"

"For a fact. Where the joints play strong, and the kootch is wide open, there's a bag man greasing the bull geese."

"With bribes? With money?"

"No, Annabelle—with cotton candy. Of course with money. My, you are green."

"You're telling me that the sheriff back in Clandel got paid to let carnies cheat his own people?"

"The last spot was worked strong. I hear the ice is in on this one, too. But that ain't got nothin' to do with how to work a hanky-pank. It doesn't pay patch money, because the joint doesn't bring heat."

"Patch? Heat?"

"The patch is paid up front for the fix by the strong joints. Heat is when a mark gets burnt. And when he beefs to the sheriff about it, the patch—Carl's the patch on this show, and a good one, too—he dings the agent an extra double or half-yard to ice it."

As I wondered what language this was, and chose not to believe what little I gathered from it, Walt burst into the room, saying, "It beats me whether Cheeks is just flat out lucky, or he's cuttin' cards. Always winnin' my goddamn money.... What's up with you gals?"

Madeline said, "I'm just educatin' my new road buddy here."

"She's a fast learner."

Madeline got up, and said, "I'll say. I'm headin' for the clean sheets. Good night, you two."

At the door, I thanked her for the talk. Walt turned on the TV, flopped onto the bed, and said, "She's Tex's daughter, ain't she?" I told him what I knew about her, which wasn't much.

I curled up next to him. Some old gangster movie was on. Somewhere after a few commercials, I felt his breathing shift to sleep. I unwrapped myself from his arm, went about some bathroom business, and got myself ready for bed. But feeling not so tired—and a mite abandoned, what with Walt murmuring snores—I slid out Isis's homemade book from where I'd vaulted it in the nightstand drawer.

Cutting off the TV and the lights, save the one above the table, I sat bare-naked in a chair, and again opened it to the first page.

If you think that you know, then you do not. Whoever knows knowledge to be unknowable—who knows that truth is simply too much for our minds to grasp, and is thus always misunderstood—knows the truth that sets one free.

Symbols are how we know what we believe we know. And what we believe we know creates our world. The first symbols were real objects, real events, their meanings evident in the animal lives of ancient men. Then, symbolic objects, replacements for what they represented, were fashioned into statues, fetishes, totems, used in ceremonies mimicking the older realities.

The first handmade symbols were small fat figurines of women, of the Great Mother Goddess—and over time, many other goddesses came to be worshipped. When some people saw the power these objects had over others, they exalted these idols for their own selfish gain. Whoever controlled these objects, controlled their power, controlled what people believe, controlled their world.

Idols other than the Great Goddess also became powerful, but nothing is so revered by people as is their mother—so she reigned supreme in the temples of old. All was from her womb. She not only represented our human mothers, she was Gaia, the earth goddess, from whence we receive all that the world gives. Her priests gained dominance, and her temples the most treasure—while the priests of other temples, other goddesses, vied for power.

Then, not long before history began, the civilizations of the ancient world were overrun by men from the north. Their spears and chariots, and their male gods and priests, vanquished the goddesses from their temples, and overthrew the beliefs of the people. On the blood-washed pedestals, these men exalted their own gods of war, lust, and power. But the people would also have their goddesses. So, in realms like those on Olympus, tales of marriage and rape brought forth pantheons of newborn deities—their myths ruling people's lives for eons.

When the Christians converted this world, they smashed the old stone idols, stole the old stories, and they bred new creeds with words on paper—now exalting the idolatry of a book. Declaring it to be the Word of God, their priests, like those of old, knew the power of symbols—whether written, chanted, painted, etched in stone, or embodied in a cathedral.

Though the Christians did not include the goddess in their trinity, the people worshipped Mary, nonetheless. However, all gods and goddesses are false gods—made by men and women to glorify aspects of their own selves. And to ascribe powers to these gods conceals the world's truth from us—our own truth.

All That Is cannot be known. Yet one may know that It cannot be known, and thus not be misled by those who believe that they speak the truth.

I closed my eyes and the booklet. Though addling me with a startling bewilderment, it felt of something that finally spoke to some long-lost sense. After sitting for a spell in the curious shadow of this different light on things, I took on a shiver, and put Isis's booklet back in the nightstand drawer.

A need came upon me to write in my diary all that had happened in the last few days. So, after pulling a sweater out of a drawer and yanking it down to my thighs, I dug the McCrory notebook out of the rucksack, and set to it like a miner at a seam of coal on Monday morning. Words came too fast for my pen, and my normally neat script shortly turned into a scrawl, doing my darndest to jot down the particulars tumbling through my mind before losing them to the next thunderbolt of thoughts. At the table into the early hours, I filled page after page until after three A.M.

Then I slipped the diary into the nightstand, cut the light, and scootched into bed next to Walt. He moaned and sat up, tore off his clothes, crawled under the covers, and pulled me close. Within a dozen breaths, he fell back to sleep—and I wasn't far behind him.

IIII

LEMPEREVR

The eagle on The Emperor's shield reflects that of the Empress, and his right hand holds upright the same orbed scepter, while his left hand rests on his imperial belt. Poised casually on his throne, he husbands her bounty with strength, logic, and order. Wearing the beard of paternal authority, The Emperor stares straight into his dominion, focused and vigilant beneath his military crown. The other half of his profile may be tyrannical or judgmental were he to become arrogant or self-righteous. His legs form the number four, aligning four-square with the dimensions of his world

Near sunup I got rousted by Walt's rock-hard rhubarb lazily pronging my hind end. I adjusted its aim, and like spoons in a drawer, we nestled up. One move led to another, and before long, he rode me like a bucking bronco. When he was shortly done for—but far from that for me—he rolled off onto his back, and I propped up on an elbow and watched his slithery manhood soften and shrivel.

Hot as a red beet, and my chances for a sight of satisfaction shrinking before my eyes, I wiped his floppy doodle off with the sheet and took in toying with it, tickling it stiff. Walt lolled on his pillow, humming with pleasure. Soon we were right back at it, rocking the headboard against the wall—Walt giving it to me from above with all he had. As I fetched up near the heights, I squealed for him to stay with me. Heaving and huffing, he searched my face for clues.

Then, in a first for me, we both came to it at the same time—thrashing like trout in a net, gasping for breath, squirming until we sank back into the waters of sweet sleep—the fishy scent of sex, our lullaby.

Later on, after wandering in and out of one dream after another—one where I'm holding my newborn baby daughter, who is somehow talking riddles to me—the next thing I know, a TV game show host was nattering about all the prizes that a contestant had just won. I opened an eye and saw Walt, in only his BVD's, straddling a chair, hind side before, with his forearms crossed atop the chair's back and his face three feet in front of the picture tube.

"What's on?" I asked, letting him know I was awake.

He curled a grin toward me over his shoulder and said, "Truth or Consequences, with Bob Barker."

He turned back to the show, and I studied him watching it, and puzzled on whether I was in love with him. My heart pulsed with wanting to be—a bewitchment clutching each breath. I'd read of such in novels and seen movie stars act it out. A few times before, I'd felt twinges of likely love, which came and went in moody storms. But this morning's love making had blown me away—off into a place where my body and his had joined forces to bring out what was there all along—a haunt of what could be, of what should be. Was this love?

With no ken of my fancy, he said, "That Bob Barker sure knows how to run his joint. He's got that woman all wrapped up in a doo-daw, playing her like a tuba in a Fourth-of-July parade."

I got up and went into the bathroom, and when I came out after my morning doings, Walt lay stretched out on the bed and propped up on pillows, chin on his chest and staring at another game show on TV. I snuggled up next to him, to try to watch it with him. The object of this game was to come up with the right question to the answer on the board quicker than the other players did—Jeopardy. Walt stared at the TV like a mule about to be fed. I nuzzled his meaty chest, to turn his attention toward me, but he paid me little mind.

He said, "I could work that joint better than this joker does."

"And how would you do that?"

"You gotta mix it up more with your players. You don't let the game run the show. You run the game. This guy gets big bucks just bein' a sap that doesn't stir the mix. I could do better with one hand tied behind my back."

"Could you do better with me with one hand tied behind your back?"

He laughed, slapped my bum, and said, "I'd still have one hand left to spank you silly."

"Try it," I dared him. He just chuckled some and turned his eyes back to his game show.

After a half-hour of Jeopardy, he jumped up, flipped the dial to another game show, and sprawled back down onto the bed, eager to take in more. I'd had enough of them for one morning, so I gathered some fresh clothes, took a long steamy shower, and got dressed. I dilly-dallied in front of the mirror, fixing my hair and makeup, and when I came out of the bathroom all prettied-up for him, as well as my first day on the job, he was still in his skivvies on the bed, watching yet another game show.

He glanced up at me and said, "Lookin' good, Belle.... But we got a four-o'clock call, and it ain't yet noon."

"So what happens till then?"

"I got one more of my shows to watch. Then we go find somethin' to eat. Okay?"

"But I'm hungry now."

He threw a look at me that so far I hadn't seen from him—a look that said he'd druther not have it my way. "Just one more TV show, Annabelle. How's about you take a walk, and come back in a half-hour or so? Or if you're so all-fired hungry, just find yourself some bacon and eggs somewhere."

"Fine... I'll do that."

I gathered up a few dollars from my rucksack, pulled on my boots, and went out the door without another word. The sunlight hit me like salvation at a camp meeting—my heels clopping across the balcony, down the treads, and off through the parking lot. Down the sidewalk to the right, stood rows of boxy brick buildings planted along Stuart's stretch of top land. Monday midday traffic rumbled to and fro, idling every block or two for stop signs.

I was the only one afoot in sight. Everyone else was wheeling by on the way to their lives. They eyed me mannerably—that is, nary at all—and I swung my boots in longer and louder steps as I neared a street lined with a cluster of storefronts and restaurants.

Stuart's downtown wasn't much larger than Clandel's—a jag more spread out, with wider streets, lower buildings, and much more sky. Similar murky windows of hardware and dry-goods stores displayed sun-aged samples—the signs over their doors lettered with faded paint. A few newer signs hung on brackets over the sidewalk in front of fixy shops—their pricey dresses and handbags, or silly knick-knacks and gifts, displayed behind shiny windows.

After a few more blocks, I crossed a set of railroad tracks, and it was like I'd entered another land—the black side of town. Many of the measly buildings leaned agley and shacklety, trash scattered about them in the weeds. A few signs, hand-scrawled with big brushes and runny paint, advertised used tires and fried chicken. As I passed, sullen black faces stared at me from stoops and doorways, appearing puzzled why I was there. Up ahead on the next block, I spotted several black teenagers bunched around a car booming funk music. I turned left at the next side street, made a U-turn around the block, and headed back toward the tracks. Down these side streets, the houses sat even more run-down, some of them deserted. The only face I saw there was an old woman's at a window—bloodshot eyes in dark leathery sockets peering out between ragged curtains.

Back on the white side of the tracks, I came to a restaurant with plate glass along the length of a low-slung building—Riley's. The place was near full, and taking that as a good sign I went on in. Loud with lunchtime caucus, all of the booths and tables were taken, save three chrome and red-vinyl stools at one end of the horseshoe-shaped lunch counter, near the clatter behind the kitchen's swinging doors. Dishes, knives, and forks slowed their clinking as I walked across the creaky floor toward the stool in the middle—many eyes upon me, especially the men's.

I grabbed a paper menu propped between salt-and-pepper shakers on the streaky Formica countertop, and studied it. Before I figured out what to have, a gangly feller—maybe thirty, well dressed in creased khaki trousers, white button-down shirt, and shiny black shoes—plunked down on the stool to my right.

His leg bumped mine as he settled himself, and when we looked at each other he said, "Beg yer pardon," with a pleasant smile.

"Granted," I replied and turned back to the menu.

"The ham and red-eye gravy here is a gooder," he said, leaning a mite too close.

"I think I'll try a burger." I hated red-eye gravy.

"Get it with all the fixin's. They don't scrimp none."

"I like my meat barefoot," I told him—the tone in my voice hinting mind your own business.

But he must have heard me different, and kept on talking at me and leaning too close. "I don't recall ever seein' you 'round here none. And iffen I had, I'd be a-knowin' it, 'cause you're about the all-overest purtiest gal I ever done set my eyes on. I do declare. The name's Kessel. How 'bout yours?"

I didn't look up from the menu, but told him.

"What parts you from, Annabelle?"

I almost told him I was from the parts between my kin's legs, but instead I made up a town, "Blinky Creek, Tennessee."

"Reckon I'd nary heard of there. What took you here to Stuart?"

"I'm with that carnival outside of town."

"You don't say."

"I do say."

The waitress fetched up and took our orders—ham and red-eye gravy for him, burger and French fries for me. The waitress asked if we were on the same check. I said no. He said yes. I said no again, louder. She raised her penciled-on eyebrows and scribbled out two slips.

"I sell insurance," he told me, half braggy, but somehow also half apologizing. "Got my own agency. Built it from scratch. It's doin' okay. Could be worse. It's no turkey shoot to sell financial protection to folks who ain't got poot to protect.... So what all do you do in that carnival?"

"I run a game."

"What kindly game?"

"A ring-toss game."

"Hot-toe-mitty. That's my favorite. I might just come on out and toss some rings with you, Annabelle."

"That's what we're there for."

"I don't see no ring on your finger. So's I take it you're not married."

"Not yet."

"I was married. But that's history now."

"Sorry to hear so."

"Lord help my time, it was terrible bad. Now things ain't so much. But I must say, Miss Annabelle, I reckon the likes of you could sure sparkle-up my eyes some."

"I'll let you know right now, Kessel, that ain't going to happen."

"Aw... Annabelle, my eyes are already sparklin' like the sun ball on a creek."

"Mine ain't."

"Then we need some sparkin' to fire up yours."

"No thank you," I told him and slid over to the empty stool to my left.

That didn't faze him any. "I like that in a woman," he said. "Hard to get is good to be. My ex-wife was easy. Too easy, if you know what I mean."

I quit saying any more, folded my arms across my middle, and swiveled the stool to show half my back to him. Still, he went on and on how his brothers had told him so about his ex-wife—and how he knew it, but didn't care, because she was his sweetheart from grade school—and now she'd gone and moved into a box house up a back hollow with some gully jumper and his goats.

I ignored him and studied the other folks in the restaurant. Most were men, and many looked like businessmen—several in ties and jackets, set in serious poses, selling deals or listening warily. Riley's Restaurant was a step up from Jake's Diner. No one in sight appeared to be a miner. A few pairs of fixy women, shopping bags at their sides, chatted across tables. Most of the others in there were likely on their lunch break from their desks or counters. A half-dozen waitresses, dressed in green uniforms, shuckled from table to kitchen. The only black faces I saw were back in the steamy kitchen when the doors swung open.

Then I spotted Walt outside squinting in through the plate glass. I waved at him, he saw me, and his big grin swaggered through the door. As he sat between me and Kessel, who was still going on and on about his ex-wife, Walt stopped him short with one eye—and raised the eyebrow of the other, in a question to me.

"Walt, this here's Kessel. He sells insurance."

Kessel offered his hand, but Walt just glared at him for a short piece, and then told him, "We don't want none of that. I'd rather cover my bets with my own bankroll."

Kessel didn't take no for an answer from me, but he sure did when he heard it from Walt. "Well," Kessel said, "To each his own."

"And what's mine is mine," Walt added, reaching for a menu.

My burger and fries came, and Walt ordered bacon and eggs, buttered toast, and black coffee. But the waitress told him that they didn't serve breakfast after eleven o'clock. He shook his head, looked down at the menu, and ordered a bacon-and-egg sandwich, with the bread toasted and buttered, and black coffee. Kessel's plate came next—a thick slice of ham and a pile of mashed potatoes slathered with red-eye gravy. He took in at it appearing eager to get out of there quick.

Walt put his elbows on the counter, rubbed his eyes with both hands, and said to me—and likely also to Kessel—"My game shows got done and I got hungry, so I came huntin' for you, Belle. This town sure don't look like much. But we'll be soon takin' our best shot at it."

Walt didn't have much to say after that. He appeared to be in a sour mood, maybe jealous because he'd found Kessel talking to me. Carnival life, so far, wasn't much different than life in Clandel—just more men wanting to have me, and more TV to get bored with.

After lunch, we walked back to the motel, and Walt showered while I sprawled on the bed and watched the nasty doings of fine-haired folks on a TV soap opera. Walt took his time in the bathroom in front of the mirror, shaving his jaw and greasing his hair—his silence turning me a mite testy. When he noticed my ashy eyes, he changed his tune some and cracked a few jokes, which I tried to not laugh at, so as to punish him.

A special news bulletin interrupted the soap opera. Student protesters had been shot and killed by the National Guard at a college in Ohio—Kent State. While I watched the pictures with horror, Walt fussed with his hair and teeth in the mirror, and rearranged some stuff in his suitcase. Though I didn't much abide with all the anti-war doings of the hippies and college kids, I figured Vietnam to be one terrible mess. I knew some boys who'd been sent there, and one who'd been killed. But to take in shooting down students?

Walt said, "It's about time they gave those smart-ass punks the what for."

"What? You think it's right?"

"No. It ain't right. That war ain't right. But what ain't right neither is those spoiled brats pissin' on America. They didn't send me off to Vietnam, but I done my stint without cryin' about it. Soon as I turned eighteen they drafted me right off the street and sent me to Fort Polk, Louisiana. After a brawl put me in the brig for a stretch, I did kitchen duty for twenty goddamn months. Them college boys, with their deferments bought and paid for, they got no right to shit on soldiers dyin' for our country. Maybe now that some of 'em got themselves shot up, they'll get a little taste of what others are goin' through."

I couldn't believe my ears. "They're not protesting the soldiers. They're against the politicians that send them to Vietnam to be killed for nothing."

He shook a finger at me, and said, "Annabelle, it's the same goddamn thing. From Nixon on down to Gomer Pyle, you're either on your country's side or you're not. Don't you know that most of those protesters are Commies?"

"They shot two girls!"

"They shouldn't've been there."

"But they were."

"Yeah, and we weren't. So count your lucky stars. The whole world is full of loaded guns. Sometimes they go off. And if you don't duck you maybe catch a bullet.... Come on now, Annabelle—that's enough of this already.... I gotta go buy some smokes."

He tore out of the room. I just stared at the newsman on the tube, who repeated the report, over and over, adding another detail now and then, until after beating the story to death, they switched back to the soap opera. I shut off the TV and paced the room for a spell, not only riled over the shootings, but also misput over Walt's politics. What was it with men and their stubborn loyalty to what was plumb wrong?

Most folks reckoned most politicians to be a bunch of liars and crooks— yet the bulk of them would follow Washington off a cliff, no questions asked. If a President ordered me to go over to the other side of the earth and kill people that I had no feud with, I'd be protesting, too. Was that because I was a coward? No. It's because it's not right. But Walt and all his patriots, why don't they see that it's plumb wrong? And if any of them do, then who are the brave and courageous?—those that go along with it, or those who don't?

I reached for Isis's booklet in the nightstand drawer, to shift my mind to something else, craving to rid myself of these questions. But when I turned the page to where I'd left off the night before, it was as if the answers were right there waiting for me. I recalled what Isis had said about synchronicity—coincidence with meaning—and chill bumps crawled up my arms as I slowly read the purple print.

> To be misled is the greatest tragedy. People use powers they have, or seize, to manipulate the actions of others. When you give yourself over to the will of others, your soul is lost.
>
> A mother and father tell their child what to do, and that is necessary. A child does not know what to do, or where, or when, or why. Children rely on their elders to guide them into the world. They are given a language of symbols, a religion of symbols, a society of symbols, and all these shape their perception of reality. Without symbols, we could not build the societies that we have.
>
> But as we construct our symbolic homes, our true natures become imprisoned behind walls. Stained-glass ceilings, held aloft by pillars of tradition, are but a barrier to the view of the real sky, and eventually come crashing down around us.
>
> One society fights with another over whose symbols are true. A revelation or a cataclysm sweeps away one system of belief, and

it is soon replaced by another. All that once was right becomes wrong, and what was important, meaningless.

Only when we see beyond the constructs of our societies, do we see what is essential, what is eternal, what is true, what is All That Is.

Right then, Walt swung into the room with Cheeks behind him. I slipped the booklet back into the drawer, and asked, "What's up, boys?"

Cheeks said, "I just scored a gram of hash, and we're going to give it the old taste test."

Walt slid the drapes shut. Cheeks pulled out a small brass pipe and a nugget of hashish wrapped in aluminum foil, near the size of a hazelnut. Sitting at the table by the window, he unwrapped it, sliced off slivers of the greenish-brown gob with his jackknife, loaded the pipe, struck a match, and puffed the flame into the bowl. Sucking down a lungful of the thin bluish smoke, he held it in—mouth pinched shut, cheeks like balloons, eyes bugging out. Half a cough snorted a wisp out his nose. Then another stifled cough, and another, jolting him like golly-whopper hiccups. But with clamped lips he held the dope down, each cough spurting smoke out of his nose. Leaning back in the chair, he walled his eyes back, and with a moan of pleasure, huffed out a syrupy cloud toward the ceiling. Then he promptly took on a fit of coughing, laughing all the while, and groaning, "Ahh... that's good. Primo. Kick-ass. Mmmm."

Meanwhile, Walt had grabbed the pipe and nursed it with tiny tokes, the hash building fire. When he got a good snootful, he passed it over to me. I'd never had hash. I'd hardly heard about it. Homegrown hillbilly weed was what I knew. Now and then, somebody would have some Mexican, but that wasn't much better. I took the pipe and peeked in the bowl. The slivers of hash in it were now mostly ashes. Cheeks motioned for me to hand the pipe over so he could put more in, and he sliced off another smidgen of the gummy gob.

I put a fire to it and cautiously sipped the smoke. It went down sweet and thick, the dope sinking into the flesh of my windpipe. Then my lungs exploded into a coughing jag that I couldn't shake for five minutes.

A powerful goomer swept through me—magnifying the space in the motel room, everything in it looming nearer, more colory, more important and meaningful. My coughing settled down, and a touch of fear mingled with the wonder of seeing through such transmogrified eyes. Cheeks' round smiley face looked like the Cheshire cat in that Disney cartoon—sly and rascally. Walt, leaning forward on the chair, legs crossed, elbow on a knee, chin in a hand, appeared to be puzzling out what to do next.

Cheeks lit the pipe again and passed it around. I sipped the smoke with more respect and tried to hold it down—but shortly it was busting out my ears. The next time the pipe went around, I shook my head and waved it away.

A stupor of silence set into the room. Walt checked his wristwatch and said, "Four o'clock call and it's a little past three. So's I guess we'd best get on out to the lot, and ready-up the joints. And Annabelle, you gotta get educated with yours."

The thought of taking up a new job, stoned as I was, beset me with a heart quake. Struck dumb by the hash, I could hardly get up off the bed right then, never mind go run a carnival game. As Cheeks gathered up his stash, I saw that Walt was antsy and raring to go—one knee jigging up and down while he swiped his comb back through his hair. But me, I dithered in a flummox, bereft of what to do next.

After Cheeks left, I escaped into the bathroom. The face in the mirror didn't look much like mine. Things about my make which I'd always been partial about—the high cheekbones under wide-set eyes, the upturned Irish nose, the mop of auburn curls, the pouty lips, the sharp-edged jawbone— now all appeared like a fixy mask that I could almost see through to someone else behind it. I fumbled for my cosmetics, fooled with some lipstick and mascara, and felt like a clown getting ready for a three-ring circus.

Walt pounded on the bathroom door. "Belle? What're you doin' in there? We gotta get out to the lot."

"Just a minute," I sang, trying to not sound forlorn. "I'm just fixing myself up."

"You look fine. Grindin' a joint ain't no beauty contest. Let's get a move on."

I lied, "I'll be right out." But after five minutes or so, which felt of an eternity, I had to come out, ready or not.

Walt sat slumped in a chair, eyeing me uneasily. "You okay?"

"Just dandy," I lied again. "Let's go."

The ride out to the lot changed my mood some. As Stuart fell behind us, and the winding tunnel of greening trees swept past, I sidled up against Walt on the wide front seat. The power of the big Mercury grabbing the road ahead, and Walt's stout presence protecting me from who knows what, soothed me enough to marvel, with doped-up awe, at the finery of wildflowers bedizening the craggy hillsides.

We rounded a bend and the carnival heaved into sight, the Ferris Wheel arching high above the tops of tents and rides. Put together only yesterday, the show now stood ready and waiting. A row of banners, strung on high poles, made up the front gate—a breeze rippling the canvases painted with fun faces, colory curlicues, and bizarre beasts. Hanging lengthwise above the ticket booth in the middle of the gate, a banner decked out with more curlicues made it known to all that here sets McCain's Magic Midway.

Walt wheeled the Mercury off the road and swung around one side of the show, over a set of ruts flattened in the grass, which led behind the line-up of games. We swayed to a stop beside Nick's two-ton truck—under which a mechanic in overalls was working on the brake line—and a few minutes later, we stood in front of the locked-up joint trailer. Nick, Brenda, Jenny, and Fred readied stacks of dishes, cups, and saucers under the center joint's blue-and-orange striped top.

Nick spotted us, came over, and greeted us with a gruff, "What it is?" Not waiting for any answer, nor getting one, he unlocked the trailer awnings, and Walt muscled them up with the pole while Nick slipped the hitch pins through the braces. I hopped in, and worked the trapdoors out of the floor behind the counter.

Nick asked me, "How's your slum?"

"My what?"

"Your slum. How's your stock of small prizes look?"

"Well, let's see." I pulled out each box of slum, one at a time, from under the counter, showed them to Nick, who penciled some notes onto a pad, and then I slipped them back under—plastic yellow whistles and red kazoos, woven straw finger-traps, chintzy key chains, candy-striped pencils, bamboo flutes, tin sheriff's badges, plastic four-hole harmonicas and plastic pocket combs, rubber knives and rubber spiders, Groucho Marx glasses with a big nose and black moustache, those feathery paper-tube things you blow into on New Year's Eve that roll out and make a squawk, and ugly hollow plastic teddy bears the color and size of a dill pickle.

Nick told me, "You'll need more blow-outs, spiders, penny whistles, and key chains for tonight. Put this scratch on the three empty big blocks in the middle. And I'll go get more slum out of the truck"

I did what he said—attached two ten-dollar bills and a twenty onto the large blocks with some rubber bands. With nothing else to do, but wanting to look busy, I once more took in tidying up the prizes on the other blocks. The big prizes included a small transistor radio, a pair of his-and-hers wristwatches, a real hunting knife in a genuine leather sheath, a boy-scout jackknife, a cap pistol, a fancy pen and pencil set, a cheap camera, a string of imitation pearls and a flashy phony diamond ring, both in black-velvet boxes. When I finished fiddling with these, still half in a hashish daydream, I turned around and flinched—startled by Nick standing there watching me, a carpenter's nail apron in his hand, and a stack of fresh boxes of slum atop the counter.

"Stow these under the counter. And this here's your bank," he said, handing me the apron. "Ten dollars in quarters and twenty in singles. Leave the same in the apron each night after you count up. Your end's twenty-five percent of what you grab. I'm goin' to break you in tonight, myself. I'll have Walt keep an eye on you, too."

"When do we start," I asked.

"When you hear the jenny's organ."

"When what?"

"When the front office turns on the Merry-Go-Round music."

"Oh.... What's the rules of this game?"

"We'll get to that when we open up." Impatiently leaving it at that, he went over to the other side of the trailer, where Walt was testing a basket by bouncing balls in and out.

"Walt," Nick said, "a basket agent named J.D. came in today, and I told him we'd give him a shot at this hole. When he shows, count out his bank in the spare apron. And keep an eye on him."

"Will do, boss."

Nick walked off and Walt flipped me a wink. There was nothing left to do but wait, so I sat up on the counter at my end of the trailer, my legs dangling against the bally cloth, and I took in what was going on around me—still gazing through a dope-addled haze.

The fat old feller I'd seen the day before, sitting with a deputy in front of the office trailer, came whirring and wobbling down the midway in a golf cart, swiveling his pink and gray noggin to and fro under his straw hat, his pinched-up eyes inspecting each ride and each joint. Several ride boys and game operators stiffened their spines as he passed, and mannerably greeted the big boss by name—Mister McCain.

His cart fetched up and creaked to a stop in front of the pitch-till-u-win. Amid mistrustful crow's feet and swaggy eyelids, he peered at me point-blank, his beady stare seizing my breath.

Before I had any chance to figure what to say, he grunted, "Go get 'em, Red," and he wheeled off, the cart groaning through the grass, the fuzzy folds on the back of his neck twisting one way then the other as he continued his overseeing.

Kitty-corner across the midway at the Tilt-A-Whirl, a ride boy busied himself wiping down the seats of the hooded tubs. At the Rock-O-Plane next to that, two others with wrenches in hand puzzled over its partly taken apart motor.

The joint to the left of me—a weathered blue tent, set square upon a red-painted nail-pocked two-by-four frame—had its awning up, but nobody in it. Its prizes were set up the same as that football-and-marbles game of the one-eyed ogre who blessed me out on Friday night.

Next to Walt's end of our trailer, a lanky carny with a ponytail—twenty-something and sporting a black gangster-style hat, a purple crepe shirt, blue jeans, and pointy-toed cowboy boots—took teddy bears out of a big cardboard box and hung them on the fishnet along the sides of his basketball game.

Out in front of me in the center joint, Brenda busied herself arranging piles of cups, saucers, dishes, and glasses, while Jenny squatted and chatted with three stuffed animals set around an upside-down box, serving them make-believe tea. And that creepy Fred leaned against a corner leg of the glass pitch, one hand slung on a brace overhead, fixing his narrow-eyed stare smack-dab on me.

I turned my eyes away from his and saw, walking up to Walt's counter, a gangly feller with a butch-waxed haircut, maybe a few years past forty, decked out in a maroon leather jacket, a canary-yellow shirt and crisp powder-blue polyester slacks, and stepping a mite doddly in tasseled brown loafers.

"You Walt?" he asked, and Walt nodded. "I'm J.D. Nick gave me a hole here."

Walt welcomed him with a handshake, and asked, "Where you comin' in from?"

"I was with the Playland show last week over in Roanoke, but got in a beef with the patch over a score. I beat this mark fair and square, he squawks to the law, then the patch wants me to kick it all back. When I give it up, he pockets half and only kicks the mark the other half. So the mark starts up again, wrangin' about it in my face. I point out the patch to him and tell him to do his squawkin' there. Then before I know what for, I'm disqualified. Now you let me know if that ain't one sorry sack of shit."

Walt shook his head and said, "That ain't gonna happen none around here. The patch with this outfit, Carl, he ices heat right. But I'll tell you somethin' else. Beefs won't set easy with Nick, no way, no how. If the patch dings him for a beef, Nick'll ding you strong. And let you know how much he don't like it none."

"I got ya," J.D. said, looking around. Spotting me at the other end of the trailer, he nodded mannerably—yet with that pruney look in his eye, I'd seen from so many Billy goats before.

Walt saw it, too, and told him, "That's Annabelle. She's with me. And green as the First of May."

J.D. hollered over at me, "Hey, Annabelle. I hope Walt's breakin' you in right." They both laughed at that a mite too much. I stuck out my tongue at them and put on a huffy little frown.

While they huddled up and talked business—as menfolk do when they stiffen their tails and sniff each other out—I fidgeted atop the counter, impatient to get the show going. The long strips of wood attached along the top edges of the counter soon dug into my thighs, so I hopped off and paced back and forth in front of the trailer for a spell. After enough of that, I jumped back in the trailer and sat on the floor. My back against the wall, I closed my eyes, hoping to ease my dope-addled stew. So far, this carnival business appeared to have much to do with waiting around for nothing to happen. Or was it just the hash in my blood, marking time—slow and heavy like cattails in a lazy breeze.

The ride boys at the Rock-O-Plane fired up its motor, and it sputtered and backfired like a dirt farmer's tractor—so they shut it down and went at it again with their tools. I checked the time on the watches on the blocks, yet they were stone dead. I wound the stem on one, but it didn't feel connected to anything, so I left it be.

Then a waltz took in pumping out from a pipe organ. On that signal, the rides fired up their motors and lights and began whirling about and blasting out rock and roll. Straightaway, the first wave of townies came down the midway, mainly scrawny white teenage boys, gawking this way and that, their hands shoved into the front pockets of their too-tight and too-short trousers. Along with them, some little kids dashed to and fro, stopping to dance from foot to foot, impatient for their ambling folks to catch up with them, pointing from this to that, shouting back at their kin, "I wanna do this! I wanna ride that!"

A pair of tow-headed boys, a sight unruly for eight or nine, rushed up to my counter and yelled at me again and again, "Wha'd'ya gotta do here? Wha'd'ya gotta do here?"

I had no good answer for that, which Walt saw, so he hopped over to my side of the trailer, scooped up two handfuls of hoops from my carefully laid out rows in the cloth under the blocks, spread them atop the counter, and told them, "You pitch till you win."

One asked, "How many hoops d' ya get, mister?"

"You toss the hoops until you ring a block. And you get the prize on that block."

The other boy yelled, "You mean you pitch till you win?"

"That's what I said."

The two looked at each other as if it couldn't be true—but that's what the man said.

"How much it be, mister?" asked the first boy.

"A quarter."

They ran out to a blonde woman, too big for her clothes, pushing a sleepy baby in a stroller, and they pleaded with her for a quarter. She just shook her head no, without even looking down at them, and waddled on-ward—her two boys following, kicking at the midway grass.

Walt said, "Those kids ain't seen a quarter since Heck was a pup.... Annabelle, just pile all the hoops on the counter, and shout out—'Pitch till you win. Prize every time.' Then just grab the money and pass out the prizes that the hoops land around. Nothin' to it."

He stepped back over into the other side of the trailer, and I heaped up hoops atop the counter, seeing now that the strips of wood along the edge were there to keep the hoops from slipping off. I took in chanting, "Pitch till you win. Prize every time. Pitch till you win. Prize every time." Over and over and over again.

Nobody paid me much attention. Some passing by would glance my way, some smiling at me, but most just eyed me warily—even the men. Most men usually looked at me with a sneaky glint of desire. Now I saw something else in their eyes that appeared to see me as somebody to steer clear of, somebody they wanted no part of. And with that, I felt a welcome freedom in this different role, no longer playing the pretty girl—still the same person as an hour ago, but now, just by standing in a hoop-toss game, seen as someone else.

Trying to act the part, I became the only one in sight bent on stirring up any hubbub, while the crowd, what there was of one, was content to just stroll past. Walt and J.D., done talking turkey, mutely leaned forward, elbows on the counter, and scanned the scarce passers-by. The tent to my left still had nobody in it. And the carny with the hat at the basketball toss busied himself spinning a ball balanced on one finger—while the rides spun empty, too.

Finally, a kid about twelve fetched up to my counter, jawing hard at his bubblegum and craning his pipe-stem neck back and forth to check out the prizes on the blocks. He dug a quarter out of his pocket, handed it over with nary a word from me, grabbed a handful of hoops, and with careful aim at the block with the twenty-dollar bill, he took in pitching, one deliberate toss after another. The hoops, made of thin wood, and about four inches across, clicked and clacked as they bounced off the blocks and dropped into the cloth slung below. After a dozen tosses or so, a hoop flipped off a big block and landed around a small block. He'd won a yellow-and-white plastic whistle.

I fetched one from under the counter and handed it over. He set down his handful of hoops, took the whistle, and tested it with a weak tweet. He narrowed his eyes and fingered a hoop, asking, "Does this here hoop fit 'round that there block with the twenty-dollar bill on it?"

"Sure," I told him, and surely hoped so.

"Show me."

I took the hoop and lowered it straight down over the block with the twenty. It barely fit—but it did. The big blocks, which alternated side by side with the little ones on four rails stepping up across the rack, were about one-inch-by-four thick and eight inches tall, with their tops cut off on an angle, the high side to the rear. Fixed to the rails next to each of the big blocks, little blocks were set—more like pegs, near an inch square and shorter than the big blocks, with their tops cut on the same pointy slant. What with the tops of the big ones cut that way, which made the top of the block facing the players wider than the hoops, chances were slim to none that a hoop could be tossed from the counter straight onto a big block. Odds-on, a hoop would bounce off a big one then flip onto a small one. And maybe once in a blue moon, bounce back from behind and flip around a big one, if it happened to hook it just so.

A sign on the back wall had drawings of hoops around two big blocks. One showed a hoop all the way down around the whole block, and was marked WINNER. The other had a hoop hanging off the point on the high end of the block, and was marked NOT A WINNER. Below, another sign read, "Hoops must go all the way around the block to win. Hoops hanging off the top corner do not win."

The kid studied on his chances, and then said, "That's harder than climbin' a ground pole with a basket of eggs."

I couldn't argue with him there, so I didn't know what to say next. Walt, watching us out of the corner of his eye, shouted over, "Try it again. You can't win if you don't play."

The kid shrugged, and likely seeing some sense in that, dug out another quarter. Taking dead aim at the big block with the twenty-dollar bill, his first toss clicked off the big block, flipped, and again clacked right around the same small block with the whistle.

As I handed him his prize, he asked, "What am I gonna do with two whistles?"

"Save one for when the other wears out?"

"I ain't never knowed abody what wore out no whistle," he said, eyeing me like I ought to be bored for the simples.

"You can be the first. Try it again?"

"Nah." With a whistle in each hand, he tweeted one then the other in a march step as he paraded off.

I'd made my first twelve-and-a-half cents—twenty-five percent of the kid's half-dollar—an eighth of a dollar—one measly bit. After nearly two days as a carny, I'd only earned these dozen pennies. How the heck was that going to soon add up? What if both sides of this hoop-toss counter were scams, and I couldn't make the cash money I'd need to live out here on the road, never mind get to New York or California.

For the next hour or so I chanted a thousand times, "Pitch till you win. Prize every time." The crowd had picked up some, but only a handful of players turned into my counter to toss hoops—all of them, after a few tries, walking away with only a gimcrack or two.

Walt and J.D. worked hard the crowd scuffing past them, hooking folks over with a finger, yelling things like, "Hey, buddy! Give this one a go." And, "Lady! Free shot for all the pretty gals tonight." Or, "Have ya seen this one yet?" And, "Let me show ya how to win the big prize." One after another, they talked folks off their feet, demonstrated their ball game, and won some dollars off most.

At the joint next door, three agents eventually showed up, ducking under the bally cloth and into the tent. One of them was the ill-eyed rullion that cut a rusty with me on Friday night, and another was Ray, the slick with the Clark Gable moustache in Cheek's room last night. Both took little notice of me.

I sat down for a minute on the floor at my end of the trailer. Out in front, nickels clinked onto glass in the center joint—Brenda and Fred making change to those around the side rails, and now and then handing over a teacup or a bowl. The rackety Tilt-A-Whirl spun circles with more and more riders smiling and screaming, flung up against each other in the tubs. Above, the high rides turned—the Ferris Wheel, the Zipper, and the Orbit—their lights burning brighter as the sun fell behind the ridge, each with speakers blaring rock-and-roll hits, all at odds in the dusty air. I sniffed fresh popcorn and my belly gurgled for some.

Coming out of nowhere, Nick scolded, "You can't make money sittin' on your keister."

"Sorry," I said, jumping up.

He hopped in over the counter and told me, "Young lady, I'll show you how to work this joint. Grind the tip and this can be one money-makin' mammy-jammer. Watch me."

He piled all the hoops in a heap on the counter, grabbed a handful, and took in waving them at the folks walking by, hollering at them, "Come on in. Pitch till you win. Prize every time. A winner every time. Just twenty-five cents. No losers here. A game for young and old, short and tall, shy and bold, one and all. How 'bout you, darlin'?" He leaned over the counter and waggled a handful of hoops toward an old woman tottering by with a grand-daughter, or maybe a great-granddaughter.

Her weary eyes glanced at Nick, and she asked, "Who? Me?"

"Why, sure enough. You and your daughter, both. How else can you have a good time? Walk around till your shoes get dusty? Come on over here and I guarantee that both of you will walk away with a prize. You pitch till you win here. Where else on this show are you gonna find that kind of deal for only twenty-five cents?'

The little girl, a cute brunette with a bird-like make, shied up against the old lady's faded frock. The old woman looked down at her and asked, "Would ye wanna win a prize, Netty Jane?" The girl nodded yes, her eyes lighting up. They shuffled over to the counter, and after the old lady found a wrinkly dollar in her calico purse, she gave it over to Nick, who fished a handful of quarters from my apron pocket and set two of them down on the counter for her change.

"I thought ye tol' me it were a quarter to play," she said, not abiding any swap off.

Nick said, "A quarter for her and a quarter for you. You're not goin' to let her have all the fun alone, are you?"

"Well... all righty."

While they chose their targets and took their aim, Nick was already working on calling in a young mom pushing a toddler along in a stroller. "Win a toy for the tot," was the line that hooked her. He took her quarter and waved hoops and shouted ballyhoo out at whoever else was passing by. Within ten minutes he had a knot of people at the counter, handing us money and flinging hoops, while all the time he called more in, chatting up a comical ruckus, and shouting, "Hey, another winner!" whenever a hoop clacked around one of the pegs. The more that gathered, the more that would turn in from the midway to see what it was about.

Before I knew it, I was busier than a goose with nine rectums—making change, heaping the hoops from under the blocks to the counter, and passing out the slum. Nick put into my apron what money he grabbed, and coached me along when I got behind, gradually leaving me to handle more and more of the action, while he called in even more players. Soon I was shouting out my own chatter, parroting Nick's, making some up on my own. I stuffed coins and bills into the apron willy-nilly, and felt it get thicker and heavier.

Several players asked us why it was now a quarter, when it was just fifteen cents last year. I had no answer for that, and each time he was asked Nick would make up a different reason that made no sense at all—because his uncle's mule wore out its tail swatting flies, because the queen of England got a different hairdo, because roses are red and violets are blue. But once he leaned to me and muttered, "It's a quarter because now we can get it."

The eve glom darkened and the hullabaloo grew. Beyond the harsh tubelights under the trailer's awnings, the carnival became a whirl of faces, a colory blur of hubbub. Next to me, Walt and J.D. hustled one hillbilly after another, the softballs thumping in and out of the peach baskets.

Nick eased up his spiel, leaving it more to me. I took the lead the best I could, but soon the play petered out, and after a spell with nobody tossing hoops, I stood there hollering into the crowd shuffling by.

"You'll do okay," Nick said. "Let's lighten your apron."

When I did nothing but look at him and await some explanation, he said, "Let's count up some of what you took in so far."

I pulled out the jumble of bills and dumped them on the cloth under the blocks. Nick gathered them up, and with our backs to the midway, he separated out forty dollars in fives and tens in front of me, pocketed it, wrote the number on a slip of paper, and stuffed that back in my apron, along with a fold of more than enough dollar bills for change of a twenty.

"Are you right handed?" he asked, and I nodded. "Then put the quarters in your apron's right pocket, the big bills in the middle pocket, and the singles and chicken feed in the left."

"Chicken feed?"

"Pennies, nickels, dimes."

He stepped over to the other side of the trailer and lightened up J.D. and Walt while I rearranged the money in the apron like he told me. Then he hopped out of the trailer, a wad of bills bulging in the front pocket of his trousers, and cut through at the trailer hitch to out back.

Walt looked over at me with that big grin and asked. "How you doin', Belle?"

"Doing fine.... What time is it?"

"Quarter past eight."

The last couple of hours had gone by like a whirlwind. I'd made more than ten dollars for myself, and had near half the night yet to go.

I said, "I got to pee," and did a hoppity little dance.

"The donniker's out behind the back end."

"What does it look like?"

"It's in a little trailer. Just let your nose lead you to it. Hand me your apron and I'll cover for you."

He stepped over to my side of the trailer, and I gave him my apron, jumped out of the joint, hurried down the midway, cut between some tents, and made my way out in back of the camp—the dark shadows silvered by a three-quarter moon overhead.

A squat trailer sat by itself at the edge of the woods. As I neared it I smelled that this was for sure the donniker. MENS was scrawled in black paint under a yellow light bulb by the door, and the other side of the trailer was set up much the same—LADYS painted by the same hand. With a step up on a flipped-over wooden crate, I climbed into the dimly lit trailer, where sat a pair of plastic commode seats atop privy holes in a settee cobbled onto the divider wall. At the far end, next to a one-faucet sink, stood a rusty white shower stall with a grimy plastic curtain. Under a lone bare light bulb, I peeped into a honey hole. On the grass below lay a battered metal tub collecting toilet paper and turds in a shallow pond of piss. After wiping off a seat with a length of t.p.—just in case of I don't know what—I gratefully tinkled in my generous contribution.

As I finished up, I heard the clitter-clatter outside of someone fooling with something metal. I scurried out and came face to face with the freckly giant that had scared me off when peeking into the backside of the Harem— the feller Madeline had told me about, Hankenstein. His big-knuckled brown hands toted a coil of hose, screwing one end onto a pipe near the trailer hitch. I hurried past him, but before I did, I met his doleful blue eyes, glinting with the show's colored lights like turquoise in starlight.

Back at the pitch-till-u-win, business in the next few hours went slower, but steady. The little kids in the crowd had dwindled—most gone home to bed on a school night—and the pitch-till-u-win was mainly for young'uns. They'd give me their quarters and toss their hoops with a glee unrelated to the fact that they were swapping something for nearly nothing. The quarter in their hand meant little to most of them—eager to trade it for a chance to toss hoops at prizes. When I'd tell them they'd won and hand them a rubber spider or plastic comb, most didn't much care about that, either. The disappointment I saw in their faces was not because they had traded a quarter-dollar for a two-cent gewgaw, it was because they couldn't toss any more hoops—they had to stop playing the game.

The older kids, those who knew what a quarter could buy—two candy bars with a nickel change, or a comic book, or a school lunch—they pitched hungrily for the cash on the big blocks. They saw a chance to trade that quarter for more money than they'd likely ever held all at once, but when they'd end up holding a plastic kazoo, they'd stare at it in defeat, some throwing it on the ground and stomping on it.

Most of the grown-ups who tossed hoops were doing so just to have some fun with their kids. They knew the game was rigged. They'd hoot a laugh or two when I'd hand them a tin sheriff's badge, make a joke about it, and then hand me more quarters for another round of hoop tossing with the family. Only a few ornery adults got serious about trying to really win something, and I felt sorrow for their grim faces.

My ballyhoo got better as the night went on. I made up little rhymes and chanted them in a voice I didn't know I had. "Come on in. Pitch till you win. Every time a prize. I'm tellin' no lies. Just twenty-five cents. Kids, ladies, and gents. Toss rings at the things. When you ring a thing, you win the thing you ring. A winner every game. Pitch-till-u-win's the name."

And I learned that if I looked people in the eye as they strolled past, and waved them over with a smile on my face, calling out to them, "Come on over and give this one a try," or "You look like a winner, and everybody wins here," or just make any kindly connection to them, then they'd step right up and check it out—especially the men, above all young lonely ones. No doubt most fellers walked up with fancies of winning from me a prize bigger than a plastic comb. I'd give them a pretty smile and sing a few rhymes, and they'd think they had a chance at me. Even after they'd figure I swapped them off, they'd grin and bear it. And before traipsing off with a handful of gimcracks, many would attempt one more smile, one last witty say-so. I made sure to thank them with my eyes, and most appeared to take a sight of satisfaction in that.

More players would try it again if I made it more fun for them. I'd make a big to-do about their kid winning a Chinese finger-trap. I'd slip their little fingers into each end, pull the straw weave tight, and watch disappointment disappear into smiles as they showed their trapped fingers to their kinfolk. I'd tell the kids to blow the whistles and kazoos they'd won, and they'd tweet and toot up a ruckus that would lift more smiles, and turn more heads toward my game.

If I made it fun, it was fun. When I'd see a face that was hell-bent to beat the game, I'd see that they weren't playing for the fun of it. They just wanted to pay a quarter for a twenty-dollar bill. When they didn't, and their faces soured, then I'd play their game. I'd egg them on, challenge their pride, bewail their failure, and goad them to try again. Next time their luck might change.

Walt, as he worked the baskets on the other side of the trailer, watched me out of the corner of his eye, now and then throwing me winks, smiles, or a thumbs-up. I could see he was well pleased that I was taking to the game like a beaver to a sapling.

His players were not having the fun that mine were. They were getting beat by they knew not what, and walking away only with less money in their pockets. Walt riled up the competitive blood in the men and older boys. With the ladies, he charmed them out of their cash money—flattering them as they walked past, quizzing them about themselves as he demonstrated the game, winning their confidence as he led them along to their losses. J.D., side by side with Walt, worked the baskets in his own manner. J.D. would point-blank bully the dollars away from folks.

At the joint to my left, with Ray and that one-eyed troll, and one other shifty rullion—playing phony football, adding up marbles in holes—I watched the suckers get hooked. Curious about the free-game card waved out at them, they'd shortly be doling out more and more money from their pokes, led on by the notion that they had a fair chance to beat the game, and baited further with the starry-eyed greed of winning much more than they'd allowed. Sooner or later, they were in over their heads, fearful they'd gone too far, squinting with dread, reckoning that they can't quit now, now that they were so close to winning back all they'd lost along with more money than they'd seen in a month of Sundays. Then, time after time, bereft of every dollar on them, they'd storm off down the midway, disgusted that they'd been hoodwinked.

Sometimes the man of a family would get gulled into dumping marbles in the box while his wife and kids tossed my hoops. I'd watch the wife grow panicky as her husband handed over more and more out of his poke. At first, as the kids tossed hoops, she'd mildly encourage him, leaving it up to him as he got in deeper. But when his bets became frightfully large she'd plead for him to stop. After he'd end up losing the rent or more, she'd gather up their kids, toying with their handfuls of slum, and they'd shuffle away—she giving him a tongue-lashing, and sometimes spitefully glaring back at me, as if it were my fault.

Later on, the crowd had thinned considerably, and stepping up to the marble game's counter—the flat store, as the carnies called it—swaggered a short, wide-shouldered, cocky young miner, with a sparse moustache and shaggy hair, framing liquored-up eyes and a grimace that said, <u>don't mess with me</u>.

Playing with Ray, the miner went from free game to empty wallet in less than fifteen minutes—clapping a hard fist into his palm each time he lost more. Nothing left to lose, he blackguarded out in front of the flat store, spitting nails at the three agents, while they mocked him with horselaughs.

Turning on a heel, he kicked at the dirt like to kill a snake, and clenching his fists he stamped over in front of my counter. Feeling sorry for him, but wary from a feel of trouble nigh, all I could say was, "Just twenty-five cents here to win a prize every time."

His coal-dust-rimmed eyes shot daggers at me. Then he dug a quarter out of his dusty jeans, slammed it down on the counter, grabbed up two armloads of hoops, and heaved them all at once, crash-bang up against the back wall of the trailer.

Walt leapt over the counter, leaned into the miner's face, and yelled, "What in high hell you think you're doin'?"

"I'm a-tossin' hoops. What's your botherment?" the miner barked, up on his toes, nose to chin with Walt.

Hauling up a head higher, Walt pointed a finger between the miner's eyes, and snarled, "That you're one goddamn botherment,"

He slapped away Walt's hand. Walt grabbed him by the throat. A switchblade flipped out of the miner's pocket. Walt let him loose and backed off. J.D. snatched up a claw hammer from under his counter and tossed it to Walt. Carnies shouted, "Hey, Rube!" and jumped out of their joints and surrounded the two circling each other like a pair of roosters—the miner in a crouch, waving the knife at anyone who came near—Walt shuffling his feet, slapping the hammer on the palm of his hand. I spotted Ray sneak a small pistol out of his jacket pocket.

On the far side of the circle, one of the ride jockeys from the Tilt-A-Whirl, a barrel-chested feller with a crew cut, charged at the miner, and then backed off, once, twice—baiting him with his feet stamping and arms flailing like a riled gorilla. The third time he did so, the miner spun around to fend him off with the knife, and Walt just stepped up from behind and cold-cocked the miner upside the head. His shaggy hair shook like a cheerleader's pom-pom, and down he went, face first in the trampled grass. Walt flung the hammer under the joint trailer and backed off into the sidelines.

The next minute, two deputies rushed up, pushing through the ring of carnies around the out-cold miner. One deputy rolled him over and gingerly shook his jaw to revive him. He twitched for a spell, his eyes walling back in their sockets—then he came to. The deputy hauled him to his feet and held on while the miner steadied himself, blood oozing through his hair.

The other deputy picked up the knife on the ground and asked anybody who might answer, "What's this all about?"

Ray, his pistol now stashed out of sight, stepped up and told him, "This boy made trouble with that knife and got his due."

"From who?"

Nobody said anything for a long moment. Then Walt spoke up. "From me."

A townie in the crowd shouted, "That's him, deputy. He whupped Dwayne in the head with a hammer."

The deputy swaggered up to Walt and asked, "And why'd you do that?"

"Because he pulled that frog sticker on me."

"And why'd he do that?"

"Because he's a simp that fancies himself to be big bad trouble."

"What started the trouble?"

"He lost some money up the midway and took it out on me and mine."

"How much did you beat him out of?"

"Not a cent."

"Yeah. Sure."

"Scout's honor, officer."

"You're comin' with me. Where's the hammer you clocked him with?"

Just then, a clean-cut feller—in a hundred-dollar suit and tie, and a nar-row-brimmed hat like Frank Sinatra wore—pushed his way through the circle. Several carnies called him Carl, and were eager to tell him their ver-sion of what had happened. He stopped them short with a wave of his hand, a long cigar between his fingers, and he took by the elbow the deputy about to arrest Walt, calmly walked him away from the scattering crowd, and cau-cused with him respectfully, in low voices. As they huddled, the deputy plainly appeared to consider Carl to be the man in charge here. Carl then waved over Walt to get his side of the story—and then J.D.'s, and Ray's.

Meanwhile the other deputy had wadded up a handkerchief into the hand of the miner, who pressed it up against the bloody side of his head. Several townies clustered around him, calling him Dwayne, and asking how he was and what had happened. Still staggering as the deputy propped him up with a hand under his elbow, Dwayne had no answers right then.

Carl and the deputy came over to my counter. Cigar in his teeth, Carl asked me, "What did you see, young lady?"

I didn't know if I was supposed to keep my mouth shut, make some-thing up, or tell them the truth. I had to say something, and I didn't know what to make up, so I simply told them, "That miner lost his money in the game next to mine, so he came over to me, mad as fire, and threw an arm-load of hoops all over the place. So Walt, my boyfriend, got in his face and told him to back off. Then the miner pulled a knife and waved it around at everybody. Till Walt hammered him upside the head."

"That's it?" the deputy asked.

"Yes sir. That's it," I told him, though I'd left out the part about Walt grabbing Dwayne by the throat.

The deputy took a long look at Dwayne, then shook his head and said to Carl, "We know this ne'er-do-well. He's one bad apple. Thing is, his uncle's the judge in this county. So this ain't likely to go lightly for you-all. We'll take him to get his head tended to, cut him loose, and hope that's the end of it."

"What about him pulling out that knife?" I asked. They both looked at me like my question was way out of line.

Nick came trotting up right then, eyes wide and darting about, and asked, "What's goin' on here, Carl?"

Carl walked him away from my counter and calmly told him the story. Nick appeared fit to be tied—hands shoved down into both front pockets, jangling nickels, shifting his weight from foot to foot, his head jerking left and right, like he couldn't figure where this was all coming from. After Carl filled him in, he strode over to the bushel-basket counter and got the tale retold by J.D. and Walt. Brenda then waddled up and calmed Nick down. From the glass pitch she'd seen it all as well. And as usual, leaning up against a corner leg of the center joint, Fred just stared at me with his dark daft deep-set eyes.

The deputies escorted Dwayne away, some townies following. The carnies drifted back to their rides and joints, and things settled back down. I took in another four or five dollars while J.D. and Walt, in the other half of the trailer, talked about the fracas, bandying it back and forth, up and down and back again—paying little attention to any stragglers wandering the midway. That last hour stretched out forever. Then at eleven, the lights on the Ferris Wheel blinked off and on several times and then went dark, and the whole show wound down with a sigh.

Nick hopped into the pitch-till-u-win, snatched the two tens and the twenty off the blocks, and said, "Let's count up."

Walt and J.D. dropped the awnings of the trailer, but didn't latch them, while Nick and I sorted and counted the bills and coins from my apron. With seventy-eight dollars stacked out on the shelf under the counter, minus the thirty-dollar bank that went back into the apron, plus the forty Nick had snatched earlier—I'd taken in eighty-eight dollars my first night.

Nick counted out my twenty-five percent, handed over twenty-two dollars, and he said, twisting the first smile to me I'd seen from him so far, "You done good, kid. Don't worry about that Gomer with the busted head. He got his medicine." Then he stepped over to the other side of the trailer, where Walt and J.D. were counting fistfuls of cash from their aprons.

While they settled up, I climbed out and looked around. The only motor now roaring was the big diesel generator in the middle of the show. The lights of the rides and most of the joints now dark, powerful floodlights burned atop a tower, casting hard shadows. Up and down the midway, carnies laced up the sides of their tents or put their rides to bed—no townsfolk anywhere in sight.

Walt snuck up behind me, spun me face-to-face, reached down and wrapped his arms around my thighs, and lifted me up, waltzing me in circles, his grin nuzzling my bubbies, laughing and saying, "You're a natural, Belle. One righteous hanky-pank hustler. I'm right proud of you. Right proud. I knew you had it in you. You'll do mighty fine. Mighty fine."

I hugged his head, my chin atop his greasy hair, and for the first time I felt that maybe I'd done the right thing running off with him and his carnival.

He set me down and said, "Let's grab a bite to eat at the cookhouse, and then go over to the G-top and get a drink."

What the G-top was, I hadn't a clue, but I smiled and eagerly nodded yes. Clutching one of his arms with both of mine, we strolled up the trampled midway to the cookhouse counter, where we wolfed down some charred chili dogs.

Standing out back by the kitchen truck, Nick appeared to be pleading his case to Carl and Old Eli, who shared a table with a pair of grim-lipped deputies. Other carnies at a few tables nearby leaned their ears toward what Nick had to say.

Walt quietly kept one eye on this powwow, while the other eye avoided whoever glanced his way. As soon as I finished up my second dog, he hurried me down the midway and out behind the line-up and into a big tent— maybe forty by thirty feet, with muddy canvas sidewalls all around, and a string of naked two-hundred-watt light bulbs slung between a pair of twenty-foot poles propping up its twin peaks.

At one side, a handful of poker players sat sprawled on metal fold-up chairs around an eight-foot oval table with green felt. At a cutout for the dealer in the middle of a long side, his back to the canvas sidewall, sat Trips, shuffling a poker deck with all three hands, a visor strapped to his balding dome, his lackadaisical eyes watching the card players ante up.

Scattered around several fold-up tables, a dozen other carnies sat on fold-up chairs, set helter-skelter amid the bent grass. Up against the middle sidewall, a beat-up refrigerator stood behind an elbow-high bar made of hinged-together sections of unpainted plywood. Behind the bar, Blackie— the fat man on the stool at The Dark Journey—sold cans of beer, swiveling back and forth between the fridge and the half-dozen carnies around the bar. At the other end of the tent, atop a pair of sawhorses, a long lone table with high sides stood shrouded with a fitted black tarp.

Walt bought us beers and we sat down at a wobbly table, the legs of my chair sinking into the soft pastureland. I leaned close to him and whispered, "What is this place?"

"The G-top," he whispered back. "The front office puts it up for the recreational pleasures of us showfolk. We got fifty-cent beer—Stroh's brought in from Ohio, not that mountain-hoojy three-point-two swill. We got a fine selection of name-brand hard liquor at a buck a nip. We got a poker game most every night. Punch boards for the brainless. And on Thursday, ride-jockey payday, the dice roll on yonder table."

"What's the 'G' stand for?"

"Gamblin'. The gamblin' top. Old Eli wins back, right here, most of what he pays his help. Plus it keeps his boys out of trouble in town. Nine out of ten gazoonies are more than glad to piss away their pay on booze, cards, and dice. After the rides shut down, they wouldn't know what to do with themselves otherwise. The G-top keeps 'em happy—except when they wake up under their truck at noon with a groggy head and empty pockets again. Keeps 'em on the payroll, too. When they're tapped out the day after payday they ain't quittin' nobody for at least another week."

A floppy-lipped feller—grizzled-up older than he likely was, and hunched inside tan coveralls splotched with stale daubs of pig-iron grease—fetched up to our table, a can of Stroh's quivering at his grimy fingertips, his herky-jerky eyes peeking out from under a striped railroader's cap.

Swiveling his daffy face back-and-forth from Walt's to mine, he told us, "That wrangy mark sure had it comin' to 'im. I's about to grab the biggest wrench I got, and put it to 'im myself. I seen what he done with y'r hoops, missy. That wer'nt right, no where, no how. Then he up and pulls out that there pig-sticker. What kind of idjit goes and does that?"

Walt told him, "The village idjit, Shakey."

Several more carnies gathered around our table, drifting away from the bar, beers in hand. They all took in yammering at each other about the fight, about what they'd seen, about what they would have done if they'd been in the middle of it. One of them bought us another round of beers, plunking two sweaty cans down on the table, along with the mumbled approval of all. Though I hadn't yet drunk half of mine, I smiled up at them all, thanking them with my grateful eyes.

Walt raised his first beer to his big grin, threw his head back, downed it in four gulps, crushed the can in his fist, grabbed up the second beer, and shouted, "Fuck that Clem and the goat he rode in on."

With a hoorah, everybody raised their beer cans high and drank to that. I followed suit. Following that, one after another of the carnies took in bragging on other brawls they'd been in. Walt's second beer gone before my first, he hurried to the bar to fetch another and left me there in the circle of taletellers. A few of them sawed off their whoppers right at me, leaning in close to my face, waving their beer cans about, saggy eyes bugging wide when they told me about their manly doings—as if to prove it true with eyes so wide.

I saw Madeline walk into the tent and go up to the bar, so I escaped from the braggarts and tapped her on the shoulder.

"Hey Annabelle, I hear Walt put a hammer to a mark's head."

I bought her a beer and filled her in on my take of the events. She shook her head and whispered, "I told you about that snake Ray. He's bad news, even for a flattie."

Right then, Ray's partner in crime, the big-assed one-eyed rullion, waddled into the G-top and took a seat at the poker table. Whispering in Madeline's ear, I asked what the story was on him.

She looked over her shoulder to see who I was asking about, then whispered back, "That's Bad-Eye Mike. He'd as soon bugger your grandma as look at you. I heard tell he shot a skillo agent in the balls, just for chillin' one of his scores. He's another one to stay clear of."

"Both of them work right beside me in the next tent," I whispered. "One-Eye Mike sure took his pleasure in riling up that townie Walt coldcocked. And the other night in Clandel he cut a bodacious rusty over me playing his marble game."

She muttered, "It's Bad-Eye, not One-Eye. And that don't surprise me none. The bad-eyed bastard is one bad-ass son-of-a-bitch."

I whispered, "What's the deal with his joint? You spill marbles into a box with numbered holes, then add them up, check that number on a chart, and get yards towards a touchdown? Tonight, I watched one after another get their pokes emptied by Ray and Mike, and then walk away with nothing but grief."

She mumbled in my ear, "It's a count store. The flattie quickly mis-counts a mark into the number on the chart he wants him to get—makes it look like you're gonna win by dukin' you the wrong totals. The marbles rarely add up to a winnin' number."

"But when I played it with Mike, I counted the numbers right along with him once."

"Yeah, when he wanted you to. What did they add up to?"

"No damn touchdown."

"More likely a bonus to double you up, I'll bet."

Walt came up between us, and beerily said with his arms around both of our waists, "Looky me, now. A thorn betwixt two roses."

Madeline said, "More like a thorn in my side. Or a prick I don't want stickin' me."

Walt threw back his head and let out a Kentucky yell, squeezed us close, and said, "You two be some sassy lasses with some classy asses. The gash with the flash. I ain't got eyes enough for the two of you at once. Thank you, Lordy, for sealin' the deal on Annabelle. My Belle. My dream come true. Just havin' one of you two lovelies is all a man can hope for in this woe-some world."

"Get off it, Walt," I told him.

"Alakazam! She tells me to get off it—I'm off it. Off it so fast I'll have to jump into that poker game over there. Off it so fast I'll have to snatch her up and plant a wet one smack-dab on her lovely neck afore I proceed."

Which he did, turning Madeline loose, sweeping me up against him in both muscly arms, and pronging his slurpy tongue under my earlobe. I pushed him away and he backed off, faking a hangdog face, then staggered to a chair at the poker table.

Madeline said, "You sure enough got yourself one rodeo cowboy there."

"For a fact, girl.... Truth be told, I've never much cottoned to fellers like Walt— handsome hunks of sure-fire derring-do. The football jocks at Clan-del High had no admiration for the bookish likes of me, and I'd nary a yen for their brash doings—compared to the tales of heroes in novels."

"Story people ain't got the meat on their bones that the genuine article does," Madeline said with a randy smirk.

I told her, "There's no shortage of meat on bone in this here land. A feller with a head on his shoulders, though, he's another guess."

She huffed a scoff over the lip her beer can, took a swig, and told me, "Men's heads swing on the ends of their dicks. Even those with half a brain upstairs can't say no to a hard-on. They strut around like the cock of the walk, posin' for the hens. But actually they're just puppies, scrambling to not end up suckin' hind teat."

Then she said, "I gotta git. Pa don't take to me hangin' out in the G-top much. I'm sleepin' on the lot tonight, and iffen I don't show at the house trailer soon, he'll come huntin' for me. And that won't be no pretty picture.... You wannna come hang out with me at the trailer?"

"I would. But I best try to get Walt out of here and back to town before long."

"Some other time then." She waggled some fingers at me, and left toting her beer.

I wandered over to the poker game. Around the green felt, seven players sat in front of their cards and money. I stood behind Walt, who had three cans of beer lined up aside a pair of nines showing after four cards of five-card stud. More carnies had bought him beers for hammering the townie upside the head.

In the center of the table, tended by the longer of Trips' left arms, a pile of one- and five-dollar bills grew as the betting went around. When a two-dollar bet came to Walt, he raised it to five. The raise went around the table and all dropped out save Bad-Eye Mike. Trips flipped out the last card and Bad-Eye paired Jacks showing. Walt caught a ten.

Bad-Eye bet five dollars. Walt pushed his cards across the felt toward Trips, guzzled half a can of beer, and said to Mike, "You lucky barrel of elephant shit. I was protecting those nines, and you go and buy an unconscious pair."

Trips swept the money to Bad-Eye, who laughed a gravelly "Haw, haw," and said, "Look who's cryin' now. The fuckin' hero with the hammer."

On the next dole, Walt got a five up, and folded when a dollar bet came to him. My hands on his shoulders, he reached behind and pulled me close, his hands running up and down the back of my knees.

"Now I got my good-luck gal behind me," he said, and reached for more beer.

Across the table, Bad-Eye gave Walt a look that would scare Satan, and said, "Good luck ain't no help when you're dumb-fuck enough to raise on nines."

"Kiss my ass, Mike."

"Haw! I'd have to get in line for that."

Trips chimed in with his soft voice, "Gentlemen, this is a poker game, not a pissing contest. Pair of sixes showing bets two dollars."

That hand went to Shakey, his eight in the hole pairing early. I'd learned to play poker with Pap. That was about the only thing he did together with my sister and me. Even that wasn't all that often to be seen. We'd play for matchsticks, and he'd beat us blind, scaring us with his bluffs, whooping a yeehaw when he'd win. After most every hand, he'd tell us what we did wrong, and what he did right. But whenever Rosalie or I would do right, or maybe catch a lucky card and win a hand, he'd be slow to find favor with any of that. Then he'd bet strong on his next good hand, and gloat over his pile of re-won matchsticks. I wouldn't give a hoot if I won or lost. I played along whether or not my cards were winners. All that mattered to me was that we were together, doing something fun.

I stood behind Walt for a dozen hands, watching him drink more beer and lose more money.

Bad-Eye, first seat to the dealer's right, jumped on his advantages as they came, his bulk swaying atop the creaky fold-up chair as he craned his good eye to inspect the cards around the table.

To Mike's right, Shakey's thin stack of dollar bills dwindled to near nothing as he cautiously played the first half of each hand, waiting fruitlessly for a sure thing.

Next to Shakey sat the lanky feller with the hippie ponytail under a black gangster hat, who ran the basketball game next to Walt's joint. They called him Hat, and he said little and bet only when he had decent cards.

Between Hat and Walt, sat Ed, a chain-smoking wiry-haired loudmouth, with something aggravating to say after nearly every card. Nobody paid much attention to Ed's complaints, and the mess of bills in front of him showed him well ahead of even.

To the right of Walt, a few empty chairs away, with that feather in his cap, sat Robin Marx, constantly fidgeting with his stack of money or his cards, and now and then sniggering at a smart-ass crack mumbled to himself. He played poker like he didn't want to make any bets, but had to anyway.

At a chair on the end of the table to Trip's left, a scarce-haired heavy feller—with thick wire-rimmed eyeglasses and a pasty face having little to say—sat hunched with his elbows on the table, always guarding his cards with his porky fingers, lifting his hands only to toss in a bet or his cards, or relight the fat cigar he slowly worked. They called him Suitcase.

Trips snapped cards off the deck, flipped them rapid-fire around the table, and moved the game along with his tinny, but commanding, voice, calling the cards as they fell, the pairs as they showed, the bets and the raises as they went around. At the end of each hand, he'd count the pot and take the house cut—five percent. Add that up, and every twenty hands the G-top won a pot, and never lost a one.

Walt's luck didn't change with me standing behind him. I hankered to go back to the motel, but when he asked me if I wanted to play a hand while he went out back to pee, I eagerly took his seat.

Walt rushed out of the tent, then hurried back to ask, "You know how to play five-card stud, don't you?" I told him I did and he rushed out again.

Bad-Eye Mike said, "Well if it ain't the feisty little gash what told me to go suck a polecat dick. I ain't sniffed one out yet, but I'm a-lookin' forward to when I do. I'm gettin' right weary of possum dick."

The boys around the table all got a chuckle out of that one. Bad-Eye fixed his good eye on me, a sour grin twisting his pockmarked jowls. While I coolly anted-up a dollar, I thought hard for something to say back at him, but figured I'd best keep my mouth shut.

Trips took in doling out the cards, and cautioned, "Now gentlemen, we have a lady at the table. Watch your French, see-voo-play."

I peeked at my face-down card—a queen. Trips flipped another queen from the deck to me face-up—a pair of queens right off the bat. My queen the high card showing, I opened with a dollar bet. Everybody but Shakey bought the next card—a six for me.

With nothing else showing after three cards, and my queen-six still high hand, I bet two dollars, figuring if I bet too strong I might drive everybody out. Ed folded, out of turn, and whined about shit for cards. Robin fussed with his money for a moment, before deciding to call the bet. Suitcase tossed in the two dollars like it was nothing.

Bad-Eye peeked around at the cards, then leering at me, picked up his stack of dollars, thumbed off four with his eye still on me, slapped them onto the table, and growled, "I raise Red a deuce."

As Hat tossed in his cards, Stuart's Chief of Police—badge, uniform, gun belt, flashlight, and all—pushed through the gap in the sidewall. As he stared me down, my heartbeat stole my breath.

Trips said, "Hey, Chief. You want in a few hands?"

He grunted, "Maybe." Peering from cards to faces, he scanned the carnies around the table.

"Two-dollar raise to Red," Trips announced, his two long arms sweeping the bets into a pile in front of him, the little hand on his third arm holding the deck ready for the next card.

"My name is Annabelle," I told them all. Looking around at the remaining cards on the table, I saw nothing that would beat my queens, so I said, "I'll call the two and raise five more."

A chorus of groans, whistles, and guffaws met that. Robin winced like I'd gone and pulled the feather out of his cap, and he shoved his cards toward Trips. Suitcase re-lit his cigar while he looked me over, his eyeballs enlarged by the thick spectacles. He shook his head and folded. Bad-Eye squinted at me through his good eye—half a smirk baring a picket fence of stained teeth.

Walt tore back in, quickly read the cards on the table, and asked, "Where's the bet?"

Trips told him, "A five-dollar raise from Annabelle to Mike."

Bad-Eye said, "Walt, you got yourself one gutsy gash there. She's playing me like Eve done Adam. She's likely got the two queens... ain't she?"

Walt said, "A fin finds out, Mike."

Bad-Eye dug a pinky finger into his hairy ear, calmly eyed the fingernail to see what it had brought out, shrugged, and tossed a five-dollar bill into the pot. The cards came out. He caught a king, and I, an eight.

He was high card showing now, and he came back with a five-dollar bet. I looked up questioningly at Walt.

Trips said, "Just one player per hand, please."

"It's your call, Belle," said Walt.

"It's your money," I told him.

Bad-Eye laughed, "Haw, haw. It's gonna be my money in a minute."

I had the pair of queens, the best he might have were kings. We'd get one more card. I counted out five ones from Walt's shrunken stakes, and laid them on top of the pile in the middle of the table.

Trips flipped the next card up to Bad-Eye. A king paired the other. A groan thundered from all around the table. My last card was a jack. Game over. He bet five more, to call me out, but I just pushed away my cards and got up off the chair.

Walt said, "Mike, you're so fuckin' lucky tonight, I swear you must've wiped your ass with a handful of four-leaf clovers."

"Walt, I'll tell ya. I win 'em when Old Ned allows, and steal 'em all the rest of the live-long day."

Walt looked at me, shook his head, swept into his pocket what money he had left on the table, and said, "We can't beat that kind of one-eyed luck. Let's git."

The Chief of Police, digging out his cash money, took a seat at the table. I followed Walt out of the G-top and across the deserted midway, over to the other side where the Mercury was parked. I told him I was sorry I'd lost his money, and he just shook it off with a wave of a hand, saying, "You played that hand like you should've, Belle. Sometimes you win. Sometimes you don't."

We wheeled off to town, and along the way, headlights cutting through the curves, I asked Walt, "That Fred, in the nickel pitch... he's weird. He's always gawking at me with a leery look to him. And it creeps me out."

"Yeah, Fred's creepy alright. Being Brenda's brother, Nick's gotta do right by him. And he tries—although a fold-up cot in the back of a Ford truck ain't much of a bed to speak of. There's somethin' I heard about Fred gettin' locked up for some sex thing. I don't know the details. Somethin' kinky I'd wager.... Nick says Fred's just a harmless dodo."

Dodo or not, it didn't set well with me. And not only that—when we rolled into the motel, a battered pickup truck sat out in the middle of the parking lot, with a half-dozen good-old boys leaning on the fenders. Walt pulled into a spot near the office, and as we got out of the car, the night clerk—a mean-looking feller, shaved head, thick neck, and devilish goatee—came around the registration desk and out the door, a shotgun crooked into his elbow. That stopped us flatfooted.

The night clerk squinted at us sidelong, his focus more on the boys over by the pickup truck, and he asked, "Y'all some a them carnival folk?"

"Yes, sir," Walt said. "That we are. You fixin' to shoot us?"

Loud enough for the whole parking lot to hear, he announced, "Abody swogglin' up any onset on my watch, they git their ass full a rabbit shot. Them boys yonder been askin' 'bout any carnival folk here. I reckon they got some sorty feud with y'all. But I ain't abidin' no bitin' and gougin' here tonight."

Walt looked over his shoulder at the bunch around the pickup, eyeing them till they shifted their poses. He turned back to the clerk and said, "I got no idea what those boys' beef is. We're just gonna walk up to our room now and get us a good night's sleep."

Shotgun dangling, legs planted wide, he stood there while we scuffed up the treads and down the balcony to the room. Out of the corner of my eye, I watched the posse follow us with theirs.

Inside the room, Walt pulled the drapes shut, switched on the TV, flopped on the bed, and said, "Don't you pay them never no mind. 'T ain't nothin' but some local yokels feelin' their oats. Tomorrow they won't even remember where they were last night."

I peeked out between the drapes. They were still there, caucusing in a circle, arms folded across their chests or thumbs hooked in their belts.

"Get away from the window, Belle."

"You don't know these mountaineers." I turned and told him, "Once they get a mind to even a score they're stone beholden to do so."

"The score's even. A mark gets stung. He jumps in your face. I jump in his. He slaps at me. I throttle him. He pulls a shiv. I warp his head. Case closed."

"You hope.... I hope."

"You go right ahead and hope all you want. I got beer to piss." Shaking his head with scorn, he got to his feet and went into the bathroom.

On the TV, politicians on a special news report were yammering on and on about the National Guard killing the four students at Kent State. Nixon invading Cambodia, students running riot, Vietnam tearing the country apart—and I thought I had problems.

In the raw, Walt swung out of the bathroom, his jemison strutting solid by the time he'd wrassled half my clothes off.

5

LEPAPE

The Pope gazes with avid eyes into what is beyond the boundaries of his card, and he is keen to interpret what revelations he receives for a pair of monks at his feet — who look up to him as God's own deputy. The twin pillars of duality stand slightly askew behind him. These, plus the two monks and himself, add up to five, as also does his blessing — he shows two fingers held up: dogma and taboo; and three folded in concealment: inquiry, quest, and discovery. Although each hand wears a tattooed cross, no crucifix is atop his scepter. It appears maybe crested with a fool's profile.

We didn't wake till near noon. Walt, jumping up to switch on the TV, muttered cusses as the last of his morning game shows came on, near done. Mother-naked, he slid the drapes open, scratched his straddle, and blessed out the weather. A mizzle blew against the window, droplets streaking down the glass. He yanked the drapes shut, visited the plumbing, switched off the TV, and crawled back under the sheets with me.

Dozing off again, a bizarre dream came upon me. I'm walking down a street with Pap, when parts of him— nose, arms, feet—drop off and are replaced by pieces of other men. I know I'm supposed to do something, but I don't know what, so I run back and fetch some of the parts he'd shucked off. When I try to hand him pieces of himself, he just gives me this half-smile he used to do—which, lips and all, then falls to the concrete and panics me something fierce. Without a mouth, Pap tries to tell me something, but can't.

Then, a knock on the door rousted us. Walt rolled over and groaned, "Yeah.... Who is it?"

The knock came again, pounding this time. Walt bellowed, "Who the hell is it?"

"Housekeeping," sang a woman's voice. Walt didn't budge. A half-minute later, she asked mannerably, close up against the outside of the door, "Do y'all want your room made up?"

"Come back later!" Walt shouted.

"I'm a-going home for the day

soon." Her tone now not so sweet.

"Go!"

"Y'all want some fresh towels?"

"Just leave 'em out there."

"Say what?"

"Just leave 'em out there!"

"I cain't. It's too wet."

I hopped up, bare-naked myself, stood behind the door, opening it a crack and leaning into the gap, and took an armload of towels from the maid—a plain girl not much older than I was, her mousey hair limp from the weather.

She eyed me like I was a piece in a chippyhouse, and said snippily, "I'm a-tradin' these here for them you got."

I went and gathered the towels slung about the bathroom and handed them out to her. Then I showered, wrapped a fresh towel around me, and took my time in the mirror, fixing my hair and my face. Walt was still sprawled across the bunched-up bedding when I came out.

"Walt, I'm hungry."

He mumbled, "I'll get goin' in a bit."

"I'm hungry now. I'm going to walk down to that restaurant again."

"Maybe Kessel's waitin' for you."

"Maybe.

"It's wet out there, Belle."

"Looks like it let up some."

"Suit yourself."

I dressed and set off toward downtown. But before I got halfway, a rain set in—a spatter of heavy drops at first, and then the dark clouds let loose a toad strangler. The only shelter nearby was in the doorway of a storefront church—The Temple of the Blood of the Cross written large in red paint across its long plate-glass window. I pressed my back against the glass door and watched it pour the rain down, an arm's-length away, splashing on my boots.

A tap on the glass spun my head around face-to-face with a clean-cut feller showing a kindly smile and caring eyes that searched into mine a tad too deeply. He motioned with a finger that he'd let me in. The door swung outward and I had to squeeze against the bricks as he opened it.

"Need some shelter from the storm, sister?"

"That would be right Christian of you," I tried to joke, hoping to appear less burdensome.

He held the door while I scurried in, his smile warming even more, and he said, "We must not only talk the talk, but also walk the walk."

Stomping and skiving my boots on the floor mat, and swatting the rain off my denim jacket and jeans, I thanked him heartily.

"Thank the Lord that we are here," he gently corrected me.

"Lordy, Lordy, thank you, thank you," I said and chuckled clumsily, feeling that I'd maybe spoken without proper reverence.

Hunting for something else to say, I cast my eyes around the church. The space, about sixty-foot square, once might have held a shoe store or a hardware. A checkerboard floor of linoleum tiles gleamed with buffed wax. In the back corner, kitty-corner to the windowless beige walls, sat a triangular red-carpeted foot-high stage with a homemade pulpit on it. Out in front, several rows of stackable brown chairs awaited the congregation. And at the opposite wall, a few fold-up banquet tables awaited their offerings. Along the front side, cheery gingham drapes hung across the lower half of the plate-glass. Only the ceiling looked the worse for wear—a few of the textured white panels missing from the metal frame they hung on, exposing wires and girders. Also, above a closet-sized privy in the back corner, several panels sadly sagged with splotchy yellow stains from a roof leak.

"Nice place you have here. My name's Annabelle Cory.

"I'm Pastor Tom. You from around these parts?"

"No..." I hesitated, wondering how he'd react to the truth. But he was too nice to fib to. "I'm with that carnival outside of town."

"I see," he said, his wide smile of welcome converting to a narrower one containing concern. "I would hazard a guess then that you haven't yet been saved by the blood of our Lord?"

"Well, I can't rightly say, Pastor Tom. I was brought up Baptist, and I've been to boodles of Sunday-go-to-meetings. So I reckon I'm in pretty-good shape with the Lord Jesus," I told him, trying to stave off what I knew would be coming.

"But have you brought Jesus into your heart? Have you renounced the sins of the world and accepted His forgiveness? Has His blood—shed on the cross for you and us all—has His blood blessed your soul with eternal life in our Father's kingdom?" His smile, now struggling to stay aloft, grew tighter, and his voice, reaching for the spirit on high, grew loud and righteous.

"Well, I can't rightly say...."

"My child. My child. The rains of heaven have washed you into our humble place of worship. Oh how the Lord works in mysterious ways. And how I pray that His mystery of salvation shall soon be in your heart. Praise Jesus. Praise Jesus. You have been delivered unto His word."

"I was just trying to keep from getting wet."

"So say you now. So say you now. But when the fire of the Holy Spirit comes to you, together we shall rejoice upon the ways of the Lord."

I reckoned that this parson wasn't one to hang up his fiddle shortly. And it still rained buckets outside. His preaching took to vexing me some, so I went at it from another angle. I asked him something that had always been a puzzle to me—"Pastor Tom, how is it that nailing the Son of God up on a cross can make me live in heaven forever?"

The question set him back on his heels. He blinked his eyes like he couldn't believe his ears, and then said, "God sacrificed his Son for the salvation of our souls."

"But how does killing Jesus save our souls?"

He looked me hard in the eyes, and told me, "Jesus Christ is not dead. He arose on the third day and ascended into heaven."

"So then... he didn't die?"

"He died on the cross and then arose from the grave on the third day."

"Okay, okay.... That being so, how does his blood and death save us from hellfire?"

"God demands sacrifice from man. In the Old Testament, Abraham was told to sacrifice his only son. But God replaced Abraham's son with a ram. In our new covenant with God, the glorious blood of His Son washes away our sins."

"So you're saying that if we kill things for God, then He'll let us live in paradise forever."

"No. I'm saying that Jesus, His only begotten Son, gave His life for us."

"Jesus committed suicide?"

"No! The Romans and the Jews condemned Him."

"So Jesus didn't give His life, it was taken?"

"Young woman, I see that logic, the spider's web of this world, has trapped you in bewilderment. Faith in the truth is the only way to resolve your confusion. The Word of God as written in the Bible is where your answers lie."

"Pastor Tom, I've read the Bible. Not the whole thing cover to cover, but most parts, and all four Gospels. And it appears to me that Jesus was a wonderful person, and said and did marvelous things. But I just don't get how the blood from nailing Him to a cross would work to my benefit. How the heck would Romans and Jews murdering Jesus save my soul from going to hell?"

"Believe, and it shall be!" he thundered off the cinderblock walls.

We stared empty-eyed at each other for a spell, and then I said, "Well, I guess that's about the size of it.... Thanks for getting me out of the rain. It looks like it's slowing down some. I'd best be on my way now."

I turned and walked out the door and down the wet sidewalk without looking back. The rain still fell heavy, tires hissing past, downspouts gurgling. I scooted from doorway to doorway, skirting close under the eaves. By the time I reached the restaurant, my jacket shoulders were sobby, my boots squishy, and my hair clung dripping.

Near two o'clock, the lunch rush over, I sat at a booth by the fogged-up window. Yanking a handful of paper napkins from a dispenser on the table, I swabbed my head, rubbing the curls back into my hair. A waitress came with a menu, and I ordered tomato soup, a grilled cheese sandwich, and coffee. Leaning into the corner of the booth, I swiped a circle of mist off the glass and gazed out into the gully washer.

I felt sorrowful about riling up the preacher. He'd been kind enough to let me in out of the rain, for which I'd swapped him a bucket of botherment. But he'd misput me so, with his god-almighty righteousness. What gave him the right to say he knew the truth, and that his truth was what I needed? My questions weren't asked to be spiteful. I wanted to know how and why about what I had no answer for. All he could tell me was that he believed it because he believed it. Simple as that.

I hardly knew what in God's name I did believe—but I knew what I couldn't believe. Maybe, as he said, I was snared in a spider web of common sense. But what could I do about that? Just choose something to believe in and then everything becomes hunky-dory?

When I was a little girl and was told that Santa Claus brought us the sorry toys and clothes scattered under our scrawny Christmas tree, I puzzled even then how this could ever be. How could a fat man in a red suit dole out gifts all over the whole world in one night, never mind in Clandel alone? This miracle appeared greater than most Bible stories in Sunday school. When the day came that my grade-school friend, Sally Jane Hatfield, told me the truth about Santa, it all made sense to me—it was simply a whopper sawed off for young'uns. But several years later when Sally Jane and her kin all got saved by a tent-revival preacher, and she gloried to me how the Son of God had bestowed eternal life upon her, my jaw dropped to my collarbone. How could Santa Claus be a tall tale, yet Jesus not?

Maybe because even though what Santa gave you was real stuff under the tree, Jesus's gift was something invisible inside you—love, joy, peace, and all that. Sally Jane had surely changed her ways when she found the Lord. She used to be one fractious misery—briggoty and always benastying others. After Jesus, her vinegar turned to honey wine. Something real had happened to her, and for a fact it was a point-blank miracle. She told me, eye-to-eye, that Jesus had come into her heart. Maybe what Jesus gives we'll never find under a Christmas tree. Maybe inside us things are as real, or more real, than Santa's gifts could ever be. That I could understand. But what did getting nailed to a cross have to do with it?

While the rain let up, I ate my lunch slowly. After sipping the last of my second cup of coffee, I paid the check and hurried back to the motel, hell-bent to beat the next dark cloud rolling over the ridge.

Up on the balcony, Cheeks' door was wide open, and he, Walt, Robin, George, Ray, and Larry sat sprawled around the room—Cheek's shoulders against the bed's headboard, Sharpy napping by his feet, the scent of reefer again floating in clouds of cigarette smoke.

"Hey, Belle," Walt said—the others in the room nodding their greetings or lifting a hand— "Did you find somethin' to eat? Come on in. You just missed burnin' one."

I said, "I'm good," stepped over outstretched legs, and sat next to Walt on the chest of drawers. Their caucus picked back up to where it was when I'd come in.

Hairy Larry said, "The fuckin' politicians are the biggest crooks there is. They're the biggest liars, the biggest thieves, the rottenest mother-fuckers on earth."

"Yeah,' Cheeks agreed, adding, "and now they're shootin' down college kids."

"Shoot all the fuckin' protesters," grumbled Ray. "They ain't nothin' but a bunch of cry-baby cowards."

George, the elephant-ear man, shouted, "Whoa," holding the palm of his hand up to Ray like a traffic cop. "This is America. If you don't like what's goin' on, you got a right to say so, and not get your ass shot."

Ray, leaning forward almost off the chair toward George, told him, "I don't like what the hell is goin' on, and I'm sayin' so."

"So Ray," asked Cheeks with a wry grin, "you gonna' to pull that pistol out of your belt and pop one into George for protestin' against you?"

Ray sat back in his chair, and said, "I should've put one into that mooch last night that pulled the shiv on Walt."

"I can square my own beefs," Walt told him.

Robin piped up, "Show folk gotta take care of each other. It's us against them, you know."

"That's for sure," Larry said. "The fuckin' townies think they got the exclusive on what's right and what's wrong. They're all just goddamn hypocrites and they don't even know it. We know we're thieves. And damn proud of it. Them self-righteous politicians, preachers, and so-called legitimate businessmen are all sellin' the suckers a pack of lies. The news is lies. Ads are lies. TV shows are just rides on a Merry-Go-Round to keep 'em smilin' while the ads beat 'em out of their money. Money made slavin' at some sucker job. The boss buyin' 'em by the hour instead of buyin' their whole sorry lives. Then after they've robbed 'em hour by hour, they duke 'em to the government when they've worn 'em out. What a fuckin' racket."

Walt said, "Man, it's dog eat dog."

Larry corrected him, "It's fuckin' wolf eat sheep. The marks are out there for the takin'. And if you don't beat them, they'll beat you. They're all out there on that midway lookin' for somethin' for nothin'. And we're out there lookin' to give 'em nothin' for somethin'. We sure as shit ain't in these two-bit towns to lose. We're here to win money. Money what if we don't get, then the preacher will, or the banker, or the union, or the moonshiner, or the stores filled with all that fuckin' crap."

Robin echoed with, "The marks know we razzle-dazzle 'em. Still they come wagerin' their wages—bettin' on beatin' another man's game. You never play another man's game. They gotta be wantin' to lose. How do you figure that?"

"They don't have much else to look forward to," George explained, in a voice as if he were telling them what they all knew already. "They do the same damn things, day in and day out. And when the carnival comes to town, for the measly price of admission they enter a whole other world. For as much as they can stomach or spend, they ride wheels within wheels, spinning amid the lights and music. Playing the games, a thin coin buys a fat chance, and they get taken for another kind of ride. Or step right up and watch cotton candy being spun. See, hear, speak to strange folk from afar.

"Out there on that midway setting in that abandoned pasture, these hill-billies leave the spirals of their lives. Kith and kin strolling in the springtime air, on a few-hour vacation into a world of danger with little risk, a world of mysteries with a price, a world of cheap thrills and precious fun. I make 'em sugar-frosted fried dough, call it elephant ears, and they line up for it. Starvin' for somethin' other than grits and gravy."

"George," Cheeks said, "you're a poet and don't know it."

"Yeah," said Ray, "fire up another reefer and maybe he'll paint us a picture, too."

Cheeks said, "That last one was free—to get y'all hooked on the good shit. Now it's a deuce a joint."

Ray dug a wad of cash out of the front pocket of his perma-press trousers, tossed a ten-dollar bill on the bed, and said, "Gimme five. I need to get way fucked up to get through this weather tonight."

Cheeks tossed him a joint from his shirt pocket, then dug out of the nightstand drawer a pack of Zig-Zag rolling papers and a plastic sandwich bag, fat with pot, and set himself to twisting up four more. Ray fired up the joint, and as it traveled around the room I had a few pulls on it.

After it burnt down, more cigarettes were lit. Cheeks wallowed sideways on the bed, grabbed his ten-dollar bill, and tossed the four joints to Ray. Then, after stowing his stash back in the drawer, he picked up a deck of cards on the nightstand, and said, "I'm dealin' blackjack, five-dollar limit. Who's in?"

They all scootched in close, on chairs, or atop the foot of the bed. Sharpy raised his sleepy head, looked around, twitched those ridiculously tufted eyebrows, snorted once through that scrunched-up snout, and wobbled off the mattress—to go curl up under the table by the window, lift a bald rear leg, and lick his tallywags.

I asked Cheeks, "What sort of dog is Sharpy?"

"He's a carny dog."

"The breed. What's the breed?"

"A half-breed," Cheeks said, doling out cards.

"Half what and half what?"

Ray cracked, "Half ugly and half stupid."

Cheeks ignored that, and told me, "I won Sharpy from a Chinaman in a poker game at the fairgrounds down in Mobile. He was just a pup then. The

Chinaman told me he was a mix of Shar Pei and Chinese Crested, which no doubt took some special efforts to conjugate. A Crested is small, wiry, and mostly hairless. A Shar Pei, bigger, wrinkly, and lumpy. But love will find a way. He gets the cowlicks and baldness from the Crested, and the roly-poly wrinkles from the Shar Pei."

Walt asked, "You want in on some blackjack, Belle?"

"No.... I reckon I'll just hang out in our room." The pot had queered my mood. The carnies, gathered up around Cheeks like that—getting out their money and eager for cards—uneased me like some weird dream.

Walt checked his watch. "Hour-and-a-half till call."

As he handed me the room key, I gave him a peck on the cheek, and turning my back on him, I silently tortured over all his gambling, smoking, and bullshitting with the boys—with nary for me to do but wait. What with my buzz from coffee and tokes, I was ready and raring for more than just sitting around in a motel. Yet, with the pouring-down rain come again, what else was there to do?

Back in our room I turned on the TV and fell onto the bed—nothing on but soap operas. I switched it off, ate a few chocolates, rearranged the roses in the vase, and moved them in front of the mirror atop the chest of drawers. Pacing the room, I told myself I needed to get some books to read. The only things to read in the room were the Bible and Isis's booklet, which I fetched from the drawer. Propped on pillows up against the headboard, I opened it again to words that appeared to be written for me, right there and then.

All people—tribes or nations, big or small, past or present, near or far—have had among their societies individuals that function as connections to the world of spirit.

The primitives had—and still have today where they are found—their shamans, their medicine men, their witch doctors, their sorceresses. These were living men and women, who all in the tribe knew face-to-face, who retold myths around their fires, who healed their sick, who made sacred the important moments of their lives, who tossed bones to reveal their futures, who advised their chiefs, and who spoke to their dead.

These shamans were often unusual individuals, some insane and some physically misshaped—their differences setting them apart from their tribespeople. However, rather than being shunned for their schizophrenic rantings or their horrible deformities, they were thought to be close to the gods, and were exalted when called by their people to reveal the divine. Often the shamans ate plants or potions—mushrooms, cacti, seeds, or herbs—which aided in their visions and divinations.

Like all skills and knowledge, theirs were passed from generation to generation, verbally and by example. And like all skills and knowledge, theirs brought power and privilege. Then, when cities and nations arose, a caste of priests took over the same functions as the tribal holy men. Among the priests were some true shamans, but most were men seeking position, power, or privilege, through associations with the temple—and many lacked true connections with the world of spirit.

As nations became empires—each after the other casting out the gods of the defeated and replacing them with pantheons of their own—the people were presented with shamans far removed from the fires of their villages. Alive only in the myths and legends of long-dead holy men, they tended to the people's spiritual needs only through the ministrations of the new religion's priests. And these priests gained even more power and wealth.

When blessed men and women arose amid the people with true spiritual gifts, the priests gathered them into their temples to sully their talents with dogma, converting them to serve the established order. Those who would not be swayed, they burned as heretics.

The Old Testament prophets denounced the pieties of their age. The Gospels tell of John the Baptist, a voice in the wilderness. And then came Jesus—healing the sick, casting out demons, raising the dead, changing water to wine, preaching against the Scribes and the Pharisees, thrashing the moneychangers in the Temple of Jerusalem. The people once more had a holy man in their midst. So the priests conspired with the governor, and murdered Him.

Then, a thousand years later—after generations of followers retold His story, exalting it with the trappings of other creeds—Christians crusaded against those who would differ from their doctrine, slaying heathens, heretics, and those who would not yield to the authority of the Pope.

Nowadays—quoting words seemingly written in stone, but actually only on paper—multitudes of priests preach salvation and damnation from pulpits, altars, and minarets. Mohammed, Jesus, Buddha, Krishna, Confucius, Zarathustra—these men once were real live shamans, ministering to their people, face to face. But now these avatars live in myths, like once did Osiris, Mithras, and Apollo, transfigured into tales in sacred books, which get wielded like thunderbolts from heaven by those who profess their version of truth to be sacrosanct, and their hold on power to be God-given.

Men use words to nail onto crosses or cathedral doors the clues to mysteries beyond our ken. From Olympus to Jerusalem, men deify such hearsay, exalt it with sanctity, when it merely hints at pieces of the puzzle. The mystery of our essence cannot be explained in words—it exists beyond our penchant for naming things. It lives in the silent stones underfoot and the far-off stars, in worms and carrots and whales, in you and me. The eternal divine power, the source of what men call God, is in All That Is.

Symbols strung in lines of holy text may spell out inklings of words to the wise—but they are insufficient to fathom the depths of The Spirit Within. Only by wordless communication with All That Is, within ourselves and within all else, may we escape from our Tower of Babel.

Joining everything else in an ineffable wilderness of unknowable glory, we then sense glimmers of the mystery of who, what, where, when, and why we are.

I slipped the booklet back in the drawer, and took in pacing the room again. Each time I'd read a page or two, it would echo what had just crossed my path. With Trip's fortune-telling cards turning face-up with my story, and now Isis's spooky little book—what in tarnation was going on? Was it too strange to be so? Too uncanny to be coincidental? Just plumb creepy?

It still rained buckets outside, with still an hour before the show opened, and I didn't know what to do with myself. Being stuck in a motel room on a rainy day in a town where I knew nobody wasn't what I had in mind when I'd packed my bags a few day back. This carnival business was turning out to be more about waiting around for not much to happen, rather than making big money or having some fun.

Just like back in Clandel, I reached for my diary to write down my complaints. But after a few pages of scribbling about the last couple of days—much as if I were a tourist writing a letter to the girl I'd been back home—I felt a need to dig deeper into the whys and wherefores of it all. Yet I was flat-out stumped. My pen went clueless—ballpoint on the paper and ready to roll, but with a witless vacancy behind my fingers. I couldn't come up with one word to riddle me why I found myself in such a funk, which stabbed with a dagger of fear what courage I still clung to.

I flopped belly-down on the bed and buried my face in a pillow. I felt a cry coming on, and let a few snubs leak out. Then I thrashed about to shake it off, sat at the edge of the bed, and got the notion to buy a joint off of Cheeks and get myself righteously stoned. Maybe that might change my mood, or help me see things differently, or at least get me thinking.

Next door, Cheeks took my two dollars and rolled me up a fat one. I sat on the floor in the corner by the window—Sharpy at my side, his god-awful face on his tufty front paws, his eyes meeting mine in sidelong glances beneath those cow-lick eyebrows—and I sucked down as much of the sweet smoke as I could take. When Larry asked me to pass it to him, I shook my head no and said nothing as I held the hit deep and stared straight at him. As the joint burnt down, space in the room grew, time slowed, and colors bloomed.

Around the bed, the boys leaned in and made their bets saying or signaling 'stay' or 'hit me', cheering or cursing their good or bad luck. I watched them toss their money back and forth over the cards, and wondered how it meant so little to them. They all were out here supposedly to make money. But for what? To gamble atop a motel bed? These carnies, Walt included, weren't living this life just to win the money they needed. They needed to keep the game going—win one, lose two, win three, lose four, win one again—with no final score to it all.

I lolled back my head into the wall's corner, my elbows atop my knees, the joint now a cold roach between thumb and finger, and I watched Walt closely. He'd glance my way now and then, and curl me a smile, yet it was plain to see that his eyes were much more interested in the blackjack game than in me. Only a few days gone after sweeping me off my feet, he'd now set me down to earth.

Oh, he was still there for me, making sure I was okay, and that I was still there for him. But lately I hadn't heard much of his romantic dream-girl talk. The roses on the motel-room windowsill were already wilting, and I'd bet there wouldn't be any more too soon. I was now his, and he took care of me in his own way—hauling me around with him, heroically coldcocking that yokum, and fucking me until I squirm like an upside-down turtle.

But was I so sure that I wanted to be his? I'd fled Clandel, where lots of boys wanted me to be theirs, where my so-called life was about to be buried in coal, where folks saw me as not one of them, not a belonger. And now here with the carnies I'd escaped into much the same damn trap. I hadn't become any more myself than I had been before. Who the heck was that so-called me, anyway? Me, a carny sorry-girl? Me, a hoop-toss operator? Me, watching the boys play cards until we go to work in the rain?

I scratched the bald folds on Sharpy's neck. He swung his tufted head to me for more of the same. I obliged him, my fingertips far away while I bewildered myself with half-baked options for my near future. With the scant money I had, I had little choice but to work out the week and see what came of it. Walt may not be the Romeo I thought he might be, but he hadn't done me so wrong, yet. What would happen next, I had no idea.

I closed my eyes and drifted into a pipedream where the lofty canyons of big-city streets embraced me like I once felt the hillsides of Clandel had. Though I wandered along crowded sidewalks with no purpose, the hustle-bustle thumped in my blood, and somehow I seemed to belong there.

The buzz of voices around Cheek's bed a whole world away, suchlike fancies swarmed through my doped-up noggin. Sharpy shifted his lumpy bulk closer to me, nosed my hand for more petting, and brought me back to the motel room. I stroked his smooth skin and tousled his tuft while I studied his glassy eyes. He gazed up at me as if he knew me all too well. And maybe he did. Likely not bewildered with his life, he saw me for what I was. With no options for much else, save to be with Cheeks, he wouldn't be fretting about what to do next. A dog's life—might that be better than having to figure it all out?

The card game broke up after a spell, and everybody went back to their rooms to ready themselves for the dank night ahead. Walt rushed me to get ready, and I fumbled with bundling myself in pantyhose, socks, my thickest jeans, and three layers of tops. As he waited for me, his thumping around the room flustered me to no end, exalting my impatience with him to new heights—my marijuana high crashing to ashy bummer.

We hopped into the Mercury, and when we got to the lot the rain had eased to a mizzle. Walt complained he'd only had a candy bar and coffee from the motel vending machines for breakfast, so we went first to the cookhouse, tiptoeing our way through the puddles and squishy grass.

At the cookhouse, where showfolk had come and gone all day, the ground was trampled into a sobby mess. Squirrel busied himself laying down armloads of straw from a broken hay bale, and as we walked across it, soupy mud oozed up through. We took a table out back near the kitchen truck. Scattered about the other tables, carnies huddled and hunched over their cups and bowls. The day was not only wet, it had gone cold as a pawnbroker's heart.

I ordered coffee. Walt, coffee and the special, a pork chop plate. Squirrel hurried our scalding coffee to us, and we blew on it and sipped steam, clutching with both hands the warm styrofoam. Waddling up to the next table, Lula took a seat and zipped down her red-hooded raincoat. Her huge hinder in black stretch pants sagged over the sides of the wooden folding chair, its scissored legs twisting and squishing into the boggy straw as she settled atop it. Along behind her stomped Sonny McCain, his gaunt frame wrapped in orange foul-weather gear. Both wore jingly unbuckled rubber galoshes.

"Hey honey," she said with a warm smile when she noticed me. "Annabelle, right? How's it goin' for you?"

"The weather today could be better."

"You ain't lyin', girl. But hey, the show must go on. No?"

"That's what I hear."

Sonny grumbled, "Tuesday night. Rainin' pitchforks 'n' bull yearlin's. I ain't eatin' no fire tonight. Buildin' a tip in this mess 'd be like tryin' to gather mourners for Satan's funeral. We'll just set in the tent with the heater goin', and if anyone chances to wander in we'll sell 'em a ticket and give 'em half a show."

Lula told him, "Sonny, that ain't no skin off my fat back." She tossed a low chuckle in my direction, and then asked Walt, "Say, was that you who knocked that mooch silly."

"The one and only."

Sonny said, "They oughta give you a medal."

"All I got so far is a fifty dollar ding from the patch."

Sonny asked, "Wasn't it the mooch that pulled his blade first?"

"Yessiree. But this mooch happens to have a mama whose sister is married to the judge."

"Lordy," said Lula, "there's a beef that'll stew in its juices till served."

Sonny warned, "These gillie-billies tend to their own payback. I'd keep a pistol with me, if I was you."

"Last night," Walt told him, "a posse of good-ole boys were hangin' around out in the motel parkin' lot, till the night clerk come out with his shotgun."

"That's what I'm sayin'," said Sonny. "I wouldn't worry about the judge. The old man'll take care of him. You watch out for that gillie's buddies."

"I hear ya."

Squirrel set down a paper plate piled with pork chops, smashed potatoes, and canned green peas, and Walt dove into it with a plastic knife and fork. As four o'clock neared, we picked our way down the sobby midway, and found Nick and Fred hoisting the awnings of the glass pitch. Walt helped them out while I took on a shiver, shuffling my feet under an awning—the all-day runoff from the canvas surrounding the tent with a swampy moat, seeping in through the sides of my cowgirl boots.

After they hauled up the trailer awnings, I jumped into the pitch-till-u-win, wrassled the panels out of the floor, and set them underfoot so I had something dry to stand on, the sod under the trailer going sobby. Inside the trailer having a feel of shelter, I eased myself to it, and took in redding up the joint for the night ahead—wiping a rag around, straightening the prizes on the blocks and under the counter, piling up hoops, checking the thirty dollars in my apron, moving mainly to busy some warmth into me. That took all of about fifteen minutes, and when done there was nothing left to do but wait, marooned in a dope-addled stretched-out time zone.

Soon a waltz tooted happily from the Merry-Go-Round, and one-by-one—no doubt grudgingly—the ride boys fired up their motors and switched on their lights. An hour later, a steady rain setting in, I hadn't yet had a customer. Only a few fool kids and teens, with neither money nor sense, sloshed back and forth on the midway, their wringing-wet clothes clinging to their bony frames, their hair smeared across their heads. Walt tried to call a few of them in, and then plumb gave up. I paced end to end and sang out my pitch-till-u-win rhymes for a spell, but then I just plunked myself down on the trailer floor and hunched up against the chill, fidgeting my toes to the beat of the ridiculous rock and roll blasting from the riderless Tilt-A-Whirl.

J.D. showed up a half-hour later, disgustedly picking his steps down the midway, with his head ducked under a rain-spattered black-plastic garbage bag slit down one side and turned upside down over him like a nun's outfit. Both hands at his lanky thighs tugged up the mud-stained cuffs of his jade-green trousers—on his gunboat feet, his white socks and tasseled penny-loafers mucky beyond salvation. Under the trailer's awning, he whipped off the bag, kicked it under the bally cloth, and muttered cuss after cuss, swiping raindrops off the sleeves of his leather jacket and shaking his head as if it couldn't be so. He hopped over into the bushel-basket joint, and for the next half-hour stood there, an elbow on a knee, one foot propped up on the trailer floor behind the counter, saying nothing.

After a spell, he turned to me, and grumbled, "We ain't winnin' eatin' money tonight."

I asked, "Will we stay open all night?"

"More 'n likely. The show must go on, do tell. It don't cost Old Eli but some diesel fuel to keep the lights on. His help draw salary, rain or shine. The independents got their nut paid up. His flatties'll steal a few scores from a mooch or two. And if we don't try to work this washout, and just stand around with nothin' but our peckers in our hand—pardon my French—we get D.Q.-ed."

"D.Q.-ed?"

"Disqualified. Red-lighted. Eighty-sixed. Thrown off the lot.... Hey, watch this." He bent his eyebrows toward a kid sloshing past, and with a come-here wave of his hand, he hollered, "Say son, over here for a second. I need to ask you."

The boy—maybe thirteen, in a sweatshirt and bib overalls wet to the skin, a cowlick jutting from his rain-plastered noggin—he said, "I ain't got no money, mister."

"Well that don't make no matter, boy. How'd you like to earn a free game?

"Sure 'nuff, mister. What all I gotta do?"

"Son, I need some light-bulb grease, and I gotta stay right here and take care of business. So how 'bout you go and fetch me some, and I'll reward you for your efforts with one free game?"

"Well... I reckon I might could. Where's this light-bulb grease to be found?"

"Ask anybody down the line-up for some. If they got none, they might know where you can find it."

"For a free game you say?"

"That's it. One free game. And if you fetch it right quick I'll throw in a few coins for your hustle."

"That sounds mighty fine by me. Be back shortly, mister."

He hurried off, swiveling his head in search at the flat store next to me—where nobody had yet shown up. I leaned out to watch him go to the next joint and ask the agent there for some light-bulb grease. He got pointed over to the other side of the midway and sloshed away in a gangly trot.

"I never heard tell of light-bulb grease," I said to J.D., who with Walt leaned out over the counter, grinning in the direction of the kid.

Walt said, "Ain't no such thing, darlin'."

J.D. sniggered. "Let's see how long the punk chases that wild goose. I'll lay even odds he's still at it in an hour."

"I ain't bettin' against that," said Walt.

A half-hour later the kid came back and told J.D., "Mister, I can't find none. I been back 'n' forth, one feller sending me to the next, but there don't 'peer to be nary."

J.D. said, "Dadgummit, boy. I was a-countin' on ya."

"I'm mighty sorrowful 'bout that. But they ain't nary to be found."

Walt said to J.D., "Don't you need the key to the midway to get some light-bulb grease?"

"Tarnation! I plumb forgot that they lock it up when it rains. Son, find me that key and I'll toss in another coin or two to boot."

The boy, now with wary eyes, asked, "Who's got the key to the midway?"

"I don't rightly know. Just ask around. Someone has it."

He muttered, "Okay, mister," and shoving his hands into his pockets, half-heartedly set off on another hunt.

J.D. muttered, "That boy's so stupid he couldn't pour piss out of a boot if the instructions was written on the heel."

The next few hours spelled even more misery. Dank and dark set in early while a downpour rattled atop the trailer. Flashing lights glinted through a streaky curtain of rain. A raw chill seeped into my shivery bones, along with trembles whenever my eyes met Fred's, slouching in a corner of the nickel pitch with nothing else to do but to stare at me. The midway sank into swamp, which oozed in beneath the trailer—the trap-door panels squishing underfoot as I paced back and forth, trying to fend off the cold. I grabbed a few quarters from waterlogged kids and their tomfool mothers—under my awning more to escape the rain than win a prize. The boy with the cowlick never came back with the key to the midway.

Around eight o'clock, up to Walt's counter walked Carl, the patch—bundled in a broad-shouldered trench coat under a black umbrella and his short-brimmed hat, his white and even teeth clenching an unlit cigar in his doughy face—accompanied by a burly deputy wearing a yellow poncho over his uniform and a clear-plastic topper fitted over his Smokey-the-Bear hat.

Carl said, "Walt, they're hanging an assault charge on you for what went down last night. This deputy'll take you over to the station to book you—but we've already posted bail, and he'll bring you right back after."

"What?" Walt hollered. "Carl, that guy pulled a knife on me."

"We all know that, Walt. And everything's been smoothed out, but we got to go through the motions."

"Go through the motions. What the fuck does that mean?'

"That means you get charged. Then you show up in court on Friday. You plead self-defense. And they let you go."

"Fuck that, Carl. I pay you for protection. This is what I get?"

"Just go through the motions, Walt. That's all you got to do."

"Ain't this the shits."

"Let's go, son," the deputy said, flipping out his handcuffs.

Walt asked Carl, "Fucking handcuffs?"

"Do we need the handcuffs, deputy?"

"Yes sir. We do."

Walt flung the softball he had in his hand, hard against the wall of the trailer, hopped over the counter, and held his wrists out for the deputy to click on the handcuffs. Holding him by an elbow, the deputy led him away, with Carl following. Walt turned to me and grimaced, shaking his head in disbelief.

The next second, Nick hurried up to J.D. asking what the hell was going on. J.D. quickly filled him in, and Nick cut mud after them.

I stood there with my mouth open. J.D. said to me, "Don't you worry none, gorgeous. Ain't nothin' bad gonna happen to your man."

"Looks to me like it just did," I said, my throat tightening up.

"You listen to me, now. The fix is in. It's all been worked out already. Otherwise that deputy wouldn't be with Carl. He'd come with another deputy or two. The front office got it all under control."

"And just how are they doing that?"

"With good-old-fashioned all-American give-and-take. Parley and money. Johnny Law and friends, they took the grease, or we wouldn't even be settin' here in this mudlot. They're with us, not agin us. Still, they got to stay here when we're long gone, so they need to make things look good for the voters, you see. It's all play-actin'. A paid performance. And Walt is the star of the show right now. They'll parade him about, to look like they'd done somethin' about his crime, if it be judged one. The fix is in, and that's all she wrote. Don't you go botherin' your pretty little head on it. Carnies take care of our own."

An hour or so later, the rain had slackened to mizzle, and Walt trudged down the midway toward us, looking fit to be tied—well, he had been tied. Word had gotten around the show that he'd been snatched up, so it took him a while to get over to me, what with one agent then another stopping him for the tale. His steam blown off by the time he reached me, he wearily brushed off my fearful questions with, "No problem," and, "It's in the bag, Belle," and, "Nothin' for you to worry about."

With the rain letting up, the midway crowd—if you could call it that—picked up somewhat, between nine and ten o'clock. Slogging through colored lights flashing off the puddles, some came dressed for the weather, in boots and raingear or toting umbrellas. Nick jumped into the pitch-till-u-win for a spell, hollering at stragglers one after another, bringing some life and some quarters into the hoop toss and sparking Walt and J.D. to action in the other half of the trailer.

After a spell, Walt set his hooks into a mark who looked like he might be a store clerk or a schoolteacher—a mannerly clean-cut feller with wire-rim spectacles, khaki trousers, and a button-down white shirt under a green rain poncho—his grit grimly set on learning to toss the ball like Walt showed him. Close behind, stood his pre-teen daughter, hunched up inside a red raincoat and fidgety with embarrassment under an polka-dot umbrella. She appeared not to know whether to scowl or smile in her role in this game at which her father, toss after toss, lost more and more money trying to win her a teddy bear.

Plain to be seen, Walt's fur was still up about the arrest, and he lit into his mark as if the poor feller had something to do with it. I peeked at a view of Walt I hadn't yet seen. So far, he'd treated his players with a blend of mutual respect and friendly guidance while he bamboozled them. But this was flat-out tearing at one like a coyote on a chicken.

The mark, appearing way too proud to walk away empty-handed, spent near thirty dollars to finally be allowed to win a dusty black-and-white bear. After he presented it to his daughter—now beaming in her role—he shook his head at his foolishness and led her away by the hand.

Walt dropped his hands behind the counter, counted his score, and folded it into his apron—his eyes pinched meanly as he scanned the midway for whoever might be next. With nobody nearby to call, he propped one sobby shoe upon the trailer floor and cocked an elbow atop his knee, his face holding what looked to be plumb disgust.

I took ill with disgust—not only with Walt playing hardball, but also with me and my part in this con game—the whole damn show swapping off a bag of tricks for folks' hard-earned dollars. Hunching up against the trailer wall, I simmered in my stew of guilt and blame and poor-poor-pitiful me. My mind a-boil with what-ifs and should-haves, I stubbornly fought shy of getting shut of all this flimflam. Yet how could I quit so soon, never mind one thing right after the other? Paid work was what I'd signed on for. I'd made a choice and now had scarce others—save go back home to shame.

By ten, the midway was a hog wallow—what grass there had been, trampled into slop. Any stragglers remaining chose each step carefully, but found little firm ground. The mud sucked the shoes right off of a few. Some kids just rolled up their pant legs, slung their shoes around their necks by the laces, and swashed about barefoot.

By the time the lights on the Ferris Wheel shut down, my bones felt like seams of coal in a shivery hill of jelly. Nick counted me up and handed me my end—four dollars and seventy-five cents. Seven hours of standing around in the cold and wet, for less than five bucks. I admired nothing about how that added up. If Walt hadn't paid for the room and the eats, I would've earned less than nothing for the whole day.

Walt helped close up the joints while I waited standing on the trailer hitch, my feet up out of the swamp. We picked our way through the muck to the cookhouse, where more hay bales had been strewn atop mud, lending some relief underfoot. At the back counter, I ate a bowl of hot and spicy chili-mac, and Walt, two chili dogs. One after another, show folk came up to Walt and quizzed him about his arrest, hardly allowing him to eat. At first, he'd narrate them a short version of the tale—but after the third or fourth query, he just said, "Ah, fuck it. No problem. The fix is in."

We washed the food down with steamy coffee, and for the first time in hours I thawed some. Walt asked, "What's your druthers? G-top or motel."

Though the motel room was heated and dry, the coffee jolted me sufficient to know I'd be bouncing off the walls there. So I said, "Let's try the G-top for a while."

Through the dark, we wound our way back behind the line-up, where the ground wasn't so churned up, to the saggy G-top. Pushing through the gap in the sidewall, we stepped into its bright lights and raucous voices.

Atop the trampled grass, which mercifully felt only damp, Blackie's bar was elbow-to-elbow, all of the tables were taken, and carnies filled the chairs around the poker game. The rattly fans of a pair of electric heaters, tied back-to-back on a tent pole, breathed out scorched air from red-hot wires.

We sidled up to the bar, where several fellers pronged Walt with some funning—"There's the jailbird."—"He's a-goin' from one joint to th' other."—"At least the jailhouse is dry."

Walt just shouted, "Ahh! Fuck 'em all. The fix is in." And bought us beers.

The G-top held a more antic bunch than the night before—clamorous and caterwauling, drinking firewater to burn away the dank in flesh and spirit after hours of standing with wet feet, hunched against the chill, minutes plodding through the do-nothing night. The gather-all bore out that misery loves company.

I spotted Isis at a table near the heaters, caucusing with Sonny McCain, and I wandered over after Walt's attention soon locked onto the poker table. She wore her emerald-green robe cinched snug around her waist, but with the hood down—her cheery eyes and cheeks peeking through her fine-spun silvery mane.

When she saw me she warbled, "My dear young Annabelle. How are you holding up on this terribly inclement evening?"

"Fair to middling."

"Would you like to sit with us?"

"Yes, Ma'am. Thanks. Mighty kind of you." I plumped down on a chair.

"Do you know our illustrious illusionist, and show-boss scion, Sonny McCain?"

"We met today at the cookhouse. And I've seen your show, Mr. McCain."

"Just Sonny's fine. You're with Walt, right?"

"Yes, sir."

He turned to Isis, "Did you hear they arrested Walt for hammerin' some sense into that wrangy hillbilly."

"You don't say..."

In the know, I told them, "The fix is in. Walt just has to go through the motions."

"And what are the motions?" Isis asked.

"I don't rightly know, ma'am. Tonight they put him in handcuffs and took him down to the jailhouse for about an hour."

Sonny said, "I heard Carl and the old man talkin' 'bout him havin' to show up for kangaroo court Friday."

"That's what I hear tell, too," I said.

He added, "They'll just parade him in, pound on their chests, cast the shame and glory of repentance upon his sins, and cut him loose."

"I sure hope so, sir."

"Annabelle," he said, fire building in his eyes, "There ain't no doubt about it. This county—as well as most all the others in this God-fearin' state, as well as most all the counties in all the countries in the whole wide world—this county's as corrupt as they come. This show wouldn't be sittin' here on this damn mudlot, the joints and the kootch show workin' strong, the G-top with Ohio beer and cash gamblin'... unless that judge got his cut."

"So I've been told, sir."

"Please call me Sonny. Now, Annabelle, I'm gonna tell you somethin' else. What burns my ass is these people gettin' their bag money, actin' like they're so almighty righteous—upstanding citizens, town fathers, pious Sunday-go-to-meeting gladhanders—and they're the biggest fuckin' hypocrites alive, with pre-paid tickets straight to hell." His gaunt face gone wide-eyed, he slapped a hand on the table, his beer can doing a little hop.

"I eat real fire. I shove real needles through my flesh, real spikes up my nose, real swords down my gullet. And they say that I'm a fake? They think we're the thieves? They think we're the devil?

"We pay off Satan every week, right there in that fuckin' courthouse. Gettin' his cut of all the action in town. Sharin' some with the preacherman on Sunday. Lordin' it over the peons, and puttin' the razzle-dazzle on 'em with good-old gaffed-up democracy."

Isis said, "Sonny, calm down. Your eyeballs are going to pop out of their sockets."

"That's gonna be my new act in the sideshow. A pop-eye. I've been workin' on pushin' 'em out. Look." He bugged out his eyes, the lids peeling back over the whites.

Isis sniggered and said, "I've seen plenty of pop-eyes and you ain't even close."

"Gimme a while and I'll get pop-eyed enough to get a rise out of the yokels."

Isis laughed her high hee-hee, saying, "You'd really have to pay off the sheriff after he's seen that face."

Still making bug-eyes, he tilted the last of his can of beer down his throat, and then said, "I gotta git back to the trailer and practice it some more. An artist ought not blunt his thrusts of creation." Then he sprang to his feet, whistling "Popeye the Sailor Man".

As he left, Isis and I shared a chuckle, and she said, "Sonny's one of the good ones, though a bit of a grouser."

"Isis, I've been wanting to talk to you about something."

"Why sure, Annabelle dear. You go right ahead."

"Well... I've been reading that little book you gave me. And every time I pick it up, I read about something to do with what's been happening to me near then and there. And it's giving me the willies."

She thought on this—leaning back in her tottery chair and eyeing me quizzically. Then she asked, "Do you remember when you told me about the Tarot cards that Trips read for you?"

I nodded.

"And when you asked me how those cards could be so true I told you about synchronicity?"

I nodded again.

"And I told you that something special was happening to you right now, and not to ignore it?"

I whispered, "Yes."

"Well, it seems you've got that going in a big way. Whatever makes such things happen is making it happen to you. What it is, I'd be foolish to hazard a guess. That it is, you'd be foolish to ignore."

I whined, "How could I ignore it? It's slapping me upside the head every time I pick up your book."

"You could give the book back to me."

I thought on that a piece, and then said, "That would likely end it, wouldn't it?'

She shrugged, and I thought on it more. What damage was being done? It frightened me some. It felt witchy and creepy. But what I'd read was what I appeared to need to know—maybe even wanted to know—even though I didn't know that I wanted to know it. My debate with the preacher today bore out that I couldn't swallow his version of the truth. But what was my version?

I then told Isis the tale about Pastor Tom, and asked her what I'd asked him—how does the bloody murder of Jesus save my soul?

"That's a good question, dear. And I can't tell you for sure, but from what I figure.... For eons before Christianity—and some places even nowadays—people worshiped blood sacrifice. Slaughter an animal, or a human, as an offering to a god. Why? To ask for favors, or forgiveness, in a bargain with the god.

"These primitive gods were not the God, capital G, that Christians call the Father, capital F. Back then there were loads of different gods put in charge of all kinds of different things—differing from one society to the next.

"What I suspect—distilled from reading and conjuring—is that these gods were the ghosts of those people's ancestors. Every tribe in the world, throughout time, has had its ghost stories. Many Chinese still worship ancestral spirits. Well, until Communism they did.

"If, when people die, we suppose that our souls live on in another realm, in the air above us, then what do they do there? If when you die, your soul, the person you became on earth, goes to heaven or the happy-hunting ground or the underworld or whatever else you call it—then it's reasonable to assume that heaven and hell would be filled with the same kinds of people that are in this world. And, just as some souls do here, some crave power in the realms of the dead. As above, so below.

"Now it's said among those who know magic, that when you want to summon a spirit, for whatever purpose, the spilling of fresh blood attracts it, allowing the ghost to partially materialize within the bloody vapors. The life force in the blood, evaporating into death, somehow connects the two worlds.

"These primitive shamans made blood sacrifices to summon their familiar spirits, a skill they'd discovered either by their own talents, or from other shamans. And when the shaman's tribe asked big favors of a ghost that craved power—it eventually assumed the role of a god.

"This god may or may not be able to deliver any favors. But it doesn't matter. Because by at least trying to do something about their problems, the tribe then felt better. They'd seek advice or forgiveness. They'd pray for rain. They'd ask what the future will bring. Whatever they felt powerless about, they were led to believe that the god could do something about it. The god then grows in influence, as does his priests, who end up with plenty of sacrificial meat on his table, as well as treasuries to build the god or goddess a temple with."

I squinted at her like she was telling me that the Easter Bunny was evil, and asked, "But what has that got to do with Jesus on a cross?"

"I'm getting to that, dear. I'm getting to that. You can't understand the present until you know what went on in the past.

"In the Bible, in Genesis, Adam and Eve had a pair of sons, Cain and Abel. Well, their story is that when time came for a sacrifice, Cain, the gardener, put fruits, herbs, and seeds on the altar, while Abel, the shepherd, sacrificed the blood of the lamb. When the Lord liked blood better, Cain got angry and slew Abel.

"So, right from the beginning of the Bible, blood sacrifice pleases the Lord God, Jehovah. Then along comes Abraham, who the Lord commands to sacrifice his son, Isaac, on top of a mountain. Abraham follows orders and was about to do it, when an angel of the Lord tells him he can sacrifice a ram instead. The Bible, especially the Old Testament, is simply a story of a primitive society.

"Also in the Bible, Jepthah made a burnt offering of his daughter after God granted him a victory in battle. Burned her alive. Sacrifices of first-born sons were common in many primitive societies—as well as the sacrificing of countless virgins. The greatest sacrifice one can offer is that of one's first-born son. Virgins are a dime a dozen. Aztec priests, for their gods, cut the hearts out of tens of thousands of people atop pyramids not that far from here and not that long ago.

"So, my dear Annabelle, after Jesus was crucified and deified, then the early Christians, who were primitive people as well, figured that the only way any sense could be made of Jesus' bloody murder was that God sacrificed His Son for us—or that Jesus offered Himself up to His Father—so that all our sins would be forgiven.

"And if you believe that, then I suppose they would be.... Does any of this make any sense to you?"

"No.... It sounds like it's all built on one hocus-pocus after another."

"That it is, dear. That it is."

"So does the blood of Jesus really wash away sins?"

"Annabelle, belief is everything. What you believe creates your world. Look around you. What do you see? You see everybody wearing the clothes that they believe in. Carnies here in this tent believe different things than do the townsfolk up the road. Townies believe in rectangular homes, a forty-hour workweek, and church on Sunday—and there's no changing their minds. They'll die for their beliefs. They'll kill for them.

"But just a few hundred years ago, other people gathered around in tents right here in this meadow—Indians in teepees who had completely different beliefs and lived completely different lives. The blood of Christ was unheard of. They had their own blood rites. Their salvation was to be in harmony with the Great Spirit of All That Is.

"What their sins were, and how they were forgiven, I haven't a clue. What I suspect though, is that if someone believes that the crucifixion of Christ redeems their souls from eternal damnation, then so it does."

I wondered aloud, "The fortune-telling cards—and your book, doing that synchronicity thing—should I believe in all that? Would any of it save me from damnation? Or maybe lead me there?"

"That's another mystery, Annabelle dear. Things happen. Why or how, I can't rightly say. We're not able to know those answers.... Maybe we could slit the throat of a sacred cow and ask the spook that shows up."

We chuckled at that some—she handily with her hee-hee-hee, and me joining in skittishly, uneasy about what I might be told next. It all struck me spellbound, but put a fright in me, too.

I twisted around, hunting for Walt, who still stood watching the game at the poker table. Turning back to Isis, I asked, "But what should I do? Give back the book, or keep on reading?"

"Dearie, I don't have an answer for that one, either. If you're not comfortable where it seems to be taking you, then that's a call you have to make. What one person needs to know, and what one does about it, that's as varied as people's faces. What you need to know, perhaps only you can know. One can come to know too much and grieve over that. Too little—well maybe ignorance is bliss. Maybe it's like Goldilocks and the Three Bears. She tries the porridge, the chairs, the beds, till she finds the one that feels just right."

"But she tried them all," I said.

"Yes, she did."

I nodded, and told her, "Thanks again, Isis. I'm going to try to get Walt back to the motel."

"Anytime, Annabelle. Anytime."

I got up, went over and stood next to Walt, and watched a few hands of five-card stud. The thickest stack of money sat in front of a tall and broad-shouldered player that Trips called Paul—apparently Tall Paul, owner of several joints on the midway. On his muscled-up chest, he sported a crisp short-sleeved yellow knit shirt with an tiny green alligator stitched above the pocket, and atop his square-jawed head was cocked a matching yellow golf cap with the name of a Florida country club embroidered above the visor. Sitting ramrod straight, Paul's wolfish eyes assessed the cards and faces of those in the game, each in their turn as the bet went around—which with his pile of money and clean-cut clothes gave him a powerful air of one sleek and cunning lucky dog.

The others, hunched elbow-to-elbow at the table, were much the same as the night before. Robin, Ed, Shakey, Hat, and Suitcase, minus Bad-Eye Mike. Plus George and Hairy Larry from Cheek's room, and three other carnies whose nameless faces I'd seen around the lot—likely other agents, by the cut of their clothes.

I whispered in Walt's ear, "Can we go back to the room?"

"Sure. This table's got too many chairs for my money." He guzzled the rest of his can of beer, lit a cigarette, and led me out of the tent and to his car.

On the way back to town, I asked, "So... what do you have to do to take care of the hammer-up-side-the-head thing?"

"Ahh... it's a bunch of fuckin' bullshit. I gotta show at the courthouse Friday, at one o'clock, for an arraignment. The wheels've already been greased, but I need to show up for appearances. The judge is catchin' heat from his wife, as it's her wrangy nephew with the dent in his noggin. So he's obliged to do somethin' about it, which'll be nothin' but hearin' that the numbskull pulled out his frog-sticker on me first."

"Won't you need a witness?"

"The only witness I'm goin' to need is already in the judge's poke. Case dismissed."

"Shouldn't I come with you and maybe back you up?"

"Annabelle, I'm gonna back you up as soon as we get to the motel room."

"I'm serious."

"I'm damn straight. And gettin' straighter, too."

Turning a deaf ear to his cagey wisecrack, I felt a mite misput that he didn't want my help. I stewed on it as we rode along with a silence between us. Me hankering to toss in his face a few of his failings—his endless games, his lack of attention to his so-called dream girl, even the miserable weather, too, as if that was his fault. Simmering in my own juices, I held off for fear of jumping out of the pan and into the fire.

At the motel, he switched off the motor, and said, "Belle, you're dead right. I might need you with me, to back me up, one way or another."

In a welcome breath of relief, his magic words, or maybe the way he said them to me, or maybe just because that's what I wanted to hear— abracadabra —turned my shorthairs from bristly with spite to tingly with lust.

Sniggering at my bereft change of mood, wondering whether forgiveness such as this was love, I cooed, "I'm coming, like it or not."

Walt fetched up his randy grin, and murmured, "I like it. Mmm-mmm, I like it."

That was enough to prime the pump, and we hardly got the room's door shut before we were at it again.

6

VI

· LA·MOVREV ·

Above in a sunburst, Cupid aims his arrow at the heart of a man whose eyes are perplexed. Cupid, blindfolded by what resembles the symbol on the scepter's orb, has one leg detached from his buttocks. To the man's left, a young woman extends an arm from her heart to his, as she narrows her jealous eyes at a stern woman to his right, who lays a wistful hand on his shoulder. His right arm is shorter than his left, which reaches toward the young woman's womb. His choices are old or new, reason or emotion, yet an arrow of destiny will soon fly. Six is the number of ambivalence.

Rode hard and put up wet, I awoke Wednesday morning with my satchel sore from one all-get-out rambunctious night. Three times, we'd gone at it. Each rut lasting longer than the last. Though I was plenty willing, Walt was rollicky as a randy otter—rolling us afire and rocking us sweaty.

Around ten o'clock, when he reached down for more, I swatted his hand away and said, "My monkey smarts. You've plumb wore me out."

He slapped my bum, hopped up— his hoe handle wagging—switched on the TV, and flipped the channel to a game show. I studied him while he pulled a corner of the window curtain aside, the sunshine pouring in. He peeked outside, scratching his straddle, and then went into the bathroom, kicked up the commode seat with a toe, and let loose his morning branch.

Right there was my man—the curve of his make, the sturdy thighs, his weight slung on one leg, like a stallion's hindquarters. Hair askew everywhich-a-ways, he grinned at me over his muscly shoulder, shook his doodle dry, and said, "What you lookin' at, girl?"

"At one handsome sight."

Grunting like a hog, he crawled under the sheets, snorting and snuffing, rooting his snout up and down the length of me. Squealing laughs, I wrassled away and pushed him off. But when his nose found what it was hunting, and then his tongue, I locked my thighs around his ears, and joined the choir of oohs and ahhs of the game show audience.

All the talk about sex that people do, talk that had made me puzzle what I was missing—all the novels and movies making it out to be the best thing there is—I'd scarcely understood until now. At last, I'd let myself go—gone to heart-strutting wildness, an animal with the hobbles off, finally free. That's what all the talk was about. Everybody, everywhere, caught in their everyday human traps, yet crawling atop each other in the dark, hungrily groping for the pleasure of becoming again the animals we all are.

By quarter to noon, I'd showered, and Walt had neared his daily dose of morning game shows. Fixing my face and hair in the mirror, I looked myself dead in the eye and wondered where all this was going. Walt had sure enough won my prize—as for my body. All what we'd done last night, I'd never had any notion that such was possible. I'd not only let him do things to me—and I to him, which just the week before I would not have thought decent—I now couldn't get my fill of it.

The pleasure I took from him I did my blamedest to give him back. And what he did to my body rendered me into a woman—not the woman I'd thought I'd one day come to be, but one with a stove in her straddle smoldering to burn more of his firewood. All those catch-as-catch-can beaus from Clandel had kindled only a sputtering flame or two. Yet after less than a week with Walt, I was stoked. I'd found a part of myself that I knew had to be there. My mistake had been that I'd reckoned it would be someday bestowed on me by some prince. Sure enough, Walt had put a match to me and fanned my flames. But only after I'd opened wide my stovepipe's damper, did this blaze arise.

For a fact, Walt had fired up the woman in me, but was he truly the man for me? On the other side of the bathroom door, he lay sprawled across the bed, stinking up the room with his third or fourth Raleigh of the morning, staring at yet another game show on the blathering TV. I'd run off with him for an adventure, for an escape, and now here I stood wondering what I'd been caught up into.

Not once since our first morning together had either of us said a word about love. What I'd told him back then about love being the good of your soul giving itself to another soul's good for the good of love—that was just something I'd read in some novel. How could I ever know what love is if I'd never been in love? How could I have known what sex was until I'd set myself loose with it?

I finished up in the mirror, swung open the bathroom door, and asked him, "Do you love me?"

He rolled his head to me, blinked away some surprise, and said, "Belle, I'm nuts about you. You're the sugar on my donut. You're the hole in my donut. You're the tires on my wheels. The gas in my tank. The key in my ignition."

"I didn't ask you that. I asked if you loved me."

"Shoot... course I do, Annabelle."

But as he said so, I wondered whether he really knew how to love. In Walt's eyes lived a look plain to see that fancied I'd hung the moon. But what was it he loved? Me, whoever that was? Or was it the me he saw behind his eyes, or felt with his tallywags? Other than when he'd beset his randiness on me, his attention was mostly elsewhere, leaving me to abide with scarce admiration.

He searched my eyes for what I might say next, and then asked, "Do you love me?"

"I'm trying to figure that out."

He smirked, turned back to the TV, and said, "Let me know when you come up with the answer."

"You'll be the first to know," I said, and left it at that for now.

Thinking I'd maybe hurt his feelings, or let him down, I curled up next to him on the bed. We watched the tail end of the game show and said nothing more. It appeared that my question, and my lame answer to his, had brought us to a stage where there was now a curtain up between us—a curtain that if we took down would reveal either what we wanted to see, or what we did not. It felt best to leave it up for now, until it lowered on its own, or one of us tore it away.

I allowed that much of what Walt said was what he'd say in order to get what he wanted. That was his game and he was good at it. Even though he told me he loved me, something just didn't quite ring true. And right then and there, for me to say I loved him echoed clunky inside me, like a loose string on a banjo.

The last few days with him had doled out comfort and excitement all at once—most of the time. But was he the man for me? Was I really the woman for him? I'd opened my satchel to Walt, but would he be open to the needments of my heart? We'd quickly learned to give and take our pleasures, but could we learn the give and take of love that lasts?

I'd thought I had a notion of what love was, yet now looking love in the face, I blinked. Trying to make out the blurry haunt of all I'd heard tell of love, the more I squinted to bring it into focus, the more I saw it wore my own face.

When the goofy music played at the end of his game show, Walt jumped into his pants, saying, "Let's go get some breakfast."

Within minutes, we were at Riley's Restaurant again in the middle of the noon rush. Again, the hungry gaze of many of the men followed me as we walked to stools at the lunch counter. But this time, Walt fended them off with a look that turned their eyes away. Being protected like that felt long overdue.

Walt ordered his bacon-and-egg sandwich and coffee, and I, a ham sandwich and coffee. After the food was set in front of us, a handsome feller in a gray pin-stripe suit sat down on the stool to my left. Reaching for a menu, he flashed me a warm smile and nodded his respects to Walt. While chewing my sandwich and sipping coffee, I studied at him from the corner of my eye. His face carried a favorance to a young Cary Grant in the old movies on TV—a sturdy forehead over eyebrows gently urging nut-brown eyes, a straight nose and trim lips, and a square jaw with a cleft like a baby's bottom.

Half an eyeful of him, and then and there, alakazam, a lusty tizzy took away my breath and throbbed through me. As he looked over the menu, I peeked at the back of his hand—the fine curly hairs on his tan skin, his clean-cut fingernails, a gold wristwatch ticking at the hem of starched white cuffs.

"What's good here?" he asked us, his voice low and musical, his accent out-of-state.

I shrugged and said, "The ham sandwich's fine by me."

Walt said, "Don't get set on no breakfast. They got banker's hours on that."

"I'm a banker," he said with an easy chuckle. "And I've always wondered about that saying. I work my eight hours or more, five days a week, sometimes six, just like everyone else."

Walt said, "Buddy, I don't make 'em up. I just say 'em."

I offered, "Maybe it's because a bank's only open from ten till three?"

"I suppose," he said, showing a killer smile. "What do you two do to keep the wolf away?"

I shot Walt a glance. After swallowing a chew of egg, he said, "We keep carnival hours. Four to eleven, Monday to Friday, eleven to eleven on Saturday. Then most of Sunday jumpin' to the next spot and settin' up.... And we are the wolves."

That dropped the banker's jaw a jig, before he asked, "How's business?"

"Well," Walt told him—pausing to take a bite of a wedge of toast, and chewing while saying—"Yesterday was a washout. And today the sun's breakin' through the clouds. I'll let you know how it is after Saturday night."

I said to the banker, "You don't sound like you're from around these parts."

"No, I live in Philadelphia. My bank sent me down here to scout out some local banks for acquisition."

Walt cracked, "So you're a bank robber."

"Well, you might say that," he said, again with his easy chuckle. "Only instead of guns, we use stocks and bonds."

"I'd bet an ink pen's robbed more men than any pistol ever did."

Walt's wisecrack put a chill on more talk. The banker ordered a steak plate—from the expensive side of the menu—and turned his attention to some papers he pulled from his suit-jacket pocket. My ham sandwich went dry in my mouth as I sat there trying to appear normal, yet gone all a-twitter like some skittish wallflower at a barn dance, suffering one powerful craving for this banker feller.

Whatever had taken ahold of me, made no sense at all. He was thirty-five or more, and wore a wedding ring. Right next to me sat Walt, who less than an hour ago I'd asked if he loved me—and I might also mention had eagerly corresponded with the whole night long. Whatever had come over me, I sat there wanting to get shut of it, but couldn't. And it spun me as confused as a termite in a yo-yo.

With as much an eye for comely menfolk as any gal, I'd known myself to take a long-distance fancy to a blade or two back in Clandel, even though they were spoken for. But there on that stool, knowing only sidelong glances and the sound of his voice, how could I be in such a red-combed swoon? It bewildered me so mightily I feared it, and him. I labored through the rest of my sandwich, clumsily picked at the potato chips, and sipped trembly coffee.

Walt eyed me curiously. I sensed he had a notion about my fluster—a hot blush in my cheekbones no doubt plain to be seen. I lifted a difficult smile to him, and whispered, "I'm off for the girl's room."

He shrugged as he swiped at the yolk and grease on his plate with the last corner of his toast.

When I turned the doorknob of the restroom, I spied back at them. Walt's gaze was on his coffee mug, but the banker's eyes were on me. I hurried inside, locked the door, and leaned into the mirror. My color up and my eyes jumpy, I ran cold water and scooped some onto my face. The paper-towel dispenser rattled empty, so I had to use toilet paper to dry my face—which left tiny rolled-up balls of it salting my freckles. I picked them off, one by one, grateful for something to do while hoping to calm down.

I hunted for some reason why I'd gotten so worked up over this stranger. Was this point-blank love at first sight? Maybe like what had done Walt in with me? Did it have something to do with the woman I'd felt I'd become? What if my opening up to Walt had switched on the woman in me, and now I was plainly in heat—another pruney sorry-girl loose upon the world, diddling one feller all night and all morning, and hankering for another by lunch.

What did that have to say about my so-called love for Walt? If I loved him, why was my satchel now slippery just thinking about that banker? And if I loved Walt, why couldn't I tell him so? For a fact, I had little notion what love really was.

Even so, I couldn't hide in the privy much longer. An impatient knock at the door hurried me out. Walt wasn't on his stool, but the banker was. Swivety as a one-eyed cat watching two rat holes, I took my seat, wanting no more of the remains of my lunch.

While I squirmed on the stool, hunting for where Walt went, the banker flipped slowly through his papers. His lunch came—French fries and snap beans stacked beside a charred and bloody slab of steak. He pocketed the papers back inside his jacket, took up his napkin, knife and fork, and leaning to me, said, "When I get done today, I might come out to your carnival and see what's going on. Where's it set up?"

"A few miles south of town," I told him. Fumbling for what to say next, I said, shocked that I did, "My name's Annabelle Cory. What's yours?"

"Richard, Annabelle. Richard Lee."

"Right pleased to make your acquaintance," I said, and managed with a mannerable smile to reach out for the handshake he offered. When he took my hand in his, electricity sizzled through me straight to my middle. Before letting go, I gave his warm fingers an extra little squeeze, and he returned the same.

Out of the corner of my eye, I caught sight of Walt coming out of the men's room, witnessing me mooning at Richard Lee. I swiveled on the stool toward Walt as he walked up.

"I had to take a quick dump," he muttered. "Let's pay up and get out of here."

On our way out, I couldn't bring myself to look back and see if Richard Lee had his eyes on me or not, though I was powerfully keen to. If I had, Walt would've seen it, plain as day.

But that didn't matter none. Walt had seen all he needed to, and hurrying us down the sidewalk, he snarled, "Next you gonna fuck that banker?"

I stopped dead in my tracks. "Say what?"

He spun around and said, "You think I'm blind? You'd like that banker to make a deposit."

"I would no such thing!"

"Baby, you can't flimflam a flimflammer."

I glared up into his face, more angry over his seeing right through me, than over his crack about fucking the banker. And angry all the more at myself for mooning at Richard Lee in the first place—doing Walt wrong, if only in my mind.

Even so, I lashed out at him, as if in self-defense, but really to hide the truth. "You think you know it all. You don't know a thing about me. I'm just some pretty thing for your damn doodle to diddle. You're more interested in those stupid TV game shows than in me."

He leaned into my face, eyes mad as fire and quivering with sore disappointment. I'd seen him beef a man with a hammer, and I feared he'd set in on me with his fists. He hissed, "Don't do this to me."

"Do what?"

"Turn it around on me."

He'd caught me there. Flummoxed, I spun on my heels and stomped away, leaving him standing flat-footed. I looked back once to see if he followed, but his back was already to me, marching off in the direction of the motel. My stride shortened, my legs heavy with dread. After a block or two,

I sat on a wall by a parking lot, and ran my fingers through my hair, trying to ease my heartbeat.

I'd stirred up hell with a long spoon—Old Scratch nigh to get his due. Walt was right. And my getting all huffy and put out about it was dead wrong. I'd set myself out on the street. But how could I own up that my twitchet had twitched for another man—a riddle to me why, without rhyme or reason. Walt surely cared for me, tolerable enough, in his own manner. For sure I held some druthers about his ways. But there was no call to chuck a polecat into his face.

I had to arsle out of this hardness, tell it on myself, smooth Walt's hackles—and the only way for that led back to the motel room. But I figured it might go easier if I let things cool down some before I showed my face. By then, Walt might even have an apology ready and waiting for me.

I hopped off the wall and bogued around town from sidewalk to sidewalk. When I found myself in front of the Stuart Public Library—a newer brick building with plate glass along both sides of the corner entrance—I went on in, and poked through the shelves of books.

It came to me that maybe I could use some schooling about love, and that there might be some book here that might ease my tortures. So I went to the card catalog, and under 'love', found a title—*The Art of Loving*. I hunted up the thin little book and sat down with it in the sunlight by the plate glass.

A couple hours later I'd read that love was not only something that you get, it's much more about what you give. It's not something that happens to you, it's what you do. And like anything else you do, you learn how to do it, like an art.

The book said that love isn't easy. It's tortured by difficulties and failures. Many will fall in love—escape from loneliness and go hogwild for a spell—and some will learn to love, through union with another. It also said that most of us usually fall in love with who we want our lover to be—we see what we want to see, which is what we project from ourselves onto the other. Yet when the masks come off at the costume ball, for love's dance to go on, our partners must be taken as-is, not as we need them to be.

But what spoke to me the loudest was the notion that since there hadn't been much love between Maw and Pap, then maybe I'd had poor schooling in it. Could it be that I didn't know how to love?

The Bible tells us to love others as you would yourself. So for the golden rule to shine, first you have to love yourself. Yet truth be told, I wasn't all that fond of whoever I was.

And on top of all this, *The Art of Loving* said that you not only had to learn how to love, you had to learn how to be lovable.

It all appeared such a chore, taking the wind from the sails of romance. After my studying on it, I was not only more bewildered, I felt plumb unfit for love.

Now near three o'clock, we had to open the joints at four. I couldn't borrow the book because I didn't have a library card. I thought of stealing it, but that went against the honesty of what I'd just read. So I returned it to its shelf, hurried out of the library, and traipsed back to the motel.

When I got to the room, the door was locked, and Walt didn't answer my rapping. His car was in the parking lot, so I knocked on Cheek's door. Half his chuffy face peeked out through a gap in the drapes, and he let me in. Walt was there with George and Diane, toking up before work. Two joints burning at once, the sweet-smelling smoke floated thick as mountain mist.

Walt eyed me with a look that asked—where the hell have you been?

I sat next to him on the chest of drawers, and Diane passed me the last half-inch of one of the joints. As I sucked in a horse dose of it, I got the feeling that maybe I'd interrupted them talking about me. Outside the door, I'd heard their antic voices, but now that I was in the room, their manner had gone clumsy. Walt sat stone silent, grim as an undertaker.

Diane, sweet enough to try to break the mood, asked, "So how's it goin' for you, Annabelle?"

I breathed out a cloud of smoke, passed the roach back to her, and coughed, "Great." She waited for more from me, but I had none.

She said to George, "We best get over to the lot and put the fire to the fat." George nodded agreement and they got up to go. I asked Walt for the room key and followed them out the door.

At the mirror in the bathroom, fussing with my hair, there I was, not far from home, but may as well be, with only a few dollars and maybe less sense, and likely about to set into a cuss fight with Walt. I'd wrapped myself into this yopped-up budget and only I could undo it. The only clue I had how, I'd found in that library book—I had to give love to get love.

Walt pounded hard at the door and I hurried to let him in. He slumped onto one of the chairs at the table as I eased onto the other. His chin tucked into his neck, he eyed me sidelong, and asked, "So did you fuck him?"

"What? Hell no!"

"So where you been for two damn hours?"

"I walked around town some, then went into the library and read a book."

"Read a book?... What book?"

"A book about love."

"And what did it tell you?"

"It said that love is what you give."

"Ain't that what you told me that first morning back in Clandel?"

"Yeah.... but now I see better that you don't just fall in love, and that's that. We've got to work at it to make it happen. I'd been led to believe that love would come to me like magic. A knight in shining armor rides up, rescues me from the dragon, carries me off to his kingdom, and we live happily ever after."

"So you figured that'd be me? And it ain't goin' like that for you?"

"I don't know what I was figuring. I was just doing what came next."

"So now what comes next?"

"Give me a couple of days, Walt... to figure it out."

We went silent for a spell, staring at our knees. Then he told me, "Annabelle, I want you to know. I may not be the most romantic pickle in the barrel, but I wasn't workin' any alibis when I said this mornin' that I love you."

"I didn't think you were."

"And baby, I ain't fool enough to not know that right now you can't say as much for me."

"Walt, honey, I'm one step off the train out here. I absquatulate from all I know, and here I am—as misput as a goose in a henhouse. You need to give me some time to sit on this egg and see what hatches. This is your world I'm in now."

"That I can do, Belle. That I can do." And with that he got up and went into the bathroom, adding sullenly, "Four o'clock call. We best get our keisters out there."

On the way out to the lot—the Mercury wheeling past pour-offs from yesterday's rain while scraps of misty clouds clung to the hillsides—I asked him, "Walt, when you say you love me, what do you mean?'

"What do I mean? What do you mean, what do I mean?"

"I mean... what are you feeling when you love me?"

"I'm on top of the world, Belle. When I look at you, I see the most beautiful gal on earth. When I'm sittin' here beside you, I'm damn glad of it. When I'm fuckin' you raw, I enter a time zone where the clocks don't tick. When I saw you eyein' that banker, my guts fell into a donniker hole. When you didn't show at the room for two hours, I was fit to kill. After our parley, a rainbow's come across the sky again."

As we rolled onto the lot, rocking over the ruts, I wondered why didn't I feel like he did. Doubtless, he was more in love with me than I was with him. What had I done for him to love me so? He hardly knew me. What was it he'd fallen in love with? My good looks? My randy and ready satchel?

That library book studied on different sorts of love. And it plainly appeared that Walt suffered from a pure-quill case of love at first sight. But what was the case with me? Maybe what with and all the love lost between Pap and Maw, I was unable to do what I've never been shown. The book said I could learn to love him—learn to love myself better, and everybody else, to boot. All that sounded hunky-dory when I'd read it, but so did lots of other things that then would never happen. One thing made sense enough, though—for love to live, I've got to give it as well as get it.

The lot was still a sobby sponge behind the joints, and out along the midway a barnful of hay had been spread over the muck. Up by the front gate where some low spots held water—one puddle nearly a duck pond—a dump truck slid off its load of sawdust and three ride boys with rakes muscled the mix about. Nick already had the awnings up at the joint trailer. Bending over with one hand atop the counter, a wet rag in the other, he swiped mud off the bally cloth.

I hopped into the pitch-till-u-win and straightened things up somewhat. Soon the Merry-Go-Round piped up its waltz and the rides roared to life, screeching with damp grease. Then nothing much happened for the next couple of hours—just Fred's eyes augering into me, and a kid now and then with a quarter or two.

Half the reason I'd left out with this carnival was to make some powerful cash money to go over the mountain with. After three days of it, I had not much more in my poke than if I had worked half as many hours at the diner. And so far, this night didn't look any too promising either. I hollered and hollered, "Pitch till you win. Prize every time. Pitch till you win. Prize every time...." again and again and again. I tried the rhymes I'd made up. I waved folks over to me as they walked past. Yet only one or two, from time to time, fetched up to my counter to swap their money for hoops.

Walt and J.D. appeared to be competing with each other, hungrily bedeviling the scattered crowd. One or the other of them would lay it on so thick to anybody ambling by, you'd think it was the most important thing on earth to toss balls in a basket.

Walt's manner was more personable than J.D.'s. He'd charm a plain Jane in under the awning with a compliment, or bait a young buck with a challenge. He played on who the marks were, or wanted to be, and he used that to get a ball in their hands.

"Say young feller, I'd guess you got a knack with a ball game. You look like maybe an infielder, or maybe a pitcher. Well this here's a game of skill for the skillful. The rules aren't complicated, so I'm gonna spell it out to you for free, along with plenty practice shots till you're good to go for the big prize. I bet you know some pretty girl that'll give you some huggin' when you hand her over one of these stuffed bears. Just come over here for a looksee, and I'll show you how it's done. "

Or—"Young lady... 'scuse me. I see your man is elsewhere tonight. May I interest you in a complimentary trial demonstration on how to win a fuzzy prize? But watch out, 'cause when you bring it home tonight he's gonna ask who won that for you. You tell him you won it by yourself. But don't say I showed you how. And I'm gonna show you how for free, no fee. Free practice shots, on me. Don't walk by. Try before you buy a try. Kindly step right up and have a ball."

J.D. though, would plumb order them to hand over their money. He'd use the brute force of his insistent voice to bulldog the sheep to their fleecing.

"Hey buddy! Yeah, you. Come over here. Hey, don't just walk away. I'm talkin' to you. That's right—you! Come over here. I'm not gonna bite. Come here. Hey!—why are you here if you're not gonna take a chance on somethin'? Either come over here now and play the game or you might as well turn around and go on home. Wait! Didn't you hear me? It's you I'm talkin' to. Where's your manners? Am I just wastin' my breath on you? Come here and get your free shot. I'll give you a free lesson on how it's done, so what's to lose? No money for a practice shot at this easy toss-the-softball game. How can you go wrong with that? Didn't your daddy tell you to get it where you can? Well here's where you get it. Get on over here afore I have to go out there and get you!"

Then J.D., or Walt, would give a ball-tossing lesson. I'd watch out of the corner of my eye as they'd work the cop ball, as Walt called it, in and out of the basket—a ball they tossed in during their demonstration that, when left in, the mark's shot would glance off of, and not bounce out off the bottom slats. But when money was passed over the counter there'd be no cop ball in the basket, and the shot would shoot back out like the basket had springs in it.

Everybody knew these games were rigged. The hoops on the pitch-till-u-win, plain as day, just barely fit around the big blocks with the big prizes. Yet its rules made simple sense—big prizes on big blocks are hard to get and little prizes on little blocks are easy to get. If the big prizes were easy to win, what would be the fun, the challenge, the excitement?

But I felt unease about how Walt's basket joint was rigged. It wasn't out in the open for all to see. Folks were bamboozled into thinking it wasn't all that hard to do. Their free practice shots would stay in the basket because of the cop balls, but those for the money would not. A plain and simple sandy got run on folks, to lead them in and lead them on. They didn't know how they were being swapped off, but they shortly found out that they were.

I wondered whether I could ever run such a game. And I wondered what sort of person Walt really was to be able to. J.D. was no puzzle—a petty thief and damn proud of it. Walt appeared to have more to him than that. I just couldn't reckon what.

Around sundown—the lights pulsing in the eveglom and the crowd growing—J.D. worked a mark up to five dollars a shot. "Chunk one in there like you just done, and you win the big green shaggy dog, plus forty dollars cash. That's more than all your money back, plus the big prize. Just five more'll do it."

The mark—a young feller, poor as a fence rail, wearing droopy mechanic's overalls smutched with crankcase drippings—he squirmed on J.D.'s hook, and sullenly fished a five-dollar bill out of his poke. With oil-stained fingers, he fondled the softball, tossed it gingerly, and it bounced off the basket's rim, plunked in, and stayed in!

The boy threw both hands in the air and let out a Kentucky yell.

But J.D. leaned into his face, pointed at a small sign on the back wall, and told him, "Sorry son, the sign says, 'Rim Shots Do Over.'"

He squinted at the sign, and then at J.D., and asked, "What in tarnation does that mean, mister?"

"It means the rules say that when a ball hits the rim of the basket, it's no good. You gotta take the shot over."

"You never said nothin' 'bout no rim shots."

"I reckoned you could read, son. And there's the sign right up there on the wall in front of your face, plain as day."

The mark peered at the sign again, and then he gave J.D. a look that said, 'I should've expected as much from the likes of you.' And, of course, his do-over shot bounced right on out.

Muttering, "Fuck you, mister," he kicked at the muddy straw and stormed off with shoulders hunched and hands shoved into his front pockets.

J.D. yelled to him, "If that be your druthers, it'll cost you twenty-five-times-five for a shot at the rim of my puckered-up asshole. My virtue don't come cheap." At that, he and Walt had a short chuckle, before they went back to calling in more passers-by.

The rim shot sign did hang in plain sight. And I'd seen Walt and J.D. make players redo shots that had hit the rim but not gone into the basket. But the rule, the alibi, was really there for when a ball would hit the rim, ricochet away from the springy slats, and stay in. Especially when the mark was about to win big.

Another alibi, used when needed, was the foul-line rule. A strip of duct tape ran across the top of their counter with the words 'No Leaning Over Foul-Line' written across it in red marker. Every once in a while, Walt or J.D. would caution a player about the foul line, telling them that their hand can't be past the line when they toss the ball. Yet from my sidelong angle, I witnessed nigh-on every shot being flung from hands that were well past the foul line—often even half a body leaning over it. But Walt and J.D. wouldn't call the rule on them then. The rule was there for when they needed it. In an alibi joint, when a mark made a winning shot, he heard an alibi about why he hadn't won.

Sure enough, the rules of the game were the rules of the game. And as every carny would tell you, they weren't out there on that midway to lose. But it didn't set right that Walt used those rules to take advantage of folks, after hoodwinking them into thinking that the game was easy by baiting them with the cop ball.

Walt didn't appear to have any problem with it. The herd on the midway was there to be fleeced and it was his duty to do so. Carnies stood on one side of the equation and townies on the other, which added up to a license to green folks out. It was only a job, like any other. Only a game. Everybody out to win, playing by the rules.

My pitch-till-u-win game, swapping off quarter-dollars for two-cent prizes, was also fixed to beat the marks. But there they were, leaning over the counter, right next to the 'No Leaning' sign, tossing hoops with hopes of beating me at my own game, their eyes on the prize—the greedy look in many an eye turning ashy when I'd hand them their plastic whistle.

If they wouldn't try to beat the game, then the game couldn't beat them. Beat them before they beat you—was that the way to win in this world? Do it unto others before they do it unto you?

In the book I'd read that afternoon, its golden rule was that before you could really love another, you had to love everybody, as well as yourself. Yet there was Walt, saying he loved me, while sticking it to whoever walked past his counter.

I'd plainly swapped one set of rules for another. Back in Clandel, the mine owners had the government in their pockets, robbing the land and the people under the rules of that particular game, promising a living, but doling out slow death from black lung and poverty. Bible-thumping preachers promised heaven, but delivered guilt. Politicians promised folks protection, but sent their boys to die in Vietnam. Televisions sold things to make lives easier, but folks struggled lifelong to pay for it. Banks loaned them money to buy homes, and then bled them dry with interest.

The diner I'd worked in fried up an egg worth less than a nickel, charged a dollar-twenty-five for it on a plate with a three-cent slice of toast, and paid me as little as they could get away with to fetch it up. Everything had a price— which mostly was however much as one could profit for one-self. And if you didn't play that game, you'd lose. You'd end up with little to eat yourself. This was the God-almighty ever-loving world, and you'd best play by its rules.

I didn't know if I could play this hoop-toss game for long, but I did know I'd need much more cash money to get where I was going, wherever that was. And the only option I had right then was to holler more of, "Pitch till you win. Prize every time."—again and again and again—and holding my palm out again, to ask, "Try again?"

The Wednesday-night crowd thickened as the sky darkened. I chanted my ballyhoo, collected quarters, made change, and passed out slum. All of a sudden, I got so busy that I lost track of who had paid and who had not, and it was all I could do to grab the money, gather up more hoops from the cloth under the blocks, heap them onto the counter, and ask loudly who had rung that plastic spider or that tin badge.

Most would ignore a hoop of theirs that had landed around a small block. They'd just keep on tossing at the cash on the big blocks until I stopped them, gave them their gimcrack, and asked them for another quar-ter. Many would not fess up that it was their hoop around the small block.

I'd seen it land there, and seen that they'd seen it, and still they would tell me that it wasn't theirs. Maybe the carnies were right—if you don't try to beat them, they'll try to beat you.

Hoops clicked and clacked on the blocks, while the hullabaloo out past my counter spun into a throbbing jangle of hubbub—voices shrieking and laughing and shouting and jowering—rides roaring and rattling amid clashing rock-and-roll tapes—colory lights flickering in the crowd's bedazzled eyes.

The crowd that night swarmed with darker faces. The first-of-the-month checks had been cashed, the bills paid, and now there was some money in pockets that the rest of the month saw little of. Waves of black families pressed up to my counter—big-butt mamas bumping the whites aside, their nappy kids weaving around legs and clustering up front, wide eyes not much higher than the counter, their fingers gathering hoops long before I could talk any money away from their folks.

Vexed whites would cock an eye, uneasily finish their games, and walk off with their teeth on edge. Then the black kids would take over the whole counter, ranging back and forth to point out the prizes they'd aim for, bragging at their brothers and sisters about what they were about to win. They'd take deliberate aim, toss with follow-throughs of body English, and stamp their feet when the hoops bounced off their targets. Their kin watched over them with hoots and chuckles, and easily handed me quarters for more kids to play, and often a quarter or two for a try at it themselves.

For a fact, they all had a heap sight more fun playing pitch-till-u-win than the white folks did. Most whites, young and old, appeared to toss hoops from a lack of anything else better to do. They'd measure their chances, and the money in their pockets, and then take in pitching as if they expected to lose. When I'd hand them a rubber spider, they'd squint at it, grunt, stuff it in their pocket, and walk off. But the black kids went at hoop tossing like it was the best thing that's happened to them so far this year—which maybe it was. When they'd win their gewgaw, they'd scowl with sore disappointment for a moment, and then show it to their kin for all to laugh out loud at.

Over on the other side of the trailer, J.D. ran a different joint. He muttered in my direction, more than twice, bigoted cracks about "these goddamn jigs." When they came up before him and asked, with money in hand, what his game was, J.D. would just look past them and say nothing.

Walt on the other hand, worked the blacks just as hard as he did the whites. His game was to treat them with respect, which at that time and place would be quite a surprise to some. He'd call them 'ma'am' and 'sir', and the younger ones, 'man' and 'girl', and he never called a boy, 'boy'. He'd suck up to the young bucks, steer them to bragging, tell them they were the greatest. But J.D., he just shook his head, stewed in his hateful notions, and appeared to wish he was in another country.

Not long after nine o'clock, when the action was at its peak, I spotted Dwayne, the feller Walt had hammered, standing over on the other side of the midway by the pipe rail in front of the Tilt-A-Whirl. With him was a trio of ridge runners—big mean-looking boys. Dwayne wore a white bandage taped on the side of his head, partially under a lop-sided feed cap. Under its visor, his eyes squeezed out a vicious stare at Walt.

I found a pencil and a scrap of paper and scribbled, 'The boy you hammered is standing over by the Tilt-A-Whirl giving you the evil eye.' I smuggled the note over to Walt, and he just shrugged, saying, "Yeah, I seen him."

Walt didn't appear concerned, but I surely was. I knew these hillbillies. Once they took in feuding they wouldn't quit until they gained some satisfaction. No matter if the law was in on it or not. It was personal—to be settled by them and their own.

The four of them eyed Walt from there for a quarter-hour, until the ride jockey from the Tilt-A-Whirl—the one who had charged at Dwayne and his knife the other night—swaggered over in front of them and stood, arms crossed on his barrel chest, staring them down. They shuffled off down the midway and glowered back at us over their shoulders.

I didn't like the looks of this. It rattled me so, the whole rest of the night I kept on the lookout for them, sure they'd return.

Once again, the crowd petered out after ten o'clock. My apron bulged with paper money and sagged with the weight of a pint of coins. Nick came over and counted up a hundred-and-ten dollars, and I still had the coins and a wad of dollar bills to add in. I told him I had to pee.

"You go ahead. I'll watch the joint. Take a little break. Get yourself somethin' to eat. You're doin' right fine, young lady. You're one money snatchin' hanky-panker."

Surprised and pleased by the warm smile he granted me, I thanked him for the praise, handed him my apron, and jumped out of the joint.

After visiting the donniker—under which the tub now brimmed with a loud soup—I cut back out on the midway between some shows at the back end, and found myself in front of a tent, maybe twenty-foot square, which I hadn't much noticed before. A long narrow banner strung corner to corner across the front read:

INSIDE! ~ THE WILD MAN OF BORNEO ~ ALIVE!

Nearby, a group of black teens goaded one another to buy a ticket. I heard one say, "That crazy nigger in there be eatin' a frog live and kickin'."

My curiosity sparked, I paid a quarter to a brown-skinned woman with a year-old baby in her arms. I'd seen her and the baby before at the cookhouse, sitting with a darker feller with a big bush of frizzy hair.

Inside the tent, a dozen people stood around a plywood pen, four-foot high and eight square. In a corner crouched the feller with the bush of frizzy hair, wearing a grimy red union suit and a silly pair of checkered Bermuda shorts, and around his neck was a leather collar padlocked to a chain staked down at the middle of the straw-strewn pen. He, by turns, cringed and snarled at the faces above him—his face smudged with what appeared to be blood, but more likely was ketchup. Once he scrambled snarling on all fours toward a woman across the pen, causing her to scream and back off. But the length of chain kept her out of reach of his benastied fingers.

Several more folks straggled in as we stood elbow-to-elbow around the pen, watching this Wild Man from Borneo hate us with his evil eye and savage scowl. After a stretch of that, the woman who sold admission out front came into the tent with one arm around the baby on her hip, and in her other hand she had a frog, a good-sized swamp frog, four inches nose to hind end. She flipped it into the middle of the pen, and without a word went back outside.

The Wild Man pounced on the frog, snatched it up, and popped it into his mouth—the whole frog, headfirst, save its feet flapping between The Wild Man's gap-teeth.

Everybody took another guess on that. Some simply stared, wide-eyed and drop-jawed. Others shrieked or laughed out loud. I tried to cough up a gasp in my throat, which instead plunged to my belly when he gulped the frog straight down his goozle.

Snaggle-toothed and bug-eyed, The Wild Man opened his mouth wide and hopped around the pen for all to see. The frog was gone! He'd swallowed it whole and kicking, which sent a horror across the flabbergasted faces circling the pen. A blonde woman, her bouffant swagging side to side, rushed out of the tent, a hand clasped to her mouth. Next to me, a pair of black girls doubled over with squeals of laughter. Other folks, with sickly frowns and dropped jaws, stared in dumfounded disbelief.

Then after a few minutes of this, The Wild Man squatted in the middle of the pen, pinched his eyes shut, and as he slowly opened them cross-eyed, out popped the frog's face between his puckered-up lips! The frog, that a moment before was swimming in stomach juices, blinked its eyes at the crowd.

A storm of shrieks, groans, and laughs, swept through the thunderstruck spectators, as the wild-eyed savage took in tearing about the pen like a franzied chimp, tossing straw in the air, frog dangling and kicking, clenched in his teeth by one leg.

And then, for the grand finale, he squatted in the middle of the pen, snatched the frog from his mouth, stretched it out like a corncob, and with a bloodthirsty sneer, sunk his snaggly teeth into the frog's guts!

After a stunned silence, this raised the biggest ruckus yet. The black gals next to me shrieked out belly laughs—the tears rolling down on one, the other hiccupping as she held her sides and staggered about. Some folks appeared queasy—grimacing under squinty eyes and pale cheeks, trembly hands clutched to mouths or stomachs. Other folks, including me, just stared blankly.

Snarling through his scattered teeth, The Wild Man of Borneo tore into the vitals of the frog, ripping them from the kicking carcass. Leaping about at the end of his chain, with innards trailing down his chin, he swung in one hand the gory carcass overhead. And then the lights in the tent cut out.

Several women screamed bloody murder. Waving a flashlight at the entrance, the woman with the baby on her hip hollered, "Show's over, folks. This way out." We all jostled out of the tent, escaping the gobbling sounds behind us in the dark.

Back out on the midway, staggering past Sonny McCain eating fire up on his stage in front of a spattering of onlookers, I calculated that with not more than twenty people in The Wild Man's tent, at a quarter apiece—then that feller had eaten a live frog for less than five dollars. And that had to be his wife, with their baby in her arms, collecting the quarters and tossing him frogs. What a way to feed a family.

Up ahead, Trudy and Janet shimmied their stuff out in front of The Harem while a gaggle of men gawked up at them—Danny's nasally spiel pimping it all through a tinny bullhorn. Who were these carnies? How could they do such things, day-after-day, week-to-week? Would I become one of them? Could I become one of them? Was I one of them already?

Where was my place in the world? Who were my people? Becoming a hustling hanky-panker for Nickel Nick promised nothing much to write home about. My being Walt's woman was likely just another game of his. New York City was as far away as ever. And what if, when and if I get there, I find the same?—myself, lost at life's starting line, with naught to offer, save my good looks.

I scuffed once around the midway through the mud-stained straw and sawdust, and hopped back into the pitch-till-u-win. Business was so slow, Nick wasn't even there.

Walt eyed my hangdog look, and asked, "You alright, Annabelle?"

"I just saw that feller eat a frog."

"Lionel's one glommin' geek, ain't he?"

"Glommin' geek?"

"He gloms frogs like they were buttered biscuits."

"Walt, how can a man with a wife and baby provide for his family by eating frogs?"

"People pay to see it."

"But how did he choose to do that? How could he? How could she?"

"You'd have to ask him about that. Everyone's got their tale about how they took up with it. Some'll tell you. Some won't. I guess Lionel digs geekin'. Geeks usually bite the heads off chickens and drink the blood. Lionel must like eatin' frogs better. They're cheaper than chickens."

I huffed, "I reckon there's a heap sight of other things a man can do to earn a living."

"Belle, I'm gonna also guess, that for a gap-toothed jig in the U.S.A., his opportunities are limited. Lionel pulls a nice house trailer down the road with a fairly new Buick. And I don't doubt he wins more money out here than most do. Get past the taste of frog guts, and the hardest thing about the joint would be findin' enough frogs to eat.

"Lionel's got himself a reputation as one top-of-the-line regurgitator. How much worse is that compared to some sucker job as a janitor cleanin' up white people's donnikers? Or heavin' their swill into a garbage truck? Lionel runs his own show. And there ain't many his color who can say that."

I said, "Even I can't say that."

"Annabelle... baby, you've been out here only four days. What're you expectin' to happen?"

"I don't know, Walt. I'm sorely lacking a clue."

"You hang in there. You hang in there."

I hung out in the pitch-till-u-win, until Nick counted us up and shut it down. My end for the night came to thirty-four dollars. That was near as much as I would make in a week at the diner. Maybe the clue I lacked was just some patience.

Walt said, "I hear tell the gypsies are barbecuing ribs tonight. Follow me."

He took my hand and led me out back to a battered green house trailer at the edge of the camp. The ribcage of half a beef sizzled on a spit over a fire in a ring of stones, cranked lazily by a ten-year-old boy—firelight a-flutter over his dusky skin and straight black hair. Around the fire, staring into it, beers in hand, stood several carnies, ride boys and agents, some faces known to me. Others sat in groups on fold-up chairs, their voices tiny under the plumping moon and the swath of stars. A flamenco guitar, flighty and scratchy from a portable record player, kept time with the snap and crackle of flames licking beef fat.

Walt led me to a cooler by the trailer where a slight and swarthy feller squatted—thirtyish, in black jeans and a black leather jacket—pushing cans around through the ice.

"What's the privilege, Yanko?"

Yanko didn't look up. "Beers a buck. Ribs, rice, and stew, a fin."

Walt told him, "A pair of both," and counted twelve dollars off his fold of cash.

Yanko fished out a couple cans of three-two Budweiser, stood up quick as a cat, and made the swap. Adding Walt's bills to the wad in his silk shirt pocket, he said as he eyed me—his side glance with a cagey spark to it— "Ribs'll be ready soon."

The trailer door wide open, I saw two gypsy women by the stove, an older and a younger, cutting up vegetables and tossing them in a steamy stewpot. The older one stopped short her chopping, turned with a big knife in her gnarly hand, and met my gaze—the same gypsy I saw when the chihuahua came at me last Friday night. I curled a mannerable smile to her, but she just narrowed her eyes at me and shortly turned back to her chore. I hunted for the dog and spotted it prancing by the boy at the spit, it's bulgy eyes swiveling from meat to boy.

Walt lit a cigarette and I followed him to the fire crackling with barbecue. The ice-cold beer in my hand sent a chill to my shoulders, so I leaned into the raw heat alongside some ride boys and a couple of other agents—Hat from the basketball joint next door, Larry from Cheek's room, Shakey and Ed from the poker table. Walt took in yarning about his legal troubles, which I'd heard more than enough about already.

My front side toasty, I turned my tail to the fire and searched the faces on the chairs. Lula and Sonny were laughing it up with George, Diane, and an older couple I hadn't seen around. On a chair off by herself at the edge of the firelight, the geek's wife held her baby to her mother-naked bubby, an empty chair beside her. Several other circles of carnies sat around drinking, smoking, and joking—some faces familiar, some not.

Walking toward us, backlit by the light towers, a short man in a cowboy hat escorted a girl on his arm. As the fire's glow grew into their faces, I saw it was Madeline and her father. After they took care of business with Yanko and dragged some chairs over into a circle of older carnies, I left Walt retelling his tale, grabbed myself an empty chair, and set it next to Madeline.

"Hey, Annabelle. How's it goin'?"

"Oh... fair to middling."

"You ain't met my pa have you? Pa, this here's Annabelle. Annabelle, Tex."

Tex leaned forward off the chair an inch, tipped his Stetson with a finger, and said, "How do, Annabelle. Those ribs turnin' on that fire smell mighty tasty 'bout now. You fixin' to git you some, too?"

"Yes sir, I surely am."

"T'ain't nothin' like Gypsy ribs I know of. 'Cept maybe Fort Worth barbecue. But Fort Worth's quite a stretch away tonight. Gypsy ribs be fine by me."

"Yessiree. Truth be told."

Tex turned his attention to the talk around the circle—predictions about how Beckley, the next spot, ought to be. I leaned into Madeline's ear and whispered, "Have you ever been in love?"

She jerked her eyes in Tex's direction, then told him, "Pa, Annabelle and I are goin' to take a little walk, for some girl talk."

"That's fine, sweetheart. Don't be tardy for the ribs."

I guzzled down the rest of my beer, tossed the empty can into a cardboard box with a pile of others, and we strolled off into the woods. Moonlit barely enough to see, we found a newly fallen hickory trunk to sit on. Madeline fished a skinny joint out of her bra and fired it up—pulling long and hard on it, the weed crackling and the burning ash casting a glow onto her pursed-up face.

She passed it to me, and as she breathed out the smoke, said, "Yeah... Love. I reckon I've been in love, once or twice. But not quite enough, I guess. Or maybe not enough with someone man enough for me to take up with. Pa and me, we're a team. It's gonna take someone extra-special for me to swap what we got for I don't know what."

I sucked in a lungful and passed it back. The dope rushed into my eyes—the space deepening between the trees around us, their trunks appearing nearer and stouter among the jumble of shadows cast from the moon. Notes of laughter and guitar sang out above the murmur of voices from the gather-all, in tune with the low thrum of the diesel generator.

After our greedy pulls on the joint cooked it down to nothing in no time, I asked her, "What was it that made you believe you were in love?"

She thought on this for a piece, and then said, "Well, maybe because those beaus felt different than the others.... The one I was most tempted to take up with, Toby, he wasn't the sharpest knife in the drawer. Cute he was. Not drop-dead handsome like Walt. But there was somethin' that perked up his eyes when he gawked at me, that told me how he favored me so.

"He had barely two nickels to rub together. Ran a bust-one balloon joint on the Williams' show, where we were with them over in Ohio last summer. At a couple of spots, our joints got located across from each other. On the sly, I'd watch him. His face, hangdog much of the time. But when he'd eye me, it lit up like a kid's in front of a birthday cake.

"We snuck off, here and there, for a little kissy-face bump and grind. I didn't let him in me, but we got hot and sweaty never-you-mind.... He was kind to me, and gentle. And he made me laugh to high heaven.

"The last spot we played together, he asked me to go with him. I fretted over it mightily. But I had sense enough to count up that apron and see the foolishness of it.... Still, I wonder."

The trees in the silence felt of wonder, too. I asked, "What do you reckon love is?"

"Shoot, Annabelle. Just another fairy tale for all I know. I can't rightly tell. What's your take on it?"

"I used to think it was something that hit you like a bread wagon. And when it did you'd know it in a heartbeat. Like in the movies."

"Honey, movies are the biggest illusion show goin'."

"Yeah. Well, like in books."

"Books are as full of hokum as anything else. One book sayin' one thing. Another, another."

"I found a book in the library today that said real love wasn't something you fell into, it was something you learned to do. Like an art."

"There you go. One book says either, the next one, neither. And it's likely neither either, nor or. It's likely both. You fall in love—but then you learn more about loving, to make it last if it's good. That don't take no book to tell you."

"No... I don't allow it does. And no book's about to tell me whether or not I'm in love with Walt."

"What's your gut feel of that?"

"Bumfuzzlement. Part of me's hot as a red beet for him. Another me wants to get shut of his ways. One minute I'm all a-torture over him. The next, I'm sorely out of heart."

"Does he treat you right?'

"Yeah.... In his way."

"That's the way with menfolk. It's their way to do things their way. And with some, it's their way or the highway.... But I'll tell you what, girlfriend. Now I'm no Ann Landers, so what I'm about to say comes from someone who don't know much more than you do. It appears to me—and I see it when you two are side-by-side—that Walt is flat-out crazy about you. Plus, I see you leanin' toward him, more than away from him.

"Annabelle, you already hopped aboard this train. So what sense is there in jumpin' the tracks till you see where you're goin'?"

"I reckon so.... It just feels of cutting up a big hog with a little knife."

She chuckled and agreed, "That it is. That it is. And I bet those Gypsy ribs are soon comin' off the fire.... Annabelle, listen, I can't say whether this'd be good for you or not, but it's turned my head around for the better in some ways. Cheeks has some acid, and I'm hankerin' to get a taste of it."

"Acid?"

"Yeah. LSD."

"Doesn't that make you think you can fly? And jump out of buildings?"

"It gets you flyin', but I never seen nobody on it wantin' to jump out of no window."

"You've tried it?"

"A couple times. Trippin' ain't no walk in the park, girl. But where it took me was well worth the ticket."

"Where's that?"

"Oh.... I'd say it took me somewhere that gave me a different outlook, both outside myself and inside. And what I saw seems to have mollified some of the foolhardy contentiousness that used to plague me so."

"Madeline... I don't know."

"You give it some ponderin'. Let's go gnaw some ribs right now."

We stepped through the trees and back to the fire. A shyness came over me as we neared, as if we, or at least I, had been dis-invited to the gather-all by what we'd smoked in the woods. I fancied their eyes to be suspicious of me—though it was plain enough that they cared only about getting their fair share of the vittles.

The two gypsy women had set kettles out on a fold-up table, along with paper plates and napkins and plastic knives and forks. Yanko and the boy had the side of ribs strung up on a limb of a nearby tree, the boy holding the beef steady while Yanko knifed off chunks and tossed them into a wide wooden bowl.

I joined the line shuffling up to the table. Walt stood five or six ahead of me and waved for me to join him, but I shook him off, shy about cutting in front of anybody. At the table, I took my plastic fork and paper plate. One kettle held white rice, the other a chunky vegetable stew. Onto clumps of rice, we ladled ourselves portions of the stew, then chose our ribs from the wooden bowl.

By the time I got through the line, all the chairs were taken. Walt sat on one by Lula and Sonny—everyone's plates on their knees save Lula, who had no lap, and who ate with one hand, holding her plate with the other. I went over beside Walt and sat cross-legged on the ground. Leaning over my food, I took in at it hungrily. The vegetables tasted of a spice I didn't know, and the ribs were spare and tough, but saucy and peppery. Not much talk was heard as we all dug in. The fire hissed and crackled as the scratchy gypsy record plinked beneath the stars—the generator thrumming deep in the heart of the sleeping carnival.

Out of the corner of my eye, I watched Lionel, the geek, who joined his wife and child, and brought her a plate along with his. He teethed his ribs much like he did the frog, and my appetite dried up. Lula scoffed her heaped-up plate in no time, sucking her fingers after gnawing each rib to the bone. Sonny nibbled on his. Walt washed his food down with another can of beer.

Before long, one after another, we got up and dumped our soiled plates and gnawed bones into a cardboard box. Some voiced their compliments and appreciation, a few asked for seconds—Yanko getting more dollars for that—but most just tossed their trash and walked off.

Walt said to me, "Let's go over to the G-top. Get another beer. See what the action is."

I winced, and said charily, "I think I'll stay here for a spell."

Well-fed, still stoned, and at ease with the music and fire under the stars, more gambling was hardly my druthers right then.

"Suit yourself." He shrugged and strode off, appearing a mite misput.

"I'll do that," I muttered under my breath to his back.

Face aglow with heat, I stood alone by the fire as the Gypsy boy dragged dead branches from the edge of the woods, stomping on them to bust them up and tossing them into the crackly flames. I asked him what his name was, and he told me, "Pesha."

Yanko changed the record on the player to a livelier tune. Lula hauled up off her chair and shuffled her feet through the grass—her hands waving over her head, her bulk jigging to the jazzy guitar and fiddle. Sonny slapped his hands to the beat. Smiles and hoots rose all around. Yanko joined in the dance, stepping out a grim-faced fandango in circles around Lula. Lionel pulled his wife out of her chair, the baby in her arms, and jitterbugged in front of her while she bounced the baby. Tex let out a yeehaw and slapped a knee while stomping his boot in time. On the chair beside him, Madeline still gnawed at rib bones.

One of the better-looking ride boys took my hand, swung me into the middle of the dance, and took in clogging to his own drummer. The outlandish fiddle and guitar carried me off into a fancy of how a Gypsy girl might dance. I spun circles with prancing steps, arms weaving with the melody, face up to the moon, shaking my hair to the fiery music.

Yanko whirled his fandango over face-to-face with me, and I echoed his steps. Everyone else, now on their feet, closed in around us, clapping top the beat, egging us on, a-hooting and a-hollering. The tune finished up with a flourish, and so did Yanko, sweeping me back off my feet, dipping me low to the ground—to hearty applause.

I fell into a chair, out of breath, returning smiles to those flashed to me. When I spotted Walt at the edge of the firelight, his mouth and brow bent downward, I got up, still panting, and sashayed over to him.

"Havin' fun?" he muttered.

"Whew-eee.... One dance with a Gypsy about tuckered me out."

"Not much action at the G-top tonight. Let's head back to the motel." With nary a nod from me, he marched off in a snit, allowing I'd follow. I waved good-bye to no one in particular at the fire. Madeline, watching with a wary cast in her eyes, waggled some fingers back to me.

I scooted after Walt, but then heard her call, "Annabelle, wait a sec." She trotted up to me, and whispered, "I'll meet you at the motel in the mornin' around ten. If you don't want to trip, will you be with me while I do?"

"Sure I will."

"Okay. See you then."

I ran to catch up to Walt—who, quills up, hurried us off the lot, and we sped wordless into town.

By the time we got in the room, I was fit to kick the cat. He lit a cigarette, flipped on the TV, and flopped onto the bed. I tried to ignore both his mood and mine, and locked myself in the bathroom to ready myself for bed. When I came out, he just kept on glaring at Johnny Carson and some blatherskite movie star, and paid me never-no-mind while I plopped in a chair, stripped to my panties, and pulled on a T-shirt.

Finally I asked, "What sort of critter crawled up your surly hinder?"

His eyes shifted to mine, and he said, "The sort that's witnessed, twice in one day, you fetchin' up to another man."

"I've done no such thing!"

He turned back to the TV, growling, "So you say."

I sat there for a short piece, a heat to my boil. Then I jumped up, switched off the TV, and paced back and forth, wall to wall, telling him, "You listen to me, Walter Ryder. I allow that banker this morning did catch my eye—because he was one handsome feller to admire. But that was it. I had no notion about no fetching up to him. Lord sakes, he wore a wedding ring."

"So you had a look-see if there was gold on his finger. I wonder why you'd wonder that?"

"Because I'm a girl, and we notice those things."

"Well, I can also notice what you notice. I've a keen eye for it, 'cause I make my livin' seein' through faces. And baby, you had the pussy-drippin' bothers for that banker. Then you come back two hours later from the so-called library. Is that what you told your mama when you were off japin' some hillbilly boy?"

"I'm telling you, I was at the library... reading a book about love!"

"Oh, that's a good one—a book about love. And what did that book say? Dance like some kootch gash with the fuckin'est Gypsy in eight states?"

"I was just dancing! Folks were dancing. That ain't no sin in my book. And I know nothing about that Gypsy."

"If I hadn't come back, you would've."

"Walt.... Fuck you. I ain't taking no more of this shit. You're plumb wrong. I ain't done a thing wrong, and I'm telling you that for the last god-damn time. Now fuck off!"

He jumped up off the bed like he was coming at me—flinching, I side-stepped away—but he just reached to switch on the TV again, and flopped back onto the bed. I grabbed my jeans, yanked them on, shoved my bare feet into my boots, threw on my jacket, and stormed out the door, slamming it behind me.

I rushed across the balcony and down the treads to the parking lot—then I stopped short. Where the heck was I headed? I had no place else to go. Even if I trudged through the moonlight out to the lot, who would take me in there? The motel office was dark, the no-vacancy sign lit. It was hours to sunup, the air biting with chill. I thought I might hide out in Walt's car till morning, but when I went over and tried the door, it was locked.

I spotted him spying down at me through a crack in the drapes, and I ducked out of sight under the balcony. Where else could I go, save back to the room? So, after punishing him with little time enough for him to regret my absence, and the chill seeping under my skin, back up the treads I stomped.

As I neared our room, I heard the TV on in Cheek's room. I hesitated, and then tried a few gentle knocks on his door. He peeked out between the drapes, smiled uneasily when he saw me, and swung open the door, wearing only his skivvies.

"There be trouble in paradise," he said, his doughy swagbelly slumping over baggy BVD's. "These walls are thin."

"Cheeks, would you let me in for a spell, till I figure what to do next."

"That might take a while, gorgeous. But, yeah. Sure. Come on in."

Sharpy, sprawled atop the bed, raised an eye at me as I plopped into a chair by the table—Johnny Carson and the movie star blathering away on Cheek's TV, too.

I fidgeted, running my fingers through my hair, searching for something to say, until I came up with, "Maybe I'll just set here a short piece while we each cool down."

"Sounds like a plan," he said, laying back down on the bed, and pulling the sheet over his bottom half. "Toot of hash?"

"No thanks. I'm fucked up enough already."

"It might calm you down some."

"No.... Thanks anyway."

"Want to talk about it?"

"Oh, Walt's just jealous about nothing. Absolutely nothing."

"Nothin' to you seems to be somethin' to him. Somethin' comes from somewhere. Don't it?"

"Cheeks, I'm much obliged for you opening your door to me. But let's change the subject."

"Ten-four. What subject you want to change to?"

A silence hung between us, until I asked, "Madeline tells me she's going to do some LSD tomorrow, and she wants me to trip with her. What's your take on that?"

"My take?"

"I mean... is it dangerous?"

"Girl, the whole wide world is dangerous. Madeline's tripped before, so I guess she knows what she's doin'. The acid I got is pure and mellow. Windowpane. She'll be fine, no doubt. But are you askin' about her, or about yourself?"

"Well... about both."

"Have you ever done acid before?"

I shook my head.

"Annabelle, I can't say do or don't. And if you and Walt are still feudin' tomorrow, it might not be the best day for it. Acid tends to make whatever's on your mind a heap more intense. Amping up a spat might not be the trip you want to take."

"What's tripping like?"

"It's like lookin' at the world, and yourself, with another set of eyes. You see things in a different light. Things important to you might turn to fiddle-faddle. And the contrary, a blade of grass might appear to be the face of God."

"Forever?"

"No, for just a few hours. But yeah, acid's been known to change people forever. For the better. And sometimes for worse."

"What about for someone like me, trying to figure out what to do next?"

"I can't say whether you'd find any answers or not. But if that's what's on your mind, then a chunk of your trip could likely be about it."

"How much does it cost?"

"Five bucks a hit."

Just then came a knock on the door. Cheeks rolled off the bed, peeked through the drapes, and said, "It's Walt. Should I let him in?"

I nodded, and he opened the door. Walt stepped halfway in the room, and said to me, "Belle, come on back to the room and we'll talk this over. No yellin' this time."

I gave him a long look, nodded once, and thanked Cheeks as I stepped out on the balcony. As the door swung shut, I hissed, "I ain't going back in that room till you tell me what I'm due."

"Annabelle, I'm mighty sorry I jumped all over you about this. I just went crazy when I seen you with those other guys. I'm crazy about you, baby. So I just went crazy stupid jealous. Ain't that the price of admission of the way I feel about you? Just the thought of losin' my dream girl to another man sets fire to my eyes. Don't run off. I'm head-over-heels for you."

"Walt, I told you there was nothing for you to worry about. Absolutely nothing. But you wouldn't believe me."

"I know, Belle. I know."

A sigh heaved from the deep of my heart. I whispered, "Come on. Let's go inside and talk."

We went in the room and sat on the chairs. I told him, "Walt, you don't own me. Even if you love me, you don't own me."

"I don't want to own you, Belle."

"Well if you want to love me, then believe me when I tell you something. All the fucking bullshit alibis that you tell folks every day doesn't mean that I'm not telling you the truth. That is that and this is me. You and I can't tell each other lies. I'll allow I was attracted to that banker. But that was all. I've watched you watch other women walk past. We all get our fancies flowing when we see someone who looks good to us. But all I did was go to the library and read a book. And I was only dancing with that Gypsy. That's what I told you, and when I tell you something you've got to believe me."

"I believe you.... And maybe I also believe you don't really love me."

"Walt, honey, I've been tumbling that around in my heart all day long. And I reckon that if I need to hunt up a library book to find out what love is, then I'm out here without a clue.... Folks are always telling me what to do and how to do it, and I just don't take kindly to that. It's like the whole world wants me to be who I ain't! Yet I don't know who I am, so I go along with whatever, because I don't know what else to do...."

"Walt, you want me to love you, but I don't hardly know how to love anybody. You want me to be a carny, but what difference is that from all them back in Clandel wanting me to be what they want me to be? I just want to be who I am. Yet I don't know who that is."

"Annabelle, you're the most beautiful gal alive."

"That's what you think I am. What I think I am—that's the puzzlement."

He whispered, "Forget about it for now. Just be my lovin' dream tonight."

"Even if I hardly know how?"

"I know how. That's enough for now."

"Walt, maybe I know little to none about what real love is. But what I do know is that you make me feel like a genuine woman."

"Oh, baby—that you are. And right here's your genuine man."

VII

LE·CHARIOR

A royal driver, posing high and mighty beneath a four-square canopy, rides inside The Chariot — its crossbar dividing the upper world from the lower, the human condition from the animal realm, and the ego's will from the forces of the unconscious. A pair of distracted horses pulls The Chariot's sideward wheels in contrary directions as the melancholy charioteer, who is without any reins, yearns for his way forward. Upon his shoulders are the masks of his two faces: his adopted persona and his true self. Seven is a sacred number of transformation and creation.

Late in the morning, we woke to a rap at the door. Walt leapt up in the raw and peeked between the drapes.

"It's Madeline," he said, and crawled back between the sheets.

I pulled a sweater over me, opened the door a crack, and squinted at Madeline's silhouette in the sunshine.

She sung, "Good mornin', Annabelle. Wonderful day for trippin'."

I gathered my wits and told her, "Let me get some clothes on and I'll be out shortly."

As I shut the door, Walt asked from beneath a pillow half over his head, "What trippin'?"

"Let me talk to Madeline. Then I'll fill you in."

With a flare of his nostrils, he started to say something, but kept it to himself. I quickly visited the plumbing, pulled on my jeans, and stepped barefoot out on the balcony's cool concrete. Madeline, leaning against the railing, sipped coffee from a styrofoam cup steaming between her long fingers.

"So, Annabelle. You with me today? Or are you with me today?"

"I can't yet rightly say.... I need to talk to Walt about it. We had this big onset last night, and ended up saying we'd be honest with each other. Give me a half-hour to chew it over and take a shower."

"Okay. It's quarter past ten. I'll be in Cheek's room."

Back in our room, Walt asked again, "What trippin'?"

"Madeline's going to do LSD today. And she asked me either to do some with her or just be there with her while she's tripping."

He propped up on both elbows, and asked, "Have you ever dropped acid before?"

"No.... And I hear tell it might help me find some answers."

"It might help you right into the fuckin' loony bin."

"Have you ever done it?"

"Yeah. Once. And it's no kiddie matinee."

"Did it help you figure out things?"

"I already had things figured out. It just fucked me up big-time for one too-long never-endin' day. Half out of this world and half pain in the brain."

"Would you try it again?"

"I never gave much thought to it."

"What would you think if I tried it?"

He eyed me hard, and then said, "Belle, I don't own you, as you've made clear. But I have to argue that you'd be playin' with dynamite, which could blow everythin' to shit. So why light the match?"

"So why did you try it?"

"I don't know. To see what the big deal was all about, I guess. I prob'ly didn't have much else better to do that day."

"Well, I'm going to take a shower and think on it. At the very least, I'm going to be there for Madeline while she's tripping.... Maybe I'll do some, too. You're welcome to tag along, one way or the other."

In the shower, I juggled yes and no, back and forth. I'd heard and read about LSD—how some thought it was the greatest thing for your soul since Jesus, and others thought it came straight from Old Scratch himself, and led straight to hell. The hippies out in San Francisco swore by it. They said it changed their lives for the better—that they saw God. Some, though, had turned into vegetables from it.

I'd heard tales from a few around Clandel who'd tripped—talking about it while back in town on college vacation or on leave from the service—and none of them appeared none the worse for it. The attitude of one feller I'd known since grade school had changed much for the better, even though he became way too hairy. Whether it was LSD that did it to him, or merely getting himself out of town, I couldn't say. But of everyone I knew that had taken some, none had ended up in a loony bin, nor jumped out a window. Though there was one boy, Brady Dobbs—long off his box—who kids said had done too much acid. But he had always been hinky, and also drank too much stump liquor every day. So was it the chicken or the egg with Brady?

I toweled off and fixed my hair, Madeline waiting on me to make up my mind, which as with most of my decisions was slow to happen. Pulling some clothes out of the chest of drawers, I saw Walt eyeing me—concern heavy on his brow while appearing to swallow words he wanted to say. Our cuss fight had bunged a stopper into his telling me what to do. But now maybe that was what I needed.

Of a mind to keep him close, no matter which way things went, I asked him, "Are you coming along?"

"You want me to?"

"Yes I do, Walt. You just lie around all morning watching those game shows, then we dawdle till call. Let's do something else today."

"You're on, Belle." He tore out of bed, washed and dressed, and was pacing by the door ready to go before I'd finished primping.

By the window in Cheeks' room, the drapes wide open, Madeline sat slouched in a chair. She saw us, waved, and let us in. Cheeks whistled a tune in the shower splashing in the bathroom.

As I yanked at the tangled blankets for a decent place to sit on the bed, Madeline said, "Cheeks is trippin' too. Do we have a threesome? Or maybe a foursome?"

"I'm in," I said before I had time to shillyshally again.

Hooking a thumb toward me, Walt said, "I'm with her."

Madeline squealed, "Hot damn. We're gonna pitch a wang-dang-doodle. Where should we go?"

"Go?" I asked.

"Well we don't want to trip here in the damn motel room all day. Do we?"

"I don't know. I reckon not. Where do you figure we ought to go?"

Walt said, "Let's go out to the lot and hang out in the woods. That way we can make it to call without me havin' to drive around all fucked up."

I added, "Yeah. There's a nice little creek across the field, and things are in bloom."

Madeline said to Walt, "So, you're gonna work your alibi joint to-night?"

"Sure. Why not?"

"Well maybe we'll see why not."

Toweling his head, Cheeks came out of the bathroom, bare-ass naked—his blonde-fringed tallywags half hidden by wispy-haired hams and a rosy roll of freckly belly fat—and he said, "By gollies, y'all best drop your hits shortly to catch up with me. I'm rushin' already."

Madeline said, "I just now did mine. Got one for Annabelle and one for Walt?"

"Yes indeedy I do. Right over here. Two hits of windowpane comin' right up. Only a fin per hit. Yes indeedy doody-doo."

He pulled a snuff tin from a suitcase pocket, and from it chose one of several tidy aluminum-foil packets. Waggling his wide and dimply ass in front of my face, he bent over the table, and with the point of a jackknife worked open the folds of the packet and flicked onto the table two glassy chips about an eighth-inch square.

"There you be. Two doses of genuine lysergic acid diethylamide," Cheeks said, and returned the packet to the tin and the tin to the suitcase pocket.

Walt stepped up to the table and flipped a ten-dollar bill on it, saying, "And one genuine sawbuck in return. You gonna put some clothes on now?"

Madeline cracked, "I like him better bare-ass."

Walt snorted half a laugh. Then he licked a fingertip, poked it onto one of the clear squares, which stuck on, and he licked it off. I followed suit. The chip clung to the back of my throat as I struggled to swallow it, and after several gulps came up short I hurried to the bathroom spigot, scooped up a few handfuls of water, and washed it down.

Madeline went to the door, saying, "I'll meet you all out at the lot, behind the dark ride. I gotta get Pa's car back."

Walt shrugged an okay, and Cheeks asked him, "Can I ride with you today? And Sharpy too?"

"Sure. Long as you put some pants on your fat ass."

Ten minutes later, we were wheeling toward the lot. I felt nothing different yet. But in the back seat with Sharpy, Cheeks giggled and grinned like a kid at a clown. He'd spot something out the window, twist his hulk to follow it as we passed, and then say, "Wow," or, "Trippy."

Walt asked over his shoulder, "Gettin' off, Cheeks?"

"Man, I'm off. I'm off," chuckling loud and long at that. "Walt, can you lower this groovy rearview window?"

The Mercury had this odd back window that slanted in at the bottom. Walt thumbed a button and the glass whirred down. Cheeks turned about face—his knees on the seat, elbows spread atop it—and stuck his head out. Sharpy paddled his front paws up onto the back of the seat to see what was going on, yawping excitedly.

Walt shouted, "Don't go jumpin' out no windows on us."

I sniggered at that some, and inside me, where laughs flow out of your middle, I felt a strange sensation—like a shudder of fear, but not scary, maybe more like the strut of a thrill. I squirmed around on the front seat, hunting what else appeared odd come short. A quivering seeped out from my bones as I studied the shifting shapes. The chrome trim on the dashboard glinted reflections from deep within. The tunnel of greening trees that we rolled through splattered buttery sunlight across the streaky windshield. The motor groaned through the floorboards, its pulse throbbing up into my legs.

I turned to Walt and he curled his big grin at me, his cocksure eyes darting back and forth from me to the road. He asked, "You feel it comin' on?"

"Yeah." And the word rang through me like a church bell. I returned a smile, but wondered if he saw through it to my skittishness. I had no idea what to allow, but now had the notion that this would be no barn dance.

We rolled out of a curve, and up ahead the carnival sat there like a fairy castle. The motionless Ferris Wheel loomed up under cottony clouds afloat in a startling blue above the gnarly ridges. We swung off the road, swayed over ruts to the backside of the show, and spotted Madeline perched on the hood of Tex's black Cadillac. Walt pulled the Mercury up, nose to nose.

Sharpy scrambled out the back window and barked prancing atop the wide trunk lid, looking for a way down. Walt hollered at Cheeks, "Get that damn dog off my car," but Cheeks just quaggled with laughter as he heaved himself across the seat and out the door. Sharpy found his own way down, with half a hop off the bumper.

Walt and I climbed out of the car and leaned our hind ends against the front grill—the oily warmth of the motor seeping into my bottom, the golden brilliance of the sun cutting through me from on high. I tilted my head back and closed my eyes. I'd heard the tales about folks on LSD who stared into the sun and went blind. A trembly web of veins appeared behind my blood-red eyelids. Squinting them open, I turned away from the dazzling sun-ball as if it were a trap, set to snare me.

Madeline asked, "Everyone copasetic so far?"

I nodded, though unsure, and Walt said, "Like a toad on a toadstool."

Cheeks said, "I gotta go get somethin'. Be right back." And with Sharpy trotting alongside, he lumbered off, a jig unsteady on his feet.

Walt lit a cigarette, and asked, "Well ladies, what do we do now?"

We shrugged back and forth at each other, until Walt said, "Let's go find a spot over by that creek to hang out at. And get out of sight before things get too weird."

For me, things were fast becoming powerfully funny-turned. The dusty fenders of both cars glowed with a luster from deep within the painted metal. Each breath I drew fetched thick and loud the crisp scent of young grass jostling with a faint stink of gasoline. Each new moment grew larger and slower than the last. Dim voices from somewhere on the lot, a gentle country song from a feeble transistor radio, the distant hammering of a nail—all felt close as the chill bumps prickling the hairs on my arms. And like a dam had burst, a flood of heart-lifting energy rushed through me.

Madeline said, "Whoa.... What's out of sight is this acid. It's workin' strong, now. Hidin' out in the bushes for a while might be the right idea."

Walt said, "Wait up for Cheeks, though. If he finds his way back to us."

Just then, Tex came around the corner of a trailer and strode up to us, saying, "There you are, Maddie. Good that yer back with the car. I gotta go to the hardware in town. I ain't yet fed Sam and the others. Can you do that for me, darlin'?"

"Sure, Pa. Is later okay?"

"Not much later. You know how Sam gets sluggish after he eats." Tex cocked his cowboy hat back a notch, curious-like. "Somethin' wrong, sweetheart?"

She slid off the hood of the Cadillac, shaking her head, and said, "No, Pa. Nothin's wrong."

I saw suspicion swim in Tex's eye as Madeline joined us leaning up against the front of the Mercury. He cast a wary look at Walt and me, and then got into his Cadillac, fired it up, and wheeled away.

Walt asked Madeline, "Who's Sam?"

"Sam's our best rat. Maybe I should go and feed him now, just in case I get too fucked-up later. Y'all want to come and feed the rats?"

I nodded yes, but Walt said he'd wait for Cheeks to come back. So she and I wound our way through the jumble of cars, trucks, and trailers, and then cut through a gap in the line-up, and out to Tex's center joint, shut tight on the abandoned midway.

After Madeline unlaced one corner enough to prop the awning open, she squeezed in over the counter, and I followed her lead. A dusky warmth glowed inside the tent—pinpoints of sunlight sparkly as stars through the weave of the canvas. Overhead hung dozens of the goofy stuffed mice, kith and kin to the one I'd won, their fluffy colors gaudy as a comic book. With daffy grins, they gazed cockeyed down at me, as if the oddity here was me, having no business being beneath their gather-all in the rafters.

Motionless atop its platform in the center of the tent, its numbered rat holes around the rim of its painted wedges, the multi-colored wheel wore a cloth skirt slung on curtain rods around the platform's sides. Madeline slid one side open, unveiling several small wire-mesh cages. A white rat in each, their beady eyes curious, their whiskery snouts sniffed up at us. A loud and blinky taint of droppings billowed out into the dusty scent of crushed grass and warm canvas.

On each cage hung a small water bottle, upside-down with a plastic tube through a cork stopper, the tube bent through the wire grid, and also a feeder, a tin cooking measure, its handle crimped onto the mesh. The rats knew it was feeding time. They skittered about and stood on their hind legs, little hands gripping the wire, their cooped-up little squeaks and squeals in a chorus happy to see us—but oh how so pitiful.

Madeline reached into one of the cages, lifted out a squirmy rat, and said, "This one's Sam. He's our star. Night after night he does himself proud. Wanna hold him?"

I wasn't so sure I did, but took Sam from her anyway, cupping him in both hands. His soft warmth tickly and twitchy, his head poked out between my thumbs—red eyes searching me out, white whiskers and pink nose sniffing, tiny ears alert, his little claws scrabbling for freedom.

"Hi, Sam," I said in a breathy whisper that laid back his whiskers. He closed his eyes and stopped squirming. After some seconds, as still as a mouse, he re-opened them and stared up at me with eyes appearing to ask would I please set him loose.

While I held Sam, Madeline unlatched the top of each cage and ladled birdseed out of a sack and into the feed cups. Working quickly with an ease of having done this many times, she unhooked a water bottle from a cage wherever one was low, and filled it from a plastic milk jug. Sam must have reckoned I wasn't going to set him free, so he took in squirming and scrabbling again. Then warm pee dribbled onto my palms.

"Yuck! He peed.... Can I give him a whirl on the wheel?"

Still working the cages, she said sure, so I dropped the rat in the middle of the wheel, gave it a spin, and wiped my hand on its cloth skirt. Sam sniffed the air as he turned, took a few jerky steps back and forth, but made no move to scurry into a hole. I bowed my head over the wheel and gazed down at the colored wedges reeling by. For a spell, the pulse of colors hypnotized me stone stupid. Yet it somehow had a feel of something important fluttering unknowable just beyond the reach of my eyes.

I hauled my head up out of this trance, and seeing Sam still turning at the center of the wheel, I asked, "Why doesn't he run into a hole?"

Madeline, finishing up her last cage, said, "Which hole you want him to go into?"

"I don't know... seven?"

She got a little bottle out from under a counter, unscrewed the cap, poked a finger in, and sloshed the liquid onto her fingertip. Grabbing the rim of the wheel at number seven, she exaggeratedly poked the finger into the hole and gave the wheel a spin. Sam lifted his nose in the air, Madeline snatched the trumpet and tooted it, and Sam scampered mickety-tuck into hole number seven.

Though I'd just seen it with my own eyes, it felt of watching a mouse in a TV cartoon. "Well don't that take the rag off the bush. What's on your finger?"

"Ammonia. Evaporates quick as spit on a griddle, and then we're good for the next go-around. Sam earns a bit of kibble after he scuttles into the proper hole. And Pa beats the percentages."

"But I saw several winners when I played this game last Friday. I won a pink mouse myself."

"When all the numbers are covered, somebody's gotta win. The last couple of days, Sam's maybe been workin' the wheel too much. He seems always dizzy. Pa has to blow harder on the horn to get him to scoot, and more than usual he runs into a hole that Pa didn't duke. But Pa's got a remedy for this—a few evenin's alone in the trailer with Bill the cat clawing on Sam's cage."

She slid out the drawer under hole number seven. Sam reared up, looking for his kibble payoff, but she just dumped him back in his cage. He scurried straight to his replenished feed tin, and going at it two-fisted, nibbled the shell off a sunflower seed.

Madeline said, "Come on. Let's get out of here." And she led me back out over the counter through the gap in the tent.

As she laced the awnings back together, an electrified surge of awe strutted out deep from my middle. Like when Dorothy fell into Oz, and the world of black-and-white turned to Technicolor, the drinted red and orange stripes of dusty canvas took on an otherworldly glow that appeared to burst forth from within the sturdy weave of the cloth—the make of each thread of it somehow appearing completely astounding.

Underfoot, the mishmash of trampled grass, scattered hay, and dried mud became a magic carpet. The mute and paralyzed rides, the shuttered tents and trailers, stood like witnesses at my trial. Overhead, bluer than a possum cod, the lofty brilliance possessed a depth within its limitless height that I could actually see—not up there like some far-away ceiling—I now beheld the vast space beyond my eyes, below, between, and above the wispy clouds, and all the way to the sun-ball, ablaze with almighty power, dazzling its living heat through everything.

As Madeline finished lacing the tent, my feet shuffling for solid ground to stand on, a golf cart wobbled down the midway, whirring and groaning, carrying Eli McCain toward us. As he neared, I mannerably turned a smile his way. But it felt of a bald-faced lie, and I knew he knew I'd smiled to hide my fear. He squinted his piggy eyes at me, slowed, and fetched up to a stop.

Tapping his silver-knobbed cane to the brim of his straw hat, he said, his voice tight-chested and nasally, "Good afternoon, ladies." His eyes narrowed and darted cannily in a once-over of us.

We chimed in return, "Good afternoon, Mister McCain."

He searched us out further with, "Y'all grabbin' yourselves plenty of scratch this week?"

I stupidly nodded yes to whatever that meant, while Madeline said, "Yes, sir. That rain sure enough washed us out Tuesday night, but it's a-dryin' up today. What's the weather man say for the weekend?"

"Looks good. Looks good."

"That'll be fine by me.... We just been feedin' and waterin' the live-stock. They'll be shortly runnin' their tails off."

Old Eli grunted a chuckle. "So the rats'll be shortly runnin' their tails off, you say."

"Yes sir, that's the way we like it."

Pawing the cart's steering wheel, and about to drive off, he then swiv-eled to ask me, "Ain't you the girl who Walt coldcocked that mark for?"

The question sunk deep into my bowels, like an urge for the privy, and it felt of forever before I found myself confessing, "Well, sir, that miner lost some powerful cash money next door, and then flung an armload of my hoops up against the wall. So Walt jumped into his face, and the next thing I know the miner's waving a knife. Then Walt beefed him with a hammer.... And that's about the size of it." The words gushed from me as if somebody else was telling it on myself.

He tilted down his chins into the folds of his neck, his earthworm lips puckering to a thought, and he said, "Yeah... I reckon it is. I reckon it is...."

Maybe you best tag along to the courthouse tomorrow. Lest Walt needs some backup."

"Okay, Mister McCain. I'll be sure to do so."

"Don't you worry your pretty little head none, though. This'll be long gone tomorrow. Your Walt'll be stompin' that mud off his shoes soon enough."

"That's fine by me. I handily thank you, Mister McCain. And we weren't hunting for any trouble. No, sir. None."

"Young lady, sometimes trouble finds you. Sometimes trouble finds you." With that, he toed a pedal, the cart groaned, and his wobbly bulk lurched to and fro as he whirred away.

My heart throbbing in my gizzard, my armpits drippy with fearful sweat, it appeared plain to me that he could tell that I was high as the moon. I hissed to Madeline, "He knows we're tripping."

She eyed me like she didn't care a hate, and said, "The only thing that old bastard knows is carnivals. He ain't got a clue about nothin' but. Let's get on back to the boys, afore anyone else bums out our trip."

I followed her along the path we came. But in the ten or fifteen minutes since, everything had become another guess. The headlights and grills of the cars and trucks we passed appeared to be the eyes and mouths of faces watching us traipse along. The sidewalls of tents and trailers loomed larger and nearer, and as we breezed past, they breathed—canvas billowing as I'd allow it might, yet the sheet-metal sides of trailers breathed too. I stopped flatfooted and drop-jawed, to watch them for a spell, to be sure. And Lord's eye on it, yes they did.

Up ahead the Mercury lay stretched out like an aircraft carrier—Walt and Cheeks leaning against a fender, and Sharpy, belly-up at their feet, writhed his bald backbone atop the grass. Walt held a fresh smoke dangling between two fingers, his arms folded across his middle. Cheeks hugged a gallon jar. As we neared, I saw it was The Frog Baby, pickled in its jug.

Madeline asked, hands on hips, "Cheeks, what the hell you doin' with that thing?"

Appearing surprised at such a question, he told her, "I'm takin' it out for a little sun. The poor thing don't get out much, you know."

Walt said, "There's no talkin' him out of it. I gave it my best shot."

We stood there in a vast silence, looking back and forth at each other, until Madeline said, "Come on then. Let's take a walk and get out of sight. Where's that creek you were talking about, Annabelle?"

I pointed toward it, and said, "Just over yonder. Follow me."

My leading us off through the field felt of that I was for once the one in the know. I'd been tagging along at everybody's elbow all week long, and now it was me who knew the way to the creek. I had something I could show them, something I could do for them. In a giddy rush of foolish glory, this puffed up my plume, and brought a briggoty bounce into my legs.

We marched single file through the bloom of wildflowers—the potpourri underfoot swishing and crunching in time to our out-of-step parade, a sweet stink seething around us, a kaleidoscopic splash of colors whispering velvety sighs as we passed. For a fact, I was tripping now.

Something almighty had kicked in. I'd been way high before on booze or pot, or both at once. But that in no way measured up to anywhere near what this had become. I floated in a whole new ocean. A breathing sea of meadow and mountainside, which had once been out there, outside of me, I now was within, or it all was in me. The flowers, the stones, the dirt, the very air itself, all breathing the same life as me.

Everything took on a powerful importance. Yet I couldn't quote what was so pure-quill meaningful. The weight it carried struck me dumb like heat lightning. Just a bumblebee buzzing around a wildflower somehow meant more than I'd ever known anything could possibly mean—this knowing fading shortly away like the memory of a dream, just out of reach, but still somehow there.

Everything appeared so astonishingly marvelous. Wildflowers throbbed with colors so deep they glowed like jewels. Amid withered brush, emerald blades of springtime grass reached up for golden sunlight. Shards of shale festooned the living dirt like scattered treasure. Greening ridges lifted up stands of trees and thickets of laurel in a grateful chorus rustling beneath the miraculous blue above.

I turned to the faces following me. Walt's ear-to-ear grin beamed at me like the sun to the moon—his proud eyes showing how much he fancied me. A joyous throb echoed my own love-struck smile right back at him. Sashaying along behind Walt, Madeline, eyes wide and lips pursed, gazed side to side at the wildflowers, reaching out here and there to brush them with her fingertips. Behind her, Cheeks lumbered along, humming something out of tune, eyes pinched tight by the smile in his cheeks, the glass jar with The Frog Baby held with both hands safari-like atop his pumpkin head—and Sharpy, so ugly he's too cute, shambling along at Cheeks' heels.

We fetched up to the flat boulder where I'd sat on Sunday morning, and there where I'd tossed it, atop the patch of devil's apple, lay the dried-up circlet of mayflowers. Crowning myself with it, I stepped upon the boulder and shouted with a glee that moistened my eyes, "I hereby claim this rock to be the center of the world."

Walt said, "You're the center of my world, Annabelle."

"Aww..." Madeline chimed in, "that's so sweet. Walt, you're not only a he-man, you're a honey."

Cheeks said, "Wow. How do you think this big rock got here?"

Walt guessed, "Probably it broke loose and tumbled off the side of that ridge."

Madeline said, "Annabelle, you got one heck of a rock here at the center of your world."

"That I do. And I'm right proud to share it with you all, as you've shared your world with me."

"Aww... you're a honey too."

"That she is," Walt said. "That she is."

Cheeks asked, "Hey, queen of the rock, can Frog Baby share your world, too?"

I said, "Frog Baby is prince of the rock," then took in laughing at nothing in particular—the senseless laughs echoing through me as if in an empty dance hall.

"Yeah, Cheeks," said Walt, "spring the little bastard from its jar, and when Queenie here gives it a kiss, maybe your star attraction will turn human... and stuff you in a jar."

That struck us so funny, we all doubled up with laughs upon laughs—laughing at the laughing—fingering tears from our eyes, then laughing even more—trapped in laughter, and glad of it. Only when Cheeks sat on the edge of the boulder, wedged the jar between his knees, and unscrewed the lid, did we all quiet down.

"I hope it don't stink bad," Cheeks mumbled. "I ain't had it out of here since the start of last season."

"It's a bouncer," Madeline said. "Latex don't stink."

As he cautiously lifted the lid, he said, "The tea it's in just might." He bent down for a sniff, jerked a scowl backward, and said, "Oh my. Frog Baby, don't you need a bath."

Cheeks tipped the jar and slowly drained the tea off into the dirt. Then he took ahold of Frog Baby, and gingerly wrested it out of the jar. Without its cloudy brine and curved-glass prison, it looked like just what it was—a rubber doll. Some carny sculptor had fashioned this puny flipper-footed monster—its webbed baby fingers reaching out on short arms, its plump baby legs bandied out at the hip like a frog's, its naked chubbiness undeterminably amphibian in the straddle, its frog eyes bugging wide at the gawkers forever looming outside its jar, day in and day out. I'd paid my half-dollar and half believed it to be real. But now, set there on the rock, it had taken on another type of real—like a stone-age idol.

Walt cracked, "They say that people end up lookin' like their pets."

Madeline added, "But Cheeks'll never have butt cheeks like Frog Baby."

That fetched up another rollick of laughs. Then somehow when the silliness became too much, we suddenly ceased, and an uneasy silence set in. We glimpsed at each other as if asking, where do we go from here?

My giddiness quickly gone to skittishness, my making any sense of anything went iffy. Doubts choked off my words. Outlandish notions tumbled into even odder ideas, blowing unrememberable in and out of the ballooning space of the inside of my head. Or was it that my mind was now outside my skull, like Frog Baby freed from behind the curved glass?

Cheeks hauled himself up and called his dog, off sniffing with interest a scent on a tree trunk, "Sharpy! Let's take a bath." Sharpy cocked a fluffy eyebrow and his short tail, a tuft like a lion's on the end of it, and swiveled his squabby face to watch Cheeks tote Frog Baby toward the creek. In a reluctant trot, Sharpy caught up to him, and by the time they reached the wax myrtle, Cheeks had shed his clothes.

"This I gotta see," Walt said, and we followed him.

Cheeks plumped himself down into a pool in the creek about a foot deep and ten wide—his pink belly and man-bubbies high and dry, his jemison dangling like fish bait, his doughy shoulders propped into the spill pouring over a slab of shale, his pumpkin head lolling back into the shimmery flow right up to his cheeky grin. And out at arm's length he held onto the hand of Frog Baby—bug-eyed underwater, feet flapping in the current, appearing alive and kicking, and apparently enjoying its bath—while Sharpy waded about, thirstily lapping up a drink here and there.

Walt said, "Now ain't that a pretty sight."

Madeline said, "It's fuckin' freakin' me out."

Cheeks raised his head toward us, and hollered, "Jump in. The water's nice."

"Yeah," Walt said. "Nice and cold. You've got layers of lard to keep your ass from freezin'."

Madeline said, "I'm a-goin' in." She shucked her shoes, socks, and jeans, yanked the hem of her sweatshirt down over her hips—her downy bum bulging out the sides of black panties—and tested the water with a toe.

"Get with it, Madeline," Cheeks yelled. "Take it all off, and splish splash."

"Not in your lifetime, Chubby," she said, wading in, waving her arms for balance. Up to her knees in a ripply mirror, she hiked up her sleeves, bent over, and scooped branch water onto her forearms and face.

Walt squatted on his heels—eyes hunting for pebbles to grab up while stealing glances at Madeline's creamy thighs. A jag of jealousy stiffened my jaw, quickly blown away by the shame of my mistrust storming through me.

Walt took in lobbing pebbles at them, not aiming to hit them, but plunking pebbles nigh about. He whispered to me, "Watch this," and tossing a pebble like a dart, he bounced it off Cheek's belly—who, jackknifing up and witnessing us sniggling, swiped an armful of water our way, swashing way short.

Madeline kicked a splash at us, which instead rained down mostly on Cheeks—who, letting loose of Frog Baby, hauled up on his haunches and scooped double-barreled armloads of sparkling splashes right back at her. She shrieked, all aglee, and fought back, scooping up handfuls in return as she sloshed about dancing to sidestep getting sobby.

Then they both turned their aim to us. I backpedaled from the splashing, but Walt grabbed up some sandy mud and took in heaving it at them. The next second we all were flinging mud at each other, caught up in some tom-fool feud. Peppered by grit, I grabbled for more mud to fling, tit for tat, to and fro. We cheered direct hits, groaned at near misses, laughing like ninnies all the while.

"Wait!" Madeline shouted. "I see a frog."

We ceased fire. I brushed gobs of mud from my clothes and hair while she stalked the frog at the edge of the pool, and shortly snatched it up. Snared by one leg, it twisted and kicked like life and death, its white belly flailing about, two little arms reaching for anything, its loose leg jabbing at some hope of escape.

I yelled, "You're hurting him."

They all looked at me like they couldn't believe I might say such a thing. Madeline grabbed the frog's body in her other hand, stopping its thrashing, and said, "Oh, we'll save him from himself for a while. Just enough so we get to know each other. Then we'll let him go. And he'll never be the same again."

Walt cracked, "Keep him far away from the geek."

Cheeks—standing spread-legged and shin-deep, swiveling his raw bulk and flopping his roly-poly arms about, casting his eyes around, the widest I'd ever seen them—cried, "Where's Frog Baby?"

We all peered into the silty stirred-up pool. No Frog Baby to be seen. Cheeks squatted and duck-walked, groping through the water like a blind man picking strawberries, and screeched, "He's not here! He's not here!"

"Maybe he turned into a real frog," Walt said with half a shrug. "The one Madeline's latched ahold of."

Holding the frog high, Madeline added, "Yeah, and now you have to kiss it, for it to change back to the pickled punk."

Showing us he reckoned that to be in noway funny, Cheeks eyes narrowed and his face lowered a black scowl. He hunted once more through the pool, coming up with nothing, and then sloshed off downstream, head swiveling to and fro—and fat-back naked.

We joined the hunt down the creek for a stretch. With the real frog still kicking in her hand, Madeline waded carefully, eyes peering into the silt stirred up in Cheeks frantic wake. Walt and I followed, jumping from stone to sand to stone, and soon fell behind.

Walt hollered to her, "He'll find the little monster. We're headin' back to the big rock."

I felt beholden to hunt further for Frog Baby—but also contrarily beholden to follow Walt. Up ahead, Madeline turned around and set free her frog into the sun-sparkly run splashing at her shins, and shouted back to us, "I'll look a while more. And meet y'all back at the center of the world."

Behind Walt as we traipsed off, my knowing that I ought to help in the hunt weighed heavily on me. But there was no turning around now. Then, with a sight of understanding that made me stumble a step, a notion struck me like a bread wagon—menfolk act as if they're the center of the world. Walt saw little sense in keeping up the search. Two were on it already—one of them bare-naked and stoned out of his gourd. Reckoning that this dog don't hunt, Walt had guiltlessly cut loose of it, expecting me to just go along with him.

Womenfolk tended to take care of each other's needments. Tending to another's druthers before their own is where a woman's caution lies. Yet, snared by a man's sway, I found myself again doing what I didn't want to—following Walt along, with at-odds parcels of myself jowering back and forth over it, torn between my concerns for myself and three other people all at once, and the dang Frog Baby, too.

So which one was Annabelle Cory—the do-for-myself me, or the do-for-others me, or the do-what-others-do me? And when would whoever I am get to live my own life? Clandel had wanted me to be one of their own. Now Walt and the carnies were at the same thing.

Stricken with a spell of dumfounded awe, I wondered who the heck am I. And this question wasn't just any same-old half-baked misgiving troubling some fleeting notion of mine. The LSD had exploded it into huge-big importance. A kaleidoscope of notions, as to who I was, raced through my thoughts—puzzlements, one after the other, zigzagging through my mind like greased lightning—haunts of riddles, echoing promises of magical answers, but just beyond my grasp.

Shambling along behind Walt on the path he trampled—the brush snuffling underfoot, the tangle of greening thicket chattering gently while the wildflowers whispered—each step of mine through the airy colors grew heavier, noisier, clumsier. I gasped, suddenly in a squall of fear. Somehow, I was me no more. Who I'd been was gone. And now what? Now who was I? This question wasn't just a curiosity, it felt of a matter of life and death. One drop of a chemical had done away with who I reckoned myself to be. If that's all it took to destroy my identity, what sort of person had I been? Now who would I become?

As we approached the flat rock, I saw it as a monument, the tombstone of my previous life of only a half-hour before. I clambered atop it and lay face-up upon the cool stone, arms and legs splayed out like an X. Dizzily afloat under the vast brilliance above, I managed to say, "Walt, I'm losing it."

"Losing what?" asked his disembodied voice from the edge of the dome of the sky.

"I don't know.... It's like I've lost who I am. Like who I was wasn't really me. And now I don't know who I am."

"You're the most beautiful gal I've ever seen. And you're mine."

"That's who I am to you. I'm talking about who I am to me."

"Belle, you're the same person you were an hour ago. But right now you're righteously stoned."

"I'll never be the same person again. I know it."

"Get a grip on yourself, baby."

"That's exactly what I should do. Get a grip on myself. And yes, I am just a baby."

On hands and knees, he crawled above me, and stroking my hips, said, "I'll get a grip on you."

I levered myself onto my elbows and turned my face away from his. "No. Not now.... Please. I'm sorry. I can't right now."

Holding up his hands as if being robbed, he knelt beside me, his face looming above, carrying a pain he shied to show. He arsled off the rock, awkwardly stood there undone and offput, and dug a Raleigh out of the pack in his shirt pocket. Yanking a match afire with a crack and a hiss, he touched it to the smoke, then shook it dead. And when he dropped it, I heard it patter down through the grass—the silence was such.

He avoided my eyes by studying his cigarette. This being the first time I'd said no to a come-on of his, we both didn't know what to do next. He pushed grass back and forth with the toe of his shoe for a spell, and then sat at the edge of the rock, his back to me, and worked on his smoke. His broad shoulders hunched over, he appeared defeated—at a loss for a reason why, and sulking at the injustice.

I cringed at what I'd done—dropping acid and losing it, whatever 'it' was—and shutting the door on Walt, putting him so out of heart—and shucking Clandel to end up, in less than a week, stoned clueless atop a rock. What good was any of that? I'd gone too far. Adrift with neither oars nor anchor, I'd lost my way. Like Frog Baby, I'd been washed downriver, out of the hands of the devil I knew and into the reach of the devil I didn't. Now I had to either find my way back up the creek, or float onward.

I sat up, pulled my knees to my chin, and said, "Walt, I need some space right now. I've got to figure some things out on my own."

His back still to me, he mumbled, "Belle, you do what you gotta do."

"I don't know what it is I've got to do. I just know I need to be alone for a spell. And maybe then I'll come up with some clue."

"Fine by me."

"Walt, please don't give down on us. I'd despise ripping the stars out of heaven for this. I'm just powerfully bumfuzzled about everything and anything right now."

With hopeful eyes, he turned to me and said, "That's what I'm here for. To fix up things for you, and make things better."

The words trapped in my throat right then were, 'What if it's you what's ailing me?' Instead I told him, "Walt, you're sweet as bee gum, and I handily appreciate all of what you've done. But I've got to figure this out by myself.... Yonder there's a pour-off a short piece up the run, splashing off the ridge. I'm going to mosey over to it and see what comes of it."

"Suit yourself."

How he said that, and how he turned away his tortured face, told me I'd wounded him. I searched for some words to salve the beal, but came up with none. So I scootched over to him, hugged him from behind, and nuzzled my face in the crook of his neck. He rolled his head against mine and raised a hand to stroke my hair. As my eyes closed, a rush of joy escaped my heart. His beardy stubble soothing me with its manliness, I tumbled blindly into my own velvety expanse of pleasure.

He stood and turned and lifted me into his arms. A tornado of desire dizzied me like a ride on the Tilt-A-Whirl. His lips sought mine and I gave them up, mashing into a tangle of kisses, our arms bundling us together. His face melting against mine with each gasp and moan, Walt shape-shifted from tormenter to victim and back again, hungry to swallow me whole, but sorely forbidden.

I shied off, gently pushing him away, and he put on a hangdog look that appeared to say: won't nothin' make, won't nothin' keep—as of crops in bad weather.

Yet he said kindly, "I'll wait here a while for you."

I spread a smile, best I could, and explained, "I just need to be alone for a spell. A few minutes? An hour? A side trip on this trip? A sideshow on this roadshow?"

"Belle, if I'm not here when you get back, I'll be right where you know where to find me."

I took his hand, lifted it to kiss, and mooned up into his wary eyes—confusion racing through them. Then I turned on a heel and traipsed off, ashamed of my relief in putting my back to him.

Winding through the bushes, I came upon the steppingstones where before I'd crossed the creek, which now ran higher after the rain two days before. Some stones now underwater, and the higher ones with the current lapping at their edges, I doubted whether I could make it from one to the next. Spying upstream and down, hunting for other ways across, I saw only that my boots were likely to get wet. Why I was even there at all, suddenly felt of a huge mystery. Yet going back to Walt felt dead wrong.

I stood there like a statue and gazed into the run—sun-diamonds dancing atop the swash—the murmur and gurgle of water over stone singing like angels might. In a pool's ripply mirror, the greening fingers of the trees wove bewitchments overhead.

Plumb sure I'd gone bereft from a horse dose of LSD, and scared stiff from crippling doubts, I feared less the hop, skip, and jump across the creek, than I did the leap into the wonderland surrounding me. But there I stood, and it appeared the only choice I had was to go where I'd set off for—to the pour-off. Although whatever had prodded me to that aim was long gone and no longer mattered a whit.

It came to me to hop barefoot across the creek—this common-sense remedy a welcome balm easing my fluster. I can do this, I told myself—

gladly taking heart at just allowing that. Down on one knee, then the other, I worked off my boots and socks, and hiked up my pant legs. With socks in boots and boots in hand, I tiptoed atop the first steppingstone. Riled by rocks in its flow, the run angrily tumbled past. I studied my straits, swinging the boots, measuring the jump to the next stone.

With two tiny steps and a scissor-legged leap, I lit upon the stone, tottered some, and then did a juba across several others, sloshing barefoot just shy of the other bank. Up between my toes, cool muddy sand oozed agreeably—so much so, I tossed my boots onto a dry ledge and waded in shin-deep.

Squishing the creek bed with my piggies, from underfoot arose a heartfelt understanding of a glorious kinship. This pebbly muck was full of the fixings of life. Down off the mountain with the rain, wind, and sunlight, feeding the greenery and the critters that feed on it and those that feed on them, I was made of this mud, too.

Sun, air, water, and earth was what I am. Everybody knew of this miracle already, from common sense, or science class, or the Bible. But right then and there, this knowing welled up within me with powerful certainty. I point-blank knew it like I'd never known anything. Not the kind of knowing that came from book learning, but a ken that came from seeing so, plain as daylight in my heart. Seeing it like I'd never seen the likes of anything. Awesome and meaningful and vital. And it had been there all along, with me blind to it.

I stood shin-deep and drop-jawed. All around me, trees, bushes, weeds, all made of the same stuff. The world wasn't only out there, on the other side of my skin, it was in me as much as I was in it. I wasn't a wanderer in the forest, I lived and breathed with the forest. The viewpoint I'd known as mine—that peephole at the world through my eyes and into my head—now saw that all that is around me lived within me as well. No longer alone inside myself, I lived out there, too.

Words would never explain it. It was a knowing more powerful than words. Words would only sully its truth. Like Isis had written, our words built notions, and notions built beliefs, and beliefs built our fool's paradise. Right there inside me, behind a door padlocked with words, awaited the naked truth, silent and deep-felt.

Like when a baby is born and sees his mother's face for the first time—in her womb till his birthday, and then, shazzam, there she is, glowing with love—I'd been delivered out of my own self and into the world I'd been in all along. Face-to-face and heart-to-heart with my maker, I staggered spellbound with the glory of it all.

Wading reverently out of the water, I gently made my way barefoot into the woods and toward the pour-off. In the cool flickery shade beneath tree limbs reaching out for the dazzling sunlight, their leaves as brilliant as emeralds, the tree trunks stood like columns in a prehistoric temple. The forest floor strewn with its moldering ruins, I breathed deep the dank air, heady with the incense of old rot and new growth.

When I was a little girl at Sunday services, when the pews lifted hymns to the rafters, I'd felt of sacredness akin to this. Yet now, within me and within the trees and stones, the glorious light of The Kingdom of Heaven dawned on this mystic paradise.

Sure enough, Isis was right as rain. Whatever the Good God was, it wasn't a man or woman set atop a throne high in the sky. He or She—or more likely It, both He and She together—was within everything and everybody, inside and outside one and all. Plain as the nose on one's face. All That Is.

For quite a spell, I stood there floating in the midst of the awe of it all, before stepping onward. Among these trees, I felt more myself than among my own kind. Above me, birds sang in the swaying treetops. Ahead, a cat squirrel startled me as it scurried through the brush and scrambled up to a crotch in a hickory, where it scolded me with chatter.

Lifting a hand, I shaded my eyes from the kaleidoscope of sun and leaves, and squinted up at the scrawny gray bushytail, righteously blessing me out. If this critter had blundered into my home, wouldn't I raise a ruckus as it now did with me? Weren't we more the same than not—with two eyes, two ears, one mouth, and a heart pumping blood—all made from the same mud? We'd no doubt never share a tree limb together, but when has the lion ever lain with the lamb?

I fixed my gaze on the squirrel, and sent that Sunday-school question straight into its beady eyes. It ceased its bluster, twitched its tail some, and crept out further on the limb, where it leaned forward for a better look at me. Motionless, we gazed at each other until I unlocked my eyes from the squirrel's, and it scampered off, leaping from tree to tree and rustling out of sight.

This critter no doubt had more sense than I did of who, what, why, and where it was. Born into its patch of the world, it gathered acorns and did what squirrels do. When it curled up in its nest at night, did it wonder if it was living the life it should? Did it fret about what was good or bad, right or wrong? Likely not. That squirrel still lived in the Garden of Eden and still possessed the innocence that Trips said we lost when Adam and Eve ate Satan's apple from the Tree of the Knowledge of Good and Evil. And ever since, we've been doomed to torment over what to do with our lives.

The echoing splash of the pour-off beckoned me through the woods as I stepped solemnly toward it—the forest floor spongy and cool. Tumbling out of the laurel hell above, the rush of water also greater after the rain, the trace splattered down the jagged and mossy cut, sighing its gossamer mizzle through the dank incense. As I neared it, last fall's leaves grew slimy and slippery underfoot, and a chill shivered my spine. So I backed off and found a dry rock to sit on, not far away in a patch of sun.

For an eternity, I gazed at the race of droplets glittering like jewels in the dappled sunlight—its whispery music gaining substance as if the sound itself had thickened. The trees, bushes, and stones glowed from deep within, while everything seethed in a slow-motion boil.

I squeezed my eyes shut, to rid myself of this mirage, and a crazed sprangle of colory shapes swarmed behind my eyelids. Chill bumps crawled over my arms and the back of my neck, and I clenched my jaw, bringing on a dull ache. Blood throbbed through my head—the wall of my skull seeming no longer there—and like a hot-air balloon billowing over a fire, my mind felt close to floating off.

When I re-opened my eyes after a spell that felt of forever, the flood of reverence that had washed over me since I'd crossed over the creek—the feel of being one with all—had evaporated into a fearsome aloneness. Unable to muster the gumption to somehow shake off this bedevilment, or to just get up and go back across the creek to Walt, I teetered on the edge of terror. Tales of bad-trip freak-outs, of ending up in loony bins, beset me with a tornado of forlorn dread. Trees that moments before were a glory to on high, now loomed around me like boogermen. With me, who was no longer the me I'd known, trembling frozen with bewilderment in a melting world.

I closed my eyes again, hoping to shuck this horror. Yet in the blood-red pulse of my eyelids, the shifting colors and shapes throbbed bright as neon ghosts. The slosh and spatter of the pour-off, and the breath of a breeze rattling the leaves, now muttered like far off voices growing with unfathomable resentment. I bent an ear to heed them while will-o'-the-wisps swarming across my eyelids danced to echoes of these wordless haunts.

Faintly, a voice, singing like an angel might, called, "Ann-a-belle....." Then again, "Ann-a-belle...."

I threw open my eyes and cast them about. The forest listened with me. Nothing. But I'd heard my name called. I stood and scanned the depths between the writhing tree trunks for any clue. Restless bushes billowed like drapes in a breeze, and here and there I suspected the movement of some other presence—but none that I could fix an eye on.

"Ann-a-belle...." The voice sang again, louder and nearer. "Ann-a-belle...."

I turned toward it, and hollered, "Hello?" The word startling me as it boomed through the woods.

"Annabelle. Where are you?"—the voice riled with aggravation.

This simple question was so mysteriously puzzling, I stood dumb.

"Annabelle... it's Madeline. Is that you?"

Relief like the joy within laughter rescued me from my panic. Madeline had found me. But then her question echoed through me—"Is that you?"—dizzying me all the more. I knew it was not me. I'd somehow become someone else. Who I'd been was long gone. And I didn't yet know who I'd become.

"Annabelle!"—this time shrieking.

"Over here," I hollered back.

"Over where?"

"Over by the pour-off. By the ridge."

"What the hell's a pour-off?" she yelled, closer already.

Spotting her weaving through the trees, I caught her eye by waving my arms, and watched her carefully walk barefoot toward me, still in only her panties and sweatshirt, her hips and hair swaying, her hands reaching out for balance as she chose where next to step. I waited till she neared before answering, "A pour-off. You know, a little waterfall."

"Why don't you call it a waterfall?"

"Because it ain't a waterfall. It's a pour-off. A waterfall's bigger."

She stopped short, squinted sideways at me, and asked, "Think there's poison ivy in here?"

"Not this early, I'd guess."

"You'd guess?" she said, eyes on the ground as she neared.

"What you been doin'?" she asked.

"Madeline, I've been tripping my brains out."

"Me too, darlin'."

As she fetched up—her heart-shaped face warping monstrously, and her words appearing to sound all around me—she said, "Cheeks found his pickled punk. Actually, Lionel, the geek, found it floatin' merrily-merrily down the stream while he was huntin' frogs to eat. He snagged it up with his net and stood there wonderin' what the hell is this. Then Cheeks comes a-sloshin' down the creek, fat-ass naked, hollerin', 'It's mine! It's mine!' Funniest thing I ever done seen, other than *I Love Lucy*. Me and Lionel went to tears splittin' our sides."

I laughed some, too—springing deep from my belly, spreading a pleasure to fingers and toes. Then I remembered Walt, and asked if she'd seen him—the question appearing to come from some other me.

"Yeah. He's been just sittin' alone on that big flat rock, waitin' for Cheeks and me. Waitin' for you, more so, I'd guess. He sent me over here to find you. Cheeks was laid out, drying his bare ass atop the rock, cuddling with Frog Baby. I'm hoping he puts his clothes back on soon. By now I've seen about enough of what he's got.... Are you okay, Annabelle?" she asked, her almond eyes pinched with concern.

I hazarded a guess. "Maybe good as I might could expect.... A sight in and out of some contrariness. But I'm hoping I'm not yet much the worse for it. Moods come and go like in dreamland. A short piece back, I was all franzied about not knowing who I was any more. The world doesn't want to stay still. Everything appears trapped in itself, and restless to escape."

That many words coming out of me all at once amazed me with both my ability to string them all together right then, and the weight of their meaning. It was as if I had said the most important thing I'd ever said. My mind grabbled for what had struck me so in these words, and straightaway any sense of what had been so important fluttered off. And the more I reached for what it was, the further off it got.

Madeline said, "I've half a hankerin' to take a shower under that waterfall. You reckon it's too cold?"

Just the mention of it threw a chill through my bones. "Too cold for me."

"Maybe I'll just test it out some," she said, and tiptoed her way over the slippery leaves and rocks. Reaching out to touch the pour-off, she flicked her fingers through it, and then cupped her palms and scooped handfuls onto her face and legs. "It's not that bad," she shouted to me, shrugged and giggled. "I'm goin' for it."

She pulled off her sweatshirt and panties, flung them aside, and braless, stood like a mother-naked Greek statue—the beautiful curves of her ivory skin set against the craggy and mossy wall of shale, the straight raven-black hair falling over her teacup breasts, the V of nappy curls tucked below her bellybutton like a smile. She turned her bum to me—a blushing upside-down heart—and grabbling at the shale, she sidestepped under the pour-off. The glistening sluice splattered down over her as she lifted her face into it, slender strands of hair clinging to her hourglass back.

Spinning around to me, arms spread wide and nipples shrunk to thimbles, she yelled, "It's fabulous! Come on. Try it."

I shook my head, and hollered, "No way."

She put on an exaggerated pout, waved a dismissive hand, and then sat on a rock beneath the sparkly flutter of living water. Gathering her hair over one shoulder, she looked like a goddess in a fountain.

I'd gone skinny-dipping with girlfriends a few times, and once with some boys as well, and I hadn't been much shy about it. Our privates jiggling as we splashed and laughed, it was big fun. But flying high on this acid, eyes locked on Madeline, a fancy arose in me that shamed my decency. Not that I lusted for any red onion. I had no mind for that. It was more a sultry pleasure within my eyes, spreading further through me with each breath and glance, feeding on her raw womanhood. Ashamed to gratify this yen, I turned away, shuffled my feet, and peered through the trees to quile my unease.

I told her, "I'm going to catch up to Walt."

"Wait for me," she said, and pussyfooted her way over the mossy rocks to her clothes.

I snuck shy peeks at her, wringing out her sable hair—long as a horse's tail and slick with shine—toweling herself with her sweatshirt. And when she bent over to dry her legs, I stood gazing at the grotesque backside of some sort of human sow—teats a-flopping, hind-end a moist dark fright—the beautiful vision of her moments before, monstrously shape-shifted.

After she pulled on the blotted sweatshirt and the skimpy panties, she changed back into herself, showing me her smile, and we set off, stepping lightly over the forest floor, silent as two deer. The woods still breathed magical colors, glowing from a deep-set space, but whatever it was that had made known to me that all this and I were kin, had vanished—save its haunt.

At the creek, Madeline waded right on across. I caught sight of where I'd tossed my boots, upstream by the steppingstones, fetched them, and half waded, half hopped, from stone to stone, over to the other side.

Atop the flat rock, Cheeks sprawled belly-down, his freckly bum rosy with sunshine. Next to him, Sharpy lay curled up with his tufted eyes and ears cocked to our approach, and Frog Baby sat back inside its jar, but without its pickling. Walt, hands jammed into the front pockets of his blue jeans, stood eyeing me as we walked up, an impatient twist to his grim grin.

"Find any clues over yonder?" he asked, his tone ornery.

That soured me point-blank. I just shrugged, and flashed a vexed glance or two at him. He walled back his eyes, shook his head a few times, and dug for a cigarette.

Madeline, sensing our testiness, tried to ease the air by saying, "There's a beautiful little waterfall alongside the ridge. I took a shower under it, and it was wonderful."

Walt muttered, "Wonderful.... Just wonderful."

"Too cold for me," I added.

Walt said, "So I'd imagine."

A sullen hush came over us all. Cheeks rolled over and sat up, saying, "Ladies and gentlemen, dog and frog, I suggest a change of scene."

Madeline, pulling on her jeans, said, "Yeah. I've seen about enough of your naked ass for one day. When you gonna make yourself decent?"

"I'll never be decent. Who in hell wants to be decent?"

"Just get some clothes on," she told him, "afore I take in whuppin' you with a switch."

"Oh my. My oh my, my Madeline. That's what I've been prayin' for since Georgia. Lay it on me, she-bitch! Can you put on some skin-tight black-leather slacks before you do me? Hot damn. I'm gettin' a chubby just thinkin' of it."

"Cheeks, go fuck yourself. If you can find your chubby little pork sausage."

He howled and hooted and hauled up on the rock, grabbing ahold of his doodle and waggling the puny thing at Madeline. She stuck a finger down her throat and gagged. Then, flashing me a sly smile, she walked off, shouting back to us, "I suddenly got a hankerin' for a hot dog with onions. See y'all later."

Walt grumbled, "Cheeks, take your joint out of your hand and get some clothes on."

"I will if you give me a ride back to town. I need some teabags to brew up some brine for Frog Baby's jar. We got a show to do in a few hours."

"Yeah, yeah. I can do that," Walt told him, and then asked me civilly, "You wanna go into town for a while?"

I shook my head. "I'll just hang around here."

"Suit yourself."

My moods as flighty as a hummingbird, I now felt sorry for him. He only wanted me to go along with his doings, and all day long I'd been giving him a hard time about it. He hadn't really mistreated me any, so why did I mistreat him? It wasn't his fault, it was mine. Yet I couldn't mollify my airs right then. Something had ahold of me that wouldn't let it be, and I didn't know what. I went over to him and reached up for a hug. He stood stony and cold as a gravestone. We searched each other's faces while Cheeks pulled on his clothes.

I said, "I'll be here when you get back."

"I'm the one who's still here, Belle. You're who's gone off."

"I know... I know."

With nothing more to say, Walt led me and Cheeks back to the Mercury, along with Sharpy and the un-pickled punk. They got in and wheeled off the lot, and I stood there with my heart choking me like I'd swallowed it whole. What the heck was I doing? Why did I push away everything and everybody in my life? Most folks yearned to cling to their own. I had no more stick-to-it-ness than chewed bubblegum on greasy glass.

Needing to pee, I set off for the donniker, glad to have any purpose in sight. I had thought that maybe the LSD had already begun to wear off some. But alone again, away from the reality of my friends—if one could call that reality—I felt scarcely out of the woods yet.

I cut through a gap in the line-up and hurried along over the midway's carpet of trampled sawdust and straw. Basking under the dazzling blue sky, the rides snoozed in their pipe-rail cribs—behemoth beasts of burden, wheels within wheels—Octopus, Orbit, Rock-O-Plane, Round-Up, Scrambler, and Saturn Six. Across the midway from them, crouched the huddled line-up of joints—awnings down, laced and latched, their temptations hidden behind dusty canvas and aluminum—lying in wait for the night's fair game. Only the moan of the generator and some muffled voices and laughs from over by the cookhouse accompanied my footfalls.

As I neared the back end, Danny came out from behind the Harem in a rush, and stopping in his tracks, said, "Hey, Red. How's it goin' for ya?"

"It's going."

With a thumb and a finger, he tweaked one scraggly end of his Fu Manchu, and asked, "You ready to dump that hanky-pank chump-change and win some serious scratch?"

Without hesitation, I told him, "No way, Danny. No way."

He snorted a scoff. "Red, there's always a way. Sometimes you just don't see it."

"Well I'm plumb blind to nary a one."

"We'll see.... We'll see," he said, touching my elbow before shuckling off up the midway.

I studied the stage in front of The Harem. What if Walt and I split up? I likely couldn't work next to him in the pitch-till-u-win. So then what would I do? Whatever dollars I'd vaulted away so far wouldn't get me too far. And if Walt weren't paying for the room and most of my food, I'd have a heap less, right quick.

Could I get up the gumption to strut my stuff for some powerful cash money? The idea of it came down on me like high winds against a barn door banging open and shut with its hinges squealing. Danny would be no charm to work for, but neither was Nick. Trudy was way too much for any human to abide, but it was Janet's problem keeping the reins on her. The swaggering crowd of brush apes would leer at me like I was a red-combed sorry-girl—their auger eyes needling me with pruney lust. But would I hate it? Truth be told, most men looked at me that way already, which often pleasured me more than I'd want to allow.

However, my trading off of it—giving them a jag of what their nasty minds hone for, so that I might prosper—took a giant step toward the chippyhouse. But what's the difference between what Marilyn Monroe and all the other movie stars do, and what goes on in The Harem? Well, one is glamorous and the other trashy. But we're not in Hollywood here—not even close. And soon, so I could shed this devilish carnival, my options might be either take the bus back to Clandel, or get up on that hootchy-kootchy stage, lure men behind the curtain, and shed my clothes.

Leaving off chewing on this any longer, I turned on a heel and cut through a gap in the back end, and marched to the donniker. There, down on his knees, dragging one of the honey troughs out from under the trailer, Hank mumbled cusses as he coaxed out the battered tin tub brimming with a slop of sallow turd-and-t.p.-mottled flux. Arsling it out from under, enough to get a grip on the side handles, he hauled himself up on his haunches, and duck-walking hind-side-first, with some of it sloshing over the sides, he slid the trough to a nearby freshly-dug hole—my innards churning at the sight and smell.

Hank stood wiping his hands on the benastied bib of his gray-striped overalls, and gave me a lengthy look that appeared to carry both puzzlement and undue hope. He nodded mannerably, and said, spluttering like he was being strangled and flailing his arms about as if he was shooing the words like flies, "This ahere be the ladies' leavin's. What I aims to bury shortly. For y'ur needments, missy, use the menfolk's privy, an' I'll keep a lookout."

I cautiously stepped up into the men's side of the trailer—calling, "Hello?" to nobody. While doing my business, I wondered what had brought Hank so low to take on such a job. Did this gangly old half-breed have no other options in life? He couldn't have just up and chosen this. Did he get stuck out here with no home to go back to, and end up tending the honey hole of carnies? Sure, somebody had to do it—but why him? Because he said yes? Or because he didn't say no? I felt an unease that if I didn't get a grip on my own doings, then I might could end up much the same.

I scooted out of the donniker, and as I walked past him, he tipped the trough on end and the slurry gushed into the hole. A stink loud enough to drown out a gather-all of riled polecats lit into my nose like coal smoke. I'd learned enough from science class to know for a fact that I'd just inhaled a cloud of molecules that not long ago had been up the hind ends of carnies, and then had stewed in a vat all week—a knowing which the LSD rang true, much too much.

With one hand over my nose and mouth, I reached forward with the other for the quickest which-a-way out of there. And—although unsure whether Hank said this or not—I thought I heard him mutter, like a prayer over a grave, "God is both good and evil."

Not slowing to find out if he actually had said that, I trotted through the zigzag maze of cars and trucks and trailers, and stumbled into Isis, sunning herself in a lawn chair beside her house trailer.

"Whoa, Annabelle. Where you headed off to in such a rush?"

"Escaping from the stink of Hank dumping the privy honey."

She tittered her melodic little laugh, and said, "There's no escape from the shit of this world, dearie. Set a while, and tell me how things are with you."

She gestured to another chair leaning against the trailer, which I unfolded next to hers and sat upon. In only her black bikini, with her green robe draped over the back of her chair, Isis's tattooed skin glowed like the funny pages from an old Sunday newspaper—drinted, withered, and discolored, yet warm and gaudy in the sunlight.

Amid silver curls tumbling from her saggy jowls, a gentle smile stretched her thin lips tight against crooked and yellowy teeth. Her merry eyes, blue as robins' eggs, studied me as if I were the most darling thing she'd seen in quite a spell.

She laid her veined and gnarly hand atop mine, and asked, "How's it going with your young man, Walt?"

"Right now, not so hot."

"Oh? What seems to be the problem?"

"Dog my hide if I can figure. Sometimes I think it's him. Sometimes I think it's me. Maybe it's both of us."

"Well," she said, "most times things are bits of both. However, you can't do much about what he does. You can only do something about you.... Are you alright, dearie? You seem a tad out of sorts."

Not wanting to let on that I was flying high on LSD, I shied from her search of my face, and blurted out, "I sometimes wonder who I really am."

She threw back her head and laughed a chorus of hee-hee's, revealing a hint of the tattoos hidden by her beard on her neck, the tattoos she'd said held the meaning of life. I tried to conjure some sense of it from pieces of what symbols I saw, before she turned to me and said, "Now you're asking the right question. Who do you think you are?"

"Just another hillbilly from Clandel."

"No, dear. Clandel has made you act like just another hillbilly from Clandel. You're really the same unique and beautiful person who was born into this world some twenty years ago."

"Nineteen years ago."

"Whenever it was when you slid out of your mother's womb, that's still who you are. Then, and now, and forever. Your family and your town, your schooling and your friends, all have tried to make you into what they want you to be."

I sat up and faced her, and said, "I'd allowed pretty near the same thing to myself not an hour or so ago."

"Who *you* are is that girl who was there before they all had their way with you.... Do you remember her?"

I leaned back and thought on this. Behind all what I'd accepted and rejected of my coal-town life, there'd been a part of me saying yes or no—a voice smothered by shoulds and musts—a girl who wanted to be, but hardly had the chance.

"Do you remember that little girl they named Annabelle?" she asked again. "She's who you truly are. And now she's about to become the woman you truly are. The person that life has created, not the one who the world has made you into."

Like someone with amnesia, I tried to recollect who I'd been before being hit over the head with West-by-God-Virginia. While Isis searched my eyes for clues, and with the LSD still spinning whirlwinds behind them, I sensed the shadow of a ghost. I knew the haunt was there, but to bring it back to life, I sorely lacked the hoo-doo.

"She's there," I said, "I'm there, in me, behind it all somewhere. Often I feel her telling me things.... But how do I reach her?"

A smile bloomed on Isis's bushy cheekbones, gleeful that I'd understood. She patted my knee, and said, "The same way you reach the soul of All That Is. By silencing your blathering thoughts. And hearing without listening."

"Say what? How?"

"By meditation. By quiet contemplation amid the essence of being."

"And how do you do that?"

"First, my dear, just sit someplace quiet and comfortable. It need not be completely silent. The gentle sounds of the world, the froufrou of wind or birds, are all okay as long as they don't hijack your attention. Concentrate on slowing your breathing, following its flow in and out of you.

"Second, cease the chatter that infests our minds. Shut off those wordy things we call thoughts. It's not easy to quiet this yackety-yack. But our deepest mind uses no words. There's a deeper knowledge within us that was known eons before the first words were ever spoken. We've built a Tower of Babel upon which we believe we can talk our way up to God. Yet what we seek isn't on high, atop a pile of words. It's in us all. It's all in us. We're all in it. The you who you are is your part of it all. You, unified—yet unique."

She let that sink in, while she searched my face for clues if it did. I sat drop-jawed dumb in the light of what I'd just been through at the creek—the ken of what she'd said ringing true, like a dinner bell jingle-jangling to my hungry soul.

"And thirdly, you must open your inner eye to witness it. If you try to see or hear it, then you won't. Remain open to it, receptive. Then, when you do see it, you won't be deceived."

"Deceived by what?"

"Deceived by your own assumptions. And by the assumptions of others."

"How will I know which is which? And what do you mean, 'it'?"

"Oh you'll know it when you see it, my dear."

A reedy voice asked, "Know what?" We turned to see Trips ambling up to us.

"All that we are, and All That Is," Isis told him, her eyes sparking with welcome.

He sniggered, and said, "M'lady, are you corrupting this gorgeous girl with your mystic malarkey?"

"Look who's talkin', you Jungian three-armed Tarot dealer. Annabelle here tells me you gave her a reading, back at the last spot."

Standing there auger-eyed, he studied me a moment—the black cape over his two left arms, his acorn-shaped head not much taller than mine when sitting, the peach fuzz under his beret glowing like a halo in the lowering sunlight—and then he said, "Oh yeah... I remember now. You cut three trumps. Three corresponding trumps, like a picture book with captions. The Fool, The Lovers, and The Wheel of Fortune. Right?"

I nodded, and he asked, "So how's the future been?"

I shrugged, and Isis joked, "You tell her. You're the fortune teller around here."

He threw his head back with a cackly laugh, and said, "Fortunes aren't told. They're sold."

"So that's your deal with fate," Isis said, smirking.

"I'd rather tempt fate with cash, than dole out free mystic mottos."

She snorted, and said aside to me, "A fool assumes it's all in the cards."

"Not so, my androgynous darlin', not so. Tarot cards have nothing on them but mirrors of what's in us."

"Are you doling out your own free mottos now?" she scoffed. "Or are they for sale?"

"They're yours to treasure, in trade for my pleasure of buying you a cup of coffee at the cookhouse."

"Only if you keep those cards up your sleeve."

"That I can do. All three sleeves."

Isis stood—I followed her lead—and she leaned to me and whispered, "Don't you never no mind us two old freaks. We're just amusing ourselves. And you'll find yourself, sooner or later. Just keep on looking inside."

She put a hand on my shoulder and drew me into a hug. My arms circled her tattooed midriff and squeezed her frail frame close. But the soft and loose skin of her bare waist, the press of her saggy bubbies against the firmness of mine, the eerie tickle of her beard on the side of my face, shied me off from our embrace.

Trips, quite the gentleman, helped Isis on with her robe, sporting three attentive hands and a doting gleam in his eye. She flipped the hood over her hair, winked one knowing eye at me, and with Trips at her elbow, they set off toward the cookhouse. I watched them stroll away—a tattooed bearded lady, wise as her snake, and a three-armed fortune teller, weird as the pictures on his cards. Even if I wasn't in such a hopped-up state of mind, they appeared beyond belief. Yet there they went, arm in arm in arm.

I wandered off to the edge of the lot, past the gypsy camp to where the tree line met the field, and found another rock to sit upon for a spell, hoping to settle back to earth. But the LSD kept on magnifying each moment huger than ought to be possible, jolting me with alternating currents of fear and glory, panic and peace, horror and beauty, confusion and clarity.

Again and again, absolute knowings of obvious truths would burst out of their hidden cocoons, and immediately flutter off like butterflies—beyond capture with any net I might wave, and never to be pinned down under glass for study. What good was a trip with no souvenirs to bring back?

The whine of tires on blacktop drew my eyes, and beyond the bushes I spied the red and chrome glints of Walt's Mercury returning from town. In no mood to deal with anybody's mulligrubs, including my own, I lit out into the woods, weaving through the trees until nothing of the carnival could be seen behind me.

I chewed over what Isis had told me. The only notion I had of meditation was of a half-naked scrawny guru in rags, cross-legged on a rug, eyes walled up in his hairy head. How could the likes of that be a remedy for the likes of me? To just sit there and try to not figure out things when you're trying to figure things out, didn't make a lick of sense.

Also, just who was this 'me' that she said was the real me? Wasn't I plainly an ackempucky of all I'd been through, all my experiences, all I'd learned? How might a bearded lady in a rag-tag carnival have the answers? She knew diddly-squat about me.

I stopped dead in my tracks, thunderstruck by a notion that the contentious argufying forever blathering on and on inside my head was what Isis had said kept me from being myself—my own notions wrassling with each other.

After only a few hours of LSD, bucketfuls of assumptions about what in the world was the world no longer held water for me. I saw that things maybe weren't what I thought them to be, unless I allowed them to be so. Starving for answers my whole life long, I'd swallowed lashings and lavins of notions about the world—other folk's answers, spoon-fed to me right along with side dishes of my own bereft concoctions.

My mind already blown to smithereens, what harm could come from giving this meditation thing a try? I looked around for someplace fitting to do so, and spotted a jade-green patch of moss carpeting a straddle of gnarly roots beneath a thick oak. The afternoon sun, not far from the top of the west ridge, sprinkled the seat with dancing dapples of light. After clearing off some twigs and feeling for any dampness, I leaned my backbone up against the bark and shifted about until sitting cozily, but not cross-legged like a swami. I wondered if that would make a difference, like not kneeling or folding hands when praying.

I closed my eyes and gently gave ear to the woodland sounds—the swish of breezes in the treetops, the chirp-chirp of birds, the murmur of the creek some ways off. Amid the shadowy murk behind my eyelids, the flutter of sunlight through the leaves flashed blood red. I fixed my attention on my breath, soughing in and out, slower and slower.

My thoughts tumbled willy-nilly, one thing after another, petty snippets of this and that, their conceits exalted by the LSD. As soon as I'd realize I was jibber-jabbering with myself again, I'd put a stop to it. When I'd hold onto the silence for a short piece, I'd float awhile amid a welling up of inner darkness. Then before I knew it, the blatherskites in my belfry would be clanging back and forth once more.

But bit by bit, I quiled them longer. More and more, a feel of expansion grew, strutting as I drew in each breath—like being inside a balloon slowly filling with tingly energy.

Somewhere above and between my eyes, within splashes of bloody sunshine, dreamlike haunts lurked in the twilight—fetching near as if to ask or tell me something, and then fading away before I could know what it was. I gathered my focus into my shuttered eyeballs and walled them upward, toward my mind's eye.

Silent lightning flashed—and the next thing I know, I'm gazing up into Maw's young face, my mouth clamped onto her firm bubby, greedily suckling her sweet warm milk.

How this could be didn't matter a lick. What did matter, what drew water from a well deep within, was my recollecting the pure-quill joy being cradled in her arms, feeding on life itself, fat with innocent love. Somehow I was there again. There from the get-go, this baby born into this world was who I truly was, and who I'd always be.

Astonished, I popped open my eyes. Through the blur of a tear the forest warmed with a wondrous comfort. A tide of courage surged into me, and anything now appeared possible.

Trying to ease the leaping of my heart, I closed my eyes, and again turned my gaze inward, seeking more of these visions. As I floated off into the darkness, snippets of my life story lit up like previews at the movies. But not like watching them from the seats. I was back inside these scenes, one after another, yet somehow all at once, understanding them as I did then, as if I were there again—somewhere in a time zone that had no clocks.....

.....I'm lying on my side, behind the bars of my crib, gumming the rubber nipple of a baby bottle, its glass smooth and hard, the lukewarm milk a smidgen blinky. Maw, her bathrobe hanging open, comes through the door to check on me, and I reach out for her soft bubbies. But she just turns and leaves the room. I push away the bottle and flail arms and legs, trying to follow her, struggling mightily just to pull myself to my feet. Eyelevel with the rail of the crib, I shriek for my birthright—my mother's milk.....

.....I'm bouncing on Pap's knee, held there by his sooty hands—big hands, strong and swollen from wrassling coal from the mine. He whistles a tune and joggles me to the beat atop his leg—me giggling near about to choke. He stops, leans back into his stuffed chair, sets me onto his solid belly, and says something in low-toned words I don't yet understand. Bundled in his safety, his power, I gaze into his rugged face, peppered with stubble, and in my adoration of him, my confidence in him, my little heart struts so proud. Then he plunks me down on the gritty carpet, reaches for a bottle of beer on the side table, guzzles half of it down, and turns his attention to the TV.....

.....We're all sitting around the dinner table about to eat—Pap, Maw, my three-year-older-sister Rosalie, and me strapped into my high chair. Maw bows her head and says a prayer, which I gather the gist to be thanking someone not here with us and who has somehow given us the food—the Lord—and I puzzle on who that can be. When I won't eat the jibbled-up hotdog and greasy beans on the plate in front of me, Maw spoons it into my mouth, jimmies it in bit by bit. I shake my head and wail and snub and spit it out, it disgusts me so—and I blame the Lord for this.....

.....My rag doll dangling in one hand, I'm toddling happily around the house, taking my baby for a walk, when my sister stamps up and snatches it away from me. I run crying to Maw about the wrong, and she tells me that it's Rosalie's turn to play with the doll. There's no way my baby can possibly also be hers, so I run back to Rosalie and try to tug it from her clutches. She swats me upside the head and knocks me to the floor—where, screaming bloody murder till my throat smarts, with Maw doing nothing about it, I cringe for what feels of forever.....

.....Maw, Rosalie, and I sit on a wooden bench at Sunday meeting. I wonder forlornly why Pap's not with us—other fathers are there with their families. As the congregation sings a hymn to the rafters, a dusty beam of sunlight through a high window catches my breath. Front and center, nailed onto a wooden cross, a painted plaster man in a diaper slumps dead—the pain on his face scaring me to dithers. The preacher man takes in hollering about Jesus saving us from Satan. I figure the plaster man to be Satan, and his punishment for being so evil is his being hung on a cross. Then, because the preacher keeps on pointing at the man on the cross as he shouts about Jesus, I get it that Jesus is the dead man! This bamboozles me to no end. In my puzzlement, I squirm atop the hard wooden seat with no further ken of what the preacher is telling us, and I wish that Pap was there.....

.....I awake on a cold Christmas morning, certain that the doll I asked Santa to bring me, exactly like the one on TV, is wrapped in one in the ribbony boxes under the sparkly tree next to the threadbare divan. Rosalie and I hop and clap and squeal into Maw and Pap's bedroom, and roust them out of bed, so we can open our gifts. We rip at ribbons, paper, and cardboard, while they sit on the divan, grinning sleepily. But in my boxes are only clothes—just dull drab clothes.....

.....On my knees with my toy shovel, I'm stabbing at a hole in my play garden, aiming to plant a dingy plastic flower. The bushes stir down in the steep below the shacklety house we once lived in, up a hollow at the edge of town. Something on the prowl is snuffing and scuffing through the brush. I get to my feet, take a few steps backward, and heft the little shovel with both hands like an ax, as it might could be a willipus-wallupus. A heart-thumping minute later, a beagle paddles into sight, nose to the ground, ears all flip-flop. Relieved it's not hungry for the likes of me, I remember a peanut-butter cookie stashed in the bib pocket of my overalls, and hold it out to the dog. Spooked at his first sight of me, he winces and arsles sideward, eyeing me charily until he lifts his nose to catch a whiff of the cookie. Then the dog fetches right up, my new best friend, half my size, tail a-wagging, sadly hopeful eyes on his prize. I dole it out to him bit by bit, my hand soon slathered with dog licking. Eating the last crumb myself, I stroke the brown and white fur, soft and oily and peppered with chaff from the bushes. There are more cookies in the kitchen, so with hand language I coax the dog up the treads and through the back door. Sliding a chair to the pantry, I climb onto it to reach for another cookie in the clown-faced jar—the beagle dancing clickety-clackety on the linoleum. Then Maw up and hollers, "What in tarnation is that hound doin' in my kitchen? Git it outta here now. You hear, missy? Now! And what's that dirt all over your knees? Can't you keep your clothes decent for half a mornin'?" I hop off the chair and scurry for the door—the dog trotting along behind me. Outside, he sees I have no cookie, sniffing the air a few times to be sure. Then swinging his snout to the ground, he trots away hunting up another scent. I follow him to the far edge of the narrow yard, where he noses into the thicket and is shortly out of sight.....

.....Newly moved into our apartment in town, I'm allowed to play in the side yard. At the far end of the scraggly lawn, between some bushes, I discover a narrow path winding into the woods, and likely made by critters coming down the hill to scavenge trash or gardens. I slowly go a dozen careful paces into the rocky shadows. Turning to look behind me, I'm shocked how bright the sunshine is on the dried-up green of the yard and the chalky paint on the side of the house. Just a few steps from my yard, there in the cool wildness of budding shoots and rotting logs, sets a whole other world, lorded over by nary a grown-up. I stand there frozen in the twilight between the sunny yard and long shadows higher on the hillside, feeling fear of what's further up, but shunning the safety of the yard. Peering up and down and side to side, I spy amid the saplings, the tree trunks, the mossy stones, for a mystery I sense is there, but can't quite catch sight of. Pap hollers my name and I scurry back into the yard. He scolds, "I thought I told you don't go up in those woods!" Then he rushes toward me to whup me one.....

.....Maw rousts me in my warm bed and tells me to get ready for school. I crave to stay home. There's an icy rain spattering on the window, and my first-grade teacher, Mrs. Moore, is such a bully that I despise being in her classroom. Old, ugly, and rambling on and on about things she's already told us, she bosses me to sit still and listen. I curl deeper under the bedcovers, clutching them tight, and my silent voice whimpers, over and over, that I don't want to go. Shortly, Maw screeches from the kitchen, "Annabelle! Git your hinder outta that bed afore I thrash it." Sobby-eyed, I crawl out and scurry across the cold floor to my dresser drawer.....

.....On my grade-school playground, Waylon and I teeter on the seesaw while a pack of kids chant, "Annabelle and Waylon, up in a tree, k-i-s-s-i-n-g. Annabelle and Waylon, up in a tree, k-i-s-s-i-n-g." I've been goo-goo with puppy love for Waylon. At the desk behind me in the third grade, he would whisper little jokes in my ear, not all that funny, but meaning to please—both of us sharing much forbidden giggling. But now—him there straddling the other end of the see-saw plank, both fists gripping the handle, head bowed in embarrassment while his eyes hunt sidelong for his escape— I see he wants no part of their mocking of us. I don't either, but his shying away from me, his shunning me in front of the other kids, casts my fancy for him out through a hole in my heart. I huff and scowl and waggle off my end of the seesaw. Waylon thuds open-mouthed to the sand as I stamp away.....

.....At Sunday school, in the church's backroom, Mr. Connors, a deacon and our teacher, stands there with his pot belly pushing his white shirt and floppy tie through his unbuttoned suit jacket, as he tells me and the other little kids scattered before him on the carpet, that unless we take Jesus into our hearts as our savior, we'll be doomed to hellfire. A question pops into my head—what then would we be saved from other than the wrath of God Himself?—which seems awful mean for the God of Love that the reverend is always talking up. I want to ask Mr. Connors about that, but I'm shy to do so because whenever I would ask him what I thought was a reasonable question, I'd get this look from his beady eyes, saying don't be so foolish. Yet being thrown into hell is no small thing. So I raise my hand, half-befuddled with my own question, and I ask him what I needed to be saved from. His eyes go beady, and he tells me, "Miss Cory, it's asking things like that, what brings doom. Faith in Jesus and in God's Bible brings us salvation from sin. With faith, we don't ask questions. We believe because it's The Word of God, and of God's Son, and the breath of The Holy Spirit. Questions only bring doubt, Miss Cory, which eats at faith like a demon, bite by bite, until faith dies. And without faith there's no salvation, only doom." But then more questions arise in me about what he just said. I flinch and fidget, not from any demons eating at me, but because his banning my questions fetches up in me a fearsome notion—maybe what dooms us instead is what Mr. Connors is teaching. And just by thinking that, the contrary of all I've ever been told, I figure I'm surely bound for hellfire.....

.....I sit in my fourth-grade classroom, bored with Mrs. Winslow going on and on about arithmetic I'd already learned how to do in the third grade. Outside the window, sunlight dances on the hillside's leaves coloring to red and gold. A crow lands atop the plank fence that borders the playground, and I watch him swivel his head and caw at something. I sorely envy his freedom. I subtract four from the twelve grades needed to graduate from school, eight more years to go, and I hate how long that adds up to. My head hanging heavy with the weight of all that time, Mrs. Winslow calls on me for the answer to what she's chalked on the blackboard. I look up, study her prim cyphers, and then shortly answer, "Thirty-four." She appears misput— likely because I'd escaped her trap, solving the problem too easily—and she turns to write a new row of numbers on the blackboard. I peek over my shoulder to see if the crow is still there, but it's flown off.....

.....In the bedroom I share with my sister, I'm pawing through my half of the closet, hunting for my favorite dress, which is not there. I rummage through Rosalie's side—not there either. I wear this dress to school as much as I can, often three and four days in a row, until Maw would snatch it into the wash, chiding me to put on something else. Shoulders flouncy, and its skirt swishy with pleats, it has an old-timey style, like on girls in cowboy movies. The tiny blue and yellow flowers printed on it have faded, and the hem has frayed some, yet I love this dress. Because no other girl in school wears anything like it, the dress gives me a feel of being someone special, another guess to them all. I figure that Maw's got it in the wash, so I sneak over to the clothes hamper in the bathroom, to dig it out. It's not there, either. Fretting now, I go ask her, as she's frying cornpone on her flat skillet, if she's seen it. "You mean that raggedy old prairie dress?" I nod timidly, suspecting what's coming. "I told you I was fixin' to pitch that out. Well, missy, I finally did. It's high time you got shed of it. Day after day lookin' like some young'un on *Death Valley Days*. Go put on that nice dress I got you for your birthday. Y'ain't hardly put no use to it yet." I stagger back into the bedroom, fall onto my bed, and snub into the pillow till late for school.....

.....Maw and Pap are in the kitchen jowering again about what the paycheck got spent on. Their contrariness is nothing new, nor is it always about money. Their voices grow louder and louder, as if whoever hollers the most will win. I'm no stranger to it, but this night I feel queer and puny about their argufying. I'm curled up beneath a patchwork quilt in the stuffed armchair in front of the TV, watching *The Donna Reed Show*, on which each week a family in starchy clothes acts up over one tame predicament after another. Yet these folks don't tear into each other like Maw and Pap do, spitting their spite back and forth. Donna Reed tends to their troubles calmly and with plain good sense. I well know this TV show isn't much more than a fairy tale. But sitting there between the voices in the kitchen and those on TV, I pine for just a smidgen of peace at home, and maybe every now and then an outcome that makes Maw and Pap smile, or swap a hug or kiss. But that appears unlikely—unlikely as all the doings on the TV show......

.....It's way past bedtime, near midnight, with a rattly winter wind outside, and I'm under the blankets with a flashlight, spellbound reading *The Pearl*, by Steinbeck—my book report due on it the next morning. At the end of a chapter, the notion comes to me that I'm not still awake reading just because I have to get my schoolwork done. It's because I can't let loose of this book. I want the story never to be over, even though I can't wait to see what happens at the end. Like Dorothy in Oz, I'm not in Kansas anymore. This tornado of words has carried me away to a native family's hut on a tropical beach, with plain-old human greed yanking levers and mashing buttons behind the wizard's curtain. Figuring this notion to be a decent forty or fifty words for my book report, I slide out of bed to scribble it into my notebook on the dresser. The creaky board in the floor complains loudly, and I have to rustle through a drawer to find a pencil. Halfway through writing it down under the yellowing oval of the flashlight, Rosalie, in her bed on the other side of the room, sits up, blinks and squints, and then whines, "Maw... Annabelle's out of bed." I scurry back under the blankets, stash the light and book at my feet, and wait for Maw to come a-hollering. But she doesn't, so I push my tongue between my lips to razz a poot at my sister, who's already breathing her sleeping sounds again. Then I wriggle down beneath the blankets—my knees like tent poles, the fading flashlight warm in the crook of my neck, *The Pearl* open across my scarce hips—and go back to where I'd left off.....

.....I'm in Maw's bedroom, decked out and primping in front of the only full-length mirror in the apartment, taped on the backside of her closet door. There's a dance and social tonight for young teens in the Church of God's basement, and I'm studying and admiring my outfit, bought with money saved up from some cleaning jobs that Aunt Jody'd got me in on—brand-fired-new leg-hugging shiny-black slacks—a sparkly-red sequined top, my skinny arms bare and pale—and pearl-gray strappy pumps with three-inch heels a size too long. The shoes and the top I found at a second-hand store. My red-leather belt, skinny and silver-spangled, perfect for the get-up, I'd filched from Celia's Lady's Shoppe. I bought the slacks there, on sale, but the belt, way too costive, I stole because I had to have it, even though I reckoned myself to hold contrary to thieving. Now, guiltily eyeing it around my middle, I wish I hadn't. Maybe one of the chaperones at the dance might know it was stolen. But it fits so perfect and looks so fixy, cinching the make of my waist and showing off my new curves between my blooming nubs and hips. I pose and pout like the girls in magazine ads, auditioning my face in the mirror—wide-eyed and high-boned, with this puny turned-up nose and a jut of jaw more than most, all surrounded with springy reddish curls—quite possibly a model's face, or an actress's. Catching glimpses of the young woman I soon will be, and posing as the cool chick I yen to be, my pride struts with the prospects. Then Maw shuffles in, eyeing me side-ways, drops her basket of laundry on the bed, and wags a finger at me, saying, "Ain't that a mite too loud for a church social? Girl, you go change into somethin' more proper. Or you'll not be goin'." I clomp to my room, slam the door, and switch on some rock-and-roll radio, way up loud. For a fact, I'm not about to change my clothes, nor go to that dance now. With a vengeance, then and there, I take in dancing my fool head off, tottering atop the heels.....

.....It's a chilly fall afternoon at a high school football game, and I'm sitting in the stands between my girlfriends, Mary Jo and Karen. The boys on the field scramble through yet another muddled play, but I'm more interested in a boy sitting a few rows in back of us, Casey Flynn, who through some flirty smiles and glances in history class has sparked my fancy. He's from the better side of town—his pap's got a drug store on Main Street—and he's sitting with a half-dozen other boys, all of them cute and cool. My heart leaping rambunctious as a foal, I ache to swivel around and see what Casey's face tells me. But the only sight of him I dare catch is in the corner of my eye when I casually turn to Mary Jo or Karen. Then the stands erupt with a roar and everybody leaps to their feet as a pass gets caught downfield and the ball is wrassled close to the goal line. Making use of the hubbub to take my jacket off, I turn to set it atop my bleacher seat and raise my eyes to

Casey. What I see is the whole pack of boys leering at me like dogs at meat. They'd all enjoyed a randy eyeful of me yanking off my jacket, twisting my curves, showing the make of my bubbies and backside. And now they all await a look from me signaling if they might have half a chance to maybe get some of that—Casey right there along with them. My shine for him goes dull in a blink, and I scowl at them my answer to their urges. Denied, one boy elbows the ribs of the boy beside him and mutters something behind a hand. They all hear it and snigger to each other. The worst of the bunch, Kevin Taylor, says plenty loud enough for me and other folks around us to hear, "Ya reckon her red onion's ruddy-tufted?"—which gets the boys all hooting manly haw-haws, Casey included. I look daggers into his eyes, turn and sit, and show them my back.....

.....Traipsing into the apartment after a sleepover at Karen's house, I cringe at the shabbiness of my home, our disorderly clattermints atop wore-out furniture. Karen's folks keep a warm and decent home, spick-and-span tidy with fixy things new as fresh paint. Both parents work jobs at the court-house, and Karen is always prettied-up with the latest fashions from Celia's window. I never invite Karen to my place—I'm shamed by it. And though she's offered many times, I'm too proud to wear her hand-me-downs. I know well that it's all to do with money—how much or how little—and I know that no matter how hard Pap works, when he is working, there's still not enough to heat our rooms proper. But that doesn't slow the dank from seeping its coldness into my heart night after night. I plop onto the couch, stare at the paint peeling off where the ceiling leaked, and shortly hear Maw snubbing behind her bedroom door. She's not one to shed tears, so I wonder what's so wrong and knock on her door, asking, "Maw... you okay?" She goes quiet, save for a lengthy sigh, then swings open the door and tells me matter-of-factly, "Your Pap's done left out for Charleston with that weed-monkey, Estelle Martin. And he ain't a-comin' back even iffen he had a mind to. We're done with that good-for-nothin'. He's dead to me now." That said, she slams the door. I stand there hypnotized by the crackly door varnish, my breath frozen, my heart clamoring wordlessly for Pap.....

.....On a glorious summer afternoon, I'm afoot downtown on my way to the library. Tucked against my side, I clutch an armload of novels, some read, some not. They're a mite overdue, but the younger librarian usually lets me slide on any fees, and she works today. Then up to the curb rolls a carload of classmates—Wint Smith in his father's huge-big Buick, along with two girls, one I know well enough, Carrie Garrett, and a pair of crew-cut football boys with reputations as skylarks. Carrie rolls down the back window and asks, "Annabelle Cory, where ever are you off to with such a passel of books?" "The library," I say. "The library? On such a fine day? Jump on in here with us, girl. We're headed for the swimming hole over by Feeny Mountain. We got a couple six-packs of three-two, and these boys here tell me they'll be skinny-dipping. What say, Annabelle?" The others chime in, "Yeah." "What say?" "Come on." But I don't know what to say. I'd never before trafficked out to swimming holes with beer and football boys. At first, the feel of I'd rather go to the library sweeps through me, but then a tidal wave of vexing embarrassment washes it away. In their eyes, I see they mark me curious, their ears cocked, awaiting what I say—which is, "But I'm toting all these books." Wint tells me, "Chunk 'em in the trunk," and gets out to open it up. Suddenly it's either say no, or don't. Yet I can only bring myself to drop them into the trunk, alongside the beer—the trunk huge enough for hundreds of books, or dozens of six-packs.....

.....I'm being led by the hand into Wade Miller's bedroom in his folk's house, who are at Bible study. After weeks of his wheedling, I've given into his beseeching me to go all the way with him. We've been steady beaus for a few months, and although I've been hot-blooded for all our kissing and groping, and I reckon myself to be in love with him, I'm now not so sure about letting him have his way with me. His smitten eyes are fixed on mine, as they've been this whole last year of high school. My bloom coming late to a skinny girl with her face always in books, our cagey smiles in class-rooms and hallways had been seen by all, gossiped about and teased about, and had led us from skittish heart-thumping dates at dances and parties, to being together daily for hours on end—much of the time mashing and grab-bing in his folk's car, or at our hideaway down along Black Creek, on our magic carpet of green moss surrounded by wax myrtle. He now pulls me toward his quilted bed. What with all the talk about how fantastic sex is, and all the romantic fireworks in novels and movies, all making me curious as a cat for what rustles behind that door, yet I still tremble at the approach of my first time—my cherry, my virginity, soon gone to unknown loss and gain. Standing there at the bedside, we blink with uneasiness. His first time too, I suspect his buddies have egged him on, as my girlfriends have me, everybody saying how wonderful and momentous it will be. He pecks a kiss on my quivery lips and takes in shedding his clothes. I fumble with mine as his strut waggles free. Many times, I'd felt its stoutness pressing in his jeans against me, and once on a black-dark night I'd fondled it to spurting. But now to see what would be shoved into my satchel turns the lust in my belly to queasiness. His electrified hands guide my naked shoulders to the pillow, and he hauls up over me while he awkwardly unrolls a rubber over his hoe handle. My cleft sobby, I spread my legs as he takes aim. At the gate, he fumbles gently, then he finds the way in, thrusting and moaning. I wince from a shot of unfamiliar pain, and I gasp as he fills my deep, again and again. After no more than a dozen strokes, with a groan and a sigh he melts on top of me. I feel him pulsing inside me, and shortly it shrivels cool and clammy. I wonder, is that all? Is this what everybody says will fetch the moon? I push him off me, sorely disappointed—feeling as if I'd helped fix a Christmas dinner and it ended up tasting like something from the high school cafeteria.....

.....On a gray and windy afternoon, I'm climbing the treads to our apartment, my rucksack heavy with schoolwork, and halfway up I turn and sit, elbows atop knees, and stare into space. The jumble of agley houses and parked cars on the hillside, the telephone poles and the power lines, the chimneys and TV antennas, all lurk beyond a notion troubling me. I wonder where in the world is all the bearm and beauty that I read of in books, that I see on TV or at a movie. I know that it's all made up, but some of it must be so. Somewhere there are sandy beaches and tall cities, all astir with much to do. Yet it's just another day for me—once again to school, then back home, to homework, supper, TV, bed—with only novels to lend me hope that there's more to it than just this. Sure enough, this townful of mountaineers acts out its own brand of drama. But like *The Beverly Hillbillies*, not much other than foolishness ever gets broadcast. And though, in the hills above the town and up the hollows along the creek, an untamed beauty lives in raw splendor, what I witness, day to day, is this coal-stained eyesore named Clandel. Here I lift my face to the early spring sun, brilliant in the pale-blue west and soon to lower beyond the thicket of trees on the ridge top. With its warm glow upon my eyes, I thank my lucky stars for my yen for books, and for—someday, somehow—their leading me to someplace else.....

.....Far off, I hear a Merry-Go-Round tooting a waltz as I await another episode to reel before me. But nothing appears....

I opened my eyes to the sun-ball dropping behind the shadowy ridge, the rocky-top tree line glimmering with golden green. The waltz was real. It meant that it was four-o'clock call already. I had no clue how long I'd been sitting there. Had I fallen asleep? If so, it was like no sleep I'd ever known. Had I been simply dreaming? If so, it was like no dreaming I'd ever done. It was like being shown one scar after another, mallyhacked into the heart of who I am.

Getting to my feet, I wobbled about some, the LSD still with its grip on me, but in a different way. The stand of trees appeared more distant, more apart, more secretive. Just a few hours before they had allowed me into their temple to show me their mysteries, but now my chance to witness more was gone. Even so, the woods shone with an eerie 3-D quality—a height, depth, and width that beset them with an otherworldliness both wondrous and frightful—though now silent and aloof, no longer having any dealings with the likes of me.

Late for work, loping and leaping over deadfall, I made tracks back to the lot. Fetching up to the pitch-till-u-win—its awning in the air and Nick behind the counter greeting me with a grouty look—I said, "Sorry I'm late, Nick. I fell asleep out in the woods."

He twisted up his face to show me his aggravation, and said, "Young lady, sleep's what the Almighty made midnight and motel beds for."

His crack stuck in my craw like bitters. But I held off saying something back at him, and hopped into the joint. Nick shook his head, climbed out, and gave over the money apron. I strapped it on and eyed Walt leaning out over the counter on the other side of the trailer. His face wore a sheepish frown that rankled me even more so. I turned away, busying myself by piling hoops onto the counter.

He swung toward me and said, "I was worried about you, Belle."

I said, "No need," and ignored him while I busied myself counting the bank in my apron. This trifling chore echoed with powerful meaninglessness amid the flim-flam fiddle-faddle all around me—the stuffed animals staring off into nowhere, strung up on the breathing walls, awash with the bluish glaze and faint pulse of fluorescent tubes in daylight—the foolish junk dangling across varnished rows of pine blocks and lying in wait under the counter in flimsy boxes from Taiwan.

Sipping on a coffee, J.D. ambled up, leaned his backside against the front of the basket joint, and studied the nothing-doing up and down the midway. J.D. never showed on time for four-o'clock call. So why didn't Nick grouse about it with him? Because J.D. was his own man, an independent agent. If Nick scolded him any about what and when, then J.D. would just light out like the fox he was—head on to his next sly doings. Nick knew that, and used J.D. for what he was worth, as long as it was worthwhile. Both of them playing each other to their own advantage.

Was this how it was with Walt and me? This notion pierced me with a pang of shame. Was this the LSD talking? In less time than it takes a poot's stink to float off in a windstorm, my contrariness had flushed dewdrops from on high straight down hell's toilet bowl. Having left behind the gods in the forest, I now appeared surrounded by devils. And yes, I likely had become one as well—suspicious and ornery, dealing in greedy deceits while swapping off kids from their quarters and me from myself. And for what? For money? The root of all evil?

Walt's game with me appeared not about money. It played by the rules of the other game that made the world go round—love. Tortured with the sight of me shucking him off—no doubt addling his own psychedelic bewilderment—Walt's hangdog glances over at me longed for my mercy, and stabbed my heart with pity. But pity doesn't grow love. And his need for my love only soured me all the more.

Thrashing about in this trap of money and love, I then and there settled on finding my escape as soon as I could.

The hundred and ten dollars I'd left Clandel with—plus the seventy I'd earned so far, minus the several dollars I'd since spent—left me with hardly enough to go very far. But if the creek don't rise, and I went at the ballyhoo barking like a big dog, what with the three days till Saturday maybe bringing in another hundred or so, chances are I could get up to New York City on a bus, and maybe find a room and a waitress job before I went flat broke. The notion of going for broke no doubt took more gumption than I could likely muster up. Yet throwing myself whole hog into hustling all the money

I could in the next few days, I figured that right now to be the only pig in my poke.

What to do with Walt's love, though, I had no clue. I only knew that if he quit me right then—or I, him—I'd have less of a chance with my scheme. So I set myself to tagging along a while longer. Be nice to him, so he would be nice to me. Give him some of what he needed, so I'd get some of what I needed. Wasn't that what most couples did much of the time? Was I so high and mighty that I couldn't, or wouldn't?

Out of the corner of my eye, I spied his mood shift ashy. Weary of my sulling over him, I stepped over to his side of the trailer, put my hands on his shoulders, and said, "Walt, I'm sorry I've been such a bitch. I don't know what's gotten into me, nor what to do about it."

He threw his arms around my waist, pulled me up against him, and whispered, "It's that goddamn LSD what's fuckin' us up, Belle. I told you that shit was dangerous as dynamite."

My measure of it was just the opposite—that the acid trip had maybe helped un-fuck me up some—and his saying of the contrary caused me to cringe a hate. But his sweeping me into his arms again, his straight-out grant of forgiveness, his plain-as-day love for me, melted my doubt-frozen heart with a welcome warmth of trust and gratefulness. Here was a man who loved me for sure. What was it in me, or him, that kept me from doing the same? I backed out of his arms, we grinned sheepishly at each other, and I climbed back over to my half of the trailer.

The midway held only a few early stragglers. My new plan of action set to mind, I badgered each and every one afoot with my feistiest pitch-till-u-win spiel. Walt chimed in with his own rowdydow, and soon enough, hoops clicked and clacked off the blocks, balls bounced out of baskets, and nickels tinkled on glass in the center joint—where when my eyes now met Fred's, mine burned with a new-found fire that melted his gaze to the ground.

The crowd thickened as the sky darkened and an oval moon rose above the ridge. Rides roared, their flashing lights whirling above the hubbub—screams and laughs and chitchat swirling again amid the blaring rock and roll and ballyhoo. Still stoned out of my gourd, but now differently, everything now appeared in a knife-edged focus—still tainted with meaningfulness, but lacking the powerful awakenings of exalted notions and puzzlements which had astounded me just a few hours before. Whatever that mysterious power had been, it had taken the mountain, and left me longing for more.

As I worked my counter back and forth, grabbing quarters and passing out prizes to and fro—to faces young and old, black and white, hopeful and doubtful, thrilled and bored, happy and angry—I saw in their eyes that they took me to be nobody in particular. Nothing personal, I was just another shady carny, snatching their money, fetching their hoops, and swapping off the junk they'd won. And though that was the role I was paid to play, I knew it wasn't me any more than who I'd been back in Clandel was me. I owned no satisfaction in either, and a newborn knowing of that gave me great comfort.

Most of the folks tossing hoops eagerly played their role as suckers, trading some of their hard-earned money and pride to have a little fun. In each of them I could now somehow see his or her own individual person— not the role they played in life, mechanic, miner, mother, schoolboy, or secretary, but the person that they were while abiding what had to be done to win something in this world. And the notion dawned on me that even though I was on one side of the counter and they were on the other in our roles at this hoop-toss game, each of us down deep sought the same prize—to be who we were. And if we just took that to heart, then maybe we'd see that we're all really on the same side.

For certain, one thing this trip had shown me was that within what I'd become lurked who I longed to be. The false Annabelle, a spider's web of notions spun with confusion and fear, held the true Annabelle prisoner. This mind-blowing day had freed me, or at least unlocked the iron bars. Due to an LSD mind-fuck of hillbilly me, now the hidden me had the chance to come to light. A body inborn amid the marrow of my bones, I'd caught sight of her. But I didn't yet know her hardly well enough. She appeared beyond what I might put into words—more likely, she was behind all my words. And though she lived deep within me, I'd also seen that much of myself was wondrously alive outside of me as well—in everyone around me, and in the stones and trees and birds and sun. So if I'm a part of all, isn't all a part of me?

I recalled Isis's little book telling me much the same. But when I'd read it a few days before, it had struck me as cloudy mumbo-jumbo. Now the thunder of that distant shudder of lightning rumbled through me—faint to my inner ear, but growing within me. And like an angel's blessing, this notion kindled in me a sense of greater kinship to those at my hoop-toss counter.

We all took our chances tossing hoops at our desires, wishing to ring the big prize—most of the time settling for life's trinkets. All of us, and all life's prizes, were more alike than not. Yet folks granted heed mainly to the differences betwixt us. Some damn bedeviled part of us had a yen to be separate from everyone and everything else, and be our own biggity person, spoon feeding our hungry pride, along with the lust low in our bellies, to the haughty appetites of our own gluttonous greed.

Maybe the game that we called our lives wasn't all about winning things for ourselves, maybe it was more about losing our selfishness. Instead of reckoning what was good for me and mine, maybe the game was really about what was good for what Isis called All That Is.

Back in the woods by the pour-off, I'd caught sight of my connection to the whole wide world. It and I were surely made from the same stuff. Its mysterious silence voiced this simple glory as if it were all that mattered. And if it was, then all these pathetic games of chance we played to get ahead in life were just wastes of time.

But what was one to do when the wolf was at the door? Or when caught up in the spider's web of this world? Or when hungry, or homeless? You had to watch out for yourself first, didn't you? Otherwise you might not last long in this dog-eat-dog land.

Wolves, spiders, dogs—was that what we were meant to be? Carnivores in a carnival? Cannibals living off the lifeblood of our neighbors? Kill to eat, or die, was the way of all life. Maybe I'd heard Hank right, and God *was* both good and evil. And if so, I'd best get used to it.

Such were some of the dope-addled fancies that washed through me in waves while tending the pitch-till-u-win. As the night rolled on, the ebb and flow of this chemical hoodoo drained off, bit by bit—its spellbinding awareness hollowing out an electrified emptiness.

Through the click and clack of hoops, I kept half an eye on Walt working his marks, one after another. And more and more, my heart softened to him. Even though, without a whit of guilt he bamboozled them out of their hard-earned dollars, he did so in such a sportive and plain-spoken fashion that they gladly gave him their money. For a fact, Walt was in the amusement business. He had big fun giving them a good time with his ball game, and most of them had big fun, too. J.D., on the other hand, stole all he could with a vengeance and a scowl—the difference betwixt the two as contrary as a puppy dog and an old possum.

Around ten o'clock, when things had slowed some, a tow-haired kid, big-eared and about ten-years old, gave me a quarter, picked up a handful of hoops, and flung one like a Frisbee. It bounced off the back row, hooked over the rear of a big block, and then flipped down right around it! Latched to the block was a necklace of 'genuine imitation pearls' in a long black box with velvety insides.

The kid stamped his foot, and said, "Dadgumit! That weren't what I aimed to git."

I looked back and forth from the kid to the block, not knowing quite what to do. The whole week long, thousands and thousands of hoops had been tossed, and finally one had rung a big block with a big prize. For a fact, they were not real pearls—I'd checked that out on the first day—but they were a decent string of fake ones, and were a damn sight better prize than all the plastic whistles, rubber spiders, and straw finger-traps that I'd been doling out. I called to Walt and pointed at the hoop around the block. He shrugged and told me to give it to the kid. I unhitched the necklace case from the block and handed it over.

The kid put on a face like a mule eating briars, and asked, "What in sand hill do I do with this a-here?"

"You got a girlfriend?"

"I got no use for none o' that neither."

"How about your maw?"

"She ain't one for puttin' on airs."

"Maybe you can swap it for something."

He glanced toward the blocks, and said, "I'll swap for that twenty-dollar bill."

"No can do."

"How 'bout that jackknife."

"Can't do that, neither."

"Well shoot. What good is it then?"

"Save it for when you get a girlfriend."

"I'd best saved my quarter-dollar for that."

"Sell it then, boy," I told him, about fed up with him. The tomfool had won a big prize, and he acted like he'd been done wrong.

Nick, catching sight of the situation from the glass pitch, hopped out and hurried over. His eyebrows arched in query, he asked me, "What's goin' on here?"

"This boy won that pearl necklace, and now he doesn't want it."

Nick's beady eyes pinched tight for a second, then he threw a glance over to Walt, who told him, "Hoop was 'round the block, Nick."

Nick sized up the kid, and asked him, "You don't want it?"

The kid shook his head. "Nary use for it, mister."

Nick told him, "I'll give you two dollars for it."

The kid's eyes perked up, then narrowed, and he said, "Ten, cash money."

Nick snorted, paused, and offered, "Three."

"Seven."

"Three-fifty."

"Seven-fifty."

"Keep it kid."

"Five-fifty."

"Son, this is the last time. Four dollars."

"Sold, mister." And he held out a hand, palm up.

From his front pocket, Walt pulled out a wad of bills thick enough to clog a commode with. The kid's eyes bulged at the sight, and his jaw hung open as Nick peeled off four dollars, one at a time into his hand. He gave over the necklace case, spun on a heel, and galumphed off.

Nick handed me the case, and said, "Here. Put it back on the block. Did you see it cop?"

"Did I what?"

"Did you see the hoop go over the block?"

"Oh. Yeah, it bounced off the back row and hooked it from behind."

"Mmm-hmm. That's how it happens.... Looks like you had a good night."

"Yeah, appears so."

"The miners got paid today. There's money in town. We'll wait till closing to count up."

He went over to J.D., though, and lightened-up his apron, before J.D. might be tempted to slip any cash, or any more cash, into his own poke. And to not show favorites he took some dollars from Walt as well. I watched Nick count up the money and wondered whether he was just a goober-grabbing tightwad, or simply a good businessman who well knew how to run his show. He treated me fair and square, and now that I'd done right by him, he allowed we could make some money together. If I were to work his game for a month or so, I'd likely lay back a decent enough stake for New York City. That made plenty more sense than carrying off with hardly enough to get there.

My back-and-forth bewilderment on whether to go or stay was wearying me feckless. The acid had left me with a connect-the-dots puzzle, which I then and there set myself to cease trying to figure out. Time would likely quile my hopped-up chemistry. What was to be, would happen soon enough. Given in to that, my dither eased—though a skittery hangover electrified my bones—and the night wound down with me sitting on the trailer floor, slouched against the wall at the far end of the counter, struck dumb by the day's doings, and staring into the colored lights burning on the motionless rides.

When the show shut down, I sorted the bills and coins from my apron into the red cloth under the blocks, while Nick added up J.D. and Walt. When he got to me, we counted a hundred-and-forty-eight dollar take for the night, and he handed me thirty-seven dollars for my end.

After Walt and Nick brought down the awnings, Walt led me off to the cookhouse, his arm across my shoulders, whispering, "You've been on my mind all day, Belle. I fear I'm gettin' this message that you're fallin' away from me. And I don't know what to do about it. I try to figure out what I did, or didn't do, and all I know is that whatever it is, I'll make it up to you somehow. If it's because I got jealous last night, forget about it. I'm over it. It was just a craziness, long gone, and it don't mean nothin' tonight."

I put my arm around his waist, and said, "Walt, I don't know what kind of mind-blowing frazzlement you've been through today. But I'll tell you, I've had a horse dose of it to chew over. And right now, I'm plumb tuckered out, beset by it all. And mighty hungry to boot."

"Fair enough. Let's eat."

At the cookhouse, we said little as we each gobbled down a bowl of steamy and spicy chili-mac, and shared a charred Italian sausage stuffed in a bun heaped with limp and oily onions and peppers. The taste and smell of the vittles, the feel of my teeth mashing it and my gullet swallowing it, the warmth of it in my belly—like everything else that day—all grew extra-magnified, and I reckoned it to be among the tastiest meals I'd ever eaten.

Walt got a coffee to go, paid Squirrel, and said to me, "How 'bout we get a nightcap at the G-top. Thursday night's payday for the ride help, and there's likely an ace-away game goin' on."

"Ace-away?"

"Come on. I'll show you." And he led me behind the joints and over to the G-top.

The big tent was thick with ride boys boozing and gambling away chunks of their week's pay—a sight loud for both ear and nose. Fellers I'd seen around the lot—at the cookhouse, or the donniker, or wrestling pig iron on the midway—now muscled beer cans elbow to elbow at the plywood bar, Blackie doling them out left and right. Among the gather-all was nigh on half the carnies in town. They filled the chairs around Trips' poker table, and stood and sat in bunches across the trampled grass. At the end of the tent opposite the poker game, a gaggle of them, shoulder to shoulder, leaned in around the dice table that all week had been shrouded beneath black canvas.

Curious, I shuffled over near it while Walt fetched us beers. Oblong and about eight feet by four, the tabletop and elbow-high sidewalls were upholstered with padded green felt. Mid-table, printed atop the felt, lay a pattern of squares and rectangles, in which were red and gold numbers and some words—come, pass, don't pass, field—all of which nobody around the table paid any attention to. Bellying up to the sidewall, stood more than a dozen ride jockeys and joint agents, and on the felt in front of several of them lay scattered piles of cash money bets.

A feller I'd seen tending the Octopus—Jimmy, they called him—his porky face sporting black-rimmed eyeglasses mended on one side with a wrap of shiny black tape, his round and suntanned noggin half-bald and half-buzz-cut, his stockiness wrapped in a tired army jacket—he pinched three, see-through-red, inch-square dice between his hammy thumb and grimy pinky, kissed them with chaw-stained lips, and flung them scuttering across the felt. Bouncing back off the sidewall at the far end and rolling to a stop, the white dots atop the dice showed a four, a four, and a one.

Jimmy pounded his fist on the sidewall rail and cussed, "Fuck my ugly mother!"

"Ace away for all that hay," announced Carl, the patch, who stood on a low platform at the middle of the table's long side—his white shirtsleeves rolled up, collar button and necktie loosened, Sinatra hat cocked on his head, and a short cigar jammed in his cheek. He hooked the dice over to him with a thin bamboo cane, while those with bets down scooped up their winnings, hooting and howling.

Carl dropped the three dice into a leather cup with two other dice, leaned over and slammed the cup in front of an agent across the table, and said, "New bank comin' out. Billy, how much in the bank?"

Billy, a muscled-up flattie sporting a turtleneck sweater and slicked-back blonde hair—I'd seen him on the other side of the midway running a phony football game played with clothespins and rubber canning rings—he peeled three twenties from his fistful of cash and dropped it onto the felt.

Carl snatched it up, checked the count, and then said to the carny on Billy's left, "Sixty dollars in the bank. How much do you want, Boyd?"

Boyd—the barrel-chested feller that ran the Tilt-A-Whirl across the midway from Nick's joints, the one who badgered Dwayne before Walt hammered him—he dropped a ten-dollar bill in front of him, which Carl swapped for one of the twenties in his hand.

To the next on Boyd's left, Carl said, "Fifty dollars in the bank. What'll you have, Tom?"

Tom, a slender baby-faced ride boy, bet five, and Carl covered it, making change. And this continued around the table, until Billy's sixty-dollar bank had been parceled out to several bets.

Walt brought me a beer, saw my interest, and explained low in my ear, "The shooter puts up the bank, any amount. The stickman goes clockwise around the table, offering any or all of it to each player, one to one, even money. If the bank gets faded, the player that takes the last bet has set down the bank. After the dice roll, if there's no money left in the bank, then whoever set down the bank has dibs on being the next bank.

"The shooter with the bank throws three dice. If he rolls any three of a kind, or any pair and a six, or a four-five-six, he scoops. All bets on the table go right into the bank. Nobody else shoots.

"If the bank rolls an ace-deuce-trey, or any pair and an ace, he loses all bets. Nobody else shoots. Ace away for all that hay. Like crapping out.

"If the bank rolls any pair and a two, three, four, or five, then that number is the bank's point. Not the pair's number—the single number.

"Next, the bet to the bank's left rolls to beat the bank's point. If he aces away, he loses. If he rolls trips, a pair and a six, or a four-five-six, he scoops—he wins his bet, and is the new bank. If his pair and a number, his point, is higher than the bank's point, he wins. Lower, he loses. If he rolls the same point, it's a push, a tie game, a split—the bet and the bank get their stakes back.

"If the dice show no trips, no pairs, no straights, it's no action. But, three-four-five and two-three-four, the big and little dillies, are also no action. The shooter rolls again, till he rolls action. Watch...."

Somehow, likely due to the doings of the LSD, I made sense of all that.

Billy, after choosing three of the five dice from the leather cup, held them high, in a fist tight as a knot, and hollered, "Four-five-six and the business," as he chunked them low and hard against the far side of the table. The dice clacked, thumped, clattered, and came up a one-three-five.

"No action," Carl declared, shifted the cigar to his other cheek, and raked the dice back to Billy,

Walt whispered, "You can bet on no action. Even money against the house. But it's a sucker bet."

Billy again held the dice high, hollering, "Four-five-six and the business," and chunked them across the table—ending up with a pair of deuces and a four.

"Four's the point," Carl announced, and raked the dice over to Boyd, who quickly shook them between both hands and scuttered them across the felt. After a couple of no-action rolls, Boyd came up with a pair of threes and a five, and snatched up the twenty dollars in front of him—his five beat Billy's four.

Tom's dice tossing style was to shuffle them around on the felt in front of his bet, and then with his fingertips lob them at the end wall. On his third toss, he rolled a pair of fives and a three. Carl bent over and picked up Tom's bet, saying, "Ten dollars now in the bank."

So it went, around the table, and at the end of the round, Billy's sixty-dollar bank had shrunk to fifty. Carl asked Billy if he wanted to press it, let it ride, or pull it down, which Walt told me meant that Billy could put more money into the bank, or let it ride for another round, or he could pull it down—take his fifty dollars, and pass the bank to the shooter to his left. Being the bank held an advantage, because the bank rolled first.

Billy let the fifty ride, and after a go-around with his point at five, the bank grew to eighty dollars. He let the eighty ride, and after rolling a deuce for his point, it shrunk to thirty. He let the thirty ride, and Boyd set him down—that is, he went the whole thirty dollars, which if Boyd won, would also win him the bank for the next round.

Billy fisted the dice up toward heaven, hollered, "Scoop-dee-doo", and threw them so hard that when they bounced off the end wall, one flew off the table and into the grass.

Carl shouted, "No dice. No dice." And after someone tossed the red cube back onto the table, Carl inspected it closely. Then he put it into the leather cup with the other dice, shook them up, and poured out five dice in front of Billy, who took his time choosing three.

Fist again held high, and hollering, "Scoop-dee-doo," as he let them fly, Billy rolled a two-three-four.

Carl declared, "A little dilly. The first one tonight. No action. Shooter rolls again."

Billy said, "New dice, Carl." Carl popped the three on the table into the leather cup with the other two, shook them up, and dumped the five out in front of Billy, who once again took his sweet time choosing the three he wanted. And once again he squeezed the dice overhead, hollering, "Scoop-dee-doo," and flung them hard against the end wall. A pair of deuces and an ace ended up atop the dice.

Carl sang out, "Ace away for all that hay. New bank comin' out."

Billy leaned his elbows onto the sidewall rail, hung his head and shook it some, then came up with a smile that appeared to say, what the hell.

Boyd, all smiles, pushed what he'd just won—his thirty and Billy's also—toward Carl. A ride boy standing in front of me, his luck as bad as his scent, gave up his spot at the sidewall and I scootched into it.

"Sixty dollars in the bank," Carl announced, and took in doling it out around the table. When he came to me and asked how much I wanted, I turned to Walt, who grinned and tossed a five-dollar bill on the green felt in front of me. Carl covered it with a five from the bank, and continued to my left until the money in his hand ran out.

Boyd poured the dice out of the cup onto the felt, shuffled the five around until he decided on three, rattled them cupped between his palms, and let them fly, rolling a pair of sixes and a three. The dice then went around the table—some winners and some losers.

When it was my turn, I snatched up the hard-edged cubes and quickly and clumsily flipped them across the felt. Only one reached the end wall.

"No dice," Carl said. "Red, all three dice got to bounce off the sidewall. Put some arm into it."

He raked the dice back in front of me, and this time I tossed them harder. They clattered and clacked and rolled to a one-four-five. No action. I rolled again. No action again. I rolled again. No action again. I went a shade shy about not being able to get anything, but when I rolled again, I hollered, "Four-five-six," and hot-toe-mitty, the dice came up four-five-six!

"Scoop! The little lady wins her bet and the bank," Carl declared. I flashed my eyes around the table, and everyone but Boyd had a smile for me. After the last shooter took his turn, Carl handed to Boyd what was left of his bank, gathered up the dice into the cup, and thumped it down in front of me, asking, "How much in the bank, Red?"

I turned to Walt, who shrugged. The ten dollars on the felt, his five and the five I'd won, didn't seem like much compared to what others had put into their banks, so with trembly hands I added a ten-dollar bill from my night's pay, and pushed it over to Carl.

He announced, "Twenty dollars in the bank," and asked the feller on my left, "Chester, how much you want of it?"

I'd seen Chester around the lot some. He ran a balloon-dart game on the other side of the midway—his pot belly always swagging out from his plaid sport coat, and his doughy face always showing shifty eyes that appeared to undress me. He peeled a twenty off the roll in his hand, and tossing it on the table, said, "Set her down."

Carl ruled, "The bank has been set down. New point coming out."

I glanced around the table and all eyes were on me. I took my time picking out three of the dice, regretting that I'd risked twenty dollars on them. Squeezing the dice in one fist, I blew on them for luck and scuttered them across the felt—a pair of aces and a four.

The Chariot

Carl raked the dice over to Chester, pulled the cigar from his cheek, and said, "Four's the point."

Chester scooped up the dice and chunked them without ceremony. No action. I let out a breath and reached behind me for Walt's hand. Chester rolled again. A pair and a three.

I won! I jumped up and down and turned and threw my arms around Walt's neck.

Carl said, "Forty dollars now in the bank, Red. Press it, pull it down, or let it ride?"

Walt whispered, "Either put more money in, or take the forty, or give it another go."

"Let it ride," I told Carl, amazed to hear myself say so.

"How much you want, Chester?"

He took twenty again, and the other twenty was covered by two five-dollar bets and a ten. I chose my dice, shuffled them on the felt some, grabbed them up in a fist, blew on them, and let them fly. After a couple of no-action rolls, I made five for a point.

Chester also rolled a five. "A push," Carl ruled, pushing Chester back his twenty and taking back twenty into my bank. The other three bets rolling against me didn't beat my five.

"Sixty dollars in the bank, Red. Press it, pull it down, or let it ride?"

My innards turning topsy-turvy, my bones hollowed out by the LSD, I doddled, sorely tempted to quit while I was ahead. Yet I squeaked, "Let it ride."

Chester bet twenty again, and around the table the other forty dollars went—mostly to smaller two- and five-dollar bets from ride boys—till I was set down by a ten from George, the elephant-ear feller from Cheeks' motel room.

I chose my dice, snatched them up and blew on them, and let them fly, hollering, "Four-five-six!" They scattered, stopped, and showed a pair of aces and a six. Cheers and groans lifted the top of the tent. Another scoop!

Carl snatched up the hundred-and-twenty around the table, and shouted, "Plenty of money in the bank. One-twenty in the bank. What d'you say, Red? Press it, pull it down, or let it ride?"

I looked around the table—everyone staring at me. Half the G-top had fetched up around the dice table to see what the excitement was all about—craning their necks behind the ring of players.

A hundred-and-twenty dollars was near what I'd made all week long. Even though I had only ten dollars of my own money at risk, all the rest of it was right there for the taking. Tortured between the need for the money and the chance for even more quick money, or the chance I might lose it all in one roll of the dice—mixed in with a pinch of guilt, or fear, that I should give them all a chance to win their money back—the bottom fell out of my spine.

Walt whispered in my ear, "Let it ride, Belle."

I turned to him and asked, "Can I take out just some of the money?'

"It's either pull it all down, or let it all ride. My call is let it ride."

Carl asked, "What's it gonna be, Red?"

"Let's go one more time," I said, and regretted doing so in the next breath.

The bank went around. Chester took only ten this time. Some at the sidewall backed off as others elbowed in with new money—Hat, Robin Marx, Hairy Larry, and Bad-Eye Mike.

When it came around to Mike, kitty-corner across the table from me, fifty dollars was left in the bank. Licking a thumb and peeling a bill off a fat fold of cash money in his hammy fist, Mike slapped a fifty on the felt and growled, "Set her down, Carl. Set her down."

His good eye, if you can call it that, augered into me with an ill will that appeared aglee with devilish pleasure. His bad eye, its lid quivering, walled around like a toad's. More than anything in the world right there and then, I hankered to beat Mike out of that fifty-dollar bill.

The dice in front of me again, I chose three, blew on them twice, and let them fly. No action. Carl sold a one-dollar no-action bet to Isis's boy, Tyrone, reaching a brown arm sideways into the game—and then paid him after I rolled no-action again. My third roll made three my point. Not too good.

One after another, each bet rolled trying to beat my three. Chester lost his ten dollars, and the other money around the table had a few more losers than winners.

The dice came to Mike. Eyeing me with his nasty grin, he rolled with a grunt and a snap of his fingers. A pair and a deuce turned up—a loser. He scowled, shifted his weight, and sniffed once.

Carl snatched up the hundred dollars in front of Mike, counted the bank, and announced, "A hundred and eighty dollars in the bank. What's your call, Red?"

I didn't hesitate. "Let it ride." I fixed my eye on Mike's, daring him to try again, and I saw his bluster rise.

Chester bet twenty this time, and when it got around to Mike, ninety was left. "Set her down," he snarled, and thumbed the cash onto the felt.

As soon as Carl dumped the dice out of the cup, I snatched three up and chunked them straight at the hundred-eighty dollars in front of Mike. He jerked back a hitch as the dice jostled the pile of cash, walloped off the sidewall, and clattered to the middle of the table—a pair of threes and a six! Another scoop!

A golly-whopper of a whoop rang out that turned every head in the tent. Those with no bets down, grinned to their back teeth and tipped their beer cans to my luck. Several of the losers at the table shook their heads in disbelief. Mike looked daggers at me, and muttered to no one in particular—his bad eye now bulging at half-staff, with me dead in its sight.

Carl raked in the dice and the money, shouting, "Plenty of money in the bank. Plenty of money in the bank." He sorted and counted it, and announced, "Three-hundred-and-sixty dollars in the bank." Then he turned to me. "What now, Red? Let it ride, or pull it down?"

Walt whispered, "Pull it down, Belle. Pull it down."

Were it not for Mike across the table, with the evil eye on me like Old Scratch himself, I'd have done so. But I'd taken on a fever, burning away any caution, ablaze with easy money to be had—and hot to stick it to Mike.

Walt grabbed me by the waist, pulled me back against him, and muttered in my ear, "Pull it down. Take what you got, Belle. Don't push your luck."

Though that made plain enough sense, I squirmed away from his grip, and addled by a lust for payout and payback, I heard myself say, "Let it ride."

Then, like flipping a switch, a jolt of regret wilted my knees. Grief quaggled my innards. That three-hundred-and-sixty dollars could've paid my way to New York City. My ticket was there on the table and I'd swapped it off for double or nothing. I blessed myself out for being dumber than a sack full of hammers.

Carl doled out the bets. Chester smelled blood and took fifty. By the time it got around to Mike, two-hundred-thirty was left. He flipped a pair of hundred-dollar bills and three tens onto the felt, and muttered, "Set her down."

I thought I spotted a flicker of fear peek out between the strutty lids of his yellowed left eye. But his right one just stared me down—a curl of amusement at the corner of his droopy lips.

The five red cubes with the white dots tumbled out of the leather cup in Carl's hand and onto the green felt in front of me. Staring down at them, I realized that the LSD still had its grip on me—a surge of it returning as the dice on the table floated like red stars on a green flag in a breeze.

I looked around the table—faces four- and five-deep, all eyes on me. I shied from their feast on my kettle of fish, dropped my gaze to the dice, and chose three with dots up that matched the least. Cupping them between both palms, and rattling them over a shoulder, I squeezed my eyes shut, conjuring up all the wish-come-true magic I could summon, and blew a one-word silent prayer on the dice—PLEASE!

I slid them into one hand, leaned over the table ready to shoot—then spun around to Walt and held them up to his lips. He nipped a kiss on a finger, the hair on my arm tingling, and I turned and flung them at the stack of money in front of Mike.

They thumped off the sidewall, clattered back over the felt, and all was silent as two rolled to a stop—a pair of fours—the third one spinning on a corner like a top. When it toppled over with four dots up, a hurrah startled me more than my shock to see that I'd won. More than seven-hundred dollars? I'd won more than seven-hundred dollars!

I hopped up and down like on a pogo stick, one hand over my squealing wide-open mouth, the other hand waving high overhead. I threw my arms around Walt's neck, and he swept me off my feet, dancing me in circles. Faces rubbernecking all around the sidelines beamed with congratulations— beer cans held high.

Carl gathered up the money, counted it, and shouted out, "Seven-hundred-twenty dollars in the bank. What now, Red? Push it, let it ride, or pull it down?"

Quick as greased lightning, I told him, "Pull it down."

This game was over. The faces at the table, especially those I'd won the money from, took a dim view of that—their eyes looking daggers at me for groundhogging their dollars and leaving no chance to win any back. Mike appeared fit to be tied, swaying his hulk from one foot to the other, hitching up his belt, choking down his damnations, and wobbling his fidgety evil eye at me.

Carl separated thirty-six dollars from the stack on the table and slid the rest in front of me. I turned to Walt and muttered, "Why did he take that money out?"

He whispered back, "The house cuts five-percent of any winning bank."

Thirty-six dollars was almost two-week's pay at the diner, and more than I'd made in the hoop toss the whole night long. Yet what else was there to do but pick up my six-hundred-and-eighty-four dollars and smile thankfully at my good luck. I folded up my first fistful of powerful cash money and squeezed it into the back pocket of my jeans.

Carl shouted, "The bank passes to the left. How much you in for, Chester?"

Chester shilly-shallied some, fidgeting with his shrunken bankroll— counting it halfway, folding it up and shoving it into his pocket, and then yanking it out to flip through again. Half-heartedly, he peeled off some bills onto the felt and swept them toward Carl—who gathered and counted them, and announced, "Fifty dollars in the bank."

Chester's bank went around the table, mostly taken up by small bets, some new money drawn to the table by my good fortune. When it got around to Mike, he set it down with a twenty-five dollar bet. Chester chose his dice, rattled them in one hand, and let fly. A pair of deuces and an ace.

Carl sang out, "Ace away for all that hay." Those with bets in front of them nodded approval of this easy knockout and snatched up their winnings. Chester spun on a heel and tore out of the tent.

At the other end of the table, Mike, who now had the bank, counted three-hundred dollars onto the felt—his eye taunting me to play his game.

I turned to Walt, and said, "Let's get out of here."

"Belle, I want some of this action, too."

I flashed him my dim view of that, but moved behind him as he took my place at the side rail. After a couple of rounds—Walt won twenty, then lost ten—he handed me a five-dollar bill to fetch a couple more beers. I'd hardly drank half of the one I had, and had no hankering for another, so I only bought one at the bar and brought it back to him with the change, which he took without turning from the game on the table.

I shuffled around the G-top. Several carnies congratulated me on my luck. I gave them big smiles and patted the lump in my back pocket. But that much cash money on me made me skittish. What's to say that one of these rascals wouldn't clobber me over the head and thieve it from me? I needed to pee, but the notion of traipsing to the donniker alone through the dark put a lid on that. Every few minutes I'd try to catch Walt's eye and cast him a look pleading to leave, but his face never lifted from the dice table.

A powerful weariness swept over me, wilting my bones while electrified heebie-jeebies still jittered through them. I figured this to be the comedown from the LSD heights. The brunt of the trip long gone, what lingered left me still buzzing, yet plumb tuckered out. I'd been drawn through a knothole backwards. The magic dance was over, with the fiddler left to pay.

When I saw Madeline walk into the G-top, my heart leapt with relief. Our eyes met and we hurried up to each other.

"How's it goin', girlfriend?"

"You're not going to believe it. I just won nigh on seven-hundred dollars over at the dice table."

"Shut up!"

"God's honest."

"Well fry me brown."

I whispered, "And the second-best thing about it is I won most of it off of that old bastard, Bad-Eye Mike."

She shook her head and muttered, "That nasty devil's been low on my list since I came on this show."

"You and me both."

"Where's Walt?"

"Over shooting dice. And likely there for a spell. Girl, I got to pee bad. But I'm shy to walk around alone in the dark with this wad of cash money bulging on my backside. Can you come along with me?"

"Sure thing. Let me fetch a beer first."

"I'm buying," I said, and did so.

Then I told Walt where we were going and asked how his luck was. He grumbled, "Okay," but appeared to be losing.

As Madeline and I made our way out back to the donniker, I asked her what she'd been doing since I last saw her.

"Oh... I hung out at the cookhouse for a while. Listenin' to Robin and some other roughies swappin' jackpots. Then Pa came along and got me to cleanin' and stockin' the joint—what I'd druther've not been doin' right there and then, but I hardly could tell Pa why. After that, I went back to the house trailer, put Canned Heat in the eight-track, and turned it way up loud while I washed and gussied-up some. Then I fixed us pork chops with smashed taters and boiled collards, and sat down with Pa for a nice dinner before openin' the joint."

I said, "That sounds like any-old normal day for you. Weren't you tripping your brains out?"

"Yeah. And that added some extra-special flavor to it. You know, with Pa and me."

I felt glad for her for that, but had to wonder if she'd swallowed the same dope I did. I said, "After you left, Walt drove Cheeks back to town. And I talked some with Isis. Then went out in the woods again."

"And then what?"

"Well... I sat under a tree and closed my eyes, and fell into some kind of trance, and had these visions of scenes from my childhood."

"Far out. What did you see?"

"The least little doings I never before remembered—but which, under this spell, somehow appeared so important."

"Like what?"

I could have told her some, but I shied from it because they eerily shamed me. So I only said, "I can't handily say, Madeline. I can't handily say."

She pried no further, and at the donniker I did my business as she waited outside, beer in hand. While my jeans were at my shins, I took the wad of money out of my back pocket, and just for the sake of running it through my fingers, I tried to count it under the dim yellow light bulb. A few hours before, I figured myself a prisoner of scarce money, trapped in this carnival, captured by Walt, with chances slim to none for my escape. My only sensible option, to go back to Maw's.

But now, these green and gray paper rectangles with fancy letters and numbers and famous dead presidents, these were my tickets to freedom. All mine now only because of how the dots on the tops of three dice happened to combine when they stopped rolling. Just one extra tumble of any one of those dice, and there'd be nothing in my hand but toilet paper.

"Annabelle?" Madeline hollered into the doorway. "You gettin' cozy in there, or have you got a problem?"

"No. No problem. Be right out." Before zipping up my jeans, I peeled some small bills off the fold, put them in a pocket, and stuffed the rest into the front of my panties. With a lump on my tummy like I was a few months along, I stepped down out of the trailer, and we headed toward the deserted midway.

"Madeline, I'm a mite fearful about toting around all this money. What if someone robs me of it?"

"Girl, everyone 'round here's got wads of cash on them. Ain't a-one of 'em gonna bust you over the head and take yours. You ever heard about honor among thieves?"

"I guess."

"There's no guessin' to it. But if you want to be safe, go to a bank and change the cash into traveler's checks. It'll cost a couple of bucks per hundred, but if it makes you feel better, it'll be worth it."

She stopped short, and said, "Looky there. That joint's afire!"

Smoke curled from the top corners of a laced-up tent in the line-up.

Madeline hollered, "Fire!"—then told me, "You run and get help from the G-top. I'll unlace the awning. Go!"

I lit out like a scalded dog, cut mud to the other side of the show, scrambled behind the line-up, and burst into the G-top, gasping, "There's a joint afire out on the midway!"

Heads spun my way. The next second, a dozen carnies rushed out of the G-top, following me back the way I came. As we scrambled around the backend, Madeline had one side of the awning half-unlaced, tongues of fire licking out through the gap.

Larry shouted, "I'll go cut the stake ropes. Y'all yank it out of the line-up."

He hurried around to the backside, a few others following, and the rest fetched up in front of the joint, awaiting Larry's signal. After a long minute—the flames now eating through the canvas top—a voice shouted, "Now!"

All grabbed hold of what they could of the awning—one carny cutting the laces with a glinty knife—and they hauled at it, once, twice, and tipped the joint over, crunching face-down onto the trampled straw and sawdust. With another heave-ho and a push from the back, they slid the joint out into the center of the midway, away from the other tents.

More carnies racked up with buckets of water and sloshed them onto the fire. A few others beat down flames by swinging teddy bears plucked from the tumbledown mess. Before long, we all stood there around it, twisting our noses at the smell, and staring at the wreck smoldering under the high moon.

Walt came up behind me, took hold of my elbow, and said, "Belle, my money was on the table so I couldn't run out sooner. You okay?" I nodded, and followed him, circling the tent to look it over. "Whose stick joint is this?" he asked to nobody in particular.

"It's one of Tall Paul's," someone said. "His six-cat."

Someone else asked, "How you reckon this got a-goin'" Another voice said, "Maybe the electric?" A couple of ride boys went over and studied the metal fuse box hanging on a two-by-four of the broken frame. One said, "Ain't no fire been in this box." They turned to the light stringer dangling inside the overturned tent and searched it for clues, shaking their heads after they found none.

Walt hunted through the remains of the scorched grass in the space where the joint had been. He kicked at something, squatted by it, poked at it, and then said, "Right here's your culprit. Some son of a bitch tossed a lit railroad flare into the joint."

Everybody shuffled over to see. Grumbled cusses filled the air. Someone guessed, "Likely snuck down to the backside from the road, then drove off."

Robin trotted up, eyes wide, squealing, "What in holy fuck happened here?"

Walt said, "Looks like someone burnt out Paul's six-cat. Come down from the road and tossed a flare inside."

Robin yanked off his cap, threw it on the ground, and kicked it like he was wanting to kill it, blessing it out as if the fire was the cap's doing.

While some carnies shuffled off, others growled to each other about what they'd do if they got ahold of the townies who did this—their faces ashy with menace and keen on pay back.

Walt told me, "That's about enough excitement for one day. Let's go back to the motel."

On the way into town, I asked him what a six-cat was.

"It's a gaffed joint. The Clems throw baseballs at a row of fringy cat dummies. The agent has a gunner to block the cats from fallin' over when he gaffs the mark."

"So folks don't win at that one neither?"

"Not a chance."

The way he said that with a smirk made me go queasy. No chance of winning was plumb wrong, and Walt didn't care a whit. Sure, all these games were fixed, more or less—as were most all the world's doings. The prize-every-time they won at my game was hardly a square deal, and the teddy bear or two that Walt doled out once in a while was more bait or bribe than something won.

I asked him, "Don't that make you feel guilty?"

"Guilty of what?"

"Guilty of being a part of it. Going along with greening folks out of their money."

He twisted skeptical looks my way while he eyed the road ahead and told me, "I'm a carny... livin' by carnival rules. I run my joint by the rules of the game. I didn't make up the game, and I didn't make up the rules. I work my joint how I see fit, and what some other agent is doin' or not doin' ain't no business of mine.

"And not only that, I'm an American, too... drivin' down the road in the U.S.A. by the rules of the road. Right now there's American boys killin' Vietcong in jungles on the other side of the world—for no decent reason save the rules of war. Is it my fault that's the way it is? Should I be guilty about those boys, too?"

"Somebody ought to," was all I could think of to say.

After a mile of silence, he asked, "What you gonna do with all that money you beat those boys out of, Belle?"

I couldn't tell him I was figuring on going over the mountain with it sooner or later. So I just shrugged.

"I was near even when you rang the fire alarm. But with a sawbuck on the table and the dice goin' around, I had to wait for my roll before I could up and rush out. Then I crap out with a measly deuce under the bank's three."

He no doubt could tell that I was out of sorts, and he was fishing for my pity. All I could give him was another shrug. Then, in the stony silence as we neared the motel, I felt him knotting up with sore disappointment at all the grief I'd given him all day long. As we swung into the parking lot, I stared out the side window, weighing how fair I'd been to him.

What chance did he have of winning me? Shadow-shy in my own darkness of what to do, was I stringing him along like an agent in the six-cat? Luring him into yet another fat chance, gaffed for my own gain? Then after I'd swapped off his heart for all he could take, for all I could take—or give—does our game get set afire and yanked out of the line-up?

He nosed the Mercury into a space near the balcony treads and switched off the key. The silence grew as we sat there. When he swiveled to face me, the creak of his leather coat on the vinyl seats sounded like a complaint. I turned my eyes to his and searched them for any clue to our riddles.

He spread that heart-melting grin of his, and asked, "So how was your day?"

I sniggered, and breathed, "It's been a trip."

"That it has. That it has.... And where do we go from here?"

"Up to the room?" I half-tried to joke.

He didn't laugh. "That's not what I meant. What I'm askin' is about me and you. Whatever we got goin', or ain't, what do you figure is happenin' to it?"

"Walt... who knows?" Dodging his question, I sunk into a wallow of shame, knowing more than I dared say, and too cowardly to fess up.

Choking for words to rescue my pride, and to save wounding his, I stammered out, "What I do know is you've been mighty good to me. And I'm grateful for it. If not for you, I'd be back where I was.

"Now, here I am... but where here is, I haven't quite settled on yet. I'm not back where I didn't want to be. Yet I'm not so sure I want to be here, either. But here we are, where I can see how crazy you are about me. And me, I'm just trying to keep my head above water....

"Walt, without you I'd no doubt be drowning in my own bathwater. But here in *your* world, I get this notion that maybe this ain't for me. Not so much you, Walt, but more this whole carny thing. And maybe... because you and the carnies are all in cahoots, then I see you more as one of them, rather than one with me."

He stared straight through me, his eyes burning scars in my heart.

"Walt, sweetie, I feel how you feel about me. Why I'm not treasuring what you've given me, gives me pause to doubt my own good graces. I suspect I'm hardly worthy of your love."

He shook his head, thumped a fist once on the steering wheel, and said, "That's not the way I see it, baby. I know when we hooked up last week I told you we could take it or leave it, a two-way street. Now I'm tellin' you I couldn't take it if you went down the road without me.

"When I called you my dream girl, could be I was tossin' you a line. But now that dream's done come true. When my eyes are on you, my smile grows, my throat lumps up, my heart thumps, my guts go flip-flop, my joint gets chubby. I'd kneel in mud to court your spark."

"Oh Walt, come on now."

"Come on now yourself, Annabelle. Do you recollect when you told me somethin' along the line of love bein' about your own goodness givin' it up to another for the good of love?"

"Yeah, sure."

"Well, I fear you ain't been true to your own sayin'."

I hung my head—feeling unfit to be a woman, his woman—and I mumbled, "You got me there, Walt. You got me there."

Ridiculed by canned laughter from someone's too-loud TV drifting out of an open window, a heavy silence set in between us in dead-of-night shadows, sliced through by shafts of moonlight.

He said gently, "Come on, Belle. Let's go up to the room."

I slumped toward him and curled up across the seat, snuggling the side of my head atop the tight jeans sheathing his meaty thigh. "Not yet," I whispered.

He stroked my hair for a spell, while I stared through the steering wheel at the wires hanging under the dash. I breathed deep the musk of his straddle, and felt his strut rise upside my head.

A fancy came to me to do what I'd never before done with a man—take it in my mouth. I'd overheard several friends, both boy and girl, bragging on it, but I hadn't admired much about it. Yet now it felt of what to do—to do something special for Walt, who loved me so and took care of me so. And rather than turning puny about it, a heat surged through me that shocked me with its blood-pounding lust.

I rubbed my skull up against his prides, and he grabbed a fistful of my hair and pressed me close. Then—before I had the chance to find out whether I'd do it there and then or not—I glanced up through the windshield and saw a man on the balcony leaning over and watching!

I jumped up like a jack-in-the-box and hissed, "Someone's up above peeping at us."

Bending over the steering wheel, Walt craned his neck for a look-see, his eyes shooting daggers upwards. I sat up and snuck a peek, and the man still leaned on the railing, but made like he was just taking in the night air. Walt swung out of his door, came around and opened mine, and gave me his hand. As the treads up to the second floor rang out with our footfalls, I heard a door slam shut, and when we stepped onto the balcony, the man had gone inside.

As we neared Cheek's room, I asked Walt if he knew what had happened to him and The Frog Baby.

"I had to haul him to a grocery so he could buy some ice-tea mix. Then I dropped him off here and went back out to the lot. When I took a donniker break, I walked by his joint and didn't see him out front. But it looked flashed. I guess he got his punk back into its picklin'."

As we passed Cheeks' door, I heard his TV on. I whispered "Should we knock to see how he is?"

Walt muttered, "Save me from that, Belle. I've had just about enough of his crazy fat ass for one day."

As soon as he closed the door to our room, Walt dropped his pants to his ankles and tore open the snaps on his shirt. Before I'd waggled my jeans halfway down my legs, he was buck naked and lifting my sweater over my head. I kicked off my boots, fell backward onto the bed, and he slid the cuffs over my feet. The wad of cash bulged in my panties, on my shorthairs like a lop-sided Kotex.

Rearing up on his knees at the edge of the bed—his double-barreled chest pumped-up beneath wide shoulders tapering like a V down to his hoe handle waggling at me from its curly bush, his randy grin proud as a pirate, ear to ear—he slid my panties down my legs and the bankroll slipped between my thighs.

A short piece later, I lay sprawled atop cash scattered all over the coverlet—Walt already in the shower and the TV switched on, Doc trumpeting the end of the Tonight Show.

The echo of the day's earlier glories had promised that this could have been our most marvelous correspondence yet—but it was wham-bam over for him, long before tearing the bone out of me. As I gathered up the crumpled bills, I felt taken from, not given to. Love had to be better than this.

8

Justice, robed and angelic, sits on her bench, a winged angel gazing with dispassionate eyes at us and all our distant truths. A hint of stunned revulsion curls a corner of her mouth. Severe yet merciful, she'll shortly cut to the quick — her right hand holding upright the double-edged sword. In her other hand balances a scale, which weighs slightly to the left, — her feminine side. Holding it hooked to her heart, she is ready to weigh our two sides — our give and our take, our haves and have-nots, our virtues, our evils. A figure eight is but two linked circles, as is her scale, as is her image cast.

Could be I'd fallen off to sleep for a spell, once or twice the whole night long, but it didn't feel of it much. Between the sheets, edgy inches away from Walt, I'd tortured, sorely put out for his slapping it to me without tolerable befores or afters. If that was how he showed how he loved me, I'd hate a look at the contrary. My vexation with him, and my frazzled state as the LSD slowly lost steam, had starched me stiff alongside of him. Then, after what felt of hours, I took in tossing and turning, thrashing about for release into sleep, and getting little to none.

My mind's eye kept rehashing episodes of the acid trip—like TV re-runs, but with riddles for outcomes. The picture of Cheeks, naked in the creek, losing his rubber monster in the run, would reel before me, and I couldn't help but snigger in the darkness. Then Sam's beady red eyes would be there asking me for sympathy, his pink nose sniffing and white whiskers twitching. From vision to vision, I leapt with neither rhyme nor reason. One after another, scenes from the day haunted me in colory 3-D stereo, appearing somehow even more real than they'd been in the dazzling light of the drug. Mixed in among them were the recollections conjured up under that tree, those haunts of my rearing. Jags of them floated behind my eyelids, their keenly magnified importance again looming within me, along with the feel of great rewards for puzzling out their riddles.

The dawn creeping into the drapes, I gave up on sleep, slid out of bed, and sat naked on the cool chair by the window. I gazed at Walt, sprawled under the coverlet, his hair all agley and clumpy with pomade, and I wondered who it was that he saw when he looked at me. With love aglow in his eyes, did he see through my masquerade to the real me, whoever that was, or did he merely admire my pretty disguise? Or maybe was it simply his dream girl he adored? A fancy of his own imagination—not me, but who he wants me to be, someone I'd likely never be—which one day when he finally sees the truth, he'll regret loving.

Was this the big mistake that lovers made—courting the ghost of one's own dreams? Do we look at others and mostly see who we want to see and what they can do for us?

Wasn't I guilty of being taken in by the same will-o'-the-wisp? I'd fallen for a feller who would set me free. Little did I know that I'd shortly be corralled again, by him and his midway. Little did I still know about him and his world. Smitten with what he might do for me, I'd been swept off my own feet by my yen for something wonderful to happen in my life. Walt, my knight in shining armor? I wasn't looking at a real person, either. The real Walt lay right there on the bed—breathing soft little snores, caught up, night and day, in dreams of games.

But, as it said in that book about loving, love wasn't all about what I get from Walt, it's as much about what I give to him. And taking measure of what he'd given to me all week, sorely put to shame all I found wanting with my own misgivings.

If I just accepted who Walt really was, as is, then would real love come to me?—allowing that Walt could fry the other side of that flapjack. And if that came to pass, would the two of us each become who we are, each be ourselves? Plus at the same time, be a couple? I figured there was no way to know unless we tried.

Plain to be seen, our ride together on this wheel of fortune, if only for one week—all our games, all our hootchy-kootchy—had glued us into our very own one-and-only sideshow on time's crowded midway, with prizes to be won or lost.

And yesterday beneath that oak tree, the haunt of the little girl I once had been, my glimpse of who I'd always been, had awakened in me a knowing as primal as animal eyes. In hiding for years from the forces of the world—defending me from the onslaught of everybody telling me what to do, when, where, why, and how—was my own soul, lurking in my depths, always there, longing to one day be freed from the clutches of others.

My ornery spite toward my kith and kin, my vexation with hillbilly life, no doubt had stewed in the juices of this denial of who I was. Like a zebra spray-painted green on St. Patrick's Day, I bogued among the herd without my stripes—a black sheep, an ugly duckling—misput at myself and everyone else, because I was not myself.

Now it was happening again, with Walt and the carnies. Though the role he played for me was one I'd bought a ticket for, it was still his show, not mine.

I both resented it and enabled it. I both regretted it and yearned for it. My man, stout in his world and in our bed—his protection, his adoration— made me feel safe and wanted. Just by being his woman, I felt like one for the first time in my life. Yet deep within me lived a need to be my own gal.

I remembered Isis's booklet and fetched it out of the nightstand drawer. Flipping a few pages to what caught my eye, I read in the mornglom.

> Dominion over one's soul is an abomination to the spirit of All That Is. Whether it be by lovers, friends, family, society, priests, kings, or gods—the repression and subjugation of an individual's unique soul is simply enslavement.
>
> Though one's body may be free to move through the world, it is the spirit that yearns to be itself, and when it has been taught to be otherwise, no amount of physical freedom will allow one to find peace in the world. The journey for happiness is not taken through the outer world, it is launched within oneself, toward the reality that is at the basis of our being, and away from the illusions of the world.
>
> Every society teaches their children the constructions that sustain their system of belief. The truths atop Aztec pyramids, the truths of an automobile mechanic in Detroit, the truths of mammoth hunters in the Ice Age, all become bygones sooner or later. The realities of an African bushman and a medieval French duchess are one in the same—structures built among the needs of people to put the outer world under their control. The survival of the group initially necessitates this, but before long, these systems petrify into societies whose members live and die for the survival of their beliefs.
>
> Lost in the bargain with each world, are the inner lives of many of its people. Only too few find their way back to themselves—mystics, shamans, sages, and artists. And the ways of the world rarely tolerate those that lead souls back to the truths within.
>
> Socrates was poisoned, Jesus crucified, and countless others ostracized or burnt at the stake. Buddha, a prince of India, left his kingdom for a banyan tree, and did not return to the temples and courts to preach his truths or argue his logic—so he was not killed, even though thousands flocked to his side. Throughout all time, some men and women, not many, have seen that all is but illusion and deception, save the connection with the Source of All Being, which is within us all, and in everything else as well.

One does not have to be Jesus or Buddha to realize this in one-self. "Be ye as little children." That is, be without the beliefs that societies impose upon us. We are given our true selves by birth-right, but we are given the dogmas of our times by the decrees of our parents and by others who lay claim to authority.

We must learn the mandates of society in order to live among others in our particular time and place, but we must also keep faith with what is essential within both ourselves and everything else, in order to live with what is real and eternal.

Once again, Isis's little book had opened to a page that read like it was written for me right there and then. The magic of this sent chill bumps down my spine, and gave me a gut feeling that I was on to something wonderful and welcome. How it could be so, mattered less than the feel of that it was so. I breathed deep the relief of it, sitting there naked, soused in a content-ment that I recognized as natural as dew on a leaf.

The sun rose, and its glow through the drape's cloth warmed the win-dow-side of me while my shadow-side chilled. I ran a tubful of hot water and slid into the bath. With knees jackknifed and my head underwater past my ears, I steeped my body in the luxurious heat, my heart throbbing amid watery echoes. With what to do next still unanswered, the questions floated far from mind in the comfort of this womb, and as the water cooled, I lay there for most of an hour, like I didn't have a care in the world.

Walt stomped in, clanked up the commode seat, and made his morning branch. I sat up with a slosh, and sang hopefully, "Good morning, sun-shine."

He waggled his jemison dry, twisted a grin my way, and asked, "Got room in there for me?"

I scootched over and curled up by the spigot. He lowered himself in, and said, "We've got to be in Clandel by noon."

"What? For what?"

"To kangaroo court for hammerin' that Clem."

"In Clandel?"

"That's where the county courthouse is. So, yeah."

"This is Black County here?"

"That's what I'm told."

"I ain't seen any county deputies around."

"It's city police here. The fix is in over at the county courthouse."

I let this sink in for a piece. I hadn't allowed I'd be back in Clandel hardly a week after leaving. I breathed for something to say, my eyes searching the tiles.

"Belle, you don't have to come along if you've no mind to. I just gotta go through the motions, and there's nothin' gonna come of it. Just drive over and show up, plead self-defense, and I'll be back before call. But it might be good to have you along in case I need a witness, or there's some kind of double-cross, or fuck-up, and they throw me in the pokey. Then you can drive back and get the patch to spring me."

I couldn't say no to that, though I wasn't keen on returning so soon. I reckoned I'd one day go back. But today? I got out of the tub and toweled off, leaving Walt soaping his beard.

Shuffling my clothes around in the dresser drawer, I hunted up what to wear. My world still a jag funny-turned from an LSD hangover—spacey and ragged, yet alert—I went into a panic about what to do when I got back to Clandel. Would I go see Maw? Would the long-tongues have spread my tale all over town by now? Would I just give up this half-baked adventure, and go back to stay?

I fumbled on some clean panties and socks, and dug out my bellbottoms and a flowery peasant blouse. Reckoning that might make me look too much like a hippy, I swapped for black slacks and a green sweater. Then I scowled in the mirror at my braless nipples, yanked off the sweater, and found a decent bra. By the time I'd fixed my hair, I'd put half a plan in place. I'd trade my cash money for traveler's checks at the bank in Clandel.

I gathered several wads of bills from where I'd vaulted them, and counted it all up. With what I'd left town with, and what I'd made in the hoop toss and on the dice table—minus some dollars spent here and there on this and that—I had eight-hundred-and-seventy-six dollars. Powerful cash money—the thickness of it in my hand startling me with its potential.

I could fly to California with this kind of money. With such a stake, I could buy an old car, and rent a small apartment, and likely find a decent job, most anywhere in America. And with two days left before the end of the week, with what I was due to make in the hoop toss, I might end up with nigh on a thousand dollars.

I hurriedly sorted out eight hundred, tucked half into the top of each sock at my ankles, pulled my cowgirl boots up over, and slipped the other seventy-six dollars into my red leather purse.

Walt swung out of the bathroom, threw on some clothes, and shortly shuckled me out of the room and into the Mercury. Wheeling out of Stuart, he told me we'd get some breakfast when we got to Clandel. Winding along the road, he took in cutting up all carefree about how stacked this courthouse deck of cards was, and about how much the law in West Virginia was in the pocket of Eli McCain. Then he bragged about a jackpot he'd once gotten in and out of down in Georgia. But I knew him well enough by now to suspect that he masked doubts of an open-and-shut case.

I listened to his tales with half an ear, smiley nods, and counterfeit sniggers. Gripping the armrest on the door—not only to keep me upright in the many curves Walt raced through—I clung to it sorely troubled about how I would be judged by my hometown jury. When I stepped out onto those too-familiar sidewalks, would whisperers point at me, would glances turn away from me, would anyone ask me questions I won't want to answer? And if I go see Maw—Lordy, what kind of nightmare would that be?

Tiring of his banter, I told Walt I hadn't slept much, and needed a cat-nap before we got there. I crawled into the back seat, and he clammed up. But it wasn't sleep I craved, it was just a chance to collect myself prior to my homecoming. Sprawled face-up behind Walt's wide shoulders as he steered us over the roller-coaster road, I stared at the flashes of sun and shade flittering through the trees like strobe lights on the windows and up-holstery.

Why I was so scared to go back puzzled me to no end. After less than one week gone, my boots were stuffed with cash, and I'd somehow recol-lected some sense of who I actually was. I'd danced a gypsy fandango. I'd made new and outlandish friends. I had a man who loved me up and down and sideways. I'd learned of another way of life, another way of thinking about life. I'd escaped the traps set for me in these hills. So why wouldn't I swagger into Clandel like I'd conquered Rome?

But maybe I'd really gone nowhere. The weak knees I'd had about leav-ing Clandel were likely the same I now had about going back. Just because I toted a wad of cash, had a studly beau, and knew how to run a hoop-toss game, didn't mean that all of a sudden I was a brand-new Annabelle. I was still pretty-much the same old scaredy-cat. Jimplicutes and willipus-wallupuses still crouched behind the trees in my forest, ready to leap out at any fractious notion of mine.

When my worry turned to Maw—and the hissy-fit she'd have if she found out I'd come back to town and not gone to see her—it appeared plain as day that my dithers had much to do about her and me. I hadn't phoned or written, even just to tell her I was alive. What sort of daughter did that? Even though Maw wasn't the kind of mother like Donna Reed on the TV show, she was the only mother I had, and I'd best make the best of it. Any hankering for a different mother was about as useless as wanting different toes.

She was much of who I was—maybe more than anything else in the world. I came out of her. She raised me. I didn't have to agree with how she did so, but I oughtn't be an ingrate, either. She likely did pretty-near as best she could, in the way she knew how. Who's to say I'd do any better?

Why carry on and on about what could be—or ought to be—while my own flesh and blood still breathes her dole of days on earth. Sure enough, she'll keep on jawing at me about what I ought and ought not do. She's a mother and can't hardly help it. Yet that didn't mean I had to swallow any of what she's always trying to ram down my throat. I never much did. And now that I'd moved out of her reach, her snarling and snapping at me about my life wouldn't be such an onset.

With that in mind, I tried to see her in a new light. I closed my eyes, and within the warm blood-red flashes through the lids, I hunted for a sight of her good side. Nothing like the powerful haunts of the day before drifted in and out of view—yet a fairy-like presence lurked in the twilight between the flashes. Not her—but not not her, too.

A feel of peacefulness washed through me. For a fact, I needed to see Maw. If only for a decent goodbye. Against the vinyl backseat, I curled up like a baby back in her arms, and let the road sway and joggle me toward welcome sleep.

Waking when the car slowed, I raised my head, and through the side window I recognized the ridge tops that had loomed over me all my life. They'd been the boundaries of my world, the walls of my prison, but now that I'd been over the mountain, they no longer held me captive. The familiar faces of houses perched across the hillside, even the power lines swagging past from pole to pole, I knew them more than I'd known. And now, seeing them anew with eyes that had witnessed less than a week of another world, the town appeared more alive, not just a stale jumble of the same-old same old.

I sat up, leaned over the front seat to peck a kiss on Walt's ear, and as we rolled past the side street that Maw's apartment was on, I pressed my forehead against the side window and caught a glimpse of the treads climbing to her door. I cranked the glass down, craned my neck out into the rush of air, and breathed in what only a week before had riled me to distraction. It now appeared all so harmless. This higgledy-piggledy cluster of houses and businesses, named Clandel, maybe no longer had its hex on me.

And if it did, I now saw that it wouldn't be because Clandel had ahold of me, it'd be because of me not letting go of Clandel. Most folks in town couldn't care a hoot whether I stay or leave out. It was me who made Clandel a problem, not Clandel. The town hadn't changed a whit in a week—yet I had. I'd blamed Clandel for my misput attitude. Now I reckoned it to be all my own doing.

If that was the case, then why wouldn't it be much the same with Maw and me? True, she'd been giving me a hard time for years on end—but I'd doled out my unfair share of fractiousness, too. I once tried to be her good little girl, and then my womanhood came on me—mine clashing with hers, her out-of-date rules graveling me to no end. Though we knew love as only kin can, we'd tear at each other in thousands of quarrels, most born not from spite, but in peevish self-defense of our contrary notions of right and wrong.

I'd suffer earfuls of her cautions and mainly pay them never no mind, while she'd hardly heed any complaints of mine. Laying down her law, the queen of me, she had beset what I wanted to be. Under siege, I'd dug a moat around myself, so that her scoldings, after bouncing off my stony fortress, would sink into the moat and drown. Then, from inside my castle, just to keep her at bay, I'd hurl my own fiery words at her.

Yet, after less than a week away, my fear of battle with her, which had bedeviled me so mightily that I'd push it out of mind as quick as it would enter—my lifelong dread of her damnation—somehow had now eased.

Maybe all it took for me was to be rescued from my castle by a knight in shining armor. Or maybe the acid trip had brought me into a new kingdom. After wandering through Oz, or after falling down the rabbit hole, maybe I'd brought back the strength to become more myself. Be no longer the girl who cringed from what Maw or Clandel might say or do to me, no longer the girl they wanted me to be, no longer on stage in a play that had little to do with me, no longer huffing about being miscast and hating to act the part.

I climbed into the front seat aside Walt, and fingered my curls in the rearview mirror. As we rolled down High Street, I searched some familiar faces we passed, and they paid us little mind. In front of the courthouse—where High met Main Street, and US-52 went on down the creek and out of town, and where storefronts and offices huddled on three sides of the square—Walt swung into a parking spot, and we slid out of the car.

The courthouse stood atop a knoll, the steep hillside behind it, its fort-like stones appearing more solid than rock. I'd been inside it three times in my life—once with a grade-school field trip, once to get my driver's license, and once when I'd wandered in stoned on Luke's pot after Johnny Bob had dropped me off in the square.

The guide for our grade-school civics lesson had herded us through the halls, lecturing on this and that, which we all gave little ear to. Yet my eyes flew from one marvelous thing to another—the fancy woodwork, the high windows, the heavy doors with the official names printed in gold, the clitter-clatter of prim women at rapid-fire typewriters aside stacks of papers, the creaky footsteps of men in suits, the waxed floorboards and domed hall ech-oing the voice of our guide. For years afterward, to me the courthouse was where our king might live, if we had one like in tales. It sat apart from the rest of Clandel, belonging more to the world on TV—where Perry Mason defended the innocent, where deputies strapped on pistols in the basement station and put bad guys in jail, where all the rules could be found in the rows of books on the walls.

The next time I went there, at sixteen when I got my driver's license, I expected a big to-do about it all, and I found myself in and out of the court-house in less than an hour. After studying the rulebook for days, the multiple-choice written test was so easy I could have done it upside-down. One of Rosalie's boyfriends owned a car, and the two of them slouched shoulder-to-shoulder in the back seat while I took my road test. Beside me, the deputy sat ramrod straight, pencil and clipboard on his knee, as I jerked gears up and down a few side streets and parallel-parked back at the square. And that was that. Walking on air down the courthouse steps, I marveled at the pink slip of paper that allowed me to drive—though I had no car to do so.

A few years later, I shuffled into the courthouse under the influence of an illegal substance—Luke's hillbilly marijuana. What had before appeared so important and official, now felt so put-on. The legal records in the foot-thick vault—the births certificates, the marriage licenses, the property deeds—hardly seemed to oblige this pompous temple of exaltation. The power of the judges, the lawyers, the police, along with all the kow-towing of the good citizens, appeared part of some charade, useful and likely necessary, but play-acting none the less.

I'd bogued about through the building, peeking into offices, a few secretaries asking me if I needed some help, to which I politely replied, "No, thank you—just looking around." After a quick and guilty tour through the sheriff's office in the basement, a deputy followed me back upstairs, eyeing me hard. I strolled out of the courthouse and across the square, and as I turned the corner, I glanced back at the deputy, who stood atop the steps, his arms folded on his chest, his suspicious glare still riveted on me.

Now, as Walt and I, hand-in-hand, scuffed up the courthouse steps, the big glass doors swung open for us, held by a janitor rubbing fingerprints off it with a rag. He mannerably gave us a nod with a smile, and a cheery, "Good luck." I puzzled on how he might know anything about Walt's court case, and then realized that he likely figured we were walking into the courthouse to get married.

The hall under the dome still echoed with its own importance—the men in suits, the secretaries typing, the hushed voices of civil servants doing the people's business. Walt led me in front of a directory with white letters set in slots on a black felt panel behind a glass frame.

Scanning the list, he said, "I'm supposed to check in with the clerk of courts. Room 214. Come on."

We clattered up a wide stairway and down a waxy hall to the clerk's office, and Walt whispered, "You wait on that bench. I'll talk to him alone. These thieves don't like witnesses."

He pushed through the door, its frosted-glass panel rattling when it shut behind him. I sat down for a long wait, but before I'd barely warmed the polished walnut bench, he was back out in the hall, saying, "Let's go get some breakfast."

"What happened?" I asked as we scooted down the steps and into the square.

"I go in front of the judge at one o'clock. First on the docket after lunch. No sweat. The bag man's done his job. Where can we get some eggs around here?"

I knew Jake would fry bacon and eggs at any time of day, but there was no way I wanted to eat there, what with Loretta and Barbara likely to feed us the evil eye, along with some poisonous words.

Across from the courthouse, squeezed between two lawyer's offices, sat La Square Peg, a narrow restaurant with less than a dozen small tables draped with white tablecloths. Peggy Jones had opened the place after she'd come back from cooking school in France a year or two before. Though I'd walked by and peeked in through the window many times, I'd never had even a cup of coffee there, mostly because I reckoned it to be fine-haired, and not for the likes of me. But now it seemed safe—where it was unlikely I'd meet with questions I wouldn't want to answer, a hideout from my usual haunts—so I pointed at it and pulled Walt's hand toward it.

Inside, Walt wanted to sit by the window, but I shook my head and led him to a table for two, back by the kitchen. Near a quarter to noon, the lunch rush hadn't yet begun. The crisp linens atop the tables were primly set with matching cloth napkins, silvery flatware, spotless glasses, and creamy china. I chose a seat with my back to the room, and Walt slid the chair under me.

Sitting facing me, he raised one eyebrow with half a smirk, and whispered, "I bet I'm about to pay large for my hen fruit."

"Think of it as your last meal before you go to the gallows," I whispered back. After he sniggered some, I added, "I've never been in here before, and it's likely that no one I know will be in here."

"You don't want to be seen with me?"

"I don't want to be seen, period. I figured I'd kicked this town's coal dust off my boots. And now, not a week later, I'm back."

"Ain't nobody gonna bite you."

"I'm biting myself in the ass for it." I said, a mite too loud.

One of the three waitresses—uniformed in black skirts and white blouses, their hair pulled back into ponytails—clacked over to us in low heels, set menus with black-leather covers in front of us, and asked with a syrupy voice and smile, "May I bring you some drinks?"

"Coffee, black, for me," Walt said.

I ordered a Co-Cola.

Walt, flipping through the pages of the menu, asked, "Can I get some bacon and eggs?"

"I'm sorry, we stop serving breakfast at eleven."

Walt stonily said nothing, and the waitress click-clacked off. I opened my menu, and the prices struck me dumb. Five-ninety-five for ground beef. Over at Jake's, hamburgers were a buck-fifteen. Other things on the menu, I'd never heard of—things with French names, "a la" this and "a la" that. A few things were near ten dollars a plate, for lunch. This was West-by-God-Virginia, not Paris.

I looked up at Walt, and suggested, "They've got something called eggs Benedict, for four-ninety-five."

He slapped the menu shut, and said, "Sounds like hen fruit to me, Belle. Fancy eggs, no doubt. Pricey eggs. But, like I say—what we can get, where we can get it. What's your druthers?"

"I don't know. I don't know what any of this French stuff means. I've sort of got a hankering for a ham sandwich."

"Well, ask the lady for a ham sandwich."

When the waitress returned with our drinks, I asked if I could get a ham sandwich. She looked down her nose at me, and asked, "A croque-monsieur, or a croque-madame?"

"What's the difference?"

"A croque-monsieur has ham and cheese. A croque-madame has ham, cheese, and egg."

"The first one, please." And while Walt asked about the eggs Benedict, I found the croque-monsieur on the menu—only three-ninety-five, which relieved me somewhat.

She took away the menus and clattered into the kitchen.

Walt cracked low, "They call this place the La Square Peg 'cause they're shovin' one right in your round asshole."

"Sorry I led you in here. I'd heard it was fixy, but I had no idea."

"C'est la vie, ma Belle. And they say carnies sell loads of hogwash? Restaurants are one of the biggest scams around. Slap ham and cheese on some bread, call it somethin' fancy, spread linen on the table, and voila—folks think they're eatin' like big shots. And speak of the devil, here come some now."

The bell above the door tinkled, and I peeked over my shoulder to see four men, in suits and ties, filing in. One of them, a balding porker with gold-rim glasses perched low on his piggy nose, I recognized from election posters plastered all over town last fall—Judge Snodgrass. I leaned to Walt and whispered, "The chuffy feller with the glasses is the judge."

He whispered back, "And the weasely one with the comb-over, he's the clerk of courts I just talked to. Both of 'em, eatin' lunch on my patch money, no doubt."

They took the table by the window, bantering with each other like they owned the place, which maybe they did. The bell tinkled again and again, and soon the tables were full of clean-cut men in dark suits and fixy women in crisp outfits—many of them likely from the courthouse—the room astir with mannerable murmuring accompanied by the music of silver on china.

Our lunch arrived on small dishes set atop larger dishes. My ham and cheese was the tiniest sandwich I'd ever seen. Actually, it wasn't a sandwich at all—a sandwich has two slices of bread with stuff in between. This was just one small square of thin toast, cut in two diagonally, with singed cheese atop it, laced with thin strips of ham. That and a sprig of parsley on the side.

Walt looked down at his eggs Benedict, walled his eyes back, and whispered with a chuckle, "Those Frenchies sure know how to make an egg look like somethin' in a donniker tub."

Half a toasted English muffin had on it a small round slice of ham under a single chalky-white poached egg—slimy, crimpy and jiggly—with a dollop of pale-yellow sauce atop it all, sprinkled with a pinch of chopped chives. That and another sprig of parsley.

He jabbed a fork into it—the yolk oozing out over the china. He said, "Remind me never to go to France," and took his knife and carved it up.

I figured to just pick up my ham and cheese with my fingers and eat it like a pizza, but peeking around the room I thought better of it, and went at it with knife and fork. Walt scarfed up the mess on his plate in three minutes flat, and then swabbed bits of the English muffin into the smear of sauce and yolk. I finished up not long after, still hungry for a real ham sandwich. I sipped my Co-Cola while he smoked a cigarette and got a coffee refill. The bill, delivered inside another smaller black-leather cover, came to over ten bucks, plus a dollar tip.

Back out on the sidewalk, he asked, "What now, Belle? Go get some French fries?"

"Walt, I've got two things I want to do here. Turn my cash money into traveler's checks, and go see my Maw."

"Well, it's twelve-thirty, and I best be settin' in that courtroom at one o'clock sharp—though I see the judge ain't yet hauled his fat ass off his chair. So how 'bout you attend to your business, and I'll see you in the courtroom."

"You don't want to meet Maw?"

"Would you if you was me?"

"I reckon not."

"She's not gonna wallop your perky ass with a switch, is she?"

"Not if I can help it."

"Good girl. See you in a half-hour or so? It's not likely, but I may need some backup in that courtroom."

"I'll be there," I said, and tiptoed him up a quick little kiss.

Scooting around the corner and up Main Street a few hundred steps, I stepped into the Clandel National Bank, another building I'd scarcely ever been in. I'd never had a bank account, but a few times did have a check to cash, written on this bank. Now, like then, I approached the tellers' windows uncertain about why they might do this for me. The huge safe with its thick steel door, the polished floor reflecting the chandeliers, the high-falutin' curlicues plastered on the walls and ceiling, the gold-striped columns and beams, the stony eyes of the guard with a thumb hooked on his pistol belt, the brass bars between me and the stern faces of the tellers—all this made me feel small and poor, unworthy to breathe such airs.

I chose the teller with the least sour face—a girl not much older than myself, but lumpy as a yam, with limp brown hair framing her professional smile. "May I help you?" she sang lightly as I fetched up.

I whispered, "Might could I swap some cash money for those traveler's checks I heard tell about?"

"Why surely, honey. American Express. They have a dollar-fifty fee per hundred dollars. And come in twenties, fifties, or hundreds."

"How do they work?"

"Well, you buy the amount you want in the denominations you want, and you sign each check in front of me. When you spend them, or cash them in, you sign them again, and the matching signatures prove they're yours. Keep the serial numbers in a separate place, and if you lose them, or they're stolen, you can get them replaced. Simple as that."

I let this sink in for a short piece, and when no warning of danger floated up, I said, "Okay, the money's stashed in my boots."

Propped against the counter, I yanked one boot off, then the other, and pushed the folds of cash through the gap under the bars. The guard, and others in the bank, eyed me, some trading dim views of it. Stomping my boots back on, I shot a phony smile toward the guard, and then leaned in close to the teller's bars as she counted the cash twice—quick as Trips shuffling cards, doling it out across her side of the marble counter in hundred-dollar piles.

"I count eight-hundred dollars here."

"That's right."

"In what denominations do you want the checks? Twenties, fifties, or hundreds."

I told her that fifties would be fine. She gathered up my money, walked into the safe, and several lengthy minutes later returned with a thin packet of checks coupled onto a blue plastic wallet, which folded in half to snap shut. She set the checks face up on the counter, her ring-laden fingers slipping them under the bars over to my side, and she flipped through the book for my look-see, counting them up as she went. Each 'cheque', as it was fixily spelled out across the top, was festooned with scrolls like what paper money has, and had cyphers of US$50 on the corners. Also, they had a picture on each of that Greek god with winged feet, near bare-naked, and toting a wand with two snakes wrapped around it.

After I nodded agreement to her count, she handed me a pen, and told me to sign each check on the top line. Sixteen nervous signatures later, she asked for the twelve-dollar fee. I dug it out of my purse, paid her, and she passed me a receipt listing the serial numbers of each check. She told me to keep the receipt in a safe place—somewhere other than where I kept the checks—because if they were ever lost or stolen, then it would be much easier to get replacements. She thanked me, and I her, as I slid the receipt and checkbook into my purse. With the guard holding the door open for me and mannerably tipping his hat, I sashayed out with a feel of poor no more.

Back on the sidewalks of Clandel, with its mid-day traffic rumbling past, I may not have been so cash poor, yet I still felt poorly about seeing Maw. The courthouse clock neared one, and what with the bank teller and the signatures taking so much time, I reckoned that I should first go see how Walt was doing in the courtroom. But when I rounded the corner back into the square, I spotted the judge and the clerk through the restaurant window, still on their chairs and in no rush to end their caucus. I figured if I hurried up the hill to Maw's apartment, breezed in, said my piece, took my medicine, and told her I had to light a shuck for the courthouse, then that might make short work of any likely fractiousness. So I hightailed it back up Main Street, and before I had a chance to chew on the contrary, I stomped up the treads and burst into the apartment.

Maw sat at her lunch on the kitchen table. A baloney sandwich in her hands, she gazed at me for a spell, and then said, "Looky here what the cat done drug on in."

"Hey, Maw. How are you?"

"A heap sight better off now as I see you ain't dead."

"No, I ain't dead. I'm more and more alive, each and every day."

"Well ain't that a basket of posies."

"Maw, I didn't come here to jower with you. I came to show you I was doing fine, and to tell you not to be troubled about me."

"Well, missy, now that you done told me so, your maw won't have no worriments to knit her brow no more. Now I can just flick off my wearying switch, and not charge my mind with any of what my child is up to."

"Please, Maw, quile your cantankerousness for a piece, and just listen to me. Ears open and mouth shut."

She eyeballed me like she was about to clinch my frames. And me, I'd been eating her aggravation for so long, my bellyful was fit to burst with shit that would raise such a stink, the smell would never leave us.

But I had no yen for any such onset. Our years of bickering had come to naught. Neither she nor I had won any battles in this foolish war—yet we'd both nearly lost each other. I stood there holding down my bait of spite, squinting into her ornery eyes. And seeing her in a new light—in the kindly shade of the LSD's afterglow—I shortly melted with sorrow for her.

"Maw, kicking the cat back and forth ain't getting us nowhere. We've been scratching each other's heart out for way too long now. You're the only mother I've got, and what's the sense of us always chewing barbed wire and spitting nails? It does us no damn good. You got your druthers and I got mine. I ain't your little girl no more. I'm my own woman now. Me. Myself!... You can't keep a squirrel on the ground, Maw. You told me that."

"I also told you you're so stubborn you'd argue with a stop sign."

"If that's the way I am, then why not just let me be?"

"Cause it's my job, as your maw, to set you straight."

"Well, now it's my turn to set *you* straight. I've got a poke full of money, and a beau who loves me, and a powerful hankering for the other side of the mountain. There's nothing you can do or say to change any of that. So get over it, and be civil to your own flesh and blood."

"You're more a-kin to your Pap, Annabelle. He up and left me, too."

"Don't put that on me. Pap had his reasons for going, and I've got mine. And the two just don't meet up."

"They meet up in the deep of your consarned gallivantin' ways."

"Maw... I reckon you can't keep that squirrel on the ground, neither."

"Girl, you're so contrary you'd float upstream."

"I'm none of your hillbilly sayings. I'm me, and you're you. And the sooner you give ken to that, the quicker we rid ourselves of this hell."

Her grim lips quivered, her eyes flailed about, and tears sopped into their corners. I came around the table and reached for a hug. She looked up at me and shook her head—with disbelief, not denial. I leaned my head into the creases of her soft warm nec, and hauled her by her flabby sides up off the chair. She pushed me away half a touch, and then heaved me up against the swag of her bosom.

Years since we'd held each other so, I felt of how old she'd become, and I choked out, "Maw... I love you all the same. Nothing in this world will change that. But I'm not your little girl any more. I'm not even who I was just a week ago. We've both got to grow up and be adults about all this.... I've got to become who I am."

She gently shunned me off, held my shoulders at arm's length, and asked, "And who would that be? Some sorry-girl carny-trash?"

"No. That's not me. And it's not what you think it is."

"No? Then what is it?"

I backed up and sunk into a chair, gathered some patience, and said, "It's fun, and exciting, and by tomorrow night I'll likely have a thousand dollars in my poke."

"What fairy tale are you livin' in?"

I reached in my purse, took out the packet of traveler's checks, snapped it open on the table, and flipped over each fifty-dollar note, counting aloud the whole eight hundred.

Her suspicion hunted back and forth from my eyes to the checks. Standing there silent for a spell, she then leaned to me, palms down on the table, and asked softly, "How in tarnation did you come by that much cash money in just one week?"

"I got lucky, Maw. For once, I got lucky. I played a game by its rules and won. Somebody's got to win, and this time it was me. The whole wide world's full of games to win or lose. And you can't win if you don't play."

She snuffled a snort that I well knew, waggled her finger at me, and spit out, "What kind of game you got goin' with that carny?"

"Maw, he loves me more than I can love him. And to me right now, that's a damn shame. But not one I sit alone with. I'll allow I don't know much about the how-to of love. You and Pap weren't much good at it. But you gave it your best shot. And now it's my turn. I'm giving it *my* best shot. And my aim is improving."

"And what's he aimin' to do?"

"Make me into the woman I am. Take me far away from where I don't want to be.... He's a good man, Maw."

"Then what's he doin' greenin' folk out of their hard-earned dollars, if he's such a gooder?"

"He's just playing games with them. Selling them something just like any other business. Except he's in the amusement business. He earns his living by giving folks a chance to win something. He sells fun. It's fun to try to win a prize by tossing balls. I work right beside him in the next booth, selling hoops to toss at prizes on pegs. Most folks are glad to swap their quarters for a little fun."

She lowered herself back onto her chair, shook her head, raised her brows, and confessed, "I never expected much from you and your sister—what with the world you were born to here. We never had much of nothin'. But we lived thankful for what we had. And now, I sit here listenin' to my child braggin' on her ill-gotten gains. My baby girl a-sportin' with a pack of thieves. Diddlin' one of 'em in hotel beds.... There's nothin' now for me to do but believe it to be so. Yet I'd sooner sleep in a pasture and pick corn out of horse droppin's."

I shot back, "Everyone to their liking, as the old woman said when she kissed her cow. Isn't that what I've heard you say, many times?"

She sighed. "Yes, you did. Yes, you did."

"Maw, we'll never see eye to eye. And, let me tell you, I don't take kindly to your knocking me down—not right now, nor all the years since Pap left—you taking it out on me, because I'm more like him. Things ain't worked out the way you want, but now that's the way they are. And the only thing to save us from this damnation is forgiveness.

"I forgive you for becoming a douncy couch potato in front of that stupid TV. If I had my druthers, it wouldn't be so. But once I forgive you, all my hellish blame is gone. You've got to do the same with me.... Forgive me, Maw, for not being who you want me to be. I have to be who I am, and right now, I don't know where that leads to.

"But don't forgive me for my sake. Do it for your own peace of mind. The blame game is just another goddamn game in this fractious world—one we don't have to play. Maw, just quit! Just forgive me and accept who I am. It's nobody's fault. It just is. There's nothing else you can do about it. Nothing but burn in hell hating it."

She glared deep into my eyes, and then said in a tired voice, "Annabelle, I allow you need your say.... And I'll try to forgive you. But've you ever tried to separate fly shit from black pepper?"

I laughed a breath or two, and told her, "That's one of my favorites of yours. Once—a long time ago, after you said that about something—I sprinkled pepper on a dog turd, figuring that flies would poop on dog-doo, and to see if I could spot the difference between the pepper and fly shit. But before I went back to find out, a rain had washed it away."

"Lordy, Lordy, after all this bitin' and gougin', I do need a drink. How 'bout you?"

"I have to go now."

"What for? You just got here."

I wrassled a few seconds with coming up with some story other than Walt's waiting for me in a courtroom, but I told her, "Monday night, Walt, my beau, whupped this brush-ape upside the head with a hammer while protecting me from him. In a few minutes, Walt's about to go face-to-face with Judge Snodgrass. And even though it's been all squared away behind the scenes, he might need a witness, and that'd be me."

Her eyes walled up, she slapped both hands atop the table and pushed herself to her feet. Turning her back to me and fetching her bottle in the cupboard, she said, "Now I really need a drink. Lord help my time."

"I've got to go, Maw."

"Go! Just git. Write when you find work."

"I will. And so I can buy a ticket home when I might need to, I'll sign over one of these checks to you." Which I hurried to do and handed it over. "Vault it with the check numbers on this receipt. And maybe send it to me to come home someday. Or maybe someday you can use it to come visit me somewhere.... You know I love you, don't you?"

"I know, sugar. I know. I love you, too. We'll be a-workin' on all that forgiveness.... The rest of your things in your room, they can stay right where they be, waitin' for when you come back."

"Much obliged, Maw."

"T'ain't nothin'."

"Yes it is. You've always tried to do right by me."

Pouring her stump liquor into a fruit jar, she snapped at me over her shoulder, "T'ain't nothin', and don't take in argufying again. Just git where you got to go. No doubt you'll be back soon enough."

The week before, that would've lit my fuse. Instead, I snuffed out any flare-up, turned for the door, and left her to her self-made misery. Clomping down the treads, I caught a glimpse of what Maw was likely seeing—her baby girl turning her back to what she'd been raised to believe.

Several minutes later, breathing heavy from rushing down the hill, I slid next to Walt on a pew in the courtroom. The judge, in his high seat behind the oaken hulk of his bench, shuffled papers in front of tiny spectacles at the tip of his hog-like snout. Across the aisle, I spotted Dwayne and a few of his buddies. The left side of his head had a patch shaved bare and a row of raw stitches.

The judge hooked a finger to the clerk, who climbed from his desk by the bench and up to the judge's side. They whispered back and forth for a piece, and then the clerk went back to his desk—on his way, passing a paper to a deputy in uniform, standing as bailiff.

The deputy read the charge—assault with a deadly weapon—and called Walt to the front, opening a gate in the oak railing and guiding him by the elbow to stand before a table.

The judge growled, "Herman Walter Ryder, how do you plea to this charge? Guilty or not guilty."

"Not guilty, your honor. I hit him in self-defense."

The judge peered over his spectacles at Walt, grunted once, and dropped his eyes to the papers.

After a lengthy spell of dutifully studying a page, the judge turned his head to Dwayne, called his full name—Dwayne Allen Williams, Jr.—told him to stand up, and said, "Mr. Williams, I have in my hand a police report which states that witnesses say you threatened Mr. Ryder with a knife. Is that so?"

Dwayne shifted his feet, scratched his neck, and whined, "Judge, they done greened me out o' my money. And when I took in a-yarnin' about it, this rascal up and throttles me by my goozle. So, yessiree, I pulled out my frog sticker to fend him off."

The judge dropped his eyes again to the paper, and without lifting them asked, "Was that before or after you accosted Mr. Ryder's associate in the next booth?"

"Accosted?" Dwayne yelped. "I didn't do no accosting. I bought a game of hoop toss from her, and gave 'em a toss."

"My report here says you threw an armload of them, all at once, violently at her."

Dwayne said nothing to that.

"Was that the game where you say you were cheated? The hoop toss?"

"No. T'were a rullion in the tent next door. Where you roll marbles into holes and count up the score, in some tomfool football game."

"So, you were angry at him, and took it out on the hoop-toss girl. And when Mr. Ryder came to her aid, you pulled your knife on him."

"Well he had no needment to crack my skull with a claw hammer!"

The judge set down the police report, picked up another paper, studied it, and then wrote something on it. He slipped them both into a manila file, and then glowered down at Dwayne, telling him, "Mr. Williams, I've seen you in this courtroom too many times concerning your violent behavior. From the evidence presented here, and your own admissions, it's you who should be charged in this incident. And furthermore, if you do not change your trouble-making ways, one day you'll be headed for the penitentiary."

To Walt he said, "Case dismissed. Not guilty by reason of self-defense. Mr. Ryder, you are free to go."

Walt said, "Thank you kindly, Judge," and then he turned, swung through the gate, led me by the arm out of the courtroom, hurried us out into the square, and fired up the Mercury.

"We best get a move on before those Clems get up a posse of vigilantes," he said, wheeling out of the square. Up Main Street and out of town, he hit the gas hard, winding up along Black Creek and over the ridge. After a few miles, he slowed down some, chuckled, and leaned a big grin in my direction—fancy-free and in high feather.

"Yee-haw! Belle, I told you the fix was in. That dumb rube, Dwayne, he didn't know what hit him. Twice. And if Judge Hogshead weren't that monkey's uncle, we wouldn't have had to work this alibi. No way, no how. Hammer Dwayne's coconut, ding the patch, and that's all she wrote. Goin' through the motions, Belle. That's what this courthouse show was all about. Dwayne's lucky the judge didn't spank him bare-ass, right there and then."

"What's that mean, 'ding the patch'."

"The patch, Carl the patch. The front-office guy with the short brim and the fat cigar. He ices heat. Collects his privilege nightly from the count stores, the gaffed joints, the kootch show, and any fireball alibi agents, depending on the action and how strong the spot's played. Carl takes his cut, pays his own privilege to McCain, and the rest goes into the sheriff's poke. Now in this here fracas, Ray no doubt gave up his whole score from Dwayne to Carl and the sheriff. Ray fucked up. He shoved it way too far up Dwayne's keister. Play 'em, for sure, but don't send 'em off fit to be tied. Extra trouble costs extra bag money."

"How much did you have to pay?"

"A yard-note to the Judge Hogshead re-election fund."

"A hundred dollars?"

"I'm drivin' down the road a free man, ain't I? Nick had to pony-up another hundred. And he ain't too happy about that, he's let me know."

"How much do you pay every night to the patch?"

"Belle, I don't work my joint strong. I juggle the balls and fairbank 'em some, but I don't burn 'em. My feature is I play 'em as they come, and quit when I'm ahead. No sense in gettin' greedy. Copasetic to win what I've won, I leave 'em with the rent money. No big beefs, no big dings to the patch.

"Nick pays Carl a privilege for the basket joint, on top of the nut for his footage. And I'll tell you, the way that gig artist J.D.'s been workin' it this week, next week Nick's ding will be more. J.D.'s been disqualified from bushels of basket joints. He don't let 'em go when they've had enough. He'd as soon send 'em home for the deed to the house, as give up a spoofer. And he hates the jigs like Hitler hated Jews. The sooner he gets himself DQ'ed, the better, if you ask me.

"I've got little to do with who's beside me in the line-up, but I've got everythin' to do with how I run my own game. I told Nick that J.D. was slow poison. But the two of them are counting up fat aprons, and Nick'll take as much of that as he can get."

I said, "I don't like J.D., either. He's cocky in a nasty way.... Does the pitch-till-u-win pay the patch?"

"No. It's a hanky-pank. What you see is what you get. No beefs there. Uh-oh."

"Uh-oh, what?"

"The posse's come up on our tail."

I swiveled to look behind us, and the same beat-up pickup truck that was in the motel parking lot the other night was closing in on our rear bumper, carrying four mountaineers shoulder-to-shoulder in the cab, and Dwayne riding shotgun —his arm out the window and his middle finger jabbing upward.

Walt stomped on the gas and we roared away from them, gaining ground until we came to a batch of bends. The Mercury was built to cruise, not race through unknown curves, so Walt had to slow down to keep us on the road, while the ridge-runner driving the pickup pushed it hell-bent through one familiar curve to the next, coming up on us in leaps and bounds. Down the straightaways, we'd draw away from them, then lose ground again through the turns. On a set of switchbacks over a ridge, their bumper nudged ours once, twice, trying to shove us off the mountain!

Walt—wrassling the wheel, stomping on the gas and brake, eyes flashing from the road ahead to the rearview mirror—yelled to me, "Can you spot if any of them has a gun?"

I knelt on the seat and studied them as we lurched side to side. "I don't see one."

"Reach under my seat. There's a holster clipped to the springs."

Fishing my arm underneath, I found the cool grip of a pistol, and slid out a small caliber nickel-plated automatic sheathed in a black holster.

"Gimmie that pea shooter."

I snapped it loose from the holster and set it on the seat. When we hit the next straightaway, along a creek at the bottom of the ridge, he steadied the steering wheel with a knee, kerchanked the pistol's action back and forth, and thumbed the safety off.

"You're not going to shoot them are you?"

"What, they don't deserve shootin'? They're runnin' us off the road!"

"You shoot someone, and you'll be off the road in prison."

"Better than bein' dead."

He slowed the car some and hugged the right side of the road. The pickup barreled up alongside. With God-awful wrath warping his face, Dwayne hefted a baseball bat out his window, and with all the give 'em Jesse he had, he leaned out and with both hands walloped the bat down onto the roof of the Mercury. Bam!

Walt muttered, "You fuckin' hoojy," and let off the gas. As the back end of the pickup passed his open window, he aimed the pistol and put a bullet into the rear tire.

The tire exploded, and Walt hit the brakes. Dragging a lame back leg— the tire thumping itself to shreds—the pickup truck swerved, skidded into the berm along the creek, and bounced to a stop.

Walt floored the Mercury and waved the pistol out the window, firing a pair of shots into the air as we roared through their cloud of dust.

"Yeehaw!" Walt hooted, setting the pistol on the seat. "That'll slow 'em down some."

My hands went all trembly, my bowels clenched off a sudden urge, and the thump of my heart strutted into my gullet. I stammered, "You ain't yet done with those boys. There's naught in these mountains held to more than a feud is. Now that the law let them down, they're bound to take it on themselves to settle the score."

"Settle what score? The score's even. I got a dent in my roof and they got a tire shot to shit."

"You listen to me, mister. I know the likes of these boys. And I'm telling you they're not going to take kindly to your pulling a pistol on them. They'll be hunting you up soon enough—with guns of their own."

He glanced at me sideways, a mean twist in the corner of his mouth, then turned back to the road, saying, "They know where I'll be."

The rest of the ride back to Stuart carried a silence between us that I was grateful for. I hadn't bargained on being in the midst of a feud. But there it was, and what I could do about it was beyond me. Walt wouldn't be backing off, and I knew that neither would Dwayne and his boys. Hell had been stirred up with a long spoon.

When we parked at the motel, Walt got out to look over the damage to the roof—a dent the size of half a football. I took the room key and left him cussing, trying to push it out from underneath. Cheeks came out on the balcony as I passed his open door.

"What it is, gorgeous?"

I gave him a short version of the story, and he shook his head, saying, "Not to worry, girl. We take care of our own out here." Then he cracked over the rail at Walt, "That crease on your roof oughta been on your noggin."

Walt lifted a look like he was chewing barbed wire.

Cheeks took in laughing out loud. Then he turned to me. "You want some smoke to settle your dithers?"

I shook my head, and he asked, "How was it for you yesterday? Did you see God?"

I said, "I saw lots of things in a new way. And I've not yet come to terms with it all. How about you?"

"Oh... I had a fun trip. When I thought I lost Frog Baby, I about freaked, though."

"You didn't see God?"

"Nope. No God. No Devil. Just my dog, my partners in crime, and my latex oddity. And the magic of this world. What more do I need?"

"You're another guess, Cheeks.... Say, tell me, what's your real name?"

"I don't have a real name. I gave it up long ago."

"Well what's it say on your driver's license?"

"I don't have one of those, either. You got to have an address in one state or another to get one of those. I've got a phony one from Alabama that I flash when need be. But the name on it ain't my real name, because I don't have a real name."

"Why not?"

"I don't know... It just don't seem right to me. Ain't I allowed that? It's a free country, the last I heard."

"If you say so."

"So I say. Once I saw a TV show about people in the jungle who wouldn't tell anybody their real name. If someone knew it, then they'd have some sort of hoo-joo power over 'em. So they kept it secret. Maybe there's somethin' to that."

"Cheeks, you are odd for a fact."

"Your number's either odd or even. And there ain't no changin' that."

Walt stomped up the treads, the mood across his face none the better, and I unlocked the room and beat him to the privy. I heard him switch on the TV and drop onto the bed. After taking care of my business, I searched my face in the mirror. Something in my reflection now seemed older, or newer. Behind the eyes that looked back, there appeared to lurk someone I was becoming. Whether it would be me—whoever that was—or someone else, I had yet to find out.

Walt pounded on the door and hollered, "You drownin' in there or what?"

I let him in and sprawled onto the bed. With more than an hour till four-o'clock call, I flipped through the channels on the TV—nothing but soap operas. Walt turned on the shower, and I opened the bathroom door a crack, peeked in, and told him, "I'm going for a walk."

His naked haunches half-visible through the spattered shower curtain, he said, "I was about to wash off the sweat of all the day's heat, and lay a fresh one to you."

"I'll take a rain check on that."

"Suit yourself, Belle."

Outside, the afternoon clouds had piled up, thickening their cottony tops, and fading to gray underneath—likely soon to be rumbling with bread wagons. The Friday streets bustled with folks, their paychecks cashed and shopping for needments. Instead of walking into town, I lit off the opposite way, along a hard road for a stretch, then up a gravel side street to its dead end, and then along a pair of ruts leading into a hollow overgrown with laurel. Whispering breezes hushed the murmur of the town behind me, as the scuff of my footfalls beat time to the birdsong.

Not far along, I came up to a box house, all slattery and agley, where on the front gallery sat an old woman smoking her pipe in a cane rocking chair.

She startled me when I saw her. But her thin lips took up a smile, and she waved me over with a frail hand.

"How do, ma'am."

The lizardy skin of her peaceful face tight across her sharp bones, her pale eyes elegant beneath silvery hair twisted into a bun, she said, "Mighty fine, missy. Mighty fine. What takes ye outen this a-way?"

"Just a walk on such a fine day."

"That it be. That it be. Set with this old sister a spell and caucus some. Won't ye?"

"Why sure. But I best be not long. I'm to be at work soon."

"And what be yer job o' work?"

"I run a game at that carnival set up south of town."

"Ye don't say. Ye don't say. Why, I ain't seen the likes of a carny show since the hogs et my brother up. Hee-hee. That's been quite a spell now. And ye run a game, ye say. What kindly game?"

"Oh, just a little old hoop-toss game."

"Hoop toss, ye say. Laws I reckon iffen that wer'n't the one I favored when I were a young'un. Tossin' hoops atop dope bottles."

"This game, you toss hoops at blocks with prizes on them. Big prizes on big blocks, little prizes on little blocks."

"What be the price fer tossin' hoops anymore?"

"A quarter."

"Ye don't say. Peers a mite costive. How many hoops d'ye git fer yer quarter-dollar?"

"You pitch till you win."

"Do which?"

"You toss the hoops until one rings a block, and the prize on the block is what you win. It might take you one toss, and it might take a hundred."

"Well, by juckies, that peers a fair shake. Iffen I had an extry quarter, and ways to git there and back, I do declare I might could toss some hoops with y'all."

"What keeps you lively around here?"

"Jist keepin' alive is lively as I git anymore. I gits my Roos'velt money, what keeps me in cornpone, sorghum, and 'backer. This a-here ol' shacklety house and my clattermints ain't much to speak of, but it's free and clear, beholdin' to nary save the tax man.

"Over yonder lay a coal shelf, what I chunk off and gather up to keep the chill off. Much else, I've nary a-hankerin' fer.... Now I wager that a purty one the likes of ye got a rollicky fella or two to lively-up with. Heh?"

"Yeah, I've got a beau."

"Uh-oh. Am I a-hearin' an air o' mulligrubs in what yer sayin'?"

"Well, he's plumb crazy about me. But I ain't so sure about him."

"Dearie... what be yer name?"

"Annabelle."

"That's a purty name. Annabelle. Mine's Clairy. Annabelle, a man what won't pass without pushin's as scarce as preachers in paradise. My Leland done little but drunk up bumblin's from his copper coil, what he didn't sell off. Idlesome, misorderly, and a braggart to boot, God rest his soul. But he was hog tight, bull strong, and horse high, and he keered for me much as Joseph fer Mary. Thought I hung the moon. And that's a sight of satisfaction, Annabelle. A sight of satisfaction."

"Don't I need to be crazy about my man?"

"I swan... truth be told, yer a woman, Annabelle. There ain't nothin' no how what keeps us from gettin' techy 'bout a man's doin'. We all ain't got it in us to not be misput by what we feel of. The moon shifts shape nary more 'n our moodiness. Everhow, iffen there be a right smart of hardness atwixt ye, then that's a contrary tale to tell. Ye jist cain't polish a turd."

"We've only been together a week."

"A week, ye say? That ain't near time enough to tear the bone out o' nothin'. Give it time to tote fair. Let it green up some."

"I take that kindly, ma'am."

"I'm a-tellin' ye right, Annabelle. I'm a-tellin' ye right. There's this itty-bitty ditty that my old maw oft sang to me, what goes like this...."

She trilled like a mockingbird, "To love is to live is to give is to live is to love." She sang three rounds of it, and then told me, "Ye take that to heart iffen you see fit."

Her putting to song what I'd lately come to realize, I more than took to heart, and could only stutter, "Much obliged, ma'am. I... I got to go now. He's likely awaiting on me."

"Tell 'im old Clairy's gonna fetch up in one o' his dreams, and set 'im on the straight and narrow. And ye be huntin' fer me in yourn as well. I'll be seein' ye in mine."

"So I'm hoping, Miss Clairy.

"We'll be talking at ye."

I shuckled back down the hollow and into town. As I scurried across the motel parking lot, Walt spotted me from the door of our room and put on a fretful face before he turned back into the room. I pounded up the treads and swung breathless through the door, to find him slouched on a chair, thrumming his fingers on the table.

"We're gonna be late for call," he scolded.

"Sorry. I met an old woman up in a hollow, and we had a nice chat."

"Nick's gonna eat that one up like candy."

"Nick can eat shit, Walt."

"Whoa. What's got you all pissy?"

"Forget it. Let's just go. Give me a minute in the bathroom."

I primped, gathered a few things, and joined him out in the car, the motor already running. Not much was said on the way out to the lot—just, "What the old woman have to say for herself?"

"She said she'd come to you in your dreams and set you straight."

"Set me straight for what?"

"For me, Walt. For me."

He shook his head and stewed on this. By the time we rounded the bend near the lot, the Ferris Wheel was already spinning. And when we fetched up to the joints, Nick, working the pitch-till-u-win, had his quills up. But it wasn't so much about us being late.

He tore the apron off, dropped it under the blocks, jumped out of the trailer, and on the balls of his feet, sputtered up into Walt's face, "Son, the police say you pulled a pistol on some boys and shot out their tire?"

"They were runnin' us off the road, Nick. I got a dent from a baseball bat in my roof, compliments of that Clem I hammered. The judge let me go, and they came after us. What else could I do? Shoot one of 'em instead of a tire?"

"Walt, this whole business is aggravatin' the shit out of me. I didn't sign you on to be bustin' heads and shootin' up tires."

"Then show me red lights!"

"See. There you go again, flyin' off the handle. Get a grip, son. Just think about what you're doin' before you do it."

"I'm thinkin' I'm about to get thrown to the dogs."

"No, no. The patch just wants you to lay low, keep out of sight tonight and tomorrow."

"Keep out of sight? I'm good to win an apron full of cash this weekend. I've been grindin' this joint all week, and now I don't play Friday and Saturday?"

"Let's just see what happens tonight. Right now the deputies are lookin' for you, and unless you want another ride to the hoosegow, wise up and lay low."

"And where am I supposed to lay low? If everyone's after me, the motel's no option. My car? They know my car. Under the trailer? Where?"

"Get your sorry ass over in the G-top. I'll have Blackie bring you a pint of whiskey and a deck of cards. Play solitary, or play with your pecker. Get drunk. Just stay out of sight, before I have to ante up for any more jackpots."

"What about Annabelle?"

"The law's not after her."

"Those hoojies might do her bad because of me."

"That ain't likely. Me and J.D.'ll keep an eye on her."

"I'm holdin' you to that, Nick."

"Don't doubt me, son."

Walt waggled a finger at J.D.—who was taking this all in, leaning over the counter at the near side of the basket joint—and Walt told him, "Anybody just looks at her cross-eyed, bug-eyed, or evil-eyed, you best jump in their face."

"I'm with it on that, Walt. Got ya covered," J.D. said, nodding like a bobble-head doll.

Walt turned to me, and asked, "You alright out here?"

"Far as I can tell."

"If anybody dares cause you any trouble whatsoever, you put J.D. or Nick on them fast. Or better yet, you just come and get me in the G-top. And come see me when you catch a break. I'll sneak around now and then, too.... Fuck. Ain't this a bowl full of cat shit."

He pecked a kiss on me and ducked around back. I hopped into the pitch, tied on the apron, and cranked up my spiel. Right off, some families and kids fetched up, passed me quarters and dollars, and took in flinging hoops.

And only minutes later, two deputies swaggered up to the bushel baskets and asked J.D. where Walt was. J.D. shrugged and said he didn't know. The deputies then eyed me. As they sidled over to find out what I knew, Nick scooted up between, asking them what was up, as if he didn't know, and then he spun a tale about Walt running off and leaving him high and dry. The deputies listened with suspicious eyes, but they took it as their duty done, good enough for now, and told Nick that if he saw Walt to be sure to let them know. Nick added, for good measure, that if they find him before he does, they should lock him up and throw away the key.

When they walked off, Nick, leaning elbows on the counter, muttered to me, "Goddamn it. Johnny Law wants him for questioning. This ain't goin' away without some serious icing. And young lady, let me tell you, I ain't so keen about ponyin' up any more bag money. That last one was enough already. And 'cause this one went down off the lot, I'd bet the front office might fight shy of it, too. You tell that man of yours he best mend his contentious ways. Or he'll be seein' our tail lights soon enough."

"You tell him," I snapped back, riled that he appeared to be forsaking Walt.

Jingling his pocket change, he squinted an eye at me and nearly said something, but thought better of it, before spinning on a heel and stamping across to the glass pitch.

I stood there fretting that Walt was soon to be in the jailhouse, with none of his carnies helping him, and then I might be beholden to use all my traveler's checks to bail him out. But would I bail him out? Why would it be on me to give over all my money to get someone I'd known only one week out of jail?—someone I'd half likely not even be with next week, due to reasons that have nothing to do with him and his pistol.

I had no answer to that right then, and the needs of the game at hand, the quarters and hoops and prizes, took my mind away from it all. Not yet five o'clock, and the midway already moved heavy with people—many of them young blacks.

J.D. bellyached to me, "Friday night's jig night. Every blue gum in town'll be out here signifyin'. And Walt's left 'em all for me. What I do to deserve the likes of this?"

A few blacks at my counter threw scowls toward J.D., who paid them no mind. I ignored him like he wasn't there, and piled hoops onto the counter, passed out the slum, and grabbed more quarters.

As eveglom set in, the stream of folks down the midway turned into a flood—waves of blacks, teens to twenties, mostly girls with girls, and boys with boys, striding and shackling round and round—islands of white kids drifting among them.

In front of Hat's basketball toss, the gather-all overflowed ten-deep out into the midway. Hat whirled like a dervish—talking it up, handing out balls left and right, making change, calling the shots, passing out teddy bears, grinding the joint to beat the stir, spinning his spiel between two shooters at a time. Along with a few white jocks taking their shots, dozens of young blacks dribbled and posed at the foul line—a day-glo orange stripe painted across the front edge of a plank stomped into the dirt. They bounced the basketballs on the plank, practiced their dry-run warm-ups, took dead aim, wound up, and uncoiled their shots with lavishes of body English. Side by side, one after another, they swapped quarters for free-throws—each shooter displaying his own self-styled basketball swagger.

Hooting it up, the blacks had themselves much more fun than the stiff-necked white boys—and also won a heap sight more teddy bears. Their jokey buddies and beaus cheered their heroes on, the girls all swanked up, several hugging fuzzy teddy bears.

The crowd around Hat's joint thickened, clogging traffic between the line-up and the glass pitch, and spilling over in front of nearly half of J.D.'s counter. He asked them again and again—right mannerably, for J.D.—to move on over some. Then he shortly turned fractious, clapping his fists and snarling, "Git out from under my awning. I got money to win here. Git!"

They'd shuffle away sideward some, the whites of their eyes brimming with righteous indignation. Then they'd soon drift back, and others would drift in, some even leaning their backsides on J.D.'s counter.

"Git your black ass offen my counter. What the fuck does this look like here, boy? A street corner?"

They'd move clear, but slowly, swiveling their heads to look daggers at J.D. After a quarrelsome stretch of fruitless shooing, J.D. gave it up, and took out his vexation on any and all white folk strolling past. Nearly grabbing them by the shirt collars, he lit into them like a hold-up man, looting their pokes by not taking no for an answer, badgering their reluctance with his in-your-face run-around. But if any blacks would want to play his game, he'd snatch a half-dollar or two from them and work it plainly disgusted to do so. He'd not sink his hooks into them, not lead them on with any cop balls. He'd just snatch up their money and let the balls bounce on out, hardly turning his head to watch.

I grabbed every quarter within reach, mostly from eager little black hands. My counter jammed up, end to end, three and four deep, hoops clicking and clacking, I scurried back and forth, piling hoops on the counter, passing out prizes, making change, chanting my spiel.

Often I'd see or hear a hoop land on a small block, and again not know who tossed it. When I'd ask who won this or that whistle or spider, no one would fess up. Sometimes I could tell whose toss it was by spotting whose face gave it away—they'd cast a glance at what they'd rung, eye me quick to see if I saw it too, then they'd act as if they knew nothing about it, and take in tossing more hoops. When I'd hand them the prize, they'd look at me puzzled and swear they didn't toss that hoop. But when I'd tell them, "Oh yes you did," they'd own up to it with either a scowl or a smile.

As daylight dimmed under grumbling storm clouds, the frenzy of lights burned brighter, and the crowd surging along the midway got so close there wasn't room enough to cuss a cat without getting hair in your mouth. I had a dozen or more players tossing hoops all at once. My bulging apron swayed heavy with coins and bills. Busier than a one-legged man in a butt-kicking contest, I'd never felt so much alive.

Around sundown, I spied Dwayne pushing toward us through the crowd, followed by his posse of good-old boys, their faces twisted up like they meant business. They fetched up to the bushel-basket counter, where a pair of black teenage girls were funning with each other, taking their sweet time tossing their softballs while J.D. paid them never no mind.

Dwayne elbowed his way in between the girls, and leaning into J.D.'s face, snarled, "Where's that other son of a bitch what works here?"

J.D. glared eyeball to eyeball, and said, "Gone."

"Gone where?"

"Gone from here."

Dwayne jerked a glance toward me, and said, "What about her? She's still here ain't she?"

J.D. swiveled a look-see my way, and then, back in Dwayne's face, said, "Yep. There she is. Still here. Just like you say. And I'm still here, too, Gomer."

One of the black girls waggled a finger at Dwayne, and said, "Mister, I'm still here, too. And I done paid my fifty-cent to chunk this here ball in that there basket. So iffen you don't mind, back off some, and give some room here."

"Shut yer nigger mouth," Dwayne said, loud enough to turn plenty of heads—a sight of black faces narrowing their eyes at him.

The girl set her hands atop her hips, and asked, "Do which? Shut my nigger mouth, you say? Is that what you told me, you mother-fuckin' squirrel-turner?"

"Fuck you, nigger bitch."

"Fuck me? Nigger bitch? It's you what's fucked. You hog-fuckin' honky. My homies is gonna fuck you up good."

By now, some of the bucks from the basketball joint had moved over and pressed in close around Dwayne's posse. Nostrils flaring, scowls afire, chests huffed-up, they surrounded them with menace. The white boys, fists clenched and backs up, stood their ground with peppery eyes and twisty sneers.

J.D. swung a claw hammer out from below, whammed the flat side of it down on his counter, and hollered, "Y'all git your sorry asses away from my joint afore someone else gets clocked up-side the head."

That sidetracked the standoff enough for Dwayne to lead a retreat, shouldering sideways through the snarl, over to my counter. Leaning into me as I backed away, he warned, "When we find that man of yourn, we're a-gonna ride him bug-huntin'. Mess him up so bad, his momma won't know him from possum shit. And iffen we don't find him, I allow you'd be next in line for the likes of such. Now tell me. Where is he?"

I lied, "I don't know. He left out this afternoon and told me naught."

He waggled a finger at me, and said, "You best be tellin' no tales, girl."

Right then, Nick pushed up behind Dwayne, yanked him around by an elbow, and near as short, toe to toe, nose to nose, hissed in his face, "We've had about enough of your goddamn aggravation. You best get yourself gone before we both regret what I do to you."

"You can't tell me shit. This a-here's a free country, old man."

"No it's not, boy. I pay rent for where you're standin'. And this trailer's my private property. And right now, you're trespassing, 'cause I'm tellin' you to get your sorry ass gone."

"Where's that rullion what whupped me upside the head."

"He ain't here no more, and neither will you be when I count to three.... One."

Dwayne looked side to side, taking measure of the situation.

"Two."

Ray, Bad-Eye Mike, and the other agent in the flat store next door—all who'd been leaning out over its counter, watching this fracas heat up—ducked under the bally cloth and out on the midway all at once, and swaggered toward us. Slapping the hammer head into his hand again and again, J.D. stepped up on the trailer floor between the hoop toss and the bushel baskets, and stood eager to dive into the onset.

Dwayne let loose a Kentucky yell. "Yeee-haw. I'm a curly-tailed wolf with a pink ass, and this feud ain't done yet, boys. Let's git." And he and his posse traipsed off, shouldering through the crowd.

Nick watched them go, one hand in a pocket loosening its grip on the lump of pistol, his feet scuffing the midway like a riled rooster. He followed them away a short piece, and then came back and jumped into the pitch-till-u-win.

"Give over your apron, young lady. Take a donniker break and go warn Walt. And make sure Dwayne and his boys don't spot you."

I did what I was told—hopping out of the trailer, ducking around to the back, and watchfully winding my way past trucks and cars to the G-top. No one in sight, I pushed through the flap in the sidewall and found Walt dead drunk on a chair at the poker table, sprawled forward atop a half-dealt solitaire hand, the pint of whisky empty, and the long ash of a burnt-out cigarette dangling between two fingers.

I shook his shoulder and said his name, but he just mumbled a senseless word or two. I shook him harder, shouting his name, again and again. The best I got out of him was a smidgen of bleary-eyed recognition of me, along with something that sounded like it might have been, "I love you, baby."

The grass under the poker table looked more comfortable, and more out of sight, so I wrassled him off the chair and rolled him underneath. He took in pawing at me and moaning his rutting sounds. I pushed myself away and stood clear. He reached blindly for me once, twice, and then passed out. Looking for something more to hide him with, I found some empty beer-can cases piled behind the bar. A few minutes later, I had Walt boxed in with them, stacked two high on four sides.

Figuring that to be about the best I could do right then, I took the opportunity to head to the donniker, and with no townies in sight, I snuck out of the G-top. After my privy business, I scurried back to the joint. A full moon peeked out from behind a towering thunderhead, casting a metallic outline onto cottony billows splashed with the last hues of sunset. Flashes like foxfire, and a far-off rumbling, churned in the cloud's belly.

Back at the pitch-till-u-win, Nick showed me a fistful of cash, and said, "I took one-fifty from your apron. Not bad for half a Friday night in the West Virginia hills. Now if only that wrangy idiot keeps his crazy pink ass out of our faces, we'll be good. What's Walt doin'?"

"He's dead drunk, sleeping it off under the poker table. I stacked some boxes around him so he'd be out of sight."

Nick measured what I told him, and then said, "Let's hope he stays put for now."

I added, "Looks like a rainstorm's brewing."

"Can't do nothin' about that, young lady. Not a thing about that," Nick muttered, and then hopped over to J.D., to lighten his apron, too.

I went back to taking in money and giving out prizes. As the night set in, the feel of the crowd changed. Most of the families with their young'uns had gone home. And more and more teens, mostly black—who were much more antic than the briggoty white teens with their gawky stiffness—all swarmed past my counter, loping past with eagerness in their faces for the

carnival night, flashing wide eyes and toothy grins amid the hullabaloo of
sounds and lights

Among them blustered many who, because of their sorry lot in America,
laid bare their anger across their brows, their eyes glaring with vengeance at
all that whitey had to offer. Out on the midway, I overheard several of them
spreading hearsay about the cuss-fight between Dwayne and the black girl.
By now, his insults had festered from ear to ear, strutting into cause for battle. The sawed-off honky with the stitches upside his head, he was in for an
ass kicking.

Also, many blacks showed their disgust for J.D., for his constant grous-
ing at the overflow from Hat's basketball joint. He'd order them to get out
from under his awning. With pinched lips they'd glare at him and spitefully
shuffle only a step or two sideways. Once in a while, one or two would belly
up to J.D.'s counter, wave a dollar at him, and sportively jerk his chain—
jiving like they were too stupid to understand the rules of the ball game,
making him explain things over and over. A few acted as if J.D. was the
white devil himself, which he just about was, and they laid into him with
loud demands for his comeuppance.

J.D. swallowed all that like a poison that slowly killed all he could
abide. Soon, he'd had his fill. At my end of his counter, as far away from
them as he could get—one foot propped on the trailer floor, an elbow leaning on a knee—he just shook his head at them, avoiding their eyes, and
saying nothing in reply to their braggy signifying and jokey questions. Done
working this crowd, he clammed up, deaf and dumb with hate. In a slow
boil, he just watched everyone walk on past.

Near ten o'clock, their money running low, the crowd took on a different feel. Clusters of young folk—spudding and shackling around, each with
their own kind, black and white, guys and gals—all had little left to do, save
get rowdier. Storm clouds threatened overhead and now hid the moon—the
growing wind, thunder, and lightning stirring up even more lust for mischief.

Then all at once, a hundred heads swiveled around to see Dwayne pa-
rading his squad of grits down the midway—maybe twenty in all, jaws set
grim, their hands without weapons, but many pockets lumpy. Dwayne led
them under our awning, and as they passed, he damned me with his evilest
eye.

When all these white boys fetched up against the cluster of blacks in
front of Hat's basketball toss, many young bucks didn't give way—they
stood their ground, jostled by whites weaving through their bitter knot.
Some got a touch pushy. Cusses were swapped. And after the gang of whites
elbowed past, many of the blacks took in trailing them.

By the time they'd all marched once around the midway, the ranks of
both gangs had strutted near to mobs. Right behind them warily stalked a
dozen carnies—Robin, Chester, Larry, Buck, Shakey, and more, hefting

wrenches and hammers. The boys from the Tilt-A-Whirl mustered in. Ray and Mike ducked out of the flat store and joined the troop—Ray's fist in a pocket gripping his pistol, and Mike's bad eye gleeful at the likelihood of a fracas.

Nick rushed across to J.D. and hollered, "Drop the awnings! I don't like the looks of this," and then he scurried back to the glass pitch to help Fred and Brenda do the same. J.D. worked the awning pole while I pulled the brace pins, and we had the trailer closed up in short order. We hurried over to help out at the glass pitch, while gusts of wind cut down on us, tossing litter about, and thwacking the canvas as we laced it up.

Nick snatched our aprons, and told me, "You best get out of sight, young lady. This could get ugly fast."

I scooted through the line-up to out back. But rather than looking for someplace safe to hole up in, I couldn't help wanting to see what would happen next, so I snuck around to the back end, where on the midway's wide sweep in front of the sideshows, battle lines had formed.

Peeking between a tent and a trailer, I watched the three gangs badger each other with taunts and gestures—blacks and whites and carnies, each bunched-up with their own—three beasts, each with dozens of arms and legs fixing to tangle at the drop of a hat.

A pair of deputies ran up and set themselves to quile things, barking orders, stomping around between the gangs and gesticulating their attempts at control. When a knot of blacks and whites up the midway a short piece took in biting and gouging, they rushed over to the onset, wrassled them away from each other, and with one deputy shouting into a walkie-talkie, they hauled a few of them up front.

Beneath the growing wind, thunder, and lightning, the standoff at the back end closed in. Gripping pistols and knives and hammers and wrenches, the cussing done, all stood silent in wait for the first move.

Three shots rang out—bam! bam! bam! But not from any of them. Heads spun toward the shooter, and I craned mine out past the tent to see Trips standing on the treads of his trailer, a hog-leg in each hand—each pointed at a gang.

Trips shrieked in his high thin voice, "What in hell is goin' on here? Are you all plain stupid? Or just gone stone crazy?"

Nobody had any answer to that. They all just stood there flat-footed from the sight of a three-armed freak waving a trio of six-shooters at them— the lightning and thunder flashing and booming, and the wind whipping at his cape.

"If y'all ain't stupid or crazy—then it must be that Satan's got you by the balls! So right here and now I'm tellin' that goddamn devil to git gone. Now! Be gone! And all you fools with him."

I didn't see any devil leaving, but I did see some pistols and knives slipping back into pockets, and some faces showing shame to be caught up in what they no longer wanted a part of. The gang of carnies held fast their wrenches and hammers, as a squad of deputies rushed back down the midway. Then the rain cut loose, slicing in steep and pelting down hard.

Given a wet, but justifiable, way out of the standoff—or maybe Old Scratch had gone back to hell—the mob scattered like goats, quickly breaking ranks as heaven's fireworks let loose, bombarding the midway with blasts of wind and rain, jagged bolts, and mountain-shaking thunder. Trips lowered his pistols and scurried back into his trailer.

I darted out onto the midway and cut mud back to the joint, to make sure we were done for the night, and get paid my end. The lights on the Ferris Wheel were still burning, and on all the rides, too—some spinning through the downpour with a handful of drenched riders. Most joints still had their awnings up, but nobody was at Nick's joints, so I ducked around back to ride out the storm in Walt's car.

Then with an arm around my middle and a hard hand over my mouth, Dwayne grabbed me from behind—my heart hurling a fury of fear through me, my innards quaggling like swamp muck. Trying to bite at the grimy hand gagging me, and squealing bloody murder, I whaled at him with my elbows, fists, and heels, as he dragged me into the gap between Nick's truck and the joint trailer.

The arm squeezing my ribs slid up over my bubbies, fingering them some, as he snarled, "I tole you if I didn't find him, I'd find you. Now where is he? His car's back yonder, so I know he's about. And iffen you don't tell me right now, I'll be puttin' on you what he's got a-comin'."

He dropped his grip from my mouth, clutched my throat, and I tried to choke out a word or two. But before I could string any together, I heard and felt something thump down on Dwayne's head, which loosened his hold on me, and I scrabbled away and jerked around. Behind Dwayne, Fred stood waggling a length of two-by-four held high with both hands, about to beef it onto Dwayne's head again—which he did, dropping Dwayne to the mud.

I backed off and watched Fred, hell-bent to kill, lay into punching and kicking Dwayne—Dwayne flopping about and flailing arms and legs to fend Fred off. Shortly, Dwayne gave up on fighting back, and Fred took in slapping him across the face, pinning Dwayne down with a knee on his chest and a shoe in his straddle. Dwayne sputtered out wimpy pleas to stop, but Fred said nothing and just kept on dope-slapping him, again and again and again.

With Dwayne snubbing muddy snot and blood, Fred unlatched Dwayne's belt buckle and wrangled off his trousers and BVD's. Then Fred flipped him over—Dwayne's puny tallywags flopping into the muck—and Fred took in slickering Dwayne's pasty backside with the flat of his hand, whupping away till Dwayne's bum went rosy.

I stood there with little disgust about it, until Fred reared up, zipped out his own strutted jemison, hoisted Dwayne's hind end up against his straddle, and grinned at me like a miner who just cashed his paycheck. Then I scrambled out of there—leaving Fred to his spoils.

The downpour had eased some, the bread wagons wandering away. Wet as I was, I shuddered clueless whether my cold-shivers were from being so rained-on, or from a terrible case of after-onset dodders—or both. I sloshed over to Walt's car, hoping maybe he was in it. He wasn't, and I crawled onto the back seat, locked the doors, curled my knees to my chest, and wrung out a good cry. Whatever I'd gotten myself into here, I ached to get shed of it soon.

A good while later, Walt fumbled with his key in the car door, slumped into the front seat, plainly still half drunk, and asked, "You alright, Annabelle?"

I sniffed, "Yeah. Fine."

"Fred came into the G-top spoutin' his tale, and wavin' Dwayne's skivvies around like a trophy. If I ever see that mother-fuckin' hoojy again, I swear I'll shoot a new hole in his ass for Fred to bugger.... But I'd lay even odds Dwayne won't be comin' around no more, after goin' home with a load of jissum greasin' his shit hole."

"Walt, just take me back to the motel, please."

"Sure enough, baby. Sure enough."

We said nothing else all the way to town. I stewed on how he ought to be comforting me somehow, with words of tender care. And when none came, that added insult to injury. I'd been attacked—throttled and dragged off kicking and screaming—then rescued by a butt-fucking creep. My heart throbbing with terror, I'd come near to being hurt something terrible. Now my blood curdled with the taint of my so-called man not being there when and where I needed him. And not only was he too drunk to save me from Dwayne, he now had no balm for my wounds.

We pulled up in front of the motel office, and Walt said, "I'm gonna go slip the night clerk a sawbuck to keep an eye on my car. Here's the room key. Meet you upstairs."

I took the key, stung that he appeared to care more for his car than me. Up in the room, I stripped off my sobby clothes, locked myself in the bathroom, turned the hot water up full blast, and stood under the shower, scrubbing away the vileness of Dwayne's clutches until the little cake of motel soap broke into thin pieces. Swiping off the steam on the mirror, I held my chin high and fingered the bruises darkening on my throat and face. Then I brushed my teeth twice, toothpaste foaming at the mouth, but failing to skive away the lingering taste of Dwayne's hand.

I could hear the TV through the door—Johnny Carson doing a skit, and Ed, ho-ho-ho-ing away. With no desire to join Walt right then, I flipped down the lid of the commode seat, and sat with elbows on knees and hands over ears, staring at the checkerboard of green and white tiles on the floor.

Ever when Pap was around, we'd play checkers once in a while. He'd let me win a few times, but mostly his kings were crowned and jumping backward before I knew what hit me. I recalled him telling me, "You don't get to the far side of the board without losing scads of checkers."

I took that to mean that some things had to be lost before you could win, and if you tried to hang on to every checker on the board, you'd end up with none. Why that came to me there and then, Lord only knows, but it was telling enough for me to decide that, at first light, I'd be jumping out of this woebegone carnival's checkerboard.

Setting plans for that in mind, I realized I hadn't yet been paid my end of tonight's apron. What with all the commotion, I'd handed Nick my apron, but we hadn't counted up. So now, I had to go back to the lot to get my money. And if I did that, then I may as well work the whole day. Who knew how long it'd be before I found another job. Saturday afternoon was the big kiddie matinee—eleven-o'clock call, and then twelve hours of hoop tossing. I'd be foolish to pass up that kind of cash money.

I settled on leaving Sunday morning—buy a bus ticket to New York City, and don't look back.

Walt could do as he pleases—suit himself, like he's always telling me. It wasn't likely he'd give up his games to traipse off with me. And he likely wouldn't look kindly on me leaving him behind. So I figured I wouldn't let the cat out of the bag until it was time to go.

My mind made up, I finished in the bathroom and opened the door. Walt lay softly snoring atop the bedcovers—chin tucked into his neck, fingers laced across his belly, clothes and shoes still on, his pistol half-hidden under his pillow. Though relieved that I wouldn't have to deal with him right then, it set my teeth on edge that here he goes again. Right there, one handsome hunk of a man in my bed, but hardly here to care for me near enough.

That sealed the deal. I'd soon be long gone like a turkey through the corn.

VIIII

· LERMITE ·

At the edge of a sea, The Hermit, curious but wary, peers beyond the lantern that his right hand raises from beneath the folds of his monk's cowl. His left hand, shrunken and lacking some fingers, grips a staff that probes into the depths. With the visage of a wise old man — long whiskers and a high forehead — The Hermit looks back to the cards he follows, examining what has been, to see what will be. With wonder all his own, The Hermit wanders alone, with splendid isolation as his forlorn penance. Nine, last of the single digits, completes the procession of primary numbers.

The long dark night had granted me scarce sleep. After crawling under the covers—Walt still sprawled atop them—I'd tossed and turned until some measure of slumber fell scattered upon me.

Not long before sunrise, I woke from a dream where I'm on some sort of long sled or toboggan, but with no snow anywhere, callahooting down a rocky and treeless hillside. The other folks on the sled, a dozen or so—me with no clue who they are—they're all cutting up and having a big-eyed time, but I'm not having a lick of fun.

As we slide down the hill, which appears to have no bottom in sight, I feel sorely trapped, and the only way out is either to jump off the sled and take my chances tumbling onto the rocks, or just wake up. But what puzzles me to no end is that I now have a choice.

Usually in my dreams things just happen to me, with no druthers of mine about it. But now I have a decision to make—either jump off, or wake up. And the shock of knowing that I could make such a choice in a dream jolts me awake.

Eyes wide open, staring at the mornglom on the motel-room ceiling, I knew the dream was all to do with the ride I'd been on that week. And it left me with no doubt that I'd soon be shut of it all. But how was it that I could make choices in dreamland? It was as if I'd woken up smack-dab in the nightmare. One timeless moment, I was powerless as usual—and the next, I could choose what to do and not be obliged to lay hold to everwhat's foisted on me in the dream's captivity. I could opt for anything—with a free hand, my own free will behind it.

A warm flood of deliverance washed through me—shortly followed by a cold rinse of dread. How would I ever choose what to do in my dreams if I could hardly do so in the daylight? The real world sat out there as-is—though after the LSD I wasn't so sure about that anymore—while the dream world was likely all of my own making. If I had my say-so with on-goings while asleep, I now might be saddled with making my nightly dream dramas myself, choosing what's to happen next, with no rest for the weary.

But wasn't I beholden to do that, anyhow? If this week had taught me anything, it was that things were up to me, much more than I'd allowed. I had set out as a victim of the world around me, and had swapped that off to victimize others. I'd felt cheated—so why not do unto others as they'd done unto me? A sucker born every minute, I'd shunned becoming one myself. Yet, hadn't I?

I'd gotten myself sucked into yet another world that wasn't mine. I'd played the game, won some money, but lost even more of my self respect. Somehow I'd won Walt's love—be that what it was—but his prize turned out to be the loss of me. Walt's sins were his own—little I could do about them—however, there was much I could do about my own wrongdoings.

And the gumption to do so came from my own doing. It wasn't only the world's fault that things weren't right. It was mine, too. If I could choose what to do in a dream, then why shouldn't I be able to do the same when I'm supposedly awake?

But what in heaven or hell was right or wrong? What folks in Clandel say? What carnies believe? Lordy, save me from either. Plainly up to my own reckoning, what's good for me is right, what's bad, wrong. If I didn't know what each is my own sorry self, then who would?

So once again I had to ask myself, 'Who am I?' Whoever I was, lately I'd become more her. That forlorn haunt who long lurked within me now appeared more nigh. It was she I must be—and yet, I was her already. Instead of listening to the babble of all the voices out there, what I needed to do was heed my own inborn whisperings. I must trust myself. Then, ever what came of it—good or bad, right or wrong—I'd at least be trying for what's better.

My own self was no devil, no willipus-wallupus, no Saint Annabelle. It was just little old me—that girl I'd once been born, that woman I was becoming. Me, right there on that motel bed. My world whirling from my past to my future.

My man asleep aside me and about to get his heart broke, Walt made his living seeing through to what folks want, to what they are. Maybe he saw through to the real me, and that was who he loved. But maybe who he loved was who he wanted me to be.

I allowed I'd done much the same. When, in shining armor, he rescued me from my coaly dungeon, I went along willingly, more grateful than smitten. Then he came up short on chivalry, as if someone else had swapped places with the feller I'd left out with. Plainly, that sort of fancy wasn't love—it was a worn-out cat's-paw. With no ken of who Walt truly might be, I'd taken the easy way over the mountain. And now that I saw him in the dawning light, he wasn't the sorriest critter in the creek—yet, he was no Sir Lancelot, neither. That fairy tale was over and done with. The roses in the vase, wilted.

But to abandon all what I'd felt of him sent a sickening dread through me. What our bodies had set in motion was not so easy to cut loose of. Our randy lust for each other had coupled us in a bond stuck fast with super-glue made of raw sex. Not yet gone, I already felt the loss of our treasure of pleasure.

Though much of Walt's doings hadn't set right with me, somehow a marvelous magnetic magic had turned me into his woman—my body his, and his body mine. Now as I lay there beside him, a distance already between us, my horny yearnings still longed for him like an addict for dope. Was that what love is?

If I asked him to go with me, would he? Would I want him to? His bold worldliness might fare well along the way. He'd brought me this far— perhaps he might get me safely to whatever lies ahead in the big city. And along the way, we might grow even closer to each other. Or was all that just another romantic fancy?

As morning poured into the drapes, I dozed in and out my troubled thoughts and conjured up my escape plan. After many tangles and knots of what-ifs and maybes of mine, a rap on the door rousted us near nine o'clock. Naked, I snuck over to the window, peeked out between the drapes, and saw two brown-uniformed deputies—one rocking on his heels, the other with a hand on his holstered pistol.

I breathed, "There's deputies here."

Walt jackknifed up, still in last night's clothes—eyes darting around the room. The knocks came again, louder this time. He grabbed the pistol from under the pillow, tiptoed around to snatch up his stuff, stuffed it into his suitcase full of wadded-up clothes, leaned on it and latched it as quiet as he could, slid it under the bed, wriggled himself under there also, and whispered, "Tell 'em I'm gone."

Another knock on the door—this time more of a pounding—shook the door's hinges.

"Who is it?" I asked, with fake sleepiness, up against the door.

"Police. Open up."

"Give me a minute to make myself decent."

I scanned the room for any evidence of Walt, saw none, and then yanked at the coverlet till it hid the gap beneath the bed. What with Walt's having slept atop the blankets, it was plain to be seen that only I had been between the sheets last night. I grabbed a bath towel and wrapped it loosely around myself, figuring they'd be less likely to stay long if I wasn't dressed. Then with just my nose in the crack of the door, I slowly opened it.

"Mornin', miss. We're a-lookin' for Herman Ryder," said the older deputy—mid-thirties and many pounds heavier than the younger one, both with buzz cuts beneath their Smokey-the-Bear hats.

"You mean Walt?"

"Herman Walter Ryder."

"He's not here, deputy."

"Miss, we know that's his car out there, and we need to question him about an incident out on the Clandel corridor yesterday."

Still peeking through the crack, I told them, "I haven't seen Walt since we made it back, safe and sound, from that so-called incident—thankfully without being murdered. Those boys in that pickup tried to run us off the road. And then dented in Walt's roof with a baseball bat. I swear I feared for my life. Dwayne Williams, he got all het up over his case being dismissed by the judge. Then he chased us down the highway, fixing to do us in.

"Did Ryder then pull a pistol and shoot out their tire?" The older deputy did all the asking—the younger one eyeing me with a taut smile across his wily face.

"I saw none of that. I jumped onto the floor of the backseat and closed my eyes when I reckoned we were done for."

"Well, miss, there's two sides to every flapjack, so we're lookin' to get Ryder's statement. Mind if we take a look-see inside?"

"No, not at all." I swung back the door, still hiding behind it, and as angrily as I could muster, I added, "That three-hundred-sixty-degree son-of-a-bitch, Dwayne Williams, he not only tried to run us off the road yesterday—last night he grabbed me in the dark, in the pitchfork rain, and throttled me. If not for someone pulling him off me, he'd a-put a lot more hurt on me than these bruises on my neck. That boy is plumb psycho. Look!"

As they swaggered into the room, I stepped out from behind the door, one hand gripping the towel, and the other fingering the welts under my chin, tilting it high for them to see. But what their eyes locked onto was my make—the towel tucked in just above my bubbies and flapping half-open at the inside of my thigh, not far below my satchel. After a few frozen seconds of taking measure of me, their eyes shied off, and hunted around the room.

The older one, for sure a bully, asked, "How is it that Ryder's car is out there, this room is registered to him, and you are travelin' with him—but you got no idee where he is? That don't add up in my book."

"Look, deputy, I just met Walt a week ago. He helped me out of a jam. And when we got back here after Dwayne and his boys tried to kill us, he gave me the keys and said to watch his car, and he'd meet up with me somewhere shortly. I asked why and what for, and he told me that you deputies, or more likely Dwayne's boys, would be after him again, and he wanted no part of this feud, no more, no how. And because it was his problem, he was ridding me of the trouble. Then he walked out that door, and I ain't seen hide nor hair of him since."

They traded doubtful glances, and the bull deputy went to check the bathroom. When the other made motions that he was about to look under the bed, I turned and reached up to slide the drapes open, and I let the towel fall to the floor.

"Oopsie doopsie," I sang.

In hardly any hurry, I bent down, picked up the towel, and re-wrapped it around me. Then, as if nothing had happened—an incident which no doubt became a twice-told tale at the jailhouse—with a peevish whine, I cried, "What about me getting attacked last night by Dwayne Williams? What about that? You going after him? He's crazy dangerous. He's who's stirring up hell with a long spoon."

The deputy by the bed, forgetting about looking under it, said, "Ma'am, if you'd like to file a complaint, we can do that for you."

"And then what? Stick around here for another week to show up at the courthouse and tell the judge what a fractious lump of buzzard shit his nephew is—which appears right well-known round here already. So why ain't the rullion been locked up yet? What, file a complaint and give him another swat at me with his bat? Or throttle me in the dark again?"

Sidestepping out of the bathroom, the bigger one bellowed, "Miss, we're well aware of the likes of Dwayne Williams. He's been in our jail not a few times. But he ain't yet pulled no pistol out and shot at no one. That's why we're after Ryder."

"Well deputies, Walt ain't here. I don't know where he is and I didn't see him shoot no pistol. I was there, whupped on with a baseball bat, and near run off the road by those ridge runners. Never mind snatched up, groped, and strangled last night. So if you two officers of the so-called peace would kindly take your leave so I can get myself dressed and go to work, I'd sorely appreciate it."

They looked at each other, shrugged, and marched out of the room. I closed the door behind them and watched them through the window until their cruiser rolled off the parking lot. Yanking the drapes shut, I shuddered at my lies, amazed at how easy they came.

"Walt, they're gone."

He sidled himself and his suitcase out from under the bed, chuckling all the while, and saying, "Belle, that was one hell of a gutsy alibi. Won't be long before you'll be workin' the baskets with me."

Not about to tell him anything to the contrary, I asked, "So what do we do now?"

He went over to the window, peeked out, and said, "I guess I'd best keep out of sight again today. Johnny Law's got a hard-on what ain't about to quit for both his bag money and me.... What say I hole up here in the room all day, and you take the Merc' out to the lot. No sense in you not workin' your joint today. Nick'll be fit to be tied if you're a no-show too. Or we could just pack up and blow this jackpot—right now. Jump on over to the next spot and wait for Nick. Or just screw the McCain show and head for another carnival."

I complained, "Nick didn't pay me what I made last night. And it's kiddie's day, Walt. The pitch-till-u-win is a kiddie's game. I want my big payday."

"Yeah. Okay. Then you tell Nick what went down here—with the law on my ass and all—and after the show sloughs, you come get me, and we'll meet up with Nick down the road. How's that sound?"

"Well... if I'm to take the car, I'd rather go early, so I can buy some girl things I need." I didn't tell him it was a bus ticket.

"It's a plan, Belle." And when he leaned in to seal it with a kiss, I gave him one that felt of another lie.

While he sprawled across the bed in front of Saturday-morning cartoons on the TV, I washed up, pulled on my clothes, and finished the chocolates for breakfast. When I was set to go, he tossed the car keys on the foot of the bed and asked would I first walk over to the market around the corner and fetch him a loaf of bread, a pack of baloney, a bag of chips, and a six-pack of beer. I said sure, but I likely couldn't buy the beer. He said to grab a quart of 7-Up instead, and I did his errand.

Twenty minutes later, I wheeled the Mercury out of the parking lot. The first person I saw on the sidewalk—a spindly young woman rolling along a baby in a stroller—I pulled up alongside, leaned over and rolled down the window, and asked her where the bus station was. She mannerably told me, and I found it with little trouble—an Esso station out past the edge of town, with a warped cardboard Greyhound Bus sign propped behind an oily plate-glass window. And $28.75 later, I held a ticket to New York City.

With more than an hour to go till eleven-o'clock call, I steered the Mercury back across town and out to the lot. There were folks I needed to see before I lit out—Isis and Madeline especially. If I told them about my leaving, they'd likely keep it to themselves.

I parked the car in its usual spot behind Nick's joints, and made my way over to Isis's trailer. The carnival drowsed in the morning sun before firing up its last day in Stuart, before tearing down and hauling itself lock, stock, and barrel down the road to the next town. At Isis's trailer door, I smelled and heard bacon frying, and knocked gently.

"Annabelle, dear. You're just in time for breakfast. Come on in and join us."

I stepped up into the trailer and saw Trips slouched into a corner of the nook—one elbow on the table, another slung over the back of the bench, and the third cocking a coffee mug up to his lips. Knives and forks and a pair of plates were set on the table for the bacon and eggs that Isis tended at the stove.

"Sit down, sit down," she warbled. "I'll put out another plate for you. Plenty here to eat. Plenty. Would you like some coffee?"

"Yes, thank you." I said gratefully, and slid into the nook, face-to-face with Trips.

He sat up and leaned toward me—all three elbows on the table—and asked, "So how was your first week in show business?"

"I'd say it was no doubt the most out-doingest week I've ever had. Yes-siree Bob. And you last night, that was the bravest thing I've ever seen—coming out guns a-blazing like that."

He said something that sounded like, "Day us ex makeena," and chuckling, added, "I offer thanks to the sky gods for the backup. I'd bet a dollar to donuts that if the rain hadn't cut loose right then, somebody would've shot off one of my arms."

Isis brought me a mug of coffee, and joked, "Then you'd be like the rest of us. And then who would pay to see you?"

"My dear, I'd still have my Tarot cards. And two hands to deal them."

I squirmed on the seat, eager to tell him through the steamy coffee, "Those fortune cards you read for me last week sure came out to be true."

"Of course they did, darlin'. That's what they do. Reflect you in their mirrors."

"Mirrors?"

"The images painted on them all exist inside you. When you look at them you see parts of yourself staring back at you, seeing deeply into what everyone is. You recognize your own life. It's not me who tells your fortune. Nor the cards. It's the archetypes within you."

"The archetypes?"

Hee-heeing, Isis laid a plate and knife and fork in front of me, and cracked, "Here we go again. The three-armed Carl Jung, juggling his theories for us."

He squinted some irritation in her direction as she turned back to the stove. Leaning closer to me, he said, "The archetypes are the forms we are built from. Father. Mother. Sun. Moon. Earth. Heaven. Hell. The basic aspects of our lives. All of them, in all of us. And likely in most everything else, as well. Each of us, both different and unique. But we're much more the same as each other than not. Much, much, much more the same."

Though recollecting that squirrel in the hickory, I couldn't do nor say a thing, save be held by Trip's cocksure eyes.

"Take me, for instance. Sure, I got more arms than the next guy, but then the other guy might have more brains, or more heart. Our destinies lie in that difference. Nevertheless, we all have more in common than we choose to admit—physically and psychologically. All us animals have to eat and shit and piss and fuck. We're all born the children of millions of years of so-called human awareness—sights, sounds, smells, tastes, feelings—experiences forming the ancestral architecture of our souls, which we inherit like our blood, and which feeds our dreams, our art, and our souls with its hunger for realization. And which, if we don't give them their due, lurk like ghosts, searching for white sheets to wear."

With a spatula, Isis doled out eggs and bacon from the sputtering pan, and shaking her beard, she said, "Those ain't the only ghosts looking for sheets. All around us wander the souls of the dead, many bent upon returning among the living."

Hearing more than I wanted to, I smiled up at her, mannerably thanked her for the breakfast, and dug in. With no yen for any more ghost stories, I changed the subject, telling them, "This morning I was having this dream, and smack-dab in the middle of it all, I appeared to somehow wake up in the dream and be able to have my druthers about what would happen next."

Trips forked his eggs, smearing yolk across the white, and Isis slid in next to me, handing me a plate to pass around, stacked with buttered toast. Using his extra left hand to snatch a slice, Trips told me, "That's something to write home about, young lady. A lucid dream. Seems that your third eye has had its first glimpse inside."

"Do which?"

"I may be the only three-armed guy around here—but we all have a third eye."

"Where?"

"Right above and behind your other two. Have you done any meditation at all?"

I shied from telling them about the LSD, and what I saw under that oak tree, so I just said, "Once... after Isis told me about it the other day."

He dunked a corner of toast in the yolk, and said, "One meditation, and you get a lucid dream? It seems you have talents to uncover."

Isis chimed in, "Annabelle's a very special person. I knew that at first sight."

I swiveled a reluctant grin back and forth between them—both eyeing me like I was the freak here—and I asked, "Shouldn't I be sleeping when I'm dreaming? What good is waking up in a dream?"

Trips enjoyed a lengthy chuckle, washed it down with some coffee, then told me, "About as good as dreaming when you're awake. Either way, you're connecting one with the other, your consciousness with your unconscious, your ego with your self. The more you do of that, the more you'll—as in the words of Socrates, and many other sages—know thyself. The more you know thyself, the more you become yourself, which is who you really are. And also who everyone else is, which is essentially the same as everything else is in this whole wide world—energy shuffling forms."

Struck dumb, I lost him there. It felt like spinning on a Merry-Go-Round of words—up and down in a swirl of ideas that had a ring of truth to them, but the brass ring far from my reach.

After a spell of only knives and forks clacking on china, Isis said, "So tell me how it's going with that handsome boyfriend of yours."

I pinched the rasher of bacon off my plate, studying it as if it might hold the answer to that, then bit half of it off and told them, "I'm leaving him tonight."

"Leaving him?" Isis softly questioned.

After chewing the bacon deliberately, and swallowing it with difficulty, I said, "I bought a bus ticket to New York City for tomorrow morning."

"Then you're leaving us, too," she said, a quiver of disappointment in the creases around her eyes.

"I fear I am."

Her lips pursing amid egg yolk and breadcrumbs in her scraggly beard, she said, "Oh... May I ask why?"

Trips slid his emptied plate aside, leaned three elbows again upon the table, and probed his teeth with his tongue. Studying me closely, he said, "Isis my dear, you know as well as I do that our way of life is only for the chosen few."

After searching my face, she pushed up out of the booth and gathered some tableware. Unable then and there to list all my reasons why, I could only say, "This carnival life just plumb ain't for me."

As she turned away and brought the dirty dishes to the sink, I ate the last bite of my bacon. Remembering that I'd forgotten to return her book, I told her, "I left your book back at the motel. Maybe I can give it to Walt to get to you?'

Rattling dishes around in the sink with her back to me, she said, "Oh, you keep it dear. I have other copies."

Trips asked, "What's up in New York City for you?"

"I don't know.

"You know the big city ain't cheap?"

"I've got near a thousand dollars. I got lucky at the dice table the other night."

"So I heard. So I heard. A grand ought to get you through a few months or so, I'd chance to guess."

Talk dropped off to nothing. Busying herself at the sink, Isis appeared misput about my leaving out. Trips studied me closely, his eyes hunting deep into mine.

After a spell of clumsy silence, Isis turned to me and said, "Well, honey, I've got to prepare to meet my public. It's been a pleasure getting to know you some. I wish you all the luck in the world." And she reached out for a hug.

I banged my knees rising from the booth, and took hold of her—her over-ripe bosom squishing against mine, her scritchy beard nuzzling the crook of my neck feeling queer as feathers on a cow, her heartfelt fondness for me plain as day and warm as sunshine.

We took a step back, her hands on my shoulders. Eyes scolding mine, she told me, "You remember now. We're not alone in this world. Ghosts swarm all around us. Some want to be angels, and some want to be devils, and some just want some peace.

"Professor Extry-Arm there will tell you that all these spirits are projections from what's inside you. I say they're out there. So watch out, dear. There are hosts of haunts in the city—spirits both dead and alive—shrewd devils conniving for their own gain. Many of them angling to snare the soul of the likes of you."

I beamed her my widest smile, and said, "I'm much obliged, Isis. You're the best thing that happened to me this week. I'll never forget you."

With a hee-hee, she spread her hands saying, "Ain't that the truth. I'm just one big tattoo on your brain."

Trips put in a last word. "I've got one more card to turn for you. It says what you seek has been within you since birth. Don't search elsewhere for what you must find in yourself. Your Self, capital 'S', contains all the ghosts you'll ever need to scare up. Become who you are, young lady. What we bring forth of ourselves is the true test of whether we have lived. We must become who we are."

Isis joked, "What, and become freaks like us?"

"That's not what I said, my dear hermaphrodite. But I'd say that everyone's a freak in one way or another. Look here at this girl. She's so beautiful it's freaky. I'll bet her beauty stands more in the way of her individuation than my arms or your beard. People want to possess beauty. Folks like us, they let be."

"I'll let you be, if you don't get off your Jungian high horse."

Their voices got louder.

"And who would be your consort then? A nebulous incubus?"

"There's plenty of two-armed men wanting what I've got."

"Hey," I hollered, raising my hands between them. "Maybe it's neither one nor the other. Or maybe it's both. Everything's both inside and outside." I'd blurted that out just to fetch some peace—but when the sense of the notion sunk in me, I warmed proud of what I'd said.

Trips arsled out of the nook and to his feet, circled his lone right arm around my waist, and said, "Aha and oho. She's a dualist."

With his other two hands waggling in front of my face, each with one finger held up, he ushered me toward the door, saying, "The Self is both inside and outside of us. Each of us, apart from it, and a part of it. Your you—this individual miraculous manifestation that you are, once a captive of dreams—is now free to listen to your own voice. Heed what who you are says. Simple as pie. I see you've got it in you. So, on your way now. The Wheel of Fortune awaits you."

I stepped out of the trailer. Turning to face them, I could only lift a hand and waggle a few fingers goodbye.

Isis warbled, "Write when you find work," and gently swung the door shut.

A few minutes later, I fetched up under the mouse game's awnings. Madeline teetered on a stepladder, hanging stock—Tex handing her up armadillos from a big cardboard box.

She beamed a smile and said, "Girlfriend... you good to win some cash money today?"

I shrugged and asked, "Can I talk with you for a piece?"

Concern fluttered into her eyes. "Sure enough. A dozen or so yet to flash, then we go get a bite at the cookhouse. How's that sound?"

Several minutes later, we sat at a table off from the cluster of carnies, all of us sipping coffee and spooning up grits. Lula was there as usual—two chairs beneath her, one under each cheek—squandering opinions into Sonny's sleepy ear about her sister's marriage. Nick, huddling at a table with Carl and Tall Paul, fidgeted with his styrofoam cup. Several ride boys sprawled around the nearest pair of tables, bragging on their doings in the fracas last night.

Madeline and I hadn't yet said much to each other, save some comments about the weather and the like. Forsaking any clever lead-ins to it, I just told her in a whisper, "I've got a bus ticket to New York City for tomorrow morning."

Her jaw dropped and her eyebrows arched—her eyes bewildered circles. She breathed, "You're shittin' me. You're screwin' the show?" She peered around to see if anyone had heard, then added, "Why?"

Leaning into her ear, I muttered the tale about being set on by Dwayne, stopping short of Fred's buggering. I whined about Walt's ways. I hissed at the foul play in the joints—varmints running them like they had a license to cheat and steal. I bitched about the rain and the mud, the boring days and the franzied nights. I yarned about the drugs and the booze, the greasy grits and the watery coffee. When I ran out of what to bellyache about, I summed it up with, "Things just taste so bad to me, I'd have to lick my ass just to get the taint out of my mouth"

While I'd gone on and on, letting loose my pent-up bile, Madeline shrank away from me, grain by grain—any admiration in her eyes shifting to a dim view of my complaints. When it finally dawned on me that I was slapping my friend's world in the face, my heart drained dry.

I offered up a balm. "The best thing that's happened to me around here has been you."

Her eyes flashed into mine, likely hunting for the truth in them.

"You've been such a friend, Madeline, I can't carry myself off without riddling it out with you. I need you to know that. And you need not set any understanding to my leaving out. This life simply ain't for me."

"So, what life is for you, Annabelle?"

"I'll know it when I see it. And this ain't it."

"Girl, you've only been with it just one week. Each week's a different spot. That's what's best about a travelin' show. One spot's full of jackpots, then you pull up stakes and haul into the next one. Maybe better, maybe worse. But never the same-old, same-old, week after week. Give show business some more time. What's to lose? Then you can lay up more foldin' money."

"I don't want more money. I want to get to New York City. Why and what for, I don't rightly know. But right now, I've got a bus ticket, and cash enough to find my way, and for once I'm going to listen to what I've been telling myself to do, and just do it."

"What about Walt?"

"Walt's plumb smitten with me.... Lord's eye on it, he's no Romeo. But for a fact, he lights my fire. Then sooner or later he douses it with his aggravating ways."

"Ain't that what men do? Stir us up sweet and then mix in the bitters? Walt is one fine feller. Far better than most."

"Madeline, I ain't but nineteen. And you're near the same. What do we know about men?"

"I know enough to say you're lucky to have the likes of Walt fawnin' over you."

"Even so, I'm taking the mountain, with or without him.... He'd never quit his games."

"Did you ask him?"

"I haven't yet told him I'm leaving out. He won't even show his face outside the motel room today. The deputies are hunting for him, and Dwayne's clan's still toting a blood feud. I left him hiding out back there on the motel bed, eating baloney sandwiches and watching cartoon shows. I'll tell him tonight, and spare him any moping and grieving for today."

"Well that's mighty whitey of you.... Tell me, what's your deal with New York City? Ain't that one gigantic nasty city full of muggers and junkies, and snoots who don't care squat about nothin' but their money? Is that better than here?"

"Have you been there?"

"No. But I got some notion of it. I watch TV once in a while like everyone else."

"Madeline, New York City's the center of the world, and I want to see it, be in it. I don't know why, I just do. Maybe when I get there it won't be where I want to be neither. But at least I'll know. At least I'll have seen for myself."

She pushed herself to her feet and said, "Me, I gotta help Pa open the joint. We'll see you somewhere down the road someday, Annabelle."

With a misput little twist across her lips, she bent down, pecked a tiny kiss on my cheek, and strode away—leaving me with the icy feel of her appearing to be let down by me.

I sat there for a quite a spell, scraping my plastic spoon at the smudges of grits stuck onto the side of my plastic bowl, and teeter-tottering from sorry to go, to can't wait to be gone.

Nick fetched up and asked, "Where's Walt?"

"Some deputies came to the motel hunting for him this morning. So he hid under the bed, and I told them I didn't know where he was, and that he'd walked out the door, and left me his car till he shows up again. They appeared to hardly buy that.

"Then I told them my tale of nigh on getting run off the road yesterday, and being set upon last night by that sawed-off miner who's caused all this ruckus. They asked if I wanted to press charges, and I told them I'd be soon gone with no looking back.

"When they left, Walt crawled out from under the bed, and told me to tell you that he was holing up all day in the motel, and that I'm to go fetch him after the show closes, and we'll meet up with you on the way to the next town."

Nick, all the while jangling coins in the front pocket of blue polyester trousers, put on a face like a pain was shooting through him, then said, "I guess that's for the best—other than bein' dinged to ice more heat.... The sooner we put this spot behind us, the better."

I said, "I'll say."

He fished some nickels out of his pocket, and looking down at them in his palm, poked them around with a finger while saying, "I heard about what Fred done last night. That tub of lard ain't got a lick of sense—but he's family. My wife's brother, my daughter's uncle, I got to stick by him."

I told him, "Fred saved my ass. There in the dark and the rain, that goddamn bastard, Dwayne Allen Williams, Jr., was about to put a hurt on me bad. Had me by the throat till Fred laid into him with a two-by-four."

"That's the sorry tale," Nick said. "But Fred's also puttin' it around that he done more than that—wavin' Dwayne's skivvies around like an Injun with a scalp."

"I can't say nothing to that. I saw Fred whup him to snubbing, and I lit out."

"Fred's harmless, most days. But watch out if you wrong his own."

Being reckoned as one of Fred's own, queered me some. But I knew there was one more thing to do before tomorrow—thank him for my rescue.

Nick dug his wad of cash out, hunted for a piece of paper tucked between the twenties, eyed a number on it, and told me, "Your end last night was sixty-seven fifty."

Plucking bills from the fold, he handed me seventy, saying, "I know you're not stealing from me, so here's a little more. You're doin' a mighty fine job, Annabelle. Fine indeedy. You're one hustling hanky-panker. I'm right pleased to have you with us."

Startled less at the praise than at Nick speaking my name for the first time, I took the money and thanked him kindly. He cocked his wristwatch for a look-see, and said, "Awnings in the air in twenty minutes." Then he strutted off on his half-pint legs.

Seventy dollars in one night. For a short piece I held a candle to maybe I should abide this a while longer—another week, maybe two, like Madeline said. Then a feel of no-way-in-hell exploded inside me, blowing that notion away like stink in a storm. I had my bus ticket. And as Maw would say, I'd sooner sleep in a pasture and pick corn out of horse droppings.

I'd made my choice. For once I'd do what I wanted to. I had enough money for it, and was on my way. At last I heard myself saying so, loud and clear. Me, saying it my own self.

Lord knows I'd never cottoned to anybody telling me what to do, or what not to do—though I'd gone along with lashings and lavins of being obliged to. Misput at everybody else, I'd bless out the world like a spitting snake riled with biting its own tail.

It wasn't the world's fault that I felt like its slave. I was born free—to free myself. Isis warned of powers lurking about, eager to snatch me up for their own ends. Trips told me to listen to my Self, capital 'S'. As selfish as that might sound, it made more sense than being hog-tied by the rules of games I didn't want to play. Walt told me never play another man's game. And now here I was, done playing it.

So, what game would I play next? First, one putting on that I'm not lighting a shuck on a northbound bus the next morning. Then, a new game, with new rules. Not some joint calling me in, to take me for what I've got—but the one I'm calling for, a joint where I call the shots.

I swallowed the last of my lukewarm coffee, dumped my trash, and if only for one more day, scuffed off to the pitch-till-u-win. As I neared, I spotted Fred bending over a cardboard box in the glass pitch and setting tea-cups atop the stacks of cheap china. Beholden to thank him, I walked straight up to the rail of the center joint. He warily eyed me, a daft grin creeping across his ill-shaved face.

"Fred, I'm much obliged to you for saving my skin last night. That was plumb bold of you."

He stood straight up and looked side to side, as if hunting for what to say. Then he explained, eyes cast down, "That boy was hurtin' you."

"He was fixing to. But you sure showed him what for."

He shummicked a few steps, dove a hand into a pocket of his baggy pants and brought out Dwayne's muddy BVD's, and told me, "I use 'em for wiping dusty dishes," as if that made all the sense in the world. Then he showed me how fine they did the job by swabbing a teacup with the piss-poor shit-streaked skivvies.

I reckoned there to be little danger of Dwayne laying a hand on me again. As long as Fred was around—or truth be told, as long as I was around—I had him to safeguard me. His tetched stare now as welcome in wet weather as that umbrella you didn't want to tote along.

I waved a howdy to Brenda and Jenny, sitting side-by-side at the far corner of the center joint, sliding nickels into paper tubes—Brenda squinting a concerned scowl toward her brother. Then I crossed the midway and hopped behind the counter of the pitch-till-u-win for one more day.

And that day wasn't much to write home about. The midway crowd built steadily through the noon hour—passels of kids running hog-wild to and fro—their folks strolling along, swapping opinions, keeping half an eye on the young'uns. The big scary rides mostly sat idle, their rock-and-roll music silent, while the kiddie rides up at front end, and the Merry-Go-Round itself, swarmed with kids rattling round and round in tame circles on painted ponies and metal tubs fashioned into cars, fire trucks, boats, airplanes, and the like.

Other than spinning an unconnected steering wheel, or waving and smiling at their kith and kin, the only mischief the kids could raise was a ruckus pushing buzzer buttons and yanking on bell clappers, which they did to high heaven. Through the clangs and buzzes, screams and shouts, laughs and chatter—through the dust-flecked sunlight—through the mouth-watering scents of hot sugar, hot dogs, and hot grease—the pipe-organ waltz from the Merry-Go-Round's calliope floated across the springtime air.

Action at the hoop toss took in early, and built through the afternoon—but at an easy pace, nowhere near the franzy of the night before. Hustling back and forth, I chanted my spiel—grabbing quarters, refilling the counter with hoops, and passing out whistles and whatnots.

The folks today, young and old, black and white, somehow appeared more kindhearted. But being that they were pretty much the same sorts who'd been there all week, the notion came to me that maybe it was me who had become more kindly. For a fact I felt partly freed from the orneriness that had beset me for so long. And maybe now, since that botherment no longer hung in the air between myself and others, then by my being more agreeable to myself, I felt more mindful of others.

Next to me, J.D. worked the white folks to little profit—most of them were only at the carnival because of the kids. Ray, Mike, and the other flattie didn't show up the whole afternoon. Hat had hung out only a dozen bears or so, and spent most of his afternoon shuffling around in front of his joint, spinning a basketball on a finger, often hypnotizing a child's upturned gaze. Across the midway, the glass pitch tinkled steadily—Brenda appearing bored to tears—Jenny in a chair, swinging her legs, turning the pages of a picture book—Fred watching nickels fly, when he wasn't watching me.

In my apron, paper dollars thickened and coins grew hefty. Near six o'clock, when Nick came around to lighten me up and relieve me, I took a half-hour break for the donniker and the cookhouse, and then I ambled around the midway one more time.

At the joints and rides, the faces who one week ago saw me as grist for the mill now knew I was with it, and many mannerably nodded their greetings. Passing by the mouse game, I saw only Tex working the wheel amid a scatter of quarters on the counter—Madeline likely on break, also. When I got to the back end, I came upon Cheeks dragging out of his tent The Frog Baby's sign board.

"Hey, gorgeous, how's tricks today?"

"Kindly sandy," was all I said. And as I watched him set the sign in place—Sharpy shummicking around Cheek's feet, like he wanted to help too—I debated whether or not to tell him I'd be soon gone. After the chilly blow-off I'd gotten from Madeline, I figured I'd stay mum. I'd been given all the advice I could take for one day—though I doubted Cheeks was one to dole out prescriptions, other than the drug-store sort.

But he said, "Maddy tells me your screwin' the show. Goin' up to the Big Apple. Good luck with that. Need any mother's little helpers for the road?"

I shook my head, smiling, saying, "No, no. Thanks anyway. And thanks for all the other stuff all week long."

"Hey, I done told you we-all were gonna par-r-r-tee."

"That you did. That we did."

"Well, Annabelle, somewhere down the road someday."

I took the chuffy hand he held out to me, gripped it for a few limp shakes, and mumbled, "Maybe so, maybe no."

He squeezed up his cheekiest smile, and told me, "Gorgeous, when you get sawdust in your shoes, there ain't no gettin' away from this carny life for long."

"We'll see. Say farewell to Frog Baby for me." I said, and dropped to my haunches to finger the folds around Sharpy's slaphappy face, nuzzling my best farewell growl into his tufted ear.

I looked up and saw Cheeks pressing through the gap between the tents, hurrying out back for something else before he opened. Sharpy followed, skipping floppy-eared away, and I continued my stroll, reckoning that as much as these carnies leave things behind each and every week, my leaving out wasn't such a big deal—save for Walt.

Back in the joint, hoops clicked and clacked off and on while day faded to evening and the afternoon's flocks of families ran short of quarters and went home. They were shortly replaced with hepped-up gaggles of white teens, eager for their Saturday night out. J.D. laid into them like a hog at the trough, gobbling up what few dollars they had, along with their hopes for teddy bears.

As the night and the crowd thickened, the rides swoggled flashing colors through the rock and roll with loads of wide-eyed grins, laughing and screaming. All manner of hillbillies thronged past—pairs of couples, some sparky, some weary, the young ones hand-in-hand, the older side-by-side— coal-stained miners liquored up for their pitiful Saturday night, lone coyotes under a full moon, on the prowl for a girly show—fixy floozies in twos and threes, strutting their week-end finery, looking to catch an eye, maybe even a man, their high heels tottering across the trampled hay and sawdust.

The flatties next door went flat-out at them, two and three at a time, emptying their pokes of tens and twenties. J.D. worked both ends of the baskets, balls flying in and out. Hat played to teams of wannabe basketball lettermen and their cheerleaders. The glass pitch, on the far side of this swarming horde of West Virginians, jingled and clinked amid a dusty choke.

I soon found out that this wasn't a pitch-till-u-win crowd. If they'd stop to toss some hoops, they'd do so for only a game or two, with little interest in it, flipping hoops like they had nothing better to do, taking their prize and lifting an eyebrow—maybe sniggering as if they should have known better, and glancing accusingly at me before turning away.

I had my thousand dollars, or near enough to it. Not caring a hate for grabbing any more quarters, and fidgety to get gone, I went through the motions, but sorely suffered the sluggish hours.

The crowd petered out near eleven, and as ride boys took in pulling apart the pipe fence around the Zipper, Nick counted me up and handed me my end for the day's work—forty-eight seventy-five—and told me to go fetch Walt. With nary a word about me never coming back, I jumped out of the joint and into the Mercury and steered into town, the moonlight glazing the blacktop.

In the motel parking lot, I sat in the car for a spell, trying to come up with what to say to Walt. He wouldn't look kindly on my leaving out. His eyes carried a heart-smitten shine for me—a hopeful yearning within them that I was really his. How this fancy had come about was part of the mystery that his love was. For a fact, he adored me as did none other, and he'd be all a-torture when I was gone.

I'd likely miss him, too. His cock-a-doodle possessiveness was only what any rooster would crow about. His game-show lunacy was no worse than most other menfolk's one-track minds. His con-man swagger was just an act, much like anybody might put on when trying to sell something.

Yet, beyond all that, he was likely more of a prize than I'd allowed. Much more than I'd ever imagined could be so, Walt had sent shooting stars hurtling through my blood. Somehow I'd been bestowed with someone who would fetch me the sun and moon if I'd ask—a gift I'd ought not think little of.

The comfortable excitement I'd often feel of when near to him, the heart-strutting bearm—as well as my many vexations concerning his ways—appeared too high-powered to toss in the trash. The first man to move me so mightily—might he also be my one and only? How rare was such a find? If I was so fixed on leaving out, then why did I already pine for his arms ahold of me, for his bold strength by my side?

No doubt, old Clairy's ditty told the truth. To love was to give was to live. As what was written in that library book, love's not only what you get from another, it's more about what you give to another. Plainly, I hadn't done near enough of that.

Yet would Walt ever give up his carnival for me? For my love, my life?

Giving up on answers to that, I searched the car for any of my things, found a few, and scouting for deputies in sight, I stepped up the treads and across the balcony to the room. The door locked and the TV up loud, I rapped on the window. Walt's eye peeked around the edge of the drapes.

He swung open the door, and said, "There's my dream girl. How was your day at the office?"

"So-so."

"So-so's better that no-no. No?"

"Sure. If you say so."

The tone in my voice melted his grin. "What's up, Belle?"

"Walt.... I don't know how to tell this to you without hurting you, so I'll just say it. I'm not going with the show to the next spot. I've got a bus ticket to New York City for tomorrow morning, and I'm headed there, with or without you."

"With or without me! You're tellin' me that it's either or? Right here and now?"

"I don't know any other way to do it, Walt. I knew you wouldn't take it kindly, and I didn't want you torturing over it all day in this room. I bought my ticket this morning. Only then did I really know for sure I'd be leaving out."

He dropped his eyes, ran his fingers through his hair, and slumped into a chair. Silence set in between us like a stopped clock. I sat on the other chair by the table, and watched him think—his eyes searching the walls for answers, his jaw clenched tight, a tiny muscle in the side of his face rippling with bewilderment.

"Walt, honey, it's not all because of you. This carny life just ain't for me. And for once I'm going to do what I want to. I want to go to New York City."

"It's not *all* because of me? So what is because of me, Annabelle? What've I done to chase you off?"

"Don't look at it that way. You've been my hero. I can't thank you enough for rescuing me from my dungeon. But now I feel like I've swapped one jailhouse for another. Clandel's ways and carny ways are worlds apart. But neither of them is my world."

"And New York is?"

"I don't yet know, Walt. And I have to find out. It's important to me."

"More important than me."

"Important in a different way. You're important to me, too.... Would you come along with me?"

"Baby, I've got my life here. This is my world. You know that. What's there for me in that rat-hole city?"

"I'll be there for you. We'll be there for us. I escaped my world with you. Now you can do the same with me."

"Belle, I don't know if I can do that. Workin' a joint's what I know—what I'm good at. I'd be tradin' somethin' for nothin'. Givin' up the devil I know for one I don't."

"That's exactly what I did last week, Walt. And now I know the carny devil. And I'm done with it."

"And you're done with me?"

"It doesn't have to be that way."

"That's easy for you to say."

"No it's not. I've been torturing over it for days. I didn't just pull this out of a hat. This is me, wanting this bad. You've got to give that some respect."

"What about what I want? Don't that get respect? What about what Nick needs? Don't that get respect?"

"All Nick cares for is his damn nickels. He's using you and he's using me. That's his game. And with us gone he'll find someone else to use."

"And you've been usin' me?"

"Walt! We had a deal. Remember? You said to be me, with you. Go for it, you told me. Be the president if I want, a sword swallower if I want, your sex slave if I want. Do whatever I want, you told me. We'll see what's what. The road goes both ways. You remember all that?"

"That was before I fell in love with you, Belle."

"So that sort of deal's no good when you fall in love?"

"If you loved me, you wouldn't be leavin' me."

"I'm not leaving you. I'm leaving that damn carnival."

"And I'm a damn carny. It's part of me and I'm part of it."

"Walt, you're much more than a carny. Just like I'm more than just a hillbilly. There's a heap sight more man in you than a two-bit con man."

"A two-bit con man? Is that what you think I am?"

"No. I think that's the game you won't stop playing because it's easier not to quit. What I think you are, is a good man following the wrong rules. I've been with you only one week, but I've seen, behind that carnival mask, someone who's better than that."

"Better than what?"

"Better than all those rullions out there—lying and cheating, swapping off folks, and then laughing and bragging on it."

"I run a square joint."

"With my own eyes, I've witnessed it get a mite crooked now and then. Walt, you're only lying to yourself, cheating yourself out of a better life."

Half-a-breath short from blessing me out, he hushed himself, then fumbled for a cigarette, lit it mad as fire, pulled smoke down deep, and asked, "Do you love me, Annabelle?"

"Walt, this week you turned me into a woman—your woman. You woke up something in me I didn't know I had. I thought I knew what love might be, but the other day I had to read a book about it, to hunt for a clue. And right now I'm so bumfuzzled I don't know what to tell you."

"Baby, that sounds like an alibi to me."

"Well, goddamn it. That's what I got."

Silence fell between us while he smoked and my eyes sobbed up. I had to give him more than just some pathetic excuse, so I reached for some truth. "Walt, there's much about you that's moved me deep inside, brought me close to you, sparked my heart. And then there's these other things you do that turn me cold."

He locked his eyes to mine, but said nothing, so I continued, "I fancied you my knight in shining armor. But truth be told, it wasn't you in that fairy tale—it was who I wanted you to be....

"Well, that fancy went over the mountain soon enough, and then I took in seeing you more so as you really are—as far as I could figure it, which most times wasn't one whole heck of a lot.

"But what I plainly see is that you really love me. And though I wonder what sort of damsel in distress that you see when you look at me, your love's a gift too precious to take lightly. I treasure it... yet I don't feel worthy of it, because I'm not sure you really see the real me.

"I scarcely know who the real me is myself. I've only just glimpsed some hints of her in the last few days. So if I scarcely know who I am, then how am I to know what-all about who I love, and why? Or know if I even *can* love."

He snubbed out his smoke, and said, "Yes indeedy. Belle, you pitch one bodacious alibi. You're a natural, damn straight."

"Don't spout that carny lingo to me. I'm trying here to tell it on my own self!"

He threw back at me, "Tell it on your own self? What kind of hillbilly lingo is that? Let me tell you my own self. Go fuck yourself!"

He jumped up and thrashed around the room snatching his things, while I watched trembly-jawed and sobby-eyed. And then, mad as all get-out, he slammed out the door, stomped down the treads, and burned rubber out of the parking lot.

I sat there snubbing tears for quite a spell—part of me glad he was gone, and part of me missing him already. But also gone was all that jowering inside me, back and forth on what to do or not do. The cake was baked. And although still swiddled with mixed-up feelings, I knew I couldn't have my cake and eat it, too. One or the other, yes or no, stay or go—those were my choices. He'd made his, and me, mine. So be it. The milk's been spilt. Now it was all over but for the crying.

I yanked together the drapes, locked the door, both the bolt and chain, and turned on the shower. Washing the midway's dust out of my hair, the money's grime off my fingers, and Walt's taint from my satchel, the ribbons of suds swirled down the drain, gone like smoke up a stovepipe.

Toweling off, I swiped a streak across the steamy mirror, and stared into my eyes—the windows of the soul, they say. Peeking through the misty glass, I caught a glimpse of mine, which made this week that was appear all worthwhile.

I pawed through the chest of drawers for a clean T-shirt to pull over myself, and I flopped on the bed, atop the hollow in the covers where Walt had lain all day. Staring at the ceiling, snippets of the week reeled through me like they already had happened long ago. Wanting to capture some before they disappeared, I reached for a pen and my neglected diary in the nightstand drawer.

I picked the Bible up, too, and riffled blindly through some pages. Here was a book written thousands of years ago. I'd read a hefty measure of it and heard plenty of its stories at Sunday meeting—some believable to me, some not. It held a magic that lived in most books, though no doubt more so in its holy scriptures.

I'd read passels of other books—some not worth recalling and some unforgettable. Most had conjured their magic spells amid my life, if only for those hours reading them. Were it not for these books, I likely would've been content to stay put in Clandel.

I slid Isis's booklet out of the drawer. Flipping through the few dozen mimeographed pages of purple print, I marveled at how such a homespun thing could have exalted my past week into such a lesson. Such was the power of a book.

A notion dawned on me. Seeing as I'd read my goodly share of them, why couldn't I write my own book?

Propping the pillows and sliding halfway under the covers, I opened my diary to a fresh page. Rather than scribbling complaints to myself as usual, I wrote a page trying instead to tell my tale of that week to an unknown reader, someone who knew nothing about me. With a voice from within gushing onto the paper, out came the first-born lines of this book, casting my own magic spell into a frenzy of my own enchantment.

I read again and again what I'd written, taking great pleasure in scratching out words and jotting in better ones—as if picking out pieces that fit together shards of a picture on a jigsaw-puzzle box.

Late into the night, with far to go the next day, I switched off the lamp, got cozy under the blankets, and slid my diary beneath a pillow—knowing then and there I'd try to write a book in New York City.

10

LA·ROVE·DE·FORTVN

Vigilant upon its platform atop The Wheel of Fortune, a crowned sphinx glowers sidelong and shoulders a ready sword on its cloaked wings. Possessing a human's head and a lion's body, the sphinx represents the victory of mind over instinct. Two other beasts ride on The Wheel of Fortune — one, an animal ascending; the other, half-human and descending. As with the ups and downs of our own lives, a turn of Fortune may be good or bad. And we cannot see the hand of Fate that cranks The Wheel's axle. Ten combines what numbers came before, beginning a new progression onward.

The morning sun steeping into the drapes, I groped for the diary and pen, and scrawled down the fleeing shreds of a dream.

I'm toting a sack full of books into a library built with columns of marble like a Greek temple, and I'm stopped short by Mr. Connors, my old Sunday-school teacher, who is tending a fire on the polished floor, ablaze with torn-up pages of print. He reaches for my sack of books, but I sidestep away in terror.

Then I know point-blank what I must do, which floods me with a glorious courage. I grab a book out of the sack, and take in reading it aloud to him. Though the words make little sense, somehow it is my book—yet it doesn't matter to me that it's just jibberish.

Mr. Connors covers his ears with his hands, and shouts, "Burn that wickedness, or you shall burn!" His damnation doesn't shock me with fear, but instead electrifies me with an unexpected mercy.

However, what again jolts me awake is my knowing what is happening, my being aware much as I would be were I not asleep. Before my eyes pop open, I tell myself to look down at the book in my hands. It has blank pages, and my hands are as gauzy as an angel's might be.

Studying on this scrap of nightmare, and recalling Trip's words about connecting the unconscious and the conscious, and his praise of my talent for it, emboldened me all the more to set off on my new adventure—though not without qualms of what might become of it. My knowing of what to do in this dream showed spunk come newly to me. Even though what I'd done had goaded Mr. Connors on, I was not afraid of him, because I knew he was wrong. Yet more than that, I knew I was in a dream of my own making, able to choose to do what I see fit.

My bus due at quarter to ten, I only had an hour-and-a-half to get myself to the bus stop. Packing up mickety-tuck, twenty minutes later I swung my bags over my shoulders and closed the door behind me. The Esso station was at a crossroads a half-mile or so outside of town, and I gave thought to asking the motel clerk to call a taxicab, but after a few breaths of the crisp blue morning, I chose instead to walk, and maybe grab a quick breakfast at Riley's Restaurant.

The Sunday-morning streets stretched out nearly vacant—a scatter of parked cars along the sidewalks, stores dark inside, a few carloads of folks wheeling past, all fixy for church and eyeing me, the sole traveler afoot in sight. Nearing a cluster of beat-up cars and pick-ups parked by the storefront church where I'd ducked out of the rain the other day, I heard a chorus lift to Jesus a tune familiar to me, but I was at a loss for nary a word of it. The church door wide open, I didn't slow half a step.

A sign in Riley's window read: Closed for Worship ~ Open Noon to Five. My bags growing heavier, I trudged onward, the straps digging into my shoulders. A far piece yet from New York City, I reckoned I'd best get stronger at toting my baggage.

At the far edge of the business district, I came upon a rail-car diner, much like Jake and Loretta's place. Seeing several faces in the windows sipping coffee, I pushed through the door and swung my bags and myself into a booth. A pimply waitress fetched up, pad and pencil ready to write, and I asked if I might get some coffee, toast, and eggs, fast, because I had a bus to catch. With a shrug, she allowed why not, and the wiry cook at a griddle behind the counter heard me and had an egg cracked before she'd hollered my order to him.

Over my shoulder, I scanned the backsides stooped along the counter—unlikely churchgoers, most likely solitary miners, nursing hangovers from too much three-two beer on their Saturday night.

And then I gasped when I spotted Dwayne hunched over a coffee mug at the far end, his stitches rusty-red across the chalk-white patch shaved in his stringy hair.

If he'd seen me walk in, he didn't show it. Yet how he scowled at his coffee put me in a panic. He wouldn't do anything to me there in the diner, but what if he followed me when I traipsed the rest of the way to the bus stop. Now I wished I'd called that taxi—maybe I'd best call one now. But that might alert him that I was there, if he didn't know already, and he might follow the taxi out to the bus stop. Fear stuck in my throat, and I swallowed hard my loss of Walt's protection. In my terror, I even honed for Fred to be near.

The back of my head to Dwayne, I shrunk down into the corner of the booth, scared spitless to turn and look. Shortly, the waitress brought my breakfast and tore my bill out of her pad. I lit into the food—all the while squinting a corner of my eye toward the devil atop his stool. In no time at all, I'd gobbled down the buttery eggs and toast, and slurped up half the scalding coffee. Praying Dwayne hadn't yet seen me, I dropped some dollars on the table, and left the coffee mug still steaming.

Swinging out the door, I dared not look back until I'd hoofed down the block a stretch. When I did, he wasn't in sight. Whether he had seen me or not—or whether he favored not dragging up what had gone down in the mud—I could only guess.

Heart pounding, lungs burning, the bags swaying side to side and weighing me down like a mule, I tore off in a burnt hurry. The sidewalk came to an end at the edge of town, and I crunched onward through the gravel along the birm of the blacktop. What if Dwayne wheeled up beside me and told me to get on in? There was nobody out here to witness me being kidnapped. Maybe traveling alone wasn't such a smart idea.

Sweat dripping, stinging my eyes, I spied the Esso sign up ahead, when all of a sudden a horn blasted behind me, startling me to a stagger. I spun around to a carny semi rolling by, hauling piggyback the folded-up Tempest. The two ride boys in the cab ogled me with goofy grins as they roared past, the driver's face hinting a touch of recognition. I waved at his rearview mirror, and he tapped the horn twice, the rig rattling onward in a swirl of dust.

I fetched up to the gas station with time to spare. It was locked up tight—likely gone to Sunday meeting also—but out in front of the smutchy plate-glass window sat a trio of old movie-house seats, the plywood chairs chipped and splitting apart, the cast-iron frame rusted raw. I tossed the bags to the side, dropped breathless into the center seat, and took measure of my situation.

I wasn't out of the woods yet. What if Dwayne were to drive by and spot me sitting there? I jumped up and hunted around for some place to hide, somewhere I could keep an eye out for the bus, but duck out of sight when anything else rolled past. In the gravel parking lot off to the side of the station, sat a junk car with a back door sprung open. I perched myself on a corner of the moldy seat, keeping a lookout up and down the road. If it wasn't the bus coming, and was a car or a truck, I ducked low while it passed.

Then I remembered my bags setting out front. What if Dwayne saw them, and was smart enough to add things up? After a flurry of cars went by, I rushed out to bring them to my hideout. As I lugged them over, behind me I heard the whine of tires rounding the bend in the road. I dared not turn around, and I put on like I didn't give a hoot about its approach, keeping my steps at the same pace, though yearning to scurry back into hiding.

As I neared the old heap, the oncoming car slowed, crunched onto the gravel, and honked! I spun around, terrified I'd see Dwayne—but there, grinning through the open side window of the Mercury, sat Walt.

"You won't get far in that bucket of bolts," he said, pointing at the junker.

My innards flip-flopping, I dropped the bags, and said, "You scared the beejeebers out of me. I thought you were Dwayne, coming to finish the job on me."

"No, Belle. It's your dream man, comin' to finish the job on you."

"What's that supposed to mean?"

"It means I'm here to haul you to New York. If you'll have me. And to say I'm sorry about goin' off like that last night."

"What about your carnival? Your games? My so-called alibis?"

"McCain's Magic Midway has seen my taillights. There's always other games goin' on somewhere else. And I've got my own alibis to deal with. Just as you do. Plus, Johnny Law's got a hard-on for me hereabouts. New York's a whole other state."

His reasons made sense enough, even though I knew they masked why he really had come back—his lovelorn admiration. For his love of me to live, he'd given up his world. His doing so, and the smitten shine in his eyes, blessed me with a forgiveness that had to be love, and a shudder of joy rushed through me.

I could only stammer, "And what would I be getting into with you again?"

"The Merc', the road, the usual. Me and you workin' it out."

"Walt, what the heck are you going to do in New York City?"

"Be with my dream girl. Help you with your dream. See the big city. Maybe even book a game show on TV. I got ideas."

"You'd do that for me? No obligations sworn? No questions asked?"

"Annabelle, baby, we gotta ask questions. This whole wide world is just one big game show. How can you play a game without askin' questions?"

"Am I just another game for you?"

He pounded a fist on the steering wheel, and told me, "If you are, it's one I want to play. One I don't want to lose. One I want to win."

I studied him, hands on my hips, much like I did on Friday night the week before.

"So," he asked, his grin unsure, "you with me?"

Right then, the bus rolled around the bend. Wheeling up alongside the Mercury, the bus driver swung open the door, and shouted, "Miss, will you be ridin' with us?"

I stood there stupified. Like in a dream, the moment seemed in a time zone where the hands of the clock don't move. Before me loomed a life-changing choice. The questioning gaze of Walt, the driver, and a dozen other faces in the bus windows, awaited my druthers. I shut my eyes, ignored my panic, and asked myself what on earth to do.

....In my mind's eye appears the ghostly image of a motley jester, frowning as he juggles a lump of coal, a toy bus, and a teddy bear that wears a mask of Walt's face! Straightaway, the coal turns into a puff of smoke—the jester, seemingly on purpose, drops the teddy bear to the gravel—and then with a kindly smirk, he offers me the toy bus in his hand....

Blinking this phantom away, I looked Walt straight in the eye, and before begetting any doubt, I hefted the bags, and marched around the Mercury to the bus door.

Walt leapt out of the car, reared up blocking my way, and said, "You get on this bus, and I'll follow it all the way to New York City."

The lovesick pain on his face, along with the determined set of his jaw, showed me he would do just that. I told him, "Walt, you can do what you choose. Just like I am."

His chin dropped to say something, but only quivered a mite. He stepped aside, and I climbed aboard.

My heartbeat walloping me breathless, the driver punched my ticket and I took a seat in the rear, marveling at my newborn gumption. As the bus roared away from the station, I looked back, and yes, Walt followed.

At first, his making after me brought on a case of the creeps. What would happen if he did trail me all the way to New York? What would I do then? Yet before a mile or two had passed, haunts of my feelings for him reappeared. I missed him already—his admiration, his desire, his protection, his cocky grin and wide shoulders. My icy dread melted into a warm relief that he was still there behind me. Maybe I really did love Walt. Or did I merely love what he did for me?

I'd taken the bus by heeding The Fool within my soul. But now other voices disagreed in the pit of my qualmy stomach, cussing about how I'd turned Walt a cold shoulder. Ashamed of my ruthlessness, I felt sorry for Walt's suffering. Nevertheless, I allowed that pity wins no prize in life's carnival.

When I stood to hoist my bags into the overhead rack, I glanced back at Walt, who still followed, and I caught sight of a sheriff's car speeding past—which then did a hasty U-turn and took in after Walt, lights flashing and siren wailing.

One lonesome arm out the window, Walt waved goodbye to me, slowed, and pulled over to the berm. As the bus rounded the next bend, he fell out of sight.

Though I knew I'd made the right choice, it was no solace for my loss.

THE END

13869734R00187

Made in the USA
Charleston, SC
05 August 2012